MORTAL DEFIANCE
BY: B.A. TURNER

When uncertainty is but a plague upon the hearts of many and doubt is cast into the souls those hearts inhabit, that is when faith shields us from the darkness and guides us toward the light.

Chapter 1
An Unsuspected Sacrifice

A week had passed, and the day was Sunday July 6th. The celebration of America's freedom and independence was now a mere backdrop for the citizens of Detroit. During that week, Dreadnight and his squad introduced another ten members of Inkubus's clan to their obscure prison. Meanwhile, Inkubus was successful in creating twelve more of his super soldiers. Neither side hesitated to utilize the time at hand, as with war, time is one's greatest weapon and one's greatest enemy.

By now, Nikolai had successfully replicated both DNA sources that had been separated during the electrophoresis process. He spent those seven days working tirelessly, looking through a microscope to develop a formulated anti-serum that could attack the DNA strands of Inkubus without harming the subject's organic DNA or brain tissue.

However, his trials thus far were ineffective, leaving Inkubus's DNA unharmed or damaging all elements subjected to the formula. These trials consisted of mixing different proteins and restriction enzymes in an attempt to force the formulated anti-serum to recognize Inkubus's DNA as foreign, resulting in the anti-serum attacking and destroying those specific cells. The problem was that there are thousands of restriction enzymes known to man and any one or combination of many could be the solution.

Such failures would not discourage Nikolai though, he was a scientist, and every scientist knows that failure is the only way one can forge a path to success.

~

As hundreds of people shuffled in and out of the bars and clubs below, Slade embraced the calm air as he scanned the heart of Detroit and its rustling streets from atop the pinnacle of the General Motors tower. Perched upon the city's tallest building with knees bent and his hands pressed down onto the structure's cold metal surface, Slade could see activity for miles and was ready for any situation that could arise. Though he was in search of distress, the night sky eased his unsteadied mind, a state Slade could rarely achieve in his past life.

Prior to the Effigiem Custos, Slade struggled daily with anxiousness and unrest. A never-ending yearning for the future and for change in his life constantly ate away at his mind as he drudged through his mundane reality. Every day he would read and watch the national news, disgusted by the atrocities plaguing mankind and the media's never-ending lies. From corrupt politics to suicide bombings, evil was everywhere ... and growing. With each news clip, an augmenting anger welt within him. Slade would wish that he could do something to change the course of humanity, dreaming of having the ability to fight back.

That life was all but a distant memory now. One he hoped to never relive.

The sound of helicopter blades spinning flooded Slade's ear drums, causing him to turn his attention away from the streets and toward the Detroit River that ran behind him. Slade focused his eyesight, zoning in on the approaching aircraft that was about a half a mile away and nearing the Ambassador Bridge. It didn't appear to be the US Military or a news copter, a realization that didn't sit well with him. Filled with suspicion, Slade quickly stood, keeping a close eye on the unknown aircraft. Seconds later, one of the aircraft's doors slid open, revealing two masked militants gripping onto a woman and child, both struggling.

Before Slade could react, the militant holding the woman released his grip and shoved her out of the helicopter, sending her plummeting down toward the river. In a knee jerk reaction, Slade dove from the tower. With his wings pulled back, his body pierced through the night sky like a bullet, plunging over three hundred feet within three seconds as the woman's horrid screams filled the airwaves surrounding him.

"What the hell was that? What's going on?" Adam shouted though the comm link.

SPLASH!

The woman's body ripped into the water like a knife, blasting water into the air as rippling waves resonated around the area of impact.

Only thirty feet from crashing into the boardwalk below, Slade released his wings and arched his back, shooting him forward like a jet over the Detroit River, all while keeping his eyes up to monitor the situation.

"Ghuaahhhhh!"

The mother's head shot above the water and her arms flailed in desperation, trying to stay afloat as she gasped for oxygen. She quickly spun around in a frantic search for her son and the location of the helicopter.

"Someone help! My son!" the woman cried.

Seconds later she spotted the helicopter.

"No!" the woman screamed.

In his peripheral vision, Slade saw the boy's body appear from the aircraft as the second militant pushed him from its edge. Legs and arms flailing, the boy plummeted toward the dark blue abyss below, his scream as sharp as a knife.

"Dear Lord!" Slade shouted in disbelief.

"What! What's wrong Slade?" Ray said in sudden concern.

Slade immediately twisted his body toward the boy's helpless descent while flapping his wings vigorously to regain altitude.

"Raydar, quick, call 911 and have an ambulance sent to my location. A boy and his mother were just dumped into the Detroit River," Slade said perilously.

SPLASH!

The boy's body crashed through the river's unforgiving waters and out of sight.

Still at least twenty yards away, Slade's eyes bulged at the sight, fearful that the boy may not have survived the impact. Slade dropped headfirst toward the water and retracted his wings.

"Slade what's happ..." Ray began to say, but suddenly their connection was lost.

BOOM!

The sound of the impact was that of a detonated bomb.

Slade's body blasted into the water like a torpedo. Water exploded into the air as Slade delved below the foamy film. His rate of descent was so rapid he was nearly twenty feet deep beneath the surface upon entry. Without hesitance, Slade shifted his eyes and activated his night vision. Within a split second, clarity returned to his eyes despite the dark murky waters. He saw the young boy about thirty feet away, eyes closed, as his unconscious body was pulled deeper and deeper into the void of the river.

Slade's arms ripped through the water and his feet kicked with desperation, hoping to retrieve the boy before it was too late. That is if it wasn't already. Holding his breath and releasing the least amount of oxygen possible, Slade strenuously swam another thirty feet down until the boy was finally within reach. With panic building up from within, Slade released a choke of oxygen and extended his right arm as far as possible. His fingers grazed the boys left wrist, wrapping themselves around it. Slade pulled his arm back and drew the boy into his branded chest.

Out of oxygen and fearful of his own drowning, Slade released his wings and swiftly forced them in a downward motion, bolting him and the child toward the star lit surface.

Come on you can make it, you must!

But as they approached their saving grace above, a series of stray bullets ripped through the water like tiny cyclones. Two of the bullets clipped Slade's wings, but thankfully the water decreased their velocity and threat. As he neared the darkness of unconsciousness, his head shot from the river with the last of his strength, followed by his monstrous body.

"Ghuaahhhhh!" Slade gasped for air.

Beads of water flew from his body as he ascended with great momentum out of the murky water, his right arm holding onto the boy while shielding him from the flying bullets. Still vigorously flapping his sprawling wings, he twisted his body to the right in pursuance of the boy's mother.

"Argh ... Argh ... Errrh!"

More bullets ripped into Slade's flesh, this time into an arm and leg, infuriating him. These were no low caliber bullets, these were military grade sniper slugs, and they hurt as such.

Ignoring the immense pain resonating from his wounds, Slade located the child's mother. With one arm reaching to the sky in sheer desperation, she fought to stay afloat amidst the river's choppy waves. But as he neared, the once white foam that capped the brisk water turned a shade of red. It was blood, seeping from the mother.

Continuing to pick up speed, Slade glided toward the boy's mother, reaching her vicinity within a matter of seconds. His body nearly grazing the water beneath him, Slade lowered his left arm and grabbed onto the women's outstretched hand. In one fowl swoop, he pulled the women from the river, lifting her body into that of his own and seating her right next to her unconscious son. Immediately after so, Slade arched his body toward the sky and to the left to regain altitude.

Twisting and swaying, Slade maneuvered in search of cover in the city of Windsor, just south of Detroit in Canada as bullets from several directions continued their relentless assault.

The ambassador bridge, perfect!

Two more sniper slugs tore through his right wing and deep into his tail, causing him to groan in agonizing pain as his blood continued to drip into the river. After reaching a height of at least eighty feet, he twisted his body slightly to the right while dropping his chest and retracting his wings back which hastily sent him into a beeline spiral directly toward the water and in the direction of the ambassador bridge.

"Oh my god! Ahhhhh!" the mother screamed as they dove downward, her blood leaking down Slade's stomach.

One after another, miscalculated bullets sailed past Slade's spiraling body.

Just before crashing back into the water, Slade released and straightened his wings, rendering his body horizontal as it grazed the water and soared underneath the gargantuan bridge, finally out of the shooting range of the snipers. Upon clearing the bridge's underpass, Slade unleashed one mighty thrash of his wounded wings, forcing his body upright and causing his feet to slice into the water below until they were met by thousands of granules of sand. Gritting his teeth and tensing up his legs, his claws dug deep into the earth as he attempted to gain traction. After leaving two ten-foot-long trenches in the beach, Slade finally came to a halt, still gripping tightly onto the unconscious boy and his now fading mother.

Slade knelt and laid them gently onto the beach just under the bridge's awning. Racing time's cruel intentions, he immediately performed CPR on the young boy.

"One ... two ... three," Slade muttered as his overlapped hands were pressed firmly into the child's chest.

"Jack, please come back to me, my baby boy!" the woman shouted, life fleeing from her paled face as she leaned toward the boy, flooded in peril. "Why...why has this happened?" She cried, ignoring her own fate and clasping tightly onto her son's hand as she ran the other through his wavy brown hair.

Ghahhh. Slade drew in a deep breath before exchanging it with the boy.

"No no no! He can't be gone!" the mother screamed, tears pouring down her cheeks as she clutched her son's lifeless hands.

The child remained motionless.

"One ... two ... three ... come on, fight kid!" Slade belted, fear swarming his heart. "Don't die on me!".

The boy's head jolted up from the ground as a stream of water projected from his mouth.

"Oh, thank God! Everything's okay, Jack. Momma's here," the mother cried joyously, wrapping her arms around the confused boy as he sat upright and incessantly coughed for life.

A few seconds later she pulled her arms back, placed her hands upon her son's shoulders, and kissed his forehead. Just a foot away, Slade looked upon the mother and her child with a smile on his face, relieved and deeply moved by their reunion. In that very moment, he felt such worthiness and such pride, more than he ever had while beating a criminal senseless or imprisoning a merc. Protecting the defenseless and saving the lives of those who are in peril, that is what Michael's gift was all about. That is what fulfilled Slade's once depleted soul.

Unfortunately, that stint of relief was short lived. The mother's face waivered and her arms lost their stability, causing them to fall from the boy's shoulders. Slade's heart dropped. He knew she had already lost too much blood as the ground beneath her was a sea of red sand. Slade leaned forward, outreaching his arms as she collapsed toward the ground. Gracefully she landed into his arms, still conscious yet fading quickly. Her blood streamed down his gray skin as he stabilized her head with his hand.

"Mom! Mom!" the boy shouted fretfully, grabbing onto her frail hand.

"It's okay son. Everything is going to be alright," the mother said, turning her head and placing her other hand upon the boy's cheek, wiping his tears away.

She redirected her weary eyes to Slade as tears flooded her porcelain face.

"Promise me … that you will make sure … he makes it home to his father … 205 Baker Street, Gross Pointe Farms" she said softly, her voice trembling.

"I need you to hang in there, okay? So that you can be the one to take him home," Slade said, attempting to reassure the woman as he held her tightly in his arms.

"I don't care what anyone says," she said weakly, losing strength with each passing second. "You are not a beast or a monster," a small smile arose upon her trembling mouth. "You are a guardian angel," she added, barely able to breathe.

"Stay with me miss … please!" Slade shouted as he attempted to put pressure on her bullet wond. "An ambulance will be here any minute."

Slade's eyes filled with tears as his swelling fear became a cruel reality.

With the last ounce of strength remaining in her soul, the woman turned her head and looked at her distraught son.

"I love you my boy," she whispered as her last breath escaped her now forsaken body.

Slade felt the poor woman's body give out as her head fell loosely in his hand.

"Mom! Mom!" The boy cried, shaking her hand in fear.

An anger so profound filled Slade's veins as he blankly stared at the now motherless child. Every fiber in his being wanted to hunt the savages that killed her and rip them to shreds.

An ambulance was nearing, its ear-splitting siren snapped Slade out of his blood-curdling trance. He needed to fulfill the mother's dying request and get her son to his father. He knew that if an ambulance was approaching then a police cruiser wouldn't be far behind, and he didn't want to risk the boy being subjected to the unwavering corruption of Reem's police force. Gently, he laid the women onto the sand, blood still dripping steadily from her side.

Slade turned to the boy and placed his hands on the boy's shoulders, which were smaller than his own palms.

"We need to get you home to your dad, okay Jack?" Slade said gently.

The boy sniffled and wiped a pool of tears from his eyes then looked up at the colossal creature before him.

"But what about my mom?" the boy whimpered.

Slade tilted his head down and looked at the blood-soaked sand beneath his feet as he contemplated how to respond to the traumatized child. He exhaled and looked back up at the boy.

"Your mom is up with the angels in heaven now," he said, pointing to the sky with his right index finger. "She is watching over us at this very moment and wants me to take you to your father so that you are safe," Slade said softly.

The boy simply nodded, confusion overwhelming his innocent face.

"Alright Jack, we are going to go flying again, okay?"

"Okay," the boy responded, unsure of what to think.

"I'm going to need you to wrap your arms around my neck and hold on tight."

The boy stepped forward and did just that, entrusting his life unto the strange creature once again, this time knowingly.

"Let's get you home Jack," Slade said. "You're safe with me, I promise."

Slade looked up to the sky and with all his might leaped from the beach and into the night's unforgiving darkness, his right arm wrapped tightly around the young boy. Lifting higher and higher through the dense air, Jack gazed upon the diminishing landscape below. Wide eyed and astounded, he seemed to become distracted from the cruel reality at hand.

After navigating about ten miles northeast, Slade found himself gliding above lines of houses, each worth at least one million dollars. That's when he knew he was in the right area. Grosse Pointe Farms, one of the wealthiest cities in the entire country, a city Slade ironically knew all too well. It was the home of the first girl he had ever loved, or so he thought. However sad that part of his life was, it was now surely worth enduring as it was the only reason he was able to locate Jack's street without Adam's guidance.

"That's my house down there," Jack said, pointing at a gorgeous three level Italian Renaissance style home, its exterior layered in gray stone and its roof laced with red brick.

Just goes to show you that no matter where you live, you are never far from evil's reach.

Slade slowly descended toward Jack's house, his body upright and wings acting as a parachute as they forcefully resisted the oncoming air pressure. Drifting in between two large oak trees at the head of the driveway, Slade's feet gently landed onto the bowing blades of grass upon the front yard that were still damp from the late-night sprinkler mist. As he relaxed his wings, he glanced around to ensure no one was in sight. The coast was clear.

Leaning down, Slade set Jack down onto his own two feet.

"Let's go see your dad," Slade said.

As the two walked side by side toward the front door of the towering three story estate, Jack reached up and grabbed hold of Slade's left pinky finger, wrapping his entire hand around it. Slade, surprised by the gesture, looked down and smiled at Jack who returned the same smile.

Knock Knock Knock

The sound of rushing footsteps resonated from behind the extravagant oak doors as Slade lowered his hand.

The door whipped open. Behind it a frantic middle-aged man standing at least six feet tall with dark black hair and brown eyes. His eyes locked onto Jack with gleam.

"Jack! Where have you ..." the boy's father began to say until his eyes widened, catching a mind-boggling glance of the monstrous creature beside his son.

The man hastily lunged toward the boy and pulled him away from Slade and into his side.

"Get away from my son you beast! the boy's father shouted.

"But dad, he saved me!" the boy cried.

"What are you talking about Jack? And where is your mother?" the boy's father said fretfully, keeping an eye on Slade.

"He saved my life dad, and he tried to save mom's," the boy said with a look of sadness on his face.

"Wait ... what do you mean tried to save your mother's life? the boy's father said in confusion, his face riddled with turmoil. He turned his face toward Slade.

"Someone kidnapped your wife and son ... They had tossed them into the Detroit River to drown," Slade said somberly. "While I was recovering your son, a series of sniper bullets were fired ... One of which hit your wife."

"No ... no no! This can't be!" the boy's father cried.

"I was able to get them to safety, but she had already lost too much blood ... I'm so sorry." Slade's eyes looked down in unbearable remorse.

Anguish overtook the father as he wrapped his arms around his son, sobbing hysterically.

A sense of immense guilt swelled within Slade, unsure if his actions were flawed while the situation reeled in his mind.

What could I have done differently? Why wasn't I faster? Why didn't I protect her?

It all sank in within a mere second. A woman was dead, a mother, all because Inkubus was trying to draw him into the open. She died for nothing. Just a pawn in Inkubus's twisted game of chess. How many more innocent people would die on account of Slade's presence? The guilt slowly ate at his conscious. He didn't know how much more he could withstand.

"I'll never forgive myself for not being able to save your wife. I should have been able to. I'm truly sorry," Slade said with great pain as he turned and looked to the sky to escape the sadness.

"Wait!" shouted the boy's father.

Slade paused and turned his head back around, the position of his body remaining unchanged. The father paced forward, eventually stepping in front of him.

"Thank you for saving my son. I don't know what I would do if he were to be taken from me," the man said, reaching his hand out toward the creature in a gesture of respect and appreciation.

"I'm glad your son is okay, and I promise ... as long as I am around, no one will ever harm your family again. You have my word," Slade said with vengeance burning in his eyes as he firmly shook the distraught father's hand.

Slade's wings emerged from his back, sprawling like a river in front of the shaken father. The boy's father watched in awe at the immeasurable supernatural sight before him.

Slade's feet sprung from the grass and into the air. With one vigorous thrash, his wings rendered him afloat, just feet from the boy's father as he looked up at the beautiful spectacle.

"What is your name?" the man shouted over the gusting air flowing from the Slade's wings.

"My name is Dreadnight, and I am here to save this city," Slade said, just before turning and ascending back into the black of night.

Both Jack and his father gazed upon the starry sky as the angel of darkness disappeared, wondering if they might ever see him again.

Chapter 2
The Pain of Tomorrow

    The next morning was unordinary compared to most thus far at St. Anne's. When Father Ephrem knocked on the door of Slade's quarters to notify him that breakfast was prepared, Slade respectfully declined, stating he needed some time to himself. For a guy who was always eager to share his night's triumphs with the best of friends, this was very unusual behavior, behavior that greatly worried the other team members. No one knew what happened after Slade's comm and video stream went dark. The entire team waited in fear for his return that night on the cathedral rooftop, a return that occurred just seconds before sunrise, eliminating any chance of discussion. Each member knew something had to of went wrong that night, terribly wrong.

    Over the next five hours, both Nikolai and Ray attempted to breakdown the emotional blockade Slade had constructed, however neither could compel him to leave or allow entry into his quarters. During those five hours, Slade stewed in his own remorse, torturing himself with the memory of Jack's mother dying in his arms, wishing he could turn back the hands of time and find a way to save her. Unfortunately, that was not one of the powers Michael bestowed upon him. For the first time in quite a while, he felt powerless and weak.

    By this point in time, Father Ephrem knew Slade better than anyone. From the countless hours they had spent together over the past month, he knew exactly how Slade reacted to the ups and downs of life and this was most certainly the lowest he had seen him since the night of his stabbing. After giving Slade the appropriate time to gather his thoughts and feelings, Father Ephrem knocked on Slade's door once again at around four in the afternoon.

~

    "Slade, mind if I come in? I have brought you some coffee," Father Ephrem said earnestly.

    A part of Slade still wanted solitude, but another part of him wanted to be consoled. Slade opened the door.

    "Thank you. Come on in," Slade said as he retrieved the cup of coffee from Father Ephrem.

    Father Ephrem pulled the chair from Slade's desk and sat down. Slade followed suit by sitting down on his bed.

"What troubles you, my son?" Father Ephrem asked with concern.

For a moment, Slade remained silent and avoided eye contact.

"An innocent life was taken last night because of me, and now a young child is without his mother," Slade said with great sadness as he bowed his head.

"I highly doubt the fault is that of your own," Father Ephrem replied with confidence.

"It may not have been by my own hands ... but it was a result of my presence."

"What happened Slade?"

Slade took a few sips of his coffee, took a deep breath, and exhaled it out.

"In an attempt to lure me out into the open, Inkubus's militants kidnapped a boy and his mother then dropped them into the Detroit River from a helicopter, leaving them to drown," Slade said, his voice wavering. "When I went underwater to save the boy, a group of snipers unleashed high caliber rounds into the water ... one of them hit the boy's mother," he added solemnly.

Slade stood and paced slowly across his quarters, his hands shaking.

"I was able to get them to shore and resuscitate the boy ... but the mother ... she had already lost too much blood," Slade said, before pausing in a failed attempt to hold back tears.

"I'm so sorry Slade," Father Ephrem said consolingly.

"She died right there, right in my arms ... In front of her own son," Slade said, sobbing yet still attempting to resist.

Father Ephrem rose, walked over, and placed his hands upon Slade's broad shoulders.

"You did everything you could, son."

"Did I?" Slade said. "I could have been faster ... I could have grabbed her first ... I could have foiled their malicious plan before it even came to be." Slade clenched his fists.

"Trust me, there was absolutely nothing you could have done," Father Ephrem added sternly. "You saved her son. If you hadn't done what you did, an innocent child would be no more."

"I know, but if it weren't for me, Inkubus would have never kidnapped them."

"You don't know that son. And if you weren't defying Inkubus's tyranny, who knows how many other innocent lives would be stolen," Father Ephrem said with passion. "It's you who has and will save all those lives Slade, just like Rachel's."

Those sobering words hit Slade like a wrecking ball to the gut. Father Ephrem was right. Had he not fought for what was right, had he not confronted Davis Knight, Rachel wouldn't be alive, and he would never had the chance to see her beautiful face again. He knew he couldn't save everyone, but that didn't make the grief of witnessing such loss any easier.

"I can't begin to imagine the responsibility, the burden, you face each and every day as a result of this bestowment. Life and death decisions an ordinary individual could never fathom are placed upon your shoulders at a voluminous rate," Father Ephrem expressed. "You must not be so hard on yourself. You are trying to protect the people of this city from a vile monster," he added.

Slade lifted his head and quaintly smiled at Father Ephrem, grateful for his affirming words and guiding wisdom. He truly didn't know what he would do without him.

"You are right," Slade replied, nodding.

"You are damn right I am," Father Ephrem said with a laugh while slapping the sides of Slade's shoulders

"Hey, you're a priest, you shouldn't be swearing!" Slade said with a chuckle.

"True. But I am also a human, as are you," Father Ephrem replied with a smile. "How about we go and have lunch with the rest of the team, huh? Ray will be heading off to the precinct shortly and I'm sure he would like to see you," he added.

"Definitely. That sounds great. I'll be up there in a few."

Just as Father Ephrem reached Slade's door to leave and head upstairs, Slade stopped him.

"Father Ephrem?" Slade said, causing him to pause and turn. "Thank you … for everything," Slade added graciously.

"You're most welcome. You know that I am always here for you," Father Ephrem replied with a smile before turning back and heading into the hallway.

Chapter 3
Depravity Reprised

Two weeks and a day had passed since the river incident, an incident that further ignited Slade's appetite for justice. In those fourteen days, Dreadnight and the Siberian Scientist faced forty-two lawless transgressors that resulted in thirty-nine fresh captives. Notching the arcane asylum's occupancy up to fifty-three inmates.

The remaining transgressors weren't fortunate enough to make it to the arcane asylum. Instead, Inkubus's trio of newly trained super soldiers joined the dead, unwilling to submit regardless of the force inflicted, enduring multiple lacerations, tranqs, and even bullets in the process. Two of the soldiers were neutralized at the hands of the Siberian Scientist, more specifically headshots from his Tokarev. The third faced a sudden demise as a result of his neck being snapped like a twig from Dreadnight's ruthless strength.

From petty thieves to convicted murders, the rap sheets of the newly captured were endless and unforgiving. Of the thirty-nine men, at least twenty-five were apparent soldiers of Inkubus that were early in their transition toward full conversion. Nikolai now had an ample subject pool to pull from.

Though the quantity of testable subjects was no longer a roadblock, time was. From his countless hours of research and reformulations to his nightly acts of vigilance, Nikolai was nearly zombified. During those two weeks Nikolai made substantial progress in formulating an anti-serum, eliminating over fifteen hundred restriction enzymes as potential key agents which narrowed his search by over fifty percent.

In addition, he concluded two key findings: The first was that he would need to neutralize Inkubus's DNA in order to stabilize neurons in a subject's temporal lobe. The second was that the only way to stabilize said neurons would be to trigger reverse polarization for a split second to allow the anti-serum to attach to the foreign DNA cells. This is where he would utilize gamma aminobutyric acid, the very amino acid that was vital in Dr. Foster's serene synthesis.

A path to a cure was now in place, all Nikolai had to do was press forward and follow his instincts, the rest would merely enlighten his journey.

Seeing Nikolai work himself into what could be an early grave, the team became increasingly worried about his wellbeing. They didn't want a lack of sleep or a high level of stress to jeopardize his safety while out in the field, as one mistake could cost him his life. After constant badgering from his comrades, he agreed to take a must needed rest day, a task he fought for days.

However, not all things would remain calm and collective.

~

Later that night, Ray sat patiently at his desk in the precinct, waiting for the clock to strike twelve for his real purpose in life to beckon. Each passing minute accentuated his already elevated anxiety as he mundanely flipped through an unending stack of police reports. With nothing to distract his rampant mind, he couldn't help but think about Lainey, contemplating if his decision to distance himself from her was the right call. He hated the fact that he lied to her but feared that his involvement in dethroning Inkubus could place her in the crosshairs of his operation. It was a risk he just couldn't stomach taking.

Since their uncomfortable conversation in the breakroom a few weeks back, the two hadn't spoken once, making it feel as if they were strangers. Ray couldn't sense if she knew he had lied about his situation or was merely embarrassed from the result of her initiation. Regardless, he hated the aura of awkwardness that crept between them each and every day as they passed each other in the hallway or elevator. Such circumstances had not caused his love for her to waiver. If anything, his love had grown in intensity from his constant fear for her wellbeing.

For the countless time, Ray looked up at clock.

11:50 p.m., ten more minutes.

Pulling his eyes from the wall, he looked around at the surrounding officers and clerks, wondering which one would strike first if he made one miscalculation and his double life became uncovered. Other than Lainey, Commissioner Reem, and Deputy Chen, he had no inclination of who was under Inkubus's poisonous influence. It could be a few, it could be many. Every single shift Ray walked on eggshells, keeping his head down in an effort to go unnoticed and be overlooked. He felt like a lone elk surrounded by a cloaked pack of wolves that were thirsting for blood.

Just as he turned his head toward the west corridor, he saw Lainey's beautiful face peer from the elevator doors. She entered the main office, glancing right past Ray, fully avoiding eye contact as she walked by.

Man, this really sucks!

To his sickened disbelief, she opened Chen's office door and stepped in, closing the door behind her. Yes, that's right, Chen now had his own office right next to Reem's. A result of his ironic promotion to Chief Deputy. A promotion everyone saw coming.

What the hell is she doing in there! What does Chen want with Lainey?

His stomach twisted into a thousand knots as he feared the worst. Ray had never seen the two converse throughout his entire career at the DPD.

Why now? Why ever?

He watched intently as the two shared laughter and smiles, intensifying his current state of torture. All Ray knew was that he wished he possessed one skill more than any other at that very moment ... the ability to read lips.

God dammit. What is going on!

Ray wanted to bust through Chen's door, grab Lainey, and get the hell out dodge more than anything. But he had to keep his composure as much more than his relationship with Lainey was at stake. Shortly thereafter, Lainey exited Chen's office and headed back toward the west corridor with eyes gleaming and a smile stretched across her face. She stepped into the elevator to presumably head back her desk on the third floor.

Screw this shit. I have to go talk to her.

Quickly, he jotted something down onto a large yellow sticky note, pulled it from its stack, and rushed to the elevator. Just as he caught a brief glance of her soft brown skin, the elevator doors pinched together, costing him the chance to join her on her trip. Anxiously he pressed the up button and after about thirty seconds the elevator returned. He stepped inside and pressed the level three button with haste. After the elevator doors opened back up, Ray turned right, and started walking to the southeast corner of the floor where Lainey's desk resided. As he approached, she looked up and quickly glanced side to side as if she were hoping he wasn't coming to her desk. With every step his nerves twitched, and his heart fluttered.

"Umm, Lainey," Ray nervously blurted out as he stepped in front of her desk.

"Yes, Ray?" Lainey replied stiffly.

"Do you have a second to talk? ... In private," Ray said, looking around himself while attempting to not turn his head.

"Uhh, I guess," she said, then stood to follow his lead.

He walked down the east corridor, opposite from where he entered, before stopping in front of the women's bathroom. He quickly swiveled his head around to ensure no one was looking, slapped the sticky note onto its door, and walked through the doorway. As Lainey ineptly followed, she read the sticky note which read "out of order". Once they entered the bathroom, Ray quickly closed the door and kicked down its doorstop, preventing anyone else from entering. In a paranoid fashion, Ray paced across the bathroom, dipping down to check each stall for occupants. The bathroom was empty.

"What is going on Ray? You're acting really weird," Lainey said with suspicion, her eyebrows lifted in discontent.

Ray paused briefly before responding, his hands fidgety and eyes wandering aimlessly.

"What did Chen want with you? I have never seen him call you into his office before," Ray asked as innocently as possible.

Lainey's face tightened, showing an obvious sign of anger.

"Not sure how that is any of your business. And why do you care?" Lainey replied, bitterly crossing her arms.

"I just wanted to make sure everything was okay."

"Well, if you really want to know, he asked me out on a date for this Saturday." Her intention at verbal reprisal for his earlier rejection a success.

Ray's face dropped and his heart felt as if it stopped on a dime. No words could have been more disturbing to his ears than what just came out of her mouth.

"Oh ... and what did you say?" Ray asked, fear spewing from every syllable spoken.

Lainey looked away and toward the floor.

"I said yes."

Ray's mind cracked like a thin layer of ice, riving fissures throughout its entirety. He couldn't move his body and he couldn't speak. He was frozen in a standing coma of shock.

"I figured why not, he seems like a nice guy, and he is a dignified policeman," Lainey said with bloated confidence.

Ray scoffed out of impulse. Hearing such a blatantly delusive judgement snapped him from his comatose, filling him with anger and contempt.

"What?" Lainey said in irritation, rolling her eyes.

"I don't think that is a good idea," Ray said bluntly.

"I don't recall asking your opinion, or for your permission for that matter," she replied in a heightened tone.

"Look, I just don't want to see you get hurt. I have heard some pretty bad things about him and who he associates himself with."

"I'm pretty sure I can take care of myself. It's just a date," Lainey replied agitatedly, the motion of her head displaying the same attitude.

"Please just be careful okay … and know if you need anything … I'm here," Ray said earnestly.

"Last time I checked you had a girlfriend. Maybe you should be worrying about her instead," Lainey said sternly, each word like a punch to Ray's gut. "If you'll excuse me, I have work to do," she added, then turned to leave.

"Look, I'm sorry, but you have to trust me," Ray pleaded.

Lainey lifted the door stop and exited the bathroom, ignoring Ray's plead.

"DAMMIT!" Ray shouted, punching a nearby stall door, denting it, and causing it to crash loudly against the stall's sidewall.

Blood dripped from Ray's hand as he stood in a stupor, his mind ravaged from the nightmare he just survived. His greatest fears were now grim realities clinging onto the horizon ahead. Realities he could not bear to see come to light.

~

CRACK!

Slade heard a distant and faint shatter as he glided through the night air. He leaned to his left as the sound seemingly came from the east. Honing his hearing, he attempted to target in on the disturbance while visually scanning the approaching building ahead.

"You are going to pay for that, slut!" yelled a muffled voice.

It was obvious the sound of the man's voice was passing through the wall of a rundown high-rise apartment building straight ahead. Slade dropped his shoulders, increasing his speed and rate of descent. The high rise stood at least twenty-five stories tall, bearing decrepit beige brick tainted with black stains and a myriad of busted windows. The sound of struggle muddled with an array of desperate matronly screams intensified as he neared.

Only ten or so yards from the building, Slade had narrowed the level from which the distress was coming from but would have to make a split decision on how to reach it. The problem was that there were no fire escapes or balconies attached to the building. The only viable point of entry were two small windows that were separated by a column of brick. Neither window was large enough for him to make a clean entrance which made it seem as if his only option was to split the pair. Aiming directly for their divider, Slade slung his wings behind his back while simultaneously crossing his forearms out in front of his head, bracing for sudden impact.

BOOM!

Slade's arms blasted through the glass and mortar like a wrecking ball, sending its fragments far and wide. As Slade's body slid face first across the breached apartment's debris laced carpet, its elderly occupant was startled out of her rocking chair, abruptly ending her cat nap.

"What in God's name!" she shouted as she attempted to discern what had happened through the mist of dust that engulfed the room, nearly having a heart attack in the process.

Pressed up against the room's east wall, Slade shook his head and coughed, still hazy from the impact. He lifted himself up onto his hands and slowly rose from the floor. Fragments of stone and glass fell from his skin and bounced onto the carpet beneath him.

Balancing herself on her cane, the elderly woman squinted her eyes as the massive shadow of a figure appeared through the film of dust just feet away.

"Oh lord! A demon!" she screamed. "Oh, Jesus help me!"

Slade stepped through the veil, exposing his beastly self.

"Don't worry ma'am, I'm on his side," Slade said with a smirk, before turning and exiting out her door.

Fearful he wouldn't reach the distressed woman in time, he rushed down the hallway to the apartment adjacent to that of the elderly lady. With one swift kick, the apartment door burst open and crashed against the wall behind it. When he crossed its threshold, he saw a large middle aged African American male, his head as shiny as a cue ball with blood running down it, holding a switchblade to the throat of a young African American woman's throat, her back forced against an old couch near the east wall. A majority of the woman's clothes had been forcefully removed and scattered across the filthy floor amongst pieces of a shattered glass.

"Help! Please help!" the woman screamed desperately, reaching out one of her arms.

Startled by the crashing door, the thug twisted his head back while steadying the switchblade.

"What the hell!" the rapist belted in a deep-seated voice.

The man stood, pulling the woman up from the coach and whipping her out in front of him like a ragdoll, the blade still firmly pressed against the skin of her throat.

"You're that damn monster that keeps killing the boss's soldiers!" the rapist shouted.

"I'm Dreadnight, and I am your worst nightmare, scum," Slade snarled.

"Stay back or I swear I'll cut this bitch!"

"I wouldn't do that if I were you," Slade said in a gruff tone, taking a step forward.

The thug jerked the woman, pressing the blade even tighter to her throat then slowly stepped sideways to his left toward the middle of the room.

"If you make her bleed but one drop of blood, you will leave here in a body bag," Slade growled, exposing his teeth.

Slade took another step toward them, causing the rapist to panic. Back peddling toward the window ten feet behind him, he dragged the woman as she kicked and screamed, his arm locked tightly onto hers.

"Take one more step man and her brains will be all over the sidewalk!" the rapist yelled, his hand shaking as he swung the large living room windowpane across, punching its screen out immediately after so.

Slade started to move his foot forward, hoping to call his bluff. However, the thug pulled the woman's body up and over the ledge, leaving everything above her waist hanging midair in the night's darkness as her screams of terror cascaded out into the city.

This asshole is crazy enough to do it.

In that moment of reverie, Slade felt a powerful jolt of déjà vu as his mind was transported back to the sight of Adam Knight's hand around Rachel's throat. This was just all freakishly too familiar, especially the rage boiling within his blood at that very moment.

"I will let her go! Don't test me man!" the rapist fretted, sweat pouring down his bashed and bloodied head.

"Then do it," Slade said rashly, curling his upper lip in confidence.

Most would think only a deranged man would spew such seemingly careless words while in such an imperative situation. But Slade was no ordinary man and his words had been thoroughly calculated. He knew the woman would be safer if she were free of that perverse man's grip versus an unsteady blade deciding her fate. It was a gamble, but Slade had a feeling, no not a feeling, a celestial conviction that the odds were on his side.

Within the blink of an eye, the thug unlinked his arm from the woman while pressing his other hand firmly into her chest, sending her plummeting off the brick ledge and into fate's hands. Without delay, Slade took two broad strides then surged forward into the air like a spear toward the window. Just as Slade's fleeting body neared the window, his left shoulder plowed into the thug's chest just as he turned back around, shattering his collarbone and sending him flying against the east wall.

CRASH!

That same shoulder busted through the stationary section of the window, causing its glass to explode into thousands of pieces as Slade's monstrous body broke through the building's breach. Free falling story by story toward the sidewalk below, Slade bulleted toward the woman's flailing body with his wings tucked behind his back and arms tight against his sides. The despairing woman's screams echoed in Slade's ears as they roared by his clenched face.

Come on you can reach her ... you have to!

In a split second, he was struck by a revelation. He closed his eyes in unbreakable focus, turning his legs to stone and exponentially adding weight to his plunging body, surging his descent. Just thirty feet from the woman becoming a stain on the nearing sidewalk, Slade outstretched his arms with all the will in his body. The woman's hands clawed forward, desperate to reach the gargantuan creature before her, her eyes bulging in fleeting hope.

Just ... a little ... more

"Aaargh!"

With one painstaking reach, Slade grabbed ahold of the woman by the skin of her fingers and pulled her into his body. Holding onto her tightly, he liberated his legs while twisting his body, directing his back to the apartment building.

WHOOSH!

Slade released his wings like a parachute, rendering his body horizontal and facing him toward the dark abyss above.

But it was too late.

His body crashed into the concrete like a meteor, shattering its foundation like glass. The ground rumbled as dust lifted, consuming all that surrounded.

Immobilized, lying in a crater of dirt and debris, dwelled Slade's body. Unharmed yet terrified, the woman lifted her head and looked around frantically. Once she realized she was unscathed, she looked at the beast's inert face, its eyes closed, and head tilted to the side.

"Wake up! You've got to wake up!"

Twenty-five stories up, the merciless thug looked out of the busted apartment window and gawked at the dust cloud below.

But just as he turned to flee, he heard the voice of his victim screaming once again. Quickly, he leaned back over the ledge and saw the dust beginning to settle, revealing the fallen angel.

Slade's eyelids slowly peeled away from one another, unveiling his disoriented state.

Once his vision cleared, he looked straight ahead to see the rapist looking out of the busted apartment window, gawking at the dust cloud below with a nine-millimeter pistol gripped firmly in between his trembling hands.

"Thank God your alive! the woman shouted in relief.

The rapist quickly leaned back over the ledge. With bulged eyes, he fretfully aimed his handgun.

Slade swept his marred right wing over himself and the woman. Ignoring the stabbing pain that resonated from it, he hardened his wing. The sound of three gunshots filled the air.

CLANK CLANK CLANK!

The bullets ricocheted off the stone appendage as the woman shrieked in fear of her life. Tucked away from harm, Slade looked into the woman's eyes.

"Run ... now!" Slade said.

"I don't want to die, please don't leave me," she fretted

"You won't. I promise. Now go!"

Quickly the woman slid out from underneath his wing and ran for her life around the corner of the apartment building.

Slowly, Slade rose from the crater, his impenetrable wing still pulled out in front of him. Debris slid from his dust covered skin and crashed to ground. As his body straightened, he moaned in pain and anger. The thug released another three bullets from his gun's chamber, all of which clanked off his wing once again.

I've had enough of this shit. This ends now.

Slade released his wing from its hardened state, preparing to take flight. However, his left wing was incapacitated, fractured from the fall. The rapist watched in debilitating fear as he realized his gun was useless and that he was no longer safe from the blood-curdling beast snarling up at him.

"You're not going anywhere bitch!" Slade roared.

Slade leaped at least ten feet in the air, grappling his front claws and the hooks of his upper wings into the cement of the building while using his feet to balance himself.

Leveraging himself against the wall with his feet, Slade squatted down, the motion straightened his arms as his claws maintained his anchor. With one powerful pull, Slade utilized his lats and biceps to drive his body upward. As his arms bent and momentum grew, he detached himself from the cement and launched himself into the air while swinging his arms and reaching as high up as he possibly could. With one strike, he sent his claws and hooks into the wall once again, placing himself ten feet higher. Wide-eyed and shell-shocked, the rapist turned and bolted away from the ledge.

From leap to leap, Slade continued to scale the high rise building until climbing back through the busted window from which he dove. Just as he entered, he saw the rapist cross through the chasm that was once the front door. Slade raced after him, barreling through any object in his way until reaching the hallway. Before the man could turn to scale the stairs, Slade twisted his body and whipped his tail across the hallway. The triangular tip of his tail smacked into the side of the man's face, knocking him sideways against the brick of the east corridor wall. Discombobulated, the man stumbled to regain his footing like a drunken sailor.

After two large strides, Slade planted his gargantuan feet square in front of the rapist, steam piling out of his nose as he huffed with intent. The man froze as if he were in the presence of a ghost. Before the man could move, Slade wrapped his left hand around his throat, thrusting him flat against the wall and sending his claws into the brick like metal stakes. The man's face flooded with blood as the fear of death likely crept into his hollowed soul. A large blue vein pressed through the skin of his forehead, pulsating with each passing second.

"Please don't kill me man. I won't do it again man, I swear!" The man gasped, the restriction of oxygen obstructing his vocal cords.

"Not so tough anymore, are you?" Slade growled. "You're lucky I don't rip you limb by limb, you sick son of a bitch," he added in a hiss, his teeth screaming at the man's face.

"Please please please!" the man begged like a starving dog.

Slade drew back his right arm, fist fully clenched with muscles bulging. The man winced as he attempted turn his sweat coated skull.

BOOM!

Slade's fist smashed through the brick wall, grazing the man's trembling face as it sped by. Hanging in Slade's gargantuan hand, the rapist remained, unconscious and numb from fainting.

"Nikolai, swing by my current location. Going to need a ride back to the Arcane Asylum with a plus one," Slade said through the comm as he pulled both of his hands from the brick, causing the rapist's body to fall to the floor.

Within minutes, the Celestial shipping truck pulled up to the apartment building where Slade quickly hopped into the cargo pod, dragging the team's newest captive behind him.

~

The Merciless Gargoyle Strikes Again
By Jessica Day
Sunday, July 20th

Last night, while mothers tucked their children in for an innocent night's sleep and the elderly closed their eyes in hopes of a brighter tomorrow, terror rained down from on high. The demonic monster, now known as Dreadnight, vandalized a local apartment complex, leaving a trail of horror and despair.

The time was approximately 1:15 a.m. when the fowl winged beast crashed through the wall of a very elderly Evelynn Gray's twenty-fifth story Oak Grove apartment. Not only did he destroy the contents of her apartment, but he also took pleasure in threatening to take her life if she made a single noise. Poor Miss Gray is currently being treated at Pinewood Hospital for severe PTSD and is barely coherent.

The beast's rampage did not stop there. Once he finished ransacking the poor old lady's home, he decided to pay her next-door neighbor a visit. However, this time destruction and mental torment wasn't enough for his cruel mind. Dreadnight physically forced himself onto the female tenant who has decided to remain anonymous, restraining her every move while attempting to rape the helpless woman. Fortunately for her, a nearby citizen by the name of Charles Glass heard her desperate cry for help and rushed into the apartment to confront the fowl creature. Someway, somehow, he was able to fight off the creature, forcing him out of the women's window but sadly falling to his own demise in the process.

Today we honor and remember a true hero, Charles Glass. A man who stood up to pure evil and risked his own life to save that of an innocent woman's. I ask all citizens of Detroit to stand up and arm yourselves in case the time comes when this "Dreadnight" comes for you and the ones you love.

Chapter 4
A Hellish Visit

    Three strings of red lights illuminated the alleyway between Ninth and Corsa street as three blacked out Ford Explorers halted midway down its eerie stretch. Four mercs, dressed in dark military gear and concealed in Inkubus's signature soldier masks, stepped out onto the damp blacktop from the front and rear vehicles. In the hands of each, an M-16 assault rifle, gripped firmly with a finger grazing each trigger. After a quick swivel view of their surroundings, they approached the center vehicle. One of the mercs proceeded to open its passenger door while the remaining mercs remained on watch out, each on high alert as if a threat was lurking.

    A shiny black dress shoe peeled out from underneath the SUV door and planted itself on the blacktop amongst the puddles and rotten trash. The dimming overhead light glared off its expensive Italian leather. Like an eclipse, the gruesome mask of Inkubus surfaced from the vehicle's headliner. Inkubus stood straight and walked forward, approaching the rusty door of the seemingly abandoned four story brick loft. His driver remained, keeping the car running yet leaving its headlamps switched off.

    Just six years ago, the building housed one of the most lavish Mexican bistros in the country. That is until arson claimed its existence, turning it into a firefighter's worst nightmare.

    Two of the mercs opened its metal door and entered the building. Inkubus followed suit, while the remaining two mercs lingered outside to stand guard. From the building's tarnished exterior, one would not imagine the interior being much different. However, such a judgement would be alarmingly incorrect. As soon as the three men entered, they were met by the most extravagant and tastefully elegant decorum. Glossy porcelanto floors checkered in red and black supported their feet as crystal chandeliers glimmered above causing the floor to shimmer. To their left, a wall sheathed in the most exquisite paintings from centuries old to new. To their right, a lounge of hand carved Victorian oak furniture pieces wrapped in red velvet cloth. Slouched in the center loveseat was a middle-aged businessman with two beautiful women draped over him, both wearing the most revealing and expensive dresses imaginable. Attempting to resist their carnal urges, the two mercs avoided gawking at the vivacious women flaunting their attributes.

    At the center of the first floor, a sprawling bar consumed the south wall, separating opposing lounge areas. Its shelves were lined with the finest and rarest of liquors from across the world. Just as Inkubus and his men passed the array of liquid gold, two stunning women in skintight black dresses strolled down the staircase hugging the north wall, their hips swaying with exuberance. Without thinking twice, the two women approached Inkubus with seductive eyes and licked lips.

"How would you like a two for one deal, mister?" the taller of the two women said as she grabbed ahold of Inkubus's tie and wrapped it around her hand.

Bad idea.

Inkubus clutched her wrist and whipped her hand away from him, cracking it in the process.

"Don't touch me whore!" Inkubus hissed, staring deep into the women's shocked brown eyes.

"What the hell, freak asshole!" the other woman yelled as she pulled her friend away from him.

The initial women clutched onto her now immobilized hand as they scurried away in fear and disgust, their heels tapping vibrantly.

If it wasn't apparent enough by now, the establishment of which they had entered was a high-end whore house, if not one of the most prominent in the United States. If you had money to blow and were looking for discrete sexual indulgence, the *Crimson Rapture* was the place to be. Businessmen and travelers alike would spend upwards to twenty grand a night to experience its exotic employees. Its operations and network were as concealed and covert as its misleading headquarters. Since his uprising, Inkubus had come to an "understanding" with the operation's ownership to not only ensure it flourished, but also that it lined his own pockets with its cash every week.

Inkubus and his mercs walked past the entirety of the first floor to its northeast corner where a curtained-off room presided. One of his mercs peeled back the sleek red curtain and the three proceeded into the room. Inside were two large heavy-set Italian men, both wearing black dress shirts with their top three buttons undone, exposing their furry chests and gold necklaces that hung from their thick necks. Their greased back hair and smug cigar puffing faces wreaked of overconfidence and arrogance. As the two sat in their armchairs, a woman sat upon each man's lap, petting them as if they were animals.

When you think about it, they were exactly that ... animals.

"Ahh Inkubus. My good friend," the portlier of the Italian men blurted, surprised by his unexpected visitor. "It is good to see you ... as always. But I wasn't expecting you for another two days," the man added.

"Well Antonio ... friend," Inkubus said cynically. "When your weekly wire transfer fails to take place, well ... my mind starts to wander," he added waving his gloved hand in the air as if he were a conductor of a musical orchestra.

"Please sit. Have a drink. Hell, have one of our finest women for the night, on the house!" Antonio said animatedly.

"Pass ... I'll just take my money ... to go," Inkubus said calmly in his hellishly deep voice.

"Ladies, if you'd please excuse us," Antonio said, snapping his fingers.

The two women brushed by the two mercs, grazing their shoulders with their freshly painted fingernails as they exited the room and out to the main lounge.

"Inkubus, we've worked together for years, and you know I would never do anything to lose your valued trust or cross you. Right?" Antonio said with a choppy voice.

Inkubus didn't respond. He just stared blankly at Antonio with his demon-esque eyes.

"Look sir, there have been a few hiccups this past week. I just didn't want to send you anything until I had the full amount, you know?" Antonio said, attempting to cover his oversized ass. "We are working on making it up. I promise next week you will receive two full weeks of your cut plus some," he added with eyes full of fright.

Inkubus remained silent then took a few steps to his right and sat down in the armchair directly across from Antonio, where only a white marble martini table stood between them.

"See that's the thing, I don't give a shit about your ... hiccups, I only care about my money," he said snidely as he intertwined the fingers of his hands while resting his forearms onto his knees and slightly tilting his head down. "I expect you to produce, not spew excuses." He cocked his head to the side a bit, accentuating his eeriness.

"But sir, it's that gargoyle ... thing. It took out a few of our pimps and botched some of our client's appointments," Antonio confessed, hoping for pity.

Something no one has ever received from such a vile man.

A mechanical zipping sound arose amongst the tenseness of the room, causing the two mercs to look at one another and the eyes of the Italians to bulge as their throats tightened. With one striking blow, Inkubus sent the palm of his mechanicalized fist crashing through the marble table, splitting it in half. The Italians cringed in fear at the sight, sweating razorblades.

"What did I say about excuses? You blubbering pile of shit," Inkubus belted in a tone that would even make Lucifer himself cringe. "I don't care how you come up with the money or where it comes from. I expect my fifty grand," Inkubus screamed in a rage that could peel paint from the walls.

Unlike most of Inkubus's associates, Antonio and his brother Angelo remained "unaltered", living free of the synapsis serum and its effects. The reason being, both were direct descendants of the "Italian Famiglia", otherwise known as the most powerful and influential branch of the Italian Mafia. Regardless of how strong Inkubus's empire became, he wanted no part in a war with the mafia and vice versa from Antonio and Angelo's viewpoint.

"I'll make it up to you I promise. I just couldn't risk shorting the famiglia's payment. They can't know of our arrangement. If they did, we would all be dead men," Antonio pleaded as drops of sweat ran down his petrified face.

Inkubus rose from his chair and reached out his gloved hand, holding it out for Antonio. Silence consumed the room. Antonio stood up and looked at the black glove with extreme hesitation and fright. With his shaky right hand, Antonio clasped onto that of Inkubus's. After two seconds, which assuredly felt like an eternity in hell, Antonio exhaled in relief.

Too soon.

Antonio attempted to withdraw his hand but couldn't. His eyes nearly popped from their sockets as he glared at the hideous mask before him, curling tentacle-esque appendages hanging from every inch of its jowls.

VVIPP!

Inkubus's mechanical sleeve became engaged, inflicting fifty pounds of force into Antonio's hand. Antonio's sweat drenched face tightened as what seemed to be gallons of blood rushed to it. He attempted to resist, but it was as if his hand was being squeezed by a vice. He just couldn't fight it.

VVIPP!

The mechanical sleeve tacked on an additional fifty pounds of sheer torture, strangling the fat man's limp hand. Antonio squealed like a pig as the sound of bones snapping like twigs bounced off the walls.

"Aaarrgghhh! Please stop, my hand! Aaarrgghhh!" Antonio belted as he dropped to his knees like a bag of lead.

Angelo sat by, digging his nails into his armchair as he quivered in angst, likely praying he wasn't next in line for punishment.

Psshhh

Inkubus released Antonio from his unforgiving grip, leaving his mangled pathetic excuse for a hand dangling in the air. In a hyperventilated panic, Antonio grabbed onto that very wrist with his opposing hand and gaped at its deformed state. Within two seconds he collapsed to the floor from unmeasurable shock. Angelo quickly lunged from his chair to aid his brother, but Antonio was out cold.

"Consider that this week's payment," Inkubus said sneeringly. "I expect you will be on time with the full amount next week, otherwise that will be your balls," he added, looking into Angelo's eyes while pointing down at Antonio's decrepit hand.

"Of course, sir. It will never happen again. I swear!" he groveled.

Inkubus turned and nodded at his two mercs, indicating it was time to leave. They proceeded back out into the main area. As they marched out, calm and collected, the bystanders of the Crimson Rapture avoided eye contact with Inkubus at all costs, acting as if he and his men weren't even there. Each exotic employee squirmed as if the fear of God had overcome each and every one of their souls.

Inkubus and his men exited out of the rusty door from which they came, filing back into their respective vehicles and off into the corrupted streets of Detroit.

~

The commixing sounds of V8 engines rumbled through the hidden tunnel of the Central Station overpass as the SUVs lit their way to the cargo bay door of Inkubus's hidden base. They were met by four armed mercs who were keeping the area secure from intruders, ready to shoot anyone not authorized to enter. The massive industrial door ratcheted itself upward until providing enough clearance for the three vehicles to enter the station's bottom level. The door quickly closed behind them. Inside and ready to greet their master, were Reem and Chen, on time as expected.

"Sir. Everything squared away with our Italian friends?" Reem asked as Inkubus stepped out his SUV.

"Let's just say they will never bite the HAND that feeds ever again," Inkubus said with a grin that could be felt from a mile away.

"That's good to hear sir," Reem replied, curious to what he was insinuating to.

"Well boys, I believe it's time this costly game of cat and mouse with this Dreadnight beast comes to an end," Inkubus said with an oddly joyous tone, causing Reem and Chen to quickly glance at one another in confusion.

"If you say so, boss," Chen replied with a nod, full of fabricated confidence.

"What do you have in mind sir?" Reem added

"Round up our ten strongest soldiers. It's time to rally!" Inkubus said animatedly.

"Of course, sir. They will be here within the hour," Reem replied.

Reem and Chen did just as they were instructed, calling upon ten of their master's most valued super soldiers to converge at the Central Station. Neither man knew whether to feel excited at this abrupt change of course or to fear for their lives as they were now surely going toe to toe with Dreadnight. Regardless, they understood their boss's sudden sense of urgency. Since Dreadnight had already destroyed Inkubus's primary coke house along with its showrunner Dante and was now inflicting his wrath upon the operations of Crimson Rapture, Inkubus had a great deal to worry about these days. For the first time, Inkubus and his empire were in jeopardy, a notion he would never accept.

Would a gang of fully converted super criminals with Inkubus leading the charge be enough to stop the monstrous supernatural being? Reem and Chen sure hoped so. Their lives depended on it.

Before the minute hand of the clock could even make sixty revolutions, each and every one of Inkubus's selected super soldiers were accounted for, arriving on time and ready to serve their master. They stood tall in a single file, shoulder to shoulder, with faces of stone as they watched the tentacles of Inkubus's mask squirm and ink seep from his mouth. Inkubus stood still with his hands clasped behind his back, looking upon his creations in admiration as if he were God while they awaited his almighty instructions like dogs.

"My children," Inkubus announced, lifting his arms and outstretching them into the air. "I have called upon you ... my chosen ones, with burning ambition, to join me in what could be my most valiant crusade. A crusade that will unleash our greatest dreams, making them reality!" Inkubus belted in a surge of passion, his profound voice swallowing the room whole.

The band of super soldiers roared in devotion, pumping their fists into the air with fervor, enthralled by their master's words. However, deep within, they remained deathly afraid of the man before them.

"Tomorrow we will bring the beast of the night to his knees ... tomorrow we make him one of our own!" Inkubus shouted like a five-star general preparing for battle. "He is the only thing standing in the way of our empire and the glory that awaits it. No longer shall we live in his shadow," he added in the same commanding tone, inducing a bout of thunderous chants from his loyal puppets.

"It is time to stop the bleeding. It is time we take back the night, my sons!"

Chapter 5
A Wrong May Just Make a Right

    Ray continued to assist Adam in analyzing surveillance feeds, a task that had become increasingly personal as a result of the team's new person of interest. That person was Lainey Ross. Ever since the previous night's discovery of her involvement with Jon Chen, Ray was a complete and utter mess. Only four days from the scheduled date, Ray nearly broke down from anxiety during dinner while the team was discussing past relationships. When asked what was wrong, Ray nearly ran out of breath from relaying the entirety of his experience with Lainey that dreadful night at the precinct.

    If anyone understood what Ray was feeling, it was Slade. The feeling of helplessness and the fear of what could come were two variables that could equate to a man's insanity. Ray found comfort from Slade's words of familiarity and empathy. But no words could entirely cauterize his wound.

    Despite the team's general concern, one member remained blunt and pragmatic, and that team member was Nikolai. In the middle of the conversation, Nikolai blurted out in a most abrupt fashion "just bug her." At first Ray was put off and offended by his demeanor, that was until Slade spoke up in agreeance saying that it could ensure her safety. The idea of invading Lainey's privacy was quite unsettling, but after some thought, Ray knew it was the only route that could ease his mind and provide him with the opportunity to protect her.

    That very night at the precinct while Lainey was in the breakroom, Ray scurried up to her desk and covertly slid a microscopic tracking device into one of the hidden pockets of her purse. This was no ordinary device though. Not only was it capable of gps signaling, but also audio recognition, providing them 24/7 access to any conversation within a ten-foot radius. Was this high-level breach in privacy immoral? Absolutely. Could the discovery of such actions destroy any chance of being with the woman he loved? Highly likely. But could such actions save her life? Ray was counting on it.

Chapter 6
Blitzkrieg Bloodshed

The sky was clear, and the air was brisk as Slade glided high above the city lights of Detroit's west side, waiting patiently for some action to arise. The damming words and fictitious virtue signaling of Jessica Day's article circulated in his mind, providing him a greater thirst for vengeance than ever before.

Her day will come. All their days will come.

"You hanging in there, Slade?" Ray typed into the comm software.

"Yeah, I'm good. Just organizing my thoughts a bit," Slade replied calmly.

"Alright, well it looks like it's going to be a pretty dead night from my end. Nothing has popped up on the DPD scanner yet," Ray typed. "But as we know that usually provides us minimal leads anyhow."

Even without being able to hear his tone of voice, Slade knew Ray wasn't doing so well. He certainly wasn't his normal enthusiastic self.

"You doing alright over there, Ray?" Slade asked, his thoughts now redirected toward Ray and his situation with Lainey.

"I suppose so. Trying not to think about Lainey and that rat's date," Ray typed. "The idea of those two being together eats away at me like flesh eating bacteria. Every time I see him ... I ... I just want to lose my shit, you know?" he added.

"I know man. Try not to think about it though. It will only harm you. I promise we won't let anything happen to her," Slade said consolingly.

"I second that, comrade," Nikolai's thick Russian voice chimed in as he drove toward the south side of the city to capture the team's last target being tracked.

"Yeah, don't worry Ray. We have ears on her wherever she goes. We've got this," Adam said into the comm from the Observatory.

"You're right," Ray keyed. "Thanks. I don't know what my life would be like if I didn't have you guys. Hell, who am I kidding, yes I do, it would suck. Ha-ha," he chuckled through text, lightening the situation a bit.

Despite his confidence, Ray's situation was a growing concern of Slade's. Was it because it closely resembled that of his own with Rachel? Maybe. But he knew one thing for certain, having to hide your true self from the those you love while trying to protect them in the shadows is absolutely heart wrenching and a scenario he wished upon no man. All Slade could do was hope and pray that one day Ray would get the chance to tell Lainey the truth, revealing everything he has done for her and how he really feels about her. Slade would be a liar if he didn't admit he wished for that same chance for each and every day.

"Oh, and by the way, I think it's about time I start going by the name my enemies are to fear me by ... Dreadnight," he added slyly.

"Ha, about time my brother! I knew it would grow on you!" Ray keyed joyously. "I think myself and Nikolai should do the same!"

"Hell yes!" Siberian Scientist blurted.

"Hell yes indeed!" Father Ephrem added unexpectedly. "But what about Mr. Unseen?"

The comm went silent. The rest of the team was unsure who Father Ephrem was referring to.

"Wait ... are you talking about me?" Adam said curiously with a hint of laughter.

"Why of course. You are hidden behind closed doors, unseen to all, yet you see everything," Father Ephrem explained pleasantly.

"Man, why didn't I think of that one! Props Father E. That is awesome," Raydar keyed enthusiastically.

"Wow! What an honor guys," Mr. Unseen said appreciatively.

"You're an integral part of this team Adam. We wouldn't be able to do what we do without your help," Dreadnight said adoringly.

"Well, Mr. Unseen will always have your back. All of you guys!" Mr. Unseen said gleefully.

It was a sentimental moment for all, one of many thus far. Not only had the five men developed an unbreakable bond, one much thicker than blood, they had also become a family.

"Forget what I said about tonight being slow. A suspected robbery has been reported at the Sunrise Credit Union off 8th and Weston."

"Perfect!" Dreadnight said with a grin. "Mr. Unseen, where am I in comparison to that location?"

"Only four miles southwest of it. I'll guide you there," Mr. Unseen replied adamantly.

Utilizing the gps of Dreadnight's comm and watching its flashing red sensor upon his array of monitors, Mr. Unseen navigated him toward the location of interest with precision. As Dreadnight neared, he realized the entire block surrounding the bank was barricaded off by construction signs and bright orange rubber cones, preventing any bystander from driving past.

Hmm, that is pretty convenient, maybe even brilliant. Too bad they won't stop me, Dreadnight thought to himself, ready to pound some criminals senseless.

~

Reem picked up his desk phone and punched away at its keys, ignoring the obnoxious dial tone.

Buzz … Buzz … Buzz

"Is it done?" Inkubus said.

"Yes sir. It has been called in. Dreadnight should be there within minutes I suspect, and our men are in position," Reem replied.

"Excellent, Harvey. Head there now and wait for my signal. I will be there shortly," Inkubus stated. "Oh and one more thing … you better not screw this up!" he snarled.

"I won't sir," Reem replied as knots consumed his stomach.

Reem quickly grabbed the keys to his cruiser and his jacket, then rushed out of his office. As soon as he closed the door behind him, he snapped his fingers in the air at Chen. Per the norm, Chen followed Reem's heels like an obedient dog awaiting a milk bone as they headed out of the precinct.

~

With his wings flared and his claws drawn, Dreadnight swooped down onto a nearby church's flying buttress that clung to its siding, providing him a bird's eye view of the bank. Once his feet were planted onto the building's cold stone, he relaxed his wings, allowing them to fold behind him as he crouched onto his hands. If it weren't for the breeze rustling his onyx hair, one would not be able to comprehend the fact that he wasn't a statue molded into the church itself.

Closing his eyes, he honed his senses, amplifying his sense of hearing and directing it at the bank just thirty yards away.

"Alright boys, I'm in striking position and I hear four separate voices coming from inside the bank," Dreadnight said softly through the comm as he opened his gleaming white eyes.

"Ditto. I now have eyes on the area. I will keep a lookout for anything trying to leave that building," Mr. Unseen responded, his eyes presumably glued to the video feed from Dreadnight's comm device.

"Take em' out, Dreadnight!" Raydar typed eagerly, waiting for Dreadnight to crash the party of crime.

"Not just yet. Don't worry, they aren't going anywhere. The bank is closed, so there are no hostages and there's no reason to go in and damage the building," Dreadnight replied.

"Good point. Sorry, I'm anxious you know. I just wish I could be there alongside you helping," Raydar keyed.

"You and me both, brother … Soon though."

"Look alive, we got three robbers exiting the east side of the bank, all carrying assault rifles," Mr. Unseen blurted with urgency.

Like a barbaric angel, Dreadnight launched from the flying buttress in a nosedive toward the three men. His body sailed through the air silently until about ten feet from impact when he unleashed his wings.

FWOOP!

Startled, the robbers turned to see a mass of dark muscle with gnarly white teeth bulleting toward them.

THUD!

Dreadnight's shoulders and wings barreled into the men, sending them firmly into the concrete while their rifles were scattered in multiple directions. This of course didn't hinder the men. Instantly, they tossed Dreadnight's heavy frame off them with strength unlike any mere human. Without hesitation, the three men sprung from the ground and charged at the beast before them. The first robber lunged with a right hook, which Dreadnight blocked with his left forearm. Before he could make a second move, Dreadnight lifted his right leg and sent it directly into his chest, sending him skidding twenty feet across the parking lot.

"AARGH!"

Dreadnight took a blow to his rib cage and another to his jaw as the other two robbers began throwing blows. Quick to react, Dreadnight threw his left elbow into the one robber's face, cracking his cheekbone, as the other robber sent a left hook into Dreadnight's face. Thick obsidian blood shoot from Dreadnight's mouth as his head twisted from the impact. That very punch lit the fuse to Dreadnight's rage bomb.

"Errrrahhh!"

Dreadnight grabbed that man's masked head with both hands, throwing it into his left knee. The man's nose exploded, forcing blood to gush from the mask's mouth slits.

Surgery certainly wouldn't fix that mess. With legs of fury, the initial robber charged at Dreadnight from across the parking lot, disregarding his assault rifle just a few feet away. Before the man could even get within striking distance, Dreadnight whipped his tail around, catching both of the man's ankles and taking his legs out from underneath him.

"Hey, you, ugly animal!" Shouted the robber with the sunken face, still dented from Dreadnight's elbow.

Dreadnight turned to his right with a raised brow.

"Something's not right, why aren't they using their guns," Mr. Unseen said over the comm.

Dreadnight's mind shifted from a state of blinding rage to apprehension as he looked upon the taunting robber.

THHOOMP! TEEWWW!

"You're right, I sense no humanity, and this just seems too eas ..." Dreadnight began to say distractedly.

"Yaaarrrgghhh!" Dreadnight screamed in agonizing pain as he twisted to see what stuck him.

Sticking out of the flesh of his mid back and only an inch away from his spine was a diagonally splintered four-point harpoon bearing a two-inch shaft. It was connected to a long steel cable that ran behind Dreadnight at least fifty yards through a window of a loft three stories up. The high-tech contraption was linked to a mounted harpoon gun with an air pressure release system, all encased in glass to silence its discord. A fourth concealed merc headed its dual triggers.

Pewww

The hidden merc hit the weapon's trigger a second time, releasing four miniaturized spears from each side of the harpoon's shaft. The spears sliced through Dreadnight's wings and deep into his lat muscles, then expanded, latching themselves underneath his thick skin and causing him to writhe in unbearable pain. Each spear felt like a point-blank shot from a high caliber sniper rifle.

"Slade!" Screamed the voices of his team members.

"What happened!" Siberian Scientist shouted.

"Are you okay? Raydar keyed frantically.

Dreadnight's vision became blurry as he watched a taunting merc approach.

Shit ... what's happening?

He stumbled and fell onto his knees, unable to keep his balance.

"Something ... is embedded ... into my back" Dreadnight said sluggishly, his mind groggy. "I think ... I have been ... drugged," he added, fighting to remain awake.

"That contraption must be laced with a tranquilizing compound!" Adam gasped.

"Don't worry Dreadnight, I'm coming!" Siberian Scientist cried tremulously.

"I'm coming too!" Raydar typed with angst.

"Raydar ... no ... you can't"

"I'm not letting them take you!" Raydar keyed.

"Your cover can't be blown ... you must protect ... Lainey."

Adding to the confusion, air began circulating in gusts around Dreadnight as the sound of helicopter blades ripping in motion filled the area. Seconds later, a black helicopter with red striping landed gently about twenty yards away in front of the loft amongst the kicked-up dust. Dreadnight sluggishly shook his head, attempting to discern what was going on.

Click ... Clack ... Click ... Clack.

~

"Oh shit! That must be Inkubus!" Nikolai gasped through the comm link as he watched the shipping truck's in-dash monitor

The blood curdling king of crime stepped closer and closer toward Dreadnight, his blood red tie swaying to and fro under his vile kraken mask. His foot already pressed to the floor, Nikolai zoomed through red lights, swerving to avoid oncoming traffic and pedestrians. Nothing would stop him from getting to his American comrade.

Like clockwork, Reem and Chen pulled up beside the helicopter, flashing the police cruiser's high beams before stepping out. Immediately after, six mercs filed out from the three-story building from which the harpoon was fired, each of them yielding a handgun. Three of them positioned themselves to the left of Inkubus, and the other three to his right.

Inkubus finally surfaced, he finally showed his vile self. The whole robbery, the police tipoff ... it was all a setup, a dupe. Fear engulfed Nikolai's heart. *How could this have happened? How could we have been so blind?*

A member of their newfound family was now in the clutches of a mass murdering savage, and he felt as if he were to blame. It was a nightmare, and he just wanted to wake up.

~

A blurred fusion of black and red spots occupied Dreadnight's vision as the sound of heeled footsteps neared. That is until those footsteps stopped.

"So, we meet at last, Dreadnight," Inkubus said tauntingly, holding his arms out with the palms of his hands facing the sky. "I sure hope you're enjoying my ruse. Clever, wasn't it?" His voice hissed like a snake. "Oh, no praise for me? Not even a response? I just don't see why everyone is so afraid of you … you freak of the night!" Inkubus added animatedly, shaking his hands in mockery.

Slowly, Dreadnight felt the effectiveness of the tranquilizing compound wearing off as his head hung in exhaustion. He knew all he needed to do was let Inkubus ramble and fool him into believing the compound was in full effect while he regained enough strength and mental coherence to break free from the contraption embedded into his back.

"Don't worry, soon you will be begging for my mercy, and shortly thereafter you will worship the ground at which my feet stand," Inkubus smugly roared, placing his gloved hand against the side of Dreadnight's face. "But for now, you shall receive penance for your sins against my empire!" His voice was as deep and dark as the ocean floor.

"Ha … for once … you will actually … do something yourself, coward?" Dreadnight said with a withered voice.

Inkubus's obsidian eyes grew like wildfire.

VVIPP!

Dreadnight felt something shift within Inkubus's hand as a mechanical clamor filled his eardrums. Then the cold leather glove was no longer there.

"Eerrrahhh!"

A punch of seismic proportion struck the side of Dreadnight's face, cocking it sideways and causing blood to fly from his mouth. Dreadnight had never felt such a powerful blow, but the existent pain only confirmed that the compound was indeed wearing off. A second punch met his jaw before he could even recover, causing a tooth to project from his mouth and roll onto the concrete amongst his splattered hemoglobin.

"That's for killing Dante you son of a bitch!" Inkubus screamed.

His pain sensors re-engaging caused him to fall onto his hands as his head drooped, blood streaming from his nose.

The merc yielding the harpoon gun, tightened its cable, locking it in place to prevent any movement from its victim.

Inkubus sent three rapid kicks into Dreadnight's ribs.

The kicks were so feeble Inkubus could have just of tickled him with a feather, but Dreadnight played along, groaning in fictitious pain and grabbing onto his rib cage.

Just a little bit longer. Let him waste his time.

"Is that ... all you've got ... little man?" Dreadnight coughed out.

Inkubus drew his arm back while actuating his sleeve for full effect, likely preparing for a knockout blow. In one powerful thrust, Inkubus sent an uppercut right to Dreadnight's jaw causing it to crack on impact.

"Ahhhh!" Dreadnight groaned in agonizing pain as his head whipped back down like a bobble toy and his jaw hung like wreckage.

But the pain was a good thing ... for once.

"The least you could do is show me some damn respect and look me in the eyes amidst your defeat," Inkubus roared before reaching down with his left hand and grabbing onto Dreadnight's rustled hair, nearly ripping it out as he lifted Dreadnight's head with force.

Inkubus drew back his right arm yet again, clenching his gloved fist with fury.

Dreadnight didn't fight it. He needed to recover, if even for a few seconds.

With Dreadnight's bruised and battered face now raised square with that of his arch nemesis, Inkubus received his first full fledge view of his saboteur.

Dreadnight closed his eyes and braced for another blow to the face from that iron fist, but nothing happened. Inkubus stood there, in striking position, just staring at him with a perplexed look upon his face.

"Finish him, boss!" Reem shouted, pulling Inkubus from his dazed state.

"No. I'll need him alive ... but not well," Inkubus provocatively said, lowering his hand and lightly slapping the side of Dreadnight's face as if he were a pet.

"Siberian Scientist, you're almost there, step on it!" Mr. Unseen cried.

"I'm giving it everything I've got!" Siberian Scientist yelled anxiously.

Inkubus released his grip from Slade's hair and stepped back, placing himself between the two sets of mercs.

"Put him down my children," Inkubus ordered the six mercs, swinging his arm down like an axe as if he were Hitler commanding his troops.

But before Inkubus's arm could fall to his side, Dreadnight heard the roar of an engine approaching at an alarming rate.

Suddenly, the Celestial Shipping truck erupted out into the open from the barricaded street to his left, crashing through and shattering its bright orange blockade sign.

At the wheel was the Siberian Scientist, a sight that put a smirk upon Dreadnight's swollen face.

Inkubus turned his head to see it coming straight for him. Without thinking, Inkubus dove for cover away from Dreadnight and the truck along with Reem and Chen, just missing the truck's front bumper. The three mercs to his right weren't so lucky. They were so focused on obeying their master's single command, their other senses had become nonexistent. One of them was introduced to the bottom of two of the truck's wheels, flattening him like a pancake and instantly killing him. The second was plastered to the windshield like a bug, his skull cracked and bloodied, but he was still alive. And the third had a personal encounter with the truck's steel grille, sending his body sailing across the way and smashing into the side of the bank's wall.

Reem and Chen immediately ran for cover and slid behind their police cruiser.

"Kill that man!" Inkubus instructed his remaining soldiers as he scrambled back onto his feet and ran toward his helicopter.

Siberian Scientist slammed on the brakes and quickly exited out of the truck's driver side, his tokarev pistol locked and loaded.

P-Taff Taft

Siberian Scientist sent two bullets from his chamber into the chest of one of the oncoming mercs, slowing him down but not stopping him. Another merc barreled into Siberian Scientist like a linebacker, smashing him into the side of the truck. With his shooting hand free, Siberian Scientist sent his right elbow into the merc's back, lowering the merc just enough for Siberian Scientist to bend his arm inward.

P-Taff

With the gun's barrel up against the side of the man's skull, he released a bullet directly into the man's brain causing blood to explode onto that of his own mask. The merc dropped like lead.

That will do the trick!

"Watch out!" Dreadnight screamed.

P-Taff P-Taff P-Taff

Before he could react, Siberian Scientist's was greeted by three bullets, two to the chest and one to his left shoulder, all thanks to Reem.

"Noooo!" Dreadnight roared, his rage growing, along with his strength.

"Shit!" Siberian Scientist writhed in pain, instantly rolling back to take cover behind the front of the truck.

Luckily, he was wearing his bulletproof vest, otherwise he would have been a goner.

The four coherent mercs along with Reem and Chen continued bombarding the truck with bullets as they inched closer, providing cover for Inkubus while ignoring Dreadnight completely.

His back up against the front bumper of the truck while the bank itself provided cover in front of him, Siberian Scientist blindly shot toward the oncoming mercs in a feeble attempt to defend himself.

"Siberian Scientist, Inkubus at three o'clock! Adam blurted out as he watched the malevolent monster flee.

Siberian Scientist rolled to his left and peered out from the front of truck and saw Inkubus, Reem, and Chen nearing his helicopter. Without delay, Siberian Scientist spun his gun around and aimed it at Inkubus who was at least fifty yards away. With one eye squinted he exhaled and pulled the trigger.

"Ahhh!" Inkubus groaned in pain as he tripped to the ground, clutching onto the back of his right leg and its newly formed flesh wound.

Reem and Chen immediately dropped to Inkubus's aid, grabbing ahold of him and helping him rise from the ground.

"Fu …" Siberian Scientist began to yell until the merc from the windshield leaped from the truck's hood, landing on top of him and forcing him face first to the ground.

With regained strength, Dreadnight thrusted forward in an attempting to break free from the harpoon's metal claws. His excruciating screams of pain filled the air as the metal wire tanged in stress. But it was no use, the spears were in too deep. As he watched the bloodied merc pin Siberian Scientist to the ground, he fretted his dear friend's death. His rage took over as a bout of surmising strength poured into his chiseled muscles like hot molten iron. Quickly, he stepped back, twisted around, and grabbed tightly onto the metal cable.

"Grrrawww" Slade screamed from exertion.

Dreadnight jerked the cable, pulling with all his might. He felt it budge as nuts and bolts shot into the air, busting off the weapon as the concealed merc attempted to brace it with his body.

"Grrrawww" Slade screamed once again, digging the claws of his feet deep into the concrete below for leverage as the muscles in his back pulsed.

The once mounted weapon sprung from its brackets and flew through the loft's window, shattering its surrounding bricks and pulling the gunman along with it. Once it cleared the building, Dreadnight immediately swung the cable to his right as if he were doing a hammer throw in the Olympics. The cable whipped around, close-lining the four mercs approaching Siberian Scientist, until smashing into the side of the bank. Its wall exploded into hundreds of pieces. In a barrage of thunderous roars, the contraption rolled to a crashing stop. Debris blasted into the face of Siberian Scientist's assailant, knocking the man off him.

Ignoring the gnawing pain emanating from his back, Dreadnight released his claws and walked toward the four mercs as they attempted to rise from the ground, taking advantage of the cable's slack.

"It's time the gloves come off!" Dreadnight snarled, blood running down the majority of his body.

In one upward swipe, Dreadnight sent the claws of his right hand directly into a merc as the he stumbled to regain his footing. The merc gasped for air as the five black pikes severed his insides and blood projected onto the street. Dreadnight ripped his hand from the man's body, causing the merc to fall senseless to the ground. He stepped over the twitching inhuman shell as it inhaled its last wasteful breaths. A second merc only a few yards ahead, sprung to his feet and lunged toward Dreadnight while yielding a switchblade. The merc swung the blade in a hammering motion, but his forearm was met with the bone crushing grip of Dreadnight's left hand, which swung and tossed the merc like a rag doll across parking lot and through a church window.

P-Taff P-Taff

Two bullets from Siberian Scientist's tokarev pierced the heart of his assailant just as the merc rolled over and reached for his neck.

"Now stay down!" Siberian Scientist shouted, relieved yet engulfed in angst.

That meant there was one merc possessing no humanity left. But he was nowhere to be found.

Did he actually retreat? How could that be?

Just fifty yards ahead, Reem and Chen lifted Inkubus into the helicopter cabin, a trail of blood following him. Immediately after, Reem and Chen turned and shot at Dreadnight and Siberian Scientist as they rolled back toward their cruiser. Siberian

Scientist crawled back toward the passenger side of the cargo truck, dodging the bullets as they ricocheted around him.

The helicopter's aluminum rails creaked as they lifted from the ground. With powerful strides, Dreadnight charged toward the helicopter in a fixated blitz, ignoring multiple incoming bullets that pierced his thick flesh. His muscles tensed and rippled with each step as the pounding of his feet caused the ground to tremble. Likely fearing a cruel fate, Reem and Chen panicked like mice, leaping into their cruiser and peeling off in a frenzy.

Cowards!

Dreadnight's pace continued to excel as the helicopter rose higher off the ground. With his heart racing and blood pumping, he launched from the concrete as if his life depended on it, stretching his body out as he surged toward the helicopter and its vortex of resistance. The wire of the harpoon contraption scraped along the blacktop as it dragged behind him.

Almost ... got ...

The edge of Dreadnight's claws scraped against the aluminum rail and slid off its polished facet.

Close, but no cigar. Dreadnight's arms flailed in failure as his body reversed its course.

"Nooo!" Dreadnight roared in mind shattering frustration.

His animal instincts kicked in as they attempted to engage his wings to recover. But they wouldn't even budge, multiple tendons and ligaments had been sliced clean apart by the harpoon's vicious splintery.

Oh shit!

Hanging out of his escape chopper, Inkubus watched as Dreadnight crash landed onto the unforgiving ground below. In a scraping skid, Dreadnight's body came to a halt.

"Slade!" A symphony of screams from the team members overloaded the comm link.

"We've lost our visual. Siberian Scientist what's happening?" Mr. Unseen frantically said.

"Slade, you okay?" Siberian Scientist slid beside his comrade.

Erruff

Rings of steam shot from Dreadnight's nose, kicking up dust. He drowsily shook his head. With a trembling body, Dreadnight lifted himself up onto the palms of his hands as his arms struggled to remain tight and steady.

"Oh, thank god you are alright!" Father Ephrem gasped in relief as the link's visual returned.

Siberian Scientist reached down to provide Dreadnight some stability.

"We gotta get you out of here before anyone else shows up," Siberian Scientist said with urgency as he helped Dreadnight to his feet.

"I'm good," Dreadnight said sternly before walking sluggishly to his left and through the shattered wall where the harpoon gun had crashed.

As soon as he entered the room brimming in dust and debris, he heard a man coughing. After a few more steps and a more discernible sense of clarity, he saw the gunman himself, impaled and suspended mid-air with a large serrated spike plugging a chasm in the middle of his chest. The merc's head and arms dangled in crucifixion as he violently coughed up blood. Dreadnight paused in a stare at the merciless drone, feeling no remorse or sympathy.

Once the merc lifted his head high enough to realize who was in his presence, the synapsis serum's decree kicked in. In a final feeble attempt to attack Dreadnight and obey his master's orders, the merc feverously jerked his body, grunting and groaning like a rabid beast as blood sprayed from his mouth. But no serum could bring him back from this and no brainwashing could prevent his assured demise. In the blink of an eye, the man's body gave out and slid down lifelessly to the base of the stake and flat against the wall from which the spike hung.

"Good riddance," Dreadnight said with disdain as the man's life force dwindled away like a charring ember sailing through the wind.

He turned his attention to the high-tech harpoon gun a few feet behind him and to his left. Dreadnight pulled back his right arm and in one quick burst, sent his fist through the glass silencer and into the gun's metal shell, bending and twisting its alloy. Separated from its mating sheets of metal, Dreadnight ripped the contorted side panel completely off the weapon's barrel. Inside was a connector hub linked to the very cable which ran all the way into the projectile embedded deep into his back. Without hesitation, he pulled the hub's latch, releasing the cable and its connector.

It's a start ... Dreadnight thought to himself, feeling a smidge of relief.

"Guys, get out of there now!" Raydar keyed adamantly. "Reem just dispatched eight cruisers filled with cops to your location."

"Copy that," Siberian Scientist replied.

Dreadnight remained silent as he exited the decimated building, pulling his metal restraint behind him, his face as cold as stone and beaten to a pulp.

After stepping into the cargo pod of the truck he hit its front wall with the side of his fist, signaling Siberian Scientist that he was good to speed off. Siberian Scientist did just that, leaving the death and destruction in his rear-view mirror.

~

Slade's mind was on spin cycle as he sat atop the ice-cold metallic surface of Nikolai's examination table, his gargantuan proportions caused its legs to creak in stress. His body remained still, and his battered face bore a portrait of defeat. Already changed into his white lab coat and wearing blue latex gloves, Nikolai analyzed the array of artillery transfixed in Slade's murky flesh. Had any other creature endured such a traumatic wound, they would have certainly died within a few breaths.

"It's a good thing you didn't remove this contraption yourself. The spears themselves were and are the only thing preventing you from bleeding dry," Nikolai said in a most serious tone.

"Hmm," Slade grunted in an emotionless nod.

"Yeah, otherwise I would have had to perform an extensive blood transfusion, an operation I have little experience with on gargoyles ... and by little experience, I mean none," Nikolai said sarcastically with a brimming grin to match.

Slade chuckled, providing his first real response since Inkubus's escape.

"Good to have you back with us," Father Ephrem said, Adam nodding and smiling in agreement as they stood just a few feet away in observation.

Slade forced out a small smile, appreciative of his team's concern.

"I just cannot believe I fell for another one of that sick son of a bitch's traps," Slade said, his voice flowing with frustration and disappointment.

"We all did," Adam chimed in.

"I was so close. He was within reach ... This could have all been over once and for all." Slade sighed, closing his eyes in sadness.

The room felt as if a dreary fog had consumed its entirety as each of the four men processed the current state of their mission. The night's affair was certainly something they were not prepared to deal with.

"Not a soul in this room has the right to feel regret or anguish," Father Ephrem said, his voice cutting through the silence like a knife. "Each one of us is human and there is no shame in defending humanity and all that it stands for. Our intention was just that. And God only knows why such challenges and strife are placed upon our doorstep," he added assuredly.

Father Ephrem's devout words penetrated Slade's heart. He was right, their intentions were pure, but their judgement had been clouded by inexperience. The question was, where do they go from here?

"We must learn from this event, dissect it, and grow from the lessons it will teach us. We will become stronger … we will defeat Inkubus," Father Ephrem said with fervor.

The dreary fog that once consumed the laboratory lifted as Father Ephrem's rays of shinning wisdom enlightened all.

"He's right guys. You two nearly captured Inkubus in an unexpected bout of defense," Ray's computerized comm voice said while he typed away at his precinct desk. "Just think, we now know what we are truly up against, and our enemy now knows we are not to be underestimated," he added, likely trying to keep his emotions in check around his coworkers and maintain his cover.

"Damn right, comrade!" Nikolai shouted out of impulse.

"It's time we up our game, boys!" Adam added, with the same desire.

And then there was Slade, the only one holding back. The team awaited the slightest bit of feedback, praying he would join in on the momentum built thus far. All eyes were on him.

Slade's eyes narrowed as if they were harnessing a fiery blaze and his head bobbed in a yearning craze.

"It's time we get vengeance!" Slade growled, providing a response that triggered a chorus of cheer from his family.

Shortly thereafter as the time neared 3:15 a.m., Ray walked into the laboratory in a hurried fashion, eager as ever to see Slade now that his drudging shift was a mere memory. They exchanged a brotherly hug of relief just before Slade laid face down onto the examination table in preparation of Nikolai's extraction procedure. Next to the table, a rolling cart was positioned, displaying various glistening surgical tools, a handful of syringes, and a pile of sterile gauze.

"Shall I give you a heavy anesthetic so that you can take a nap, or would you prefer localized numbing agents?" Nikolai asked.

"The numbing agents. I don't want to take any risks considering the sun will be rising in just a few hours," Slade replied.

"You got it," Nikolai acknowledged.

Wasting no time, Nikolai reached onto the cart and pulled a large syringe filled with a green commixture of mepivacaine and epinephrine, a strong concoction typically used on cattle. With great caution, Nikolai injected an eighth of the syringe's contents near each laceration of the eight splitter spears, lifting and adjusting Slade's monstrous wings to reach each wound. Once complete, he grabbed a second and even larger syringe containing the same liquid and injected it into four spots that surrounded the main harpoon blade itself. Lastly, Nikolai applied a lavish amount of a five percent eutectic mixture of two local anesthetics, lidocaine and prilocaine, on Slade's entire back and wingspan.

"Okay, let's just give this stuff a few minutes to work its magic. Soon you should have little to no feeling in your back," Nikolai said.

"Thanks doc," Slade chuckled, causing Nikolai to smile.

Thanks to Adam's fine thinking, he and Ray wheeled the mobile monitoring system out in front of the examination table. His thought, to review the contents of the night's video feeds from Slade and Nikolai's comms. Not only would this provide Slade with ample distraction during the operation at hand, but also provide the team with their first step toward progressing forward.

For the next hour and a half, Nikolai meticulously disjoined the metallic spears from the flesh of Slade's back, cutting and digging with the steadiest of hands. Meanwhile, the other team members did just as Adam suggested, watching the replay of the night's video feed over and over with the utmost diligence. They analyzed every movement, every sound, and every mannerism of Inkubus and each of his drones, looking for the slightest of patterns or clues. Each member fed off each other's thoughts and ideas as they worked like detectives from the golden days, leaving no stone unturned.

By the end of the operation, Slade's back looked like a field of freshly plowed flesh, shredded and dilapidated from the numerous incisions and lacerations. No stitches or staples were applied since Slade believed his upcoming transformation back to human form would clean up the mess. So, for the time being, Nikolai applied a thick layer of antibiotic prophylaxis over the exposed flesh and covered Slade's entire back and the affected portions of his wings with gauze and bandaging for safe measure. Lying in a bloody mess next to the examining table, the contraption of torture that once inhabited Slade's body, a now crude reminder of the enemy at large.

In addition to the successful extraction operation, Father Ephrem, Ray, and Adam had logged a multitude of notes concerning the video footage. Out of all the footage, two particular items stuck out like a sore thumb. The first was the fact that Inkubus's soldiers were so fixated on his directive that they were oblivious to all else. This was on full display when Nikolai crashed into three of them like a freight train and not a single one of them flinched. This lapse in Inkubus's treatment procedure would surely become a most exploitable loophole while battling his goons in the future.

The second and more peculiar observation was that of the sleeve apparatus upon his right arm. Its design and unrecognizable mechanical properties were simply mind boggling, not to mention the incredible magnitude of force it generated. It was as if the apparatus was stolen straight out of a steampunk novel or even the mind of Jules Verne. After seeing such a sight, Adam was determined to not only uncover its origin, but also the source of its power.

As the glow of the morning sun ever so slowly crept above the horizon, the entire team headed upstairs to witness Slade's mystical transformation and its essence. Slade assured the team he would be fine and that they should get their rest, but none of them would budge. They insisted they be present to ensure his well-being and there was no telling them otherwise. Within minutes the ritual had begun. The warm rays of earth's brightest star slowly sealed Slade's feet and legs in stone. Slade clutched onto Rachel's charm to ease his nerves as the stone continued to sprout up his body, ignoring all principles of gravity and laws of nature as the team watched in unbridled awe.

And just like that there were two statues upon the cathedral rooftop yet again. But not for long. The air suddenly chilled as Slade's stone mask heated up like a furnace, causing it to glow like the sun itself. Seconds later, that stone mask began to wither away, turning into a swarm of embers that drifted far … far away. Before Slade's naked body could collapse, Father Ephrem rushed and caught him, ignoring the burning embers that seared his exposed face. Nikolai quickly examined Slade's back. It was indeed intact, just marred with a map of contusions, an outcome each man on that rooftop would be forever grateful for.

Though the beginning of that night was filled with misfortune and mayhem, it developed into one of mental expansion and brotherhood. Just when the team thought their alliance was rock solid, an experience as such made it ironclad.

Chapter 7
Unforeseen Fortune

The time was 7:55 p.m. on Friday, July 25th, the day Ray had been dreading for the past week. By now his nerves were fried and his stomach a mass of knotted chords. But finally, it was time to face the music. He impatiently tapped his fingers upon the rustic round table of the observatory, his heart pounding like never before.

Though his mind had to bear the weight of painstaking uncertainty, Ray wasn't alone, he was never alone. The entire team sat alongside him, making their best attempts to distract his mind and keep him grounded. Though predominately unsuccessful, Ray appreciated the gesture dearly, he just couldn't focus enough to express it at the moment. But as they had already proven time and time again, they were a family, and at that very moment their brother needed his family more than ever.

The room smelled like coffee and pancakes, yes pancakes, Ray's comfort food, as the voices of Lainey and her roommate Michelle radiated from the speakers of Adam's station. The two girls gleefully chatted while Lainey applied the finishing touches to her already flawless face, awaiting Chen's arrival to her apartment.

"Could someone just grab me a bucket? I feel like I should just vomit now and get it over with," Ray said half sarcastically, his face painting a fitting visual. "What could she possibly see in him? I mean seriously the man couldn't be a bigger douche." His voice cracked in frustration. "Why am I so in love with her?" Ray added dejectedly, dropping his head into his hands.

Slade gripped Ray's left shoulder and gave him a little shake.

"I don't know, man. But there is one thing I do know ... sometimes when a person cannot be with the one they truly desire, they become so blinded by the idea of simply being loved that they overlook any and all uncertainties, leaving their vulnerabilities fully exposed."

Ray lifted his head in contemplation.

"So, you're saying that the only reason she said yes to Chen was because I turned her down?" Ray asked with a distraught look upon his face.

"Essentially, yes," Slade replied.

"You really think I'm the one she truly desires?" Ray asked optimistically, his face now displaying a small bout of hope.

"I do, man."

"Huh," Ray said raising his eyebrows. "I'm not sure whether to feel good about that or not," he added, torn with emotion.

"You should feel very good about it, son. You're a damn good man and all this proves that," Father Ephrem said consolingly.

Rrriiinnngggg

The team's attention turned toward the speakers, stopping all conversation. Chen was there and it was time. The sound of her footsteps took over as they traipsed down the stairs, each one like a punch to Ray's gut. Then they heard the creak of a door.

~

"Evening Lainey," Chen said suavely.

"Hi Jon," Lainey replied with a brimming smile.

"Shall we?" He asked, directing his hand toward the sidewalk in an inviting fashion.

The air was calm and tepid as the two headed down the sidewalk together toward Chen's police cruiser that was just twenty yards away. The sky was dimming as the sun continued its descent below the horizon, causing the clouds to discolor.

"You drove the squad car?" Lainey asked curiously.

"Yeah. I mean why not enjoy the perks of our job, you know?"

Once they reached the car, Chen opened the passenger door for Lainey and closed it behind her once she was settled. He himself got into the car, started the engine, and drove down the street. The two participated in some general small talk regarding work and hobbies, sprinkled with some awkward silence as they headed to their destination

"Remember those perks I mentioned?" Chen said with the grin of a snake as he hit the cruiser's siren and blew through a red light, causing Lainey to wince.

"Haha, now that's fun, huh?" Chen said with laughter.

Lainey thought elsewise.

"I'd prefer if you didn't do that again ... car sickness you know," she replied, attempting to soften her already diluted response.

"God, what an asshole!" Ray blurted, shaking his head in disgust, a feeling that was mutual amongst the entire team as they listened to the covert feed.

After driving a few more miles, Chen and Lainey had arrived at *Bistro El Bilantro,* the most upscale restaurant in all of Detroit. Immediately upon realizing where she was,

Lainey felt underdressed and flat out uncomfortable. She had expected them to go to a more well ... middle class restaurant. She didn't need to be wined and dined as she just wasn't that type of girl. Apparently, Jon never caught onto that. The two exited the car as the valet man retrieved Chen's keys then hopped in to park it. Lainey couldn't believe Chen was letting a civilian drive a police issued vehicle. Suffeced to say, she was not impressed thus far, not even the slightest.

The restaurant's interior was intricate and gaudy to say the least. Glimmering chandeliers and lush tapestry as far as the eye could see surrounded the two as they entered the cesspool of overbearing money grubbers stuffing their gullets. The two were seated and immediately greeted with the finest of wines.

"Wine, miss?" The young female server asked, her black and white uniform pressed and spot free.

"Yes, please. Thank you," Lainey replied, figuring she might as well numb the mental suffering she was about to endure.

Chen of course declined and asked for a glass of their most aged scotch, his tone as haughty as could be.

"So, what do you think of this place?" Chen asked.

"It's nice. I have never been here before, but I am sure their food is great," she replied, hiding her true feelings.

"Oh, it is. Their service is lacking though apparently," Chen said arrogantly, gesturing to his hand being without a drink.

Coincidentally, the poor waitress was just approaching their table from behind Chen, her face wore a look of saddening frustration from the rude comment. Nevertheless, she was cordial and professional, neither of which Chen deserved at this point.

"Here you are sir. Sorry for the wait ... crazy night," the young waitress said. "And here are two loaves of our complementary freshly baked bread," she added politely.

"Sure," Chen replied unappreciatively.

Man, could he be a bigger ass? Ray was right all along.

"Are you two ready to order?" the waitress asked.

Both Lainey and Chen nodded and said yes.

"Go ahead Lainey. Order anything and as much as you'd like, the precinct's treat," Chen said with a devilish grin.

"I mean seriously Slade, can't we just kidnap the bastard right now? I mean why not, right?" Ray said sarcastically with a laugh tainted in anger.

"Don't worry, he will get what is coming to him and it will be much harsher than a kidnapping," Nikolai said with a smirk.

The effervescent smell of looming incense candles invaded Lainey's nostrils as she attempted to wrap her mind around the setting in which she was trapped in. Across the table, Chen drank away, already halfway through a second scotch and the second loaf of bread. For the following fifteen minutes, they chatted about work and their aspirations in regards to it while awaiting their main course, an amount of time that was deemed unacceptable by Chen which was of course expressed to the poor waitress.

That seemingly small portion of time was nearly unbearable for Lainey. She listened in disgust as Chen ranted and raved about how he was determined to become commissioner one day and of all the absurd laws he would convince the mayor to impose. At most, Lainey spoke twenty words through it all, words that innocently expressed her desire to get some real field time in place of being chained to a desk all day. Chen showed little sympathy or concern for her situation, a situation a man in his position could surely provide support toward.

Finally, their food had arrived, as well as a third scotch for Chen.

Oh thank God. I hope all of the chewing will shut him up for a bit. If I wanted to hear someone talk about their own interests all night, then I would have gone out with my mother.

However, those words were replaced by the sound of a rare steak the size of her face being barbarically dissected by a knife, blood spitting on and around the plate. Though disgusted, she somehow retained a straight face and a steady stomach as she dug her fork into her Mahi Mahi filet. The remainder of the meal continued in the same fashion, Chen rambled on about Reem, the precinct, and all his dreams laced in greed. Not a single ounce of substance was spoken the entire meal.

It was over ... finally. Chen paid the check, leaving a measly five-dollar tip on a nearly one-hundred-and-fifty-dollar bill.

Asshole ... she busted her ass for over an hour, and for what? To be verbally spit on and disrespected.

As they stood up to head toward the exit, Chen leading the way, Lainey discretely pulled two twenty-dollar bills from her turquoise satchel and set them down onto the table. Luckily, Chen was not paying attention, no surprise there. It was the kindest of gestures, one the waitress immediately noticed. The two girls exchanged smiles for a brief second before Lainey turned and walked away.

"Try to stay relaxed brother, it's almost over," Slade said, turning and looking at Ray who was jittery and uneasy.

"Not until she is at home safe, and he is far far away, man," Ray replied, his foot tapping against the floor like a rabbit as he continued to eat his pancakes.

"Well if it makes you feel better at all, I sure as hell don't foresee a second date. We all heard how horribly that date went, and it was obvious she lost all interest in Chen the minute they walked into that restaurant," Slade said.

'Yeah, it does, a little. Thanks guys … for everything … I mean really," Ray said with an innocent and shy smile.

Lainey crossed her hands as her and Chen cruised on M-10, the sounds of a random hip hop group playing throughout the car. She was glad she survived the dinner and was ready to go home to simply sleep the night away and imagine the date was all a bad dream.

Chen had other plans though.

"How about we head back my place and have a nightcap?" Chen asked, breaking the mind-numbing silence, a silence Lainey much preferred.

"Oh, that son of a bitch!" Ray blurted, standing up from his chair and migrating into a nervous pace.

"Umm, sorry I'll have to pass. I don't think that fish is agreeing with me. Probably would be better to just take me home," Lainey nervously said, thrown off by the blunt proposal.

"Yes! That's my girl!" Ray shouted, pumping his fist in joy and relief.

"Are you sure?" Chen asked, pushing the subject.

"Yes, I'm sure." Lainey said as gently as possible even though she wanted to punch Chen in the throat.

"If that's what you want," Chen replied nonchalantly, clearly taking a blow to his massive ego.

Minutes later, which to Lainey felt like hours, Chen pulled up to Lainey's townhouse. She politely thanked him for dinner and told him she would see him at the office the next day. His pride likely bruised and battered, he just nodded and told her he would see her soon. Lainey then exited the car and headed to her front door with a little more pep in her step than usual.

She closed her door behind her, leaning back onto it immediately after, mentally exhausted and full of regret. Suddenly, she realized her hands were empty.

You have got to be kidding me!

She was in such a rush to get out of that wretched car that she left her purse on the center console.

I'm such an idiot …

~

"Wait … why are we still hearing this music? Didn't she leave the car?" Ray said out of confusion, a feeling that the entire team was experiencing as well.

"Haha, the bitch forgot her purse," Chen said with in an arrogant cackle. "Window of opportunity number two. Guess we will just have to rendezvous tomorrow," Chen added with the same tone, re-inflating his ego.

"What are the odds," Ray scoffed, shaking his head.

"I sure hope he doesn't go through her purse," Adam said with concern. "Who knows what would happen if he found out she was carrying a bug."

The sense of relief that had once pooled over the observatory did a full one eighty, now mutating into fear.

Rrrirnng Rrrirnng

The team continued to listen closely to the bug's feed.

"What's up Harvey?" Chen answered.

"Come pick me up at the Green Stables Tavern. We need to have a chat about the big score coming up Sunday," Reem said. "Don't worry, I'll bring the booze," he added with a chuckle.

"Of course, boss. On my way. Be there in five," Chen replied.

"Holy shit, guys, this could be huge! Ha-ha, our luck just turned around," Nikolai said excitedly.

"Big score huh? I think it's time we get us some dirt on these boys and set up a trap of our own," Slade said with a grin.

"Wow, who would have guessed," Ray said in awe.

Just like that, Ray's emotions somersaulted, turning into a collection of excitement, drive, and a hunger for vengeance. The team sat along the table, ears glued to the speaker, impatiently awaiting Chen to pick Reem up.

What could this big score be? Could this be the team's own big break? The wait was simply unbearable.

~

Chen pulled up to the Green Stables Tavern and Reem hopped into the cruiser, a fifth of scotch clutched in his left hand. Reem told him to head to their favorite boozing spot, a section under the Antietam Avenue Bridge off Dequindre Road. Every night they had off from the precinct they would drink the night away like two alcoholic trolls under that very bridge. Tonight, was no exception. Rolling toward the discarded bridge, Chen turned off his headlamps and crept up underneath one of its arches. Once parked, he shut the engine off and turned the key to battery only, allowing the music to continue playing.

Until 1975, The Antietam Avenue Bridge posed as a major highway packed with rush hour traffic and gas fumes. Forty years later, it was a desolate memory of the once thriving motor city. Its crumbling concrete slabs were tainted with moss and overlaid graffiti, like most of the city's skeleton that remained from its manufacturing hay day. The bridge's presence was a perfect reflection of the city, its people, and its decaying existence.

Reem reached forward and pulled two clear glasses from the glove compartment, handing one of them to Chen. He cracked open a 1951 bottle of Glendale Scotch and poured a generous amount of its contents into each glass. The two men clanked their glasses together like ancient romans and sipped on its potency with a smug look covering both of their faces.

"So, Jon, did you give that fine piece of police ass the old nightstick?" Reem cackled, nudging Chen's arm.

"No. That bitch is a prude. But don't worry, I will get what I want, I always do," Chen replied with a grin.

"I don't doubt that," Reem replied with the same devious grin while raising one of his eyebrows.

"You said you wanted to talk about Sunday's arrangement?" Chen asked.

"Yes, of course. This is the big one Jon. This is the deal that will make us millions … This will be the beginning of the city becoming ours my friend!" Reem said with fervor and widened eyes.

A smirk grew upon Chen's face as he seemed to drift off into a daydream of bliss. Seconds later, he snapped back to reality and the topic at hand.

"Has anything changed or is the plan still as Inkubus detailed last night?" Chen asked.

"No change. It is still going down at 2:00 a.m. on Sunday at the Ambassador Shipping Docks of course," Reem replied before taking another thick sip of the aged scotch.

"Okay. And the shipment is still coming by rail from Mexico and up through the Midwest?"

"Yes. It may not be the fastest method, but's certainly the safest and most discrete," Reem said. "Railway security checks are basically a joke down there. How do you think so many illegals enter this country?" He added with laughter.

"Ha! Those gringos have no idea what they are getting into. Wish I could see their faces when they realize they received the last of Dante's spiked cocaine filled with amino acids and ephedrine. Meanwhile, we will be swimming in military grade artillery," Chen gloated.

"Ha-ha! Within a matter of days those half-wit Libyans will be paying us millions to fulfill a weapons demand they have been waiting years for."

~

"You recorded all of that, right?" Slade asked with urgency.

"Yes sir. I record everything," Adam replied with a smile.

The entire team was enthralled by what they had just overheard, feeling as if they needed to pinch one another to ensure it wasn't a dream. For once it seemed like they were finally catching a break and would get a glimpse of prosperity after a heart wrenching couple of weeks.

"This is beyond big guys," Slade said, his face flabbergasted with awe. "We have an opportunity to bust their biggest deal yet and maybe, just maybe, get our hands on that filthy Inkubus!" he added, a storm brewing in his striking blue eyes.

"It sure is, but we have to play this right … we have to execute with precision," Nikolai added.

"Well, we have one day to draw up a plan. So, let's get to it. I won't rest until I get to personally ruin Chen." Ray said, standing up from the table with beaming eyes of extreme focus.

This was a monumental moment for the team. A moment that provided them with the fuel they had been yearning for. Not one man in that room could have guessed or even imagined that night would unravel as it did, turning from a nerve-racking stakeout into an abundance of unforeseen fortune.

Chapter 8
Fear of the Future

With the schematics fully prepared and only a few hours separating the team from their most perilous feat yet, Slade peeled away from the observatory to collect his thoughts and prepare himself mentally. This had become routine for Slade. Every night prior to his transformation he would spend an hour of solitude in his room without interaction or distraction.

As Slade walked through the dark and dingy tunnel to cross over to St. Anne's, he paused and placed his hand against the cold stonewall beside him, stricken by an overwhelming flood of anxiety. Tonight, was not like other nights, in fact he himself hadn't been the same ever since his encounter with Inkubus. After exhaling a large breath, he continued onward, but didn't stop at his room per the usual.

Knock Knock

Slade's knuckles echoed through the hallway.

"Come in," Father Ephrem said.

Slade turned the cast iron handle and entered Father Ephrem's room, closing the door behind him and having a seat on Father Ephrem's bed.

"Everything all set for tonight's ambush?" Father Ephrem asked.

"Yep. The team worked through the night and I think we have a hell of a plan honestly," Slade replied in a less than enthusiastic tone.

"Is everything okay son? You seem troubled," Father Ephrem asked with concern.

Slade's face tightened in a reluctant pause as he attempted to put his thoughts into words.

"Yeah, I'm uhh ... having a hard time overcoming some anxiety or fear I guess," Slade said despairingly. "This is something I battled with greatly in the past and it has come back in full force. I'm just really struggling mentally right now."

"I'm really sorry to hear that Slade," Father Ephrem said empathetically. "My ears are wide open. You mustn't be afraid to express yourself as you will receive no judgement."

Slade nodded his head as he built up the courage to leak his most guarded feelings.

"Well, it all hit me after that night Nikolai and I came face to face with Inkubus," Slade started to explain. "That night as I sat there on Nikolai's examination table, I realized that all that I live for, all my hopes and dreams, were nearly taken from me." Slade's eyes tightened. "Prior to this gift, this unbelievable blessing, everything I had ever worked toward or dreamed of accomplishing in my life had been stripped from me at one point or another. Sometimes by sheer misfortune, other times by the cruel hands of others. To be honest … I'm deathly afraid of that happening again." Slade's voice weakened and his eyes swelled.

Father Ephrem rose from his chair and accompanied Slade, placing his arm around him.

"There is no shame in such fears. You're no ordinary man, Slade. Like myself, it is your passion, your dreams, that mold you and make you who you are," Father Ephrem said adorningly. "See, most people allow the outside world to influence who they are and dictate who they become, essentially turning into autonomous bodies of acceptance, of adherence. That just isn't you, or me for that matter. We are unique and we are proud," Father Ephrem said ardently.

A small smile of appreciation crept upon Slade's teary-eyed face.

"You're right, and I am proud just as you said. I wouldn't want to be any other way. But I just can't shake this fear, this immense uncertainty. I just want to defeat Inkubus and continue Michael's quest so badly … I can't imagine otherwise."

Father Ephrem stood and walked over to his desk, grabbing the picture of himself and a beautiful woman, then turned and sat back down on the bed.

"I'm going to share something with you that I have never told a single soul since its occurrence," Father Ephrem said as he held onto the picture frame and glared through its glass. "See this man here, this was me when all of my hopes and dreams were within grasp. This was when my life first had purpose. That purpose, those dreams, well they were that woman right there," Father Ephrem stated, pointing at the young woman. "Her name was Abigail Greene, and she was my fiancée." A look of sadness overcame Father Ephrem's aged face, a look Slade had yet to encounter since befriending him.

"What happened?" Slade asked earnestly.

"The world took her from me. See, I know exactly how you feel as I have felt such fear many times over the past few decades."

Thirty-six unforgettable years ago, Ephrem and his fiancée Abigail were walking the streets of New York City after watching Kraft & Morrow's live rendition of "A Christmas Story" at the Broadhurst Theater. It was a cold and snowy December night. The air was filled with the sound of buzzing street cars and the gleam of flashing billboards. Without a care in the world they joyfully conversed, clutching each other's arms to keep warm as they walked back to Ephrem's apartment on eighth street. It was a picture-perfect moment, a glimpse into their foreseeable future together as a married couple.

Or so Ephrem thought.

Just as they rounded the corner onto Ephrem's street, they were greeted by a mugger yielding a pistol, his face covered in a black ski mask. The man nervously waved the gun at Abigail demanding she hand over her purse, a gift from Ephrem the Christmas before. Ephrem urged Abigail to just hand over the purse, hoping the mugger would just take it and leave.

However, the man's greed was much harder to overcome. After Abigail handed over the purse, he pointed the gun at the gold clasp around her right wrist, demanding she surrender it. Ephrem knew the significance of that clasp, it was a gift from her late mother would had died just months before and he couldn't bear to see her lose it to some street thug. Ephrem pleaded that the man just take his wallet and his watch instead. But when Ephrem reached for his back pocket to retrieve his wallet, the mugger became startled and swung the gun in Ephrem's direction.

"No!" Screamed Abigail.

P-TAFF!

The gunshot cracked into the air like thunder as the weapon's chamber jarred violently, spitting the bullet's casing into the air. Leaning face to face into Ephrem was Abigail.

"I love you," she whispered with her final breath.

In that split second, just as the mugger had swung his arm across, Abigail had spun her body in front of Ephrem, shielding him from the bullet and sacrificing her own life for his. The mugger's eyes bulged in unbridled fright as he dropped his arm and ran in cowardice, knocking people over as he frantically fled the scene of his cold-blooded killing. Every bone in Ephrem's body wanted to chase down that bastard and beat him to a bloody pulp, but he couldn't leave his love. Abigail's body loosened as Ephrem squeezed her tightly, watching the life he had dreamt of fade away before his very eyes.

Snow calmly swayed down onto Ephrem's face and all surroundings seemed to freeze as he screamed in agonizing horror at the night sky and police sirens amassed in the distance. One man, one action, deprived him from a life of happiness, a life of fulfillment. Ephrem would never be the same after that long December night.

The next three years of Ephrem's life were that of self-deprivation, solitude, and copious amounts of alcohol. He was without hope and without a will to live. He became a mere shell of a once thriving young man. That is until he met a man who went by the name of Father Riccardo.

One dreary fall night, much like many others, Ephrem stumbled with liquor in hand down eighth street and past the very spot where his love was taken from him. However, this night he didn't want to end up back home, in fact, he didn't want to "be" at all.

A previously religious man, Ephrem found himself in a confessional booth of a nearby cathedral. He didn't quite know why he was there. Maybe it was to make one final plea to God to end his misery, or to ask forgiveness for what he was planning on doing that night. Regardless, he voiced his feelings, assuming only God could be listening at such an hour. A few minutes deep into his stammering speech, a voice appeared from the receiving end. It was the voice of Father Riccardo, who just happened to be visiting from Croatia for a seminar.

Too drunk to care, Ephrem continued, spilling his words through the mesh grate that separated the two men. His words were that of great despair, loneliness, and sheer hopelessness. It was apparent to Father Riccardo what Ephrem's intentions were that night, he intended on ending his life, an occurrence Father Riccardo would not allow.

These were the very words Father Riccardo spoke that saved Ephrem's life that very night:

"My son, the pain you feel, that anguish, that is your humanity, your soul. Your will to love and live were so immense and so true, that when they were taken, your heart could no longer bear the weight of your soul. But you see, the heart can heal, as can the soul. Now you can leave here tonight and stop your heart, ending the pain that cripples it, but it would only tarnish your soul and relinquish your humanity. Tell me, what good does that do? Does it bring back your love? Does it bring vengeance upon the one who stole your will to live? It won't, I promise you that. But if you could find the strength to persevere, to endure, then you might just be able to prevent another from pulling that trigger or losing the one that they love. Is that not what the one you lost would want you to do? Would that not provide you the slightest bit of redemption? That power is within you, and unlike most things in this world, it is within your control. Now what are you going to do with it?"

Those daggers of truth, of realism, rendered Ephrem speechless. Within a matter of twenty minutes, he went from a drunken stupor into a sober epiphany. Being a coward and escaping his pain wasn't what Abigail would have wanted, in fact, she would have been sickened by the man Ephrem had become. That alone was a notion Ephrem could not live with, one he refused to let prevail if even for one second longer.

With a reformed mind and a gracious heart, Ephrem thanked Father Riccardo dearly and asked if there was a number he could reach him at in case he needed advice in the future. Father Riccardo eagerly wrote his number down onto a small piece of paper and expressed he would always be available to help a friend. Ephrem left that cathedral a new man, while Father Riccardo went to sleep knowing there was indeed a future in line for the troubled young Ephrem.

"See Slade, that is what truly led me to the priesthood. Father Riccardo saved my life that night. He made me realize that life was still worth living and that I just needed a purpose. That purpose was to do the same as he did for others. To provide them hope and to save them from the darkness within … to prevent others from enduring the pain that once consumed my soul," Father Ephrem said.

"Wow … I am so sorry you had to go through that. I can't even imagine … surviving that. But am I sure glad you did," Slade said, his face still tightened in awe.

"This life of mine has taught me that one has to survive long enough to live," Father Ephrem expressed.

Such a statement really hit Slade, forcing him to reflect upon his own past struggles.

"And you know what, though they never found the man that took my sweet Abigail, I still obtained that redemption that I longed for."

"Really? But how?" Slade asked, bewildered by such a daunting result.

"Yes. The night I found a dying young man who had risked his life to save another's. It was you who provided what I sought," Father Ephrem said with a smile. "It gave me the chance to do what Father Riccardo did for me. The difference was, you were able to for Rachel what I could not for Abigail, and I could not let that sacrifice claim your life as it was much too vital to this earth," he added as his own eyes filled with tears of joy.

Slade smiled as he became overwhelmed with a sense of gratefulness, not only for what he provided Father Ephrem, but for his presence, and life for that matter.

"That really makes me happy, Father Ephrem. You deserved that and so much more," Slade replied.

"So, in terms of the fear you are feeling and the anxiety that presses your mind, you must realize that it is simply your humanity and your soul making you recognize that you have a life worth living. A life too important to squander. You simply cannot allow that fear and anxiety to hold you back, instead it should serve as a reminder that you must live your life to the fullest and hold nothing back. Let your passion and your dreams push you to your true potential. Because only then will your dreams become your reality."

"You're right. You're exactly right. I need focus on the task at hand. I need to keep my eye on the prize and let my dreams fuel me," Slade said with momentum.

"Let me ask you this Slade, what do you fear the most?" Father Ephrem asked.

Slade pondered the question for a moment, but only a brief moment as he thought of this very subject every day.

"Daylight."

"Daylight huh? And why is that?"

"It reminds me of the life I once had and the life I hope to obtain one day," Slade said with sincerity.

"And what does that life that you hope to obtain entail?"

"A life where I can bask in the sunlight with Rachel. A life where Inkubus and the scourge of this city have been brought to their knees in reverence of my creed," Slade replied with a serious face and a tone to match.

"Every time fear or anxiety attempts to cloud your mind, think of that life. Let it calm you, let it wash over you. That very dream will push you to do great things, to be the man we both know this world needs."

Father Ephrem's wise words were exactly what Slade needed to hear. It wasn't a coincidence Slade ended up in his quarters that night, it was a calling. One that prepared him to take on the greatest of missions yet.

Chapter 9
Karma Unleashed

The Ambassador Shipping Docks were yet another faint reminder of the city's once thriving economy. For the longest time, it served as the heart of the city's transcontinental capacity, pumping natural resources throughout the United States and Canada. Now it wore the face of a desolate wasteland consumed by broken windowpanes and soot-stained walls. Even the water that splashed alongside its moss capped bedrock was tainted green from years of unsolicited pollution. It was an obviously perfect place for a covert weapons deal, out of sight and out of mind.

Mr. Unseen and Father Ephrem sat behind the monitoring station with keen eyes, viewing for the first time the new three-sixty panoramic camera system that Mr. Unseen developed for Dreadnight, Raydar, and Siberian Scientist. After their most recent harpoon fiasco, Mr. Unseen realized he needed much better visibility to ensure he could provide the best surveillance possible. He couldn't stomach the idea of missing any key details that could put his team in jeopardy.

Thus, he integrated the technology from the comm modules into a wearable belt attachment for Raydar and Siberian Scientist, and into Rachel's charm necklace for Slade. Essentially, the belts and necklace chain were modified to retain eight six-millimeter spherical casings which were evenly distributed around its circumference. Mounted inside of each sphere was a microscopic camera of the highest quality. The casings were made of high-resolution tempered glass which act as magnifiers to ensure the best of clarity. The technology's enhanced wiring system combined with the precise placement of the spheres provides a view of perfect synchronization as if you had the view of God himself. It was truly a thing of brilliance and beauty. Now as they viewed their heroes video feeds, they could see the entire picture, warranting the name which Mr. Unseen deemed the technology, "The Eyes of Divinity."

Circling high above as the clouds camouflaged his grayed skin, Dreadnight observed the docks below, awaiting the arrival of both Inkubus's crew and the Mexican cartel. Just a block away from the docks land entrance, Raydar and Siberian Scientist sat quietly in the shipping truck with their eyes peeled, ready for action.

"Man, I can't wait to wreak havoc on Reem and Chen's big moment!" Raydar blurted unexpectedly.

For the first time, Raydar had the opportunity to join his teammates in their nightly mission,

"You and me both brother," Dreadnight replied.

In order for Raydar to conceal his identity from his renowned co-workers, he of course needed a cover, more specifically a mask and a voice modulator. Unfortunately, due to time constraints, Adam couldn't procure an elaborate disguise such as Siberian Scientist's. Fortunately, Raydar wasn't one for being flashy or picky for that matter. So, he took it upon himself to design a simple mask that not only reflected his personality but also his state of mind. With a sheet of glossy black satin fabric, a pair of scissors, a stencil, and one can of white spray paint, he created just that.

Two strips of the fabric running from the face of the mask were seated above and below each ear, tying together with its coinciding strips at the back of his head, providing a snug fit throughout the face. The front of the mask was cut along the jawline and tapered down into a "v" until ending at his collarbone. Holes were cut out around his eye placements and their borders were stiffened with plastic strips along the inside. In the design of an Orthodox cross, white paint stretched across the entirety of the eyes from ear to ear and from the tip of his forehead down to his collarbone in a width of an inch. To add to its sheer fierceness, the brows were bunched inward and down in anger which complemented the white out contacts that covered his pupils. It was simple yet strikingly effective, just like the man behind it, representing his morally guided soul and his vindictive mindset.

"Alright boys. I see two semi-trucks approaching the docks, one from the south and one from the north. Looks like it's game time," Dreadnight said through the comm.

"Confirmed. We see them as well. The one approaching from the south is three-point-five miles out and the one coming from the north is only two-point-two miles out," Mr. Unseen acknowledged. "Raydar and Siberian Scientist, I will signal you to move into position once the trucks have entered the docks."

Two red dots suddenly popped up onto their shipping truck's in-dash screen displaying the coordinates of the two semi-trucks.

"Copy that Mr. Unseen," Raydar's newly deepened and modulated voice replied. "Whew, man I love this thing!"

The rest of the team chuckled at Raydar's child-like joy.

Within minutes of each other, the two semi-trucks entered the shipping docks and drove to the eastern most building which sat above the Detroit River. The building was supported by a myriad of beams that rose above the water about ten feet and deep into the riverbed. The drivers cautiously backed their trucks directly inside the building through two separate cargo bay slots.

"Okay guys, go ahead and get in position at the entrance and set up the blockade," Mr. Unseen announced.

Raydar and Siberian Scientist started the truck and drove through the dock's entrance, parking just inside the front of it. They immediately hopped out and opened the truck's hatch where inside was a series of spike strips. With caution, they pulled each section out, laid them out onto the ground, and connected them until the entire width of the entrance was lined with tire shredding spikes.

"That ought to stop them from any attempt to escape," Siberian Scientist said as they got back into the truck.

"Okay, go ahead and follow the directions I just relayed to your GPS. The indicated location should provide you some good cover as well as a good vantage point for the ambush," Mr. Unseen said.

A blue line lit up on their in-dash screen with a specific path drawn out. Raydar and Siberian Scientist did as directed then waited for further instructions.

"Dreadnight, how to do you want to approach this?" Mr. Unseen asked.

"I'll go in solo and catch them off guard. Raydar and Siberian Scientist, after about thirty seconds I want you to neutralize the truck drivers then enter through the cargo bay doors. All of their attention will be on me so you should have free pickings," Dreadnight said like the true leader he was.

"Got it boss," Raydar confirmed.

"And where will your point of entry be Dreadnight," Mr. Unseen asked.

"Right underneath their feet," Dreadnight snarled.

The entire team smirked as they imagined the utter shock those scumbags inside that building were about to experience.

"May the grace of Michael with be you, my son," Father Ephrem chimed in.

"Thank you, Father Ephrem. May it be with all of us," Dreadnight replied.

Raydar watched with great anticipation as Dreadnight's body sliced through the air like a knife as it headed toward Windsor, just across the river. Before he could blink, Dreadnight's body dropped like a rock, causing his body to bullet toward the river with haste. With the swift release of his wings, Dreadnight was caressing the dingy water of the river, reaching a speed of at least sixty miles per hour. The dock was only seconds away.

"Here we go!" Dreadnight shouted as he sailed underneath the building and in between its supporting beams.

~

"Gentlemen, as you can see, we have upheld our end of deal. Five hundred kilos of Detroit's finest nose candy," Reem said, pointing at the stacks of cocaine bricks to right of the cartel's semi.

Next to those stacks stood eight of Inkubus's M-16 yielding super soldiers wearing their usual attire.

"How do we know the product is of the quality you speak?" The cartel leader asked in his Spanish accent as seven of his own armed militants stood attentively behind him, all donning green state issued gear.

Reem walked over to the stacks of bricks and motioned for Inkubus's men clear the way. He pulled an army knife from his utility belt and sliced an opening into one of the bricks, coating the topside of his blade with a line of the powder. Of course, this particular brick actually contained high grade blow whereas the remaining bricks were that of Dante's amino spiked product.

"I insist you try some then. I would never expect you to leave with such a product without having a taste first," Reem said as fraudulently earnest as he could.

The cartel leader approached Reem and pulled out a twenty-peso bill from his one of his cargo pockets. After rolling the bill up tightly, he leaned over and snorted the line of cocaine off Reem's blade. The cartel leader quickly rubbed his nose with intent, tilting his head back and closing his eyes repeatedly.

"Okay, yeah ... wooh ... that's what I am looking for right there," the cartel leader said erratically.

"Beautiful. Well, you already proved the worth of the artillery, so I say we both pack up and ship out," Reem said assuredly.

"Agreed. Pleasure doing business my friend," the cartel leader said.

Both men reached across to exchange a departing handshake while the militants from both sides walked toward their respective product for exchange.

~

Dreadnight arched his back, pulled back his wings, and gritted his teeth. With a deafening boom, his monstrous body blasted through the wooden floor, sending it splintering into the air and causing multiple men to crash down into the river below. The remaining men dived for cover in various directions. At least six of Inkubus's remaining mercenaries,

Reem, Chen, and five of the Mexican cartel members were dispersed amongst the surrounding area, stunned and confused. Naturally, the cartel members panicked at the sight of the beast, yelling frantically in Spanish and concluding that the entire event was a setup of Inkubus's.

Meanwhile, Inkubus's mercs immediately sprung to action, raising their weapons to fire. As the cartel members scurried toward their semi-truck, Inkubus's men had their heads on a swivel like a squad of navy seals, however they couldn't find anyone or anything for that matter.

Thirty feet up in the dimly lit rafters and hidden underneath a shell of stone wings was Dreadnight, his claws stuck into the wooden roof like nails as Rachel's necklace dangled freely.

"Tell me when, Mr. Unseen," Dreadnight whispered into the comm, his wings shielding all others from hearing him.

"Wait for it ... wait for it ... now!" Mr. Unseen shouted, likely realizing that all of Inkubus mercs as well as Reem and Chen had their eyes away from Dreadnight's vicinity.

Dreadnight released his claws from the ceiling, sending his body plummeting like a boulder falling from a mountainside. Once the men below realized what was approaching, it was too late. Dreadnight twisted his body and released his wings from their stoned state and out like a parachute. His sprawling body crashed into at least five men including Chen, flattening them like pancakes, especially the one whose ribs were crushed beneath his gargantuan feet. The mercs and their unnatural strength quickly shoved Dreadnight off them and a few feet away, just missing the gaping hole that led to the river.

"Three gunmen at nine, twelve, and three o'clock!" Mr. Unseen yelled through the comm.

Reem and the two mercs who avoided Dreadnight's fall began shooting their assault rifles. Out of instinct and thanks to Mr. Unseen's warning, Dreadnight leaped across to a nearby wall, then catapulted himself from that very wall over to the nearest gun yielding merc as bullets followed closely behind. Dreadnight slammed into the merc, grabbing ahold his assault rifle in the process as they went rolling across the floor.

He and the merc bounced onto their feet in a struggle to obtain possession of the gun in a battle of unnatural strength. His finger still on the trigger, the merc pressed into its curved steel, sending stray bullets in the direction of Reem. Reem ducked for cover as he fled behind the line of nearby crates containing the artillery located in front of the truck hatch.

Using his wits, Dreadnight ended his fight to remove the rifle from the merc and instead used him for his own cause. Redirecting his effort, he forced the merc to twist his body, sending the gun and its straying bullets in a rounding line, hitting each and every one of Inkubus's approaching mercs. Two of the six mercs fell dead to the ground from fatal impact while those remaining continued their rush toward Dreadnight, ignoring any inflicted wounds.

Spared from the bullets, Chen crawled like an ant behind stack of cocaine bricks, cowering in a ball once behind them as bullets burst their plastic encasings sending white powder into the air.

CRACK!

Dreadnight bashed his skull into the forehead of the struggling merc, sending him stumbling backward in a daze while releasing his grip from the gun. Dreadnight tossed the gun across the room and sliding across its floorboards. He then lifted his knee and sent his foot into the dazed merc's chest, projecting him like a torpedo through the northwest wall of the building and out of sight. One of the three oncoming mercs jumped him from behind, snaking his arm around Dreadnight's neck in a choke hold. Enforcing his brute strength, the merc squeezed with all his might, causing Dreadnight to gasp for air as he failed to grasp ahold of his slithering assailant. The other two mercs burst out in front of him, punching him relentlessly in the abdomen and face. Dreadnight endured the sting of the blows, focusing on the annoyance upon his back as his oxygen neared depletion.

Dreadnight arched back far enough to get the claws of his right hand into the flesh of the merc's right shoulder. Clenching his hand, his claws dug deep into the man's muscle like and anchor. Violently he pulled the merc over his head, whipping him into one of the two mercs facing him. Just as those two crashed to the ground, the third merc pulled a blade from his vest and drove it deep into the beast's left shoulder.

"Arrgh!" Dreadnight groaned in pain.

Before the merc could remove the blade, Dreadnight grabbed ahold of the side of the man's head with his left hand and thrusted it downward with lightning speed into a nearby wooden crate, splintering the crate's lid along with the man's jaw. The man's contorted face bounced off the wooden surface as his back thumped against its sidewall. But he was still coherent and began to push himself off the floor. Dreadnight's monstrous presence hovered over the merc as he pulled the blade from his own shoulder, gritting his teeth in utter agony. Just as the merc rose onto his feet, preparing to strike yet gain, Dreadnight sent the blade deep into his heart with godlike momentum, returning the favor.

"When you go to hell, say hello to your friend Adam Knight for me," Dreadnight snarled as he stared into the merc's doomed face, his jaw cocked completely to the side.

Meanwhile outside of the building, Raydar and Siberian Scientist used a pair of long-range sniper rifles with automated focusing and carbon silencers to neutralize the two semi-truck drivers. Siberian Scientist sent a lethal shot in between the eyes of the driver of Inkubus's truck, whereas Raydar sent a tranq laced silicone slug into the right shoulder of the Mexican cartel driver. Immediately they switched to their weapon of choice, pistols, each of them yielding two, one for lethal use and the other for tranquilizing. With extreme focus, they headed to their respective cargo bay door, armed and ready in a crouched hurry. As they neared, one of the cartel members popped out from the cargo door carrying an assault rifle. Without hesitation, Raydar aimed his tranq pistol and sent a dart straight into the man's neck. The man fell in a sleeping stupor to the ground before he could even lift his own weapon. As Raydar approached the cartel's truck he heard violent pounding blended with screaming in Spanish from the inside of its trailer.

SMASH!
The lone standing gunman, now out of ammunition, sent his elbow through the glass of an "in case of emergency" pod hanging from the south wall twenty feet from Dreadnight. Ignoring the two rising mercs a few feet to the right of him, Dreadnight withdrew the blade from the now corpse and tossed it aside before turning to his left to acknowledge the sound of breaking glass. Instead of a gun, the merc now gripped a fire axe tightly in his hands, blood dripping from his elbow.

Head-to-head, both the merc and Dreadnight took off in a sprint toward each other in roaring grunts. Their gap closing, the merc pulled back the axe behind his right shoulder preparing for a home run slice. Just as the merc began to swing the axe forward, Dreadnight dropped onto his right hip while kicking his left leg forward, sending him into a full speed slide. Continuing it's swing, the axe's blade grazed Dreadnight's hair as he arched back, dropping his upper body down toward the floor.

Slice!

Dreadnight outstretched his right arm, sending his claws deep into the flesh of the merc's right quadricep as he slid by. The merc barreled to ground, his leg now a useless bleeding extension.

"Dreadnight, behind you!" Mr. Unseen blurted.

P-Taff P-Taff P-Taff P-Taff

Bullets from both Raydar and Siberian Scientist's lethal pistols met the craniums of the two trailing mercs. Both dropped like rocks. Dreadnight turned and grinned at the sight of his teammates.

"Thanks guys," Dreadnight said with a smile before turning and sticking the axe yielding merc with five claws to the throat.

Brum-rum-rum-rum

The engine of Reem's semi turned over and smoke piled out of exhaust pipe.

"Shit! Reem!" Dreadnight shouted, now realizing he had forgotten about him.

As Siberian Scientist entered the building from the passenger side of the truck, Reem must have coincidentally snuck out the driver's side of the cargo bay and into the truck cabin, pulling the dead driver's body out in the process.

"Wait, what about Chen!" Raydar blurted.

"Forget about Chen. We have to go get Reem!" Mr. Unseen interjected.

"Leave him," Dreadnight replied bluntly. "I want Inkubus to know what we did here. I want him to know he's next. Plus, Reem's disappearance would place us under a city-wide microscope. We need him running the precinct since he's our tether to Inkubus's network."

Dreadnight focused his hearing, seconds later he heard heavy breathing coming from behind the stack of cocaine bricks just right of the cartel's trailer hatch and tucked away in the corner of the building. He walked over to the cartel truck's hatch. When he looked inside he saw five Mexican men hovered in fear from the display of wrath he had just unleashed upon Inkubus's men. Apparently, they knew better than to fight such a supernatural spectacle of fierceness.

"Por favor! Por favor! 'No nos maten!" The group's leader shouted, pleading for mercy.

Humanity was present, so tonight was their lucky night. Dreadnight pulled the hatch door and flung it closed, sliding its locks over afterword.

"That makes things a bit easier," Father Ephrem said through the comm with a chuckle.

Phhhssssss! Phhhssssss!

The tires of Reem's semi-truck popped loudly as its rims grinded upon the street.

Dreadnight continued his approach toward the bricks of cocaine. When he looked behind them, he saw a whimpering Chen, his hands held to the sky.

"He's over here," Dreadnight said, his eyes tightened in a death stare at Chen. "Would you like to do the honor Raydar?" Dreadnight asked.

"It would be my pleasure," Raydar replied in a snickering tone.

Raydar placed his guns back into their holsters and walked behind the bricks. He stood tall in front of the quivering Chen.

"I want him to know who brought him down though," Raydar said in a darkened grumble.

"Please! I'll do whatever you want just don't …"

Raydar lifted his mask and grabbed onto Chen's bullet proof vest.

"Ray!" Chen gasped in disbelief.

"That's right bitch. This is for Lainey," Raydar replied before sending a knockout punch across Chen's face.

"Man, that felt good!" Raydar shouted joyfully as he released his grip and Chen's body met the wooden floor.

"Raydar, tranq him and throw him in the front of the cartel's truck then drive it back to the Arcane Asylum for unloading," Dreadnight directed. "Siberian, you and I will do clean up. Set this cocaine and this artillery ablaze however you see fit while I neutralize the remaining super soldiers and round up the remaining cartel members for transport."

"Gladly, comrade!" Siberian Scientist replied while nodding in agreeance, clearly excited to blow some shit up.

"A few of each fell into the river so they can't be far away. I'll assist with the lookout of course," Mr. Unseen added.

"Alright boys, keep constant contact and let's meet back up at the observatory for some post mission briefing."

~

With his head held low and a gut full of knives, Reem entered through the base of the Central Station near the holding cell. He knew he was about to face hell on earth for failing his master yet again, in fact, he didn't know if he would be leaving at all that night.

"Ahh Harvey, about time. Is the truck parked in the tunnel?" Inkubus asked, suspecting nothing out of the ordinary.

Reem lifted his head and swallowed the little saliva that remained in his drying mouth.

"Umm … about that sir," Reem nervously said. "It's been compro …"

CRACK!

Inkubus sent a right hook across Reem's jaw, followed by a left hook, throwing his blood spitting face from side to side.

"You stupid son of a bitch! Out of all of tasks I have given you, you manage to screw this one up!" Inkubus screamed in a hellish rage.

"Sir, it was Dreadnight!" Reem frantically replied, his hands guarding his now battered face.

Vvviip!

"Oh God no!" Reem gasped

Inkubus's mechanical sleeve was engaged before his fist was sent deep into Reem's stomach.

"Hhhhhau!" Reem gasped as he fell onto his knees and clutched onto his stomach with both arms, feeling as if he were struck by a cannonball.

"And how did he find out about our arrangement?" Inkubus yelled as he stood over Reem's crippled body.

"I … I … don't know sir. I swear I didn't tell anyone," Reem blurted. "But he wasn't working alone! There were two others in masks … and they got Chen," he added in desperation.

"That doesn't answer my question!" Inkubus roared, pulling back his sleeved fist.

Oh God, I'm gonna die!

Vvviip!

Then a switch flipped within Reem's mind, as if the fear of oncoming death opened his subconscious. He knew exactly how they found out.

"Wait!" Reem belted, causing Inkubus to hesitate. "I know who told them!" He added frantically. "It was Lainey Ross sir. She had left her purse in Chen's car the night he and I discussed the exchange. That bitch must have had it bugged. There's no other explanation sir."

Inkubus lowered his arm and demanded Reem stand up.

"That name ... It sounds familiar," Inkubus voiced in contemplation. "Isn't that the officer who makes the deliveries to that damn priest at St. Anne's?" He added curiously.

"Yes sir," Reem confirmed in agonizing pain.

Inkubus's eyes shifted back in forth briefly as he seemingly attempted to connect the misplaced dots inside his mind.

"It all makes sense now."

"What's does, sir?"

"St. Anne's, the statue on its rooftop. That is where I recognized Dreadnight's face from," Inkubus said with wide eyes, now in a trance like state.

~

Inkubus was only sixteen years of age when he found himself at the St. Anne's cathedral, attending his late parents' funeral. Upon wandering off from the service, he climbed the spiral staircase to the rooftop where he was met by a cold and snowy winter's night. Dressed in black slacks, a clean white dress shirt, and a blood red tie, the frigid gusts of wind slapped his pale cheeks as the snow matted his hair. Stepping through a half-foot of snow, he fought the weather's cruel might, walking toward a snowcapped statue just ten feet away. Upon reaching it, he stepped onto its base and reached up, dusting the snow from the statues head. After leaping back down, he stood motionless in a stare at the stone figure before him, his eyes as cold as the air and as sharp as the wind.

"So, you are supposed keep evil from entering God's house and vanish it from within? Seems to me, just like God, you are a mere hoax, a fictitious figure of deception. Otherwise, neither of you would have let me step one foot into this glass house for the weak."

He spat on the face of the statue then turned and walked back toward the door. Just before reaching it, he turned his head back to look at the statue one last time, his snow-covered hair blowing in his eyes.

"Just wait, one day this whole city will be mine and there will be nothing that you or your little God will be able to do to stop me. Mark my word, when that day comes, I'm going to burn you and this place to ground, leaving no evidence of your existence!" he hollered snidely with a smirk spread across his face.

~

"Sir?" Reem asked, confused by Inkubus's frozen state.

Inkubus snapped out of his trance, shaking his head as his mind rejoined the present moment.

"Lucky for you, the discovery that your failure uncovered might just turn out to be our silver bullet. We can use this. We can use her to solidify my master plan!" Inkubus bellowed, his fist clenched and eyes wide.

Reem was seemingly spared. For the time being that is.

~

With the addition of the eight members of the Mexican cartel and Chen, the Arcane Asylum now housed a total of sixty-three frightened occupants, each clinging onto their iron barricades with no freedom in sight. Partaking in one of their most favored traditions, the team sat around the observatory's round table with a glass of vodka in hand and a calmed expression upon each of their faces. The sight was most peculiar to say least as four seemingly ordinary humans engaged in joyous conversation with a colossal gargoyle, bearing a smile of all things.

It was a time they deemed as post mission briefing. A time where they discussed the night's events and reviewed the team's video feeds for any details that may have been missed while in action. That night, the atmosphere was much more jubilant than the preceding nights since their plan went exactly as hoped and for once fortune seemed to be on their side. However, the night's success was only a steppingstone to their ultimate goal, a goal in which the lives of Benjamin Foster and his family depended upon its achievement.

Chapter 10
Perceptional Pyromania

  Three days after the disastrous undoing of the Mexican cartel exchange, Reem found himself posted twenty stories high on the rooftop of a rundown office tower with his eyes peering through military grade binoculars. His newest task, to perform personal reconnaissance of Dreadnight in search of the fowl beast's weakness. That is if he had one. For the first time since the birth of Inkubus's empire, Reem was without his partner in crime Jon Chen, a situation he didn't know if he would ever come to terms with. Tonight, his only friend would be a bottle of Jack which sat perched upon the building's cement ledge, awaiting its neck to be choked.

  Two hundred yards away through the binocular's looking glass was the statue known as the "Spirit of Detroit". It was an iconic bronze monument of a large seated man bearing outstretched arms and open hands which held two items of great significance. In its left hand, a gilt bronze sphere emanating rays to symbolize God. In its right hand, a bronze sculpture depicting the idea of a family. Altogether, the three adjoined sculptures expressed the undeniable connection between man, family, and God. Or as many would call it, spirit.

  Crrrcht

Reem's walkie talkie ended the mind-numbing silence.

  "Light the explosives on my count," Reem said into the unit. "Five … four … three … two … one … hit it!" Reem blurted, the alcohol in his system fueling his conviction.

  The blast's booming roar radiated out into the distance for miles as a display of bursting flames and blooming smoke erupted into the air. The once adored statue crumbled to the ground and into nothingness. Nearby street walkers ran in a frenzy as passing cars veered off the road to avoid the flying debris. Dust quickly replaced the fire and smoke in a swelling cloud. A man and a woman engulfed in flames appeared from that very cloud, eventually stumbling to their painstaking deaths just feet away at the center of the monument's brick courtyard.

  "That ought to get his attention," Reem said with a smirk as he reached for his trusty bottle for another swig.

  Surely enough, just moments later when Reem lifted the binoculars back up to his face, he saw a pair of spanning wings fill his view as the beast gracefully landed in the courtyard. Reem watched with gleeful antsiness as Dreadnight realized he was too late to save the lives of the two poor saps who were now burnt to a crisp.

Crrrcht

"Get ready," Reem said through the walkie talkie, nearly dropping it from anticipation.

Without hesitation, Dreadnight rushed into the dust cloud in search of others.

"Drop it, now!" Reem shouted.

A pool of liquid fell from a tarp which hung from the side of the municipal center ten feet behind where the monument once stood, drenching the impacted area and clearing the dust in the process. Standing smack dab in the middle was Dreadnight, looking up in confusion with his nostrils flaring and his body soaked from head to toe.

"Hit him, now!" Reem shouted, his body jolting along with his voice.

A controlled surge of flames shot from the burning hedges just south of where Dreadnight stood, swallowing him whole and lighting him ablaze.

That pool of liquid ... was high octane gasoline.

"Burn baby ... burn!" Reem snarled as he watched his revenge unfurl.

A man wearing a fireproof suit appeared from the bushes, continuing to blast a wave of flames from a flamethrower clutched tightly between his hands. Dreadnight violently whipped his body around in a dire attempt to extinguish the flames, however they continued to burn with undying rage.

Suddenly, Dreadnight stopped, motionless in a frozen state.

"What the ..."

Right before Reem's eyes, the gargantuan creature instantaneously turned to stone, relinquishing all the flames that had consumed his body just seconds ago. Steam emanated from the stone figure as it remained unmoved and the man's flamethrower ran out of its nitrogen supply, rendering it useless. Bystanders watching the event unravel stood aghast at the incredible spectacle before them. Then, like the flick of a switch, the stone was no more. The beast of flesh and blood reappeared, his eyes now blazing with inexhaustible fury.

"Oh shit!" Reem's heart sunk from his chest.

Dreadnight turned his head toward the man who had just lit him like a candle. In the blink of an eye, he whipped his tail around, knocking the flamethrower from the man's clutches and sending it flying into the street to the right of him. Before he could take a breath, Reem watched the beast leap at the pyro, grab him, and shoot off into the sky.

Reem had seen enough. He quickly grabbed his bottle of Jack and raced down twenty flights of stairs to his car to get the hell out of dodge.

His hands shaking and palms sweating, Reem drove as if the devil himself was chasing him.

"Dammit dammit dammit!" Reem yelled as he beat his fist against the steering wheel, an ever-growing fear swelling within him from the thought of reporting back to Inkubus.

Soon that thought would become a reality.

He reached down and grabbed his trusty friend Jack, taking three final swigs in hope that it would numb the pain he was about to endure.

Reem entered the Central Station just as Inkubus and Dr. Foster had finished a successful treatment upon their newest super soldier, the third that very night.

"Prep my next subject," Inkubus directed Dr. Foster before hearing Reem's footsteps from afar. "Ahh Harvey, back with good news I presume?" Inkubus said with cynicism dripping from every word.

"Unfortunately, no sir. He isn't weakened by fire. He's like a walking extinguisher, sir," Reem replied, sweat dripping from his forehead and burning into his eyes.

"Hmm interesting," Inkubus said, his mask hiding any and all emotion. "Well, I suggest you keep trying, or else you will develop a new weakness of your own … the inability to breathe," Inkubus said candidly.

"Yes of course, sir. I'll get right on it, sir," Reem said with a wavering voice as he swallowed the fear shooting up his esophagus.

Blades, bullets, and now fire. What else could I possible expose that wretched creature to that I haven't already. If I don't figure something out, and fast, I will never see the light of day again.

Wait a minute …

Chapter 11
Confronting Crossroads

"Eerraagghh!" Nikolai hollered, whipping his roller table across the room and into a medical cabinet in a fit of rage. Instruments and vials flew from its surface and crashed all around as books tumbled from atop the cabinet and onto the floor.

"None of it works! Every damn sequence is flawed" Nikolai said glumly, his hands gripping his bowed head.

By now Nikolai had attempted thousands of mixtures and considered an unfathomable number of variables, yet each and every potential antidote he developed ended up killing the cells of the host. Upon injection of many of these antidotes, the restriction enzyme of choice would successfully begin the neutralization of Inkubus's DNA within the subject matter. After a calculated two point eight second count, Nikolai would then inject a localized dose of five grams of gamma aminobutyric acid, triggering reverse polarization as anticipated and allowing the anti-serum to begin attaching to the foreign DNA cells.

Time and time again, each trial would appear favorable. However, such fortune would be very short lived. Without rhyme or reason, Inkubus's DNA cells would suddenly attach to the DNA cells of the host, eventually swallowing them whole and leaving a petri dish of systematic failure. From early-stage hosts to full-fledged super soldiers, the results remained the same, leaving Nikolai in a state of infuriated confusion. He was at a point of dissolution, his mind devoid of further theories or avenues.

Grazing his hands down his wearied face, Nikolai lifted his head to see the mess he had made. But it wasn't a mess that he saw, no, it was a shocking revelation. His eyes were affixed upon a very specific book, one that changed his entire train of thought ... one labeled, "Stem Cells: The Body's Miracle." Nikolai jumped from his chair and rushed over to the book and feverishly flipped through its pages.

"Of course! What was I thinking!" Nikolai belted in disbelief of his mental blunder. "Stem cells are the only organic material that can initiate differentiation! Modified with the right restriction enzyme and neural inhibitor, I will be able to shut down all nonfunctional genes within the host, leaving only the host's organic DNA behind to dismantle and destroy the foreign DNA cells."

Excitement coursed through Nikolai's veins. He had finally uncovered the key that would unlock the minds of those controlled by Inkubus and end the synapsis serum's fowl infectious spread once and for all.

Then reality set in, nullifying all excitement.

Such a discovery left him with one final, yet seemingly unattainable conclusion. Nikolai would need to obtain the stem cells straight from the serum's source ... Inkubus. It was the only conceivable possibility that remained. One that required the capturing of the demon himself.

Slade, Ray, and Adam rushed through clean room doors of the laboratory after hearing the sudden commotion.

"You alright Nikolai? Slade asked, his face scrunched in concern.

"Yeah man. Sorry. I just need a drink," Nikolai replied, frustration emanating from his eyes.

"It's only 11 a.m., a little too early for a drink don't you think?" Ray said sarcastically, his right brow lifted.

"Not in Russia it isn't," Nikolai replied coldly.

"I can get behind that logic," Slade said with a smile. "Let's take a break and chill in the observatory for a bit," he added.

The four men filed out of the lab and seated themselves in the observatory. Within minutes, Father Ephrem joined the party. Slade distributed five glasses and poured a generous amount of Winter's Bite vodka into each of them. If it weren't for Nikolai having a crate shipped over directly from Russia, they would have run out of their drink of choice the week of his arrival to the states. After a few sips, Nikolai explained his mind-bending dilemma, leaving the team just as bewildered as he.

As much as the team wanted to raid the castle known as the Central Station, they knew it was too risky. They had no idea what lied behind its deceptive walls, what technologies or weapons that could be present. Even with the seizure of Chen and the knowledge he possessed, there was no telling what had developed over the past few days. If there was but a sliver of chance that Inkubus could enslave Dreadnight, it was too significant. The game of carnal chess would be over, the city would be damned, and soon the country.

"So, this could be the early morning liquor talking, but I have an idea," Ray said with hopefulness.

"What is it?" Nikolai asked curiously, his interest peaked.

"The city's District Attorney, Sandra Daley, has been trying for years to indict Reem but could never get legislative backing for a court order," Ray said, his excitement growing with each word spoken. "We have Chen, we can use him as a pawn to rat out Reem and get the FBI to issue a search warrant on the Central Station."

The wheels of the men's minds turned in rumination at such an idea.

"I must have him physically here though to obtain the necessary stem cells, otherwise I will never find a cure," Nikolai said.

"I'm sure we can make deal with her. She'll do anything to see Reem behind bars."

"Why is she so adamant on bringing him down?" Adam asked.

"Because of our city's former District Attorney, who just happened to be her father. About five years ago, he was brutally murdered then hung in the middle of Campus Martius for all to see. Some say he had uncovered a mass crime ring amidst the city's top officials and that his murder was a warning to anyone who dared to investigate them. Others believe he took his own life in fear of his own corruption becoming public." Ray's conviction seemed to grow with each passing second. "Needless to say, the case was swept under the rug and his death was deemed a suicide. Oh, and all her father's files and records were seized by the police. Ironic, huh?"

"Maybe he had uncovered Reem's connection with Inkubus ... or even Inkubus's identity," Slade said with a distraught expression upon his discolored face, still bruised from the previous night's incineration.

"Seems to me she could be a viable ally. Our goals are one in the same and she has already put herself in harm's way to uncover the truth," Father Ephrem added.

"I say we take a vote. Anyone disagree?" Slade asked the team.

The team nodded in agreeance.

"All in favor of Ray's proposal, raise your hand," Slade announced.

All five men raised their hands in a unanimous accord.

"Well then it's settled, we will involve Sandra Daley," Slade said, raising his drink.

The team clanked their glasses together and participated in a harmonized swig of cohesion, eager to see this development unravel.

~

The only problem that the team now faced was the fact that they couldn't bring her to the Arcane Asylum or reveal the homestead of Dreadnight, considering their own "illegal" activities. Thus, they concluded that it would make the most sense to have Ray transport Chen to a neutral location to meet with Ms. Daley alone. That location would of course be the untraceable Celestial Shipping warehouse. However, before such a plan could take place, it was imperative that Chen be convinced of the importance of selective disclosure. That was a task Slade graciously accepted.

Over the course the day's remaining hours of sunlight, both Ray and Slade went to work in preparation of their upcoming tasks. Utilizing his voice modulator and his stealth phone to conceal any trace of his identity, Ray contacted Sandra Daley, referring to himself as Mr. Dar. He told her that he had a witness to Harvey Reem's crimes upon this city and that she might be interested in what the man has to say. Despite her initial skepticism, it seemed that Sandra's innate inquisitiveness convinced her to accept Mr. Dar's meeting proposal.

The meeting was set for the following night at 12:30 a.m., coinciding perfectly with Slade's transformation time and allowing him the opportunity to be posted nearby to ensure everything goes smoothly. Meanwhile, Slade prepared himself for his "motivational" speech, that he would be giving Chen upon his transformation.

Creeeeak

The hinges of the Arcane Asylum's cast iron door screamed, causing its inmates to turn their heads in fearful anticipation. Appearing from the dark unknown was Dreadnight, followed closely by Raydar and Siberian Scientist, both in their appropriate attire. The inmates watched as the three heroes walked in a powerful stride through the cell corridor, making all else seem motionless in their wake. Fear in the form of silence engulfed the Asylum, leaving only the sound of footsteps echoing amongst the cement walls. Quivering and clutching onto his cell bars, Chen likely realized they were heading straight toward him.

Raydar reached forward and unlocked Chen's cell, the bright white cross of his mask staring Chen right in his petrified face. Chen immediately stumbled backward, bumping his back into the cell bars directly behind him as the door swung open. With a menacing look sprawled across his bestial face, Dreadnight stepped into Chen's cell, his body so gargantuan it could barely fit within its confines. Quickly, Raydar shut the door behind him and locked it back up.

"Wh ... what do you want from me? Please don't hurt me!" Chen pleaded like a frightened child.

"It's time we have a little chat, don't you think?" Dreadnight snarled, stepping within inches of Chen's body.

"Yeah sure, whatever you say," Chen said, looking as if he were going to vomit.

CLANG!

Dreadnight rattled Chen's body up against the cell bars, his hand gripping onto the chest of Chen's police uniform, causing him to wince profusely.

"You are going to do me a favor, rat, and you are going to do it exactly how I say," Dreadnight growled, his teeth exposed. "Aren't you!" Dreadnight shouted, rattling Chen's body like a ragdoll.

"Yes. Yes of course. Whatever you want!" Chen cried, avoiding eye contact at all costs.

"That's more like it." Dreadnight grinned in pleasure. "So, tomorrow you will be introduced to our city's district attorney, and you are going to tell her everything you know about Inkubus's operation and your buddy Reem. Got it?"

"I … I …" Chen stuttered.

"I guess you need more than words to motivate you," Slade growled, drawing his left arm back, ready to beat an answer from Chen.

"I can't. He'll kill me!" Chen shrieked throwing his hands in front of his face.

"And you don't think I will? Guess you need some convincing," Dreadnight said, flaring his eyes and placing his clenched fist with his index finger straightened out directly in front of Chen's face.

Like a ballistic missile, an obsidian cylindrical claw shot from the flesh of Dreadnight's index finger, causing light to glare from its sleek surface and into Chen's bulging eyes.

"No no no! Please don't hurt … eeeyyaaaahhh!"

Dreadnight lowered his hand and sent the tip of that very claw into the lower part of Chen's abdomen, slightly above his right hip, and just deep enough to pierce his muscle lining.

"Oh god oh god, ahhhh!" Chen shrieked as tears ran down his tensed face.

"I wouldn't move if I were you," Dreadnight sneered. "So, either you comply with every word I say, or I move my claw a centimeter to the left and puncture your appendix, leaving you to bleed out in this very cell." Dreadnight smiled like a crazed lunatic, his face nearly grazing Chen's.

Dreadnight ever so slightly jerked his finger to the left, only pressing up against muscle lining to Chen's unknowingness.

"Okay okay! I will do whatever say you man, I swear."

In the not-so-distant background, Raydar and Siberian Scientist watched observantly, their arms crossed, and bodies poised.

"Man, this guy sure is a pansy, ay?" Siberian Scientist said.

"Yeah. Not much of a tough guy now, huh?" Raydar replied in his deep modulated voice.

Chen let out another pathetic whimper, his eyes glued to the ceiling as he likely imagined the damage Dreadnight was inflicting to his abdomen.

"You're enjoying this, aren't you? Siberian Scientist asked, his Russian accent thick as always.

"Oh, you betcha, comrade," Ray replied, causing the two to chuckle joyously at Chen's expense.

"So, here are how things are going to go, rat. You are going to spill your guts to the DA, telling her everything you know about Inkubus and your buddy Reem. Information you will of course share with us first. Secondly, you will answer all her questions to the fullest extent … excluding anything relating to myself or my two friends over there. As far as you are concerned, we do not exist. Understood?"

"Yes, of course," Chen nodded nervously.

"If you disobey me in any way, I will be the one spilling your guts … with my claws. Got it?"

"Got it. I promise I won't."

Dreadnight withdrew his claw from Chen's flesh and released his grasp from his uniform. Chen sighed in immeasurable relief as he attempted to catch his breath. He immediately lifted his uniform to see blood seeping from his lower abdomen, reigniting his panic within.

"But what about this hole in my stomach man? I'm going to bleed to death!" Chen pleaded.

"Don't worry, my friend here will bandage you up," Dreadnight said, his back turned as he walked away and grinned at Siberian Scientist, knowing full well Chen's wound was nothing more than a minor laceration.

~

The time was 11:50 p.m. as Raydar pulled up to the rear entrance of the Celestial Shipping warehouse, his guest of dishonor chained to the ceiling of the cargo pod. Once parked, he and Mr. Unseen scanned the area quickly to ensure he had not been followed.

The coast was clear. Wasting no time, Raydar opened the cargo pod hatch and unlocked the chains that were linked from the ceiling to the shackles behind Chen's back.

See, unlike most inmates in American facilities, Chen wasn't being treated like your average prisoner, merely confined by comfortably situated handcuffs. Thanks to the advice of Siberian Scientist, Raydar implemented the tactics from Russian prisons into action. Instead of the standard forward positioning of handcuffs, Chen's hands were locked tightly behind his backside with his palms facing away from his body to maintain constant vulnerability. Additionally, his mouth was gagged with a strapped rubber ball to ensure no unwelcomed noises were made.

To further such security precautions, Chen's eyes were blindfolded with opaque black fabric, preventing him from learning his captor's movement patterns and his location, all while mitigating his reaction time if something were to go wrong. As Raydar escorted Chen from the cargo pod, he rendered Chen powerless in a constant stressed position, pulling his arms upward while bent at the waist. These tactics provided Raydar with the utmost control over his prisoner, ensuring his own safety in the process.

Continuing his pressure upon Chen's arms, Raydar walked him to the back door of the warehouse where he slid his right hand from its glove and pressed his bare hand against the fingerprint scanner bolted against the building wall. The scanner beeped, providing him clearance to open the door. Quickly, he opened it and shoved Chen through, closing it behind them. Utilizing his left hand, Raydar pulled a flashlight from his utility belt, switching it on to provide a visible path to his destination amongst the pitch-black internals of the building. After approximately thirty steps, Raydar opened a second door, entering an unlit room with Chen still securely grappled. With the flick of a switch, the room was lit, revealing its black soundproofed walls which surrounded a single metal table, two matching chairs, a set of chains, and nothing more.

Ignoring his muffled screams, Raydar tossed Chen's senseless body into the one of the chairs, its legs bolted to the tile floor. Raydar chained Chen's cuffs to the chair. Chen didn't resist, likely a result of Dreadnight's words of encouragement. Pacing back and forth in the small room, Raydar awaited the arrival of Ms. Daley.

Buzzzz

Raydar's stealth phone vibrated wildly in his cargo pocket. It was Ms. Daley alerting him that she was at the back door.

"Don't go anywhere," Raydar said with a deep menacing laugh as he exited the room.

Chen rattled his chair in a panicked response.

Raydar reached the back door and placed his eye up against its peephole. As he expected, standing behind it was Ms. Daley, alone and holding a dark brown briefcase.

Standing a slender six feet tall, Sandra Daley was intimidating to say the least. With beauty to match her toughness, she wore a tailored gray pant suit accompanied by a black button-down shirt which matched her three-inch heels. Her dark brown hair was pulled tightly back into a ponytail that accentuated her sharp cheekbones and striking green eyes.

"Mr. Unseen, anything of concern showing up from the cargo truck's camera?" Raydar asked, referring to the camera installed upon the truck's rooftop.

"No sir. She arrived alone and her only movements were getting out of the car to walk up to the door and sending a text message to your phone," Mr. Unseen replied.

"Dreadnight?" Raydar asked.

"Everything looks clear, no suspicious activity or nearby disturbances," Dreadnight replied attentively while perched upon a nearby scaffold.

"Perfect, here we go ..." Raydar swung the door open.

Ms. Daley shrieked as her body jolted in fright from Raydar's chilling appearance.

"Quiet, come with me," Raydar said, grabbing ahold of Ms. Daley's arm and pulling her inside the building. As soon as her body crossed the doorway, he immediately shut the door and place his left hand tightly over the young woman's mouth to prevent and further noise.

"There is no need to be afraid miss. I'm one of the good guys," Raydar said gently.

Ms. Daley nodded, prompting Raydar to remove his hand. He switched on his flashlight once again and aimed it toward the interrogation room.

"Please, follow me."

She didn't provide a response, but she did however follow his lead. The two entered the room where Chen presided.

"What in God's name is this?" She shouted, her face distorted in disgust by the sight of a gagged and blindfolded man.

"I call it security, ma'am," Raydar replied nonchalantly. "Don't worry, he hasn't been harmed. This is just to prevent any mishaps," he added as he walked behind Chen and unlatched his gag, setting its saliva coated ball onto the table. "Ain't that right Jon?"

"Uh yeah, I'm fine," Chen nervously replied, as if a hundred tiny spiders were crawling up his body.

"Go ahead proceed with your questions Ms. Daley," Raydar said as he walked back around to the front of the table and crossed his arms.

Ms. Daley set her briefcase onto the table and sat in the opposing chair facing the prisoner. Once settled, she pulled out a pen, a legal notepad, and a voice recorder.

"Could you please remove the man's blindfold so that I can identify him with city records, Mr. Dar?" she asked, her voice shaky as she looked upon Raydar's masked face.

Raydar reached into a small slot in his utility belt, pulling out two plastic cards and tossing them onto the table and out in front of her.

"There's his driver's license and DPD ID card. That gives you more than enough to identify him. He doesn't need to see you, nor does he deserve to," Raydar said bluntly.

Clearly frustrated yet too afraid to act on it, Ms. Daley shrugged off the denial of her request and turned back to look at his ID cards.

Click

She switched on the voice recorder.

"What is your name sir?" She asked, her face serious and steady.

"My name is Jon Chen," he replied.

"Okay Jon, you report to Harvey Reem at the DPD, correct?"

"Yes."

"Tell me then, is Harvey Reem, commissioner of the DPD, working with or for anyone involved in illegal activity?" she asked sternly.

"Yes."

"And who might that be?" Her hands were shaking in blatant anticipation, awaiting his response.

Chen opened his mouth to speak, but no words came out, instead his head just shook nervously. Raydar walked behind Chen's chair and firmly slapped his hands onto Chen's shoulders causing him to tremor in fear.

"Shall I remind you of the consequences you will face if you decide to hold back any information? Raydar said exuberantly as he squeezed and shook Chen's shoulders with force.

Chen wasn't the only one feeling discomfort at that very moment in that confined room, Ms. Daley's unsteady eyes made that obvious.

"Okay okay! A man that goes by the name of Inkubus. But I swear I do not know who he is or what he really looks like," Chen pleaded, desperation clinging from his voice.

Ms. Daley's eyes lit up like a Christmas tree. Could this be the connection her father gave his life to uncover?

Ray walked back in front of the table and crossed his arms a second time.

"And where does this Inkubus operate out of?" The blatant anticipation nearly causing her to pass out.

"The old Central Station," Chen said with regret, bowing his head upon finishing the statement.

Ms. Daley scrupulously wrote notes onto her legal pad. Raydar watched with a brimming smirk, hidden underneath his militant mask.

"Who else is involved in this operation you speak of?" she asked.

"More like who isn't involved," Chen replied with a scoff.

"What do you mean by that?" she eagerly asked, the wheels of her mind likely spinning ruthlessly at his open-ended statement.

"Inkubus has this whole city wrapped around his finger, with the exception of you it seems. Governing officials, statesmen, media outlets, you name it, his hand is up their backs," Chen replied with subtle resentment dripping from his mouth.

Ms. Daley sat there speechless, her hand frozen as if she had seen a ghost. She turned and looked at Raydar with astonishment in her eyes.

"Told ya you would find this interesting," Raydar said sarcastically, causing her to smile for the first time since their meeting. "But that's not all," he added, raising his brows. "Tell her about the serum and Dr. Foster, and don't even think about leaving out a single detail."

Chen did just that. For nearly thirty minutes he provided insight on the synapsis serum's procedure, its effects, and how it had been administered to hundreds of the city's worst criminals who roamed the streets at night in cooperation with the DPD. Last but certainly not least, he explained how Dr. Foster had been blackmailed to do Inkubus's bidding and the location that he and his family were being kept hostage.

To the ears of an average citizen, the story would have seemed to be fiction or something you'd read in a comic book, causing one to laugh as if it were a silly joke. That certainly was not the case for Sandra Daley. It appeared Inkubus was her holy grail, the missing puzzle piece she had dedicated her life to finding.

Ms. Daley's pen nearly ran dry from her excessive logging of notes, her hand shifting a million miles an hour to capture ever shard of detail, no matter its significance. But that writing came to a sudden halt as she blankly stared at the words before her.

"What's the matter?" Raydar asked, uncrossing his arms, concerned at her abrupt loss of elation.

"I need to talk to you ... in private," she said sternly, turning toward Raydar with a face of worry.

Raydar nodded his head toward the door, gesturing for them to exit the room. She stood as he opened the door for her, then they walked out into the main hangar of the warehouse, closing the door behind them.

"Give us a little light Mr. U," Raydar said into his comm.

Seconds later, a section of overhead lights just above them became dimly lit, thanks to Mr. Unseen's mobile lighting capabilities linked from his monitoring station to the warehouse. Ms. Daley looked around in confusion at the sudden production of light, clearly intrigued at what just happened.

"What's wrong Ms. Daley?" Raydar asked as the two stood in the barren area outside of the interrogation room, out of Chen's sight.

"Even though everything I heard in there is literally a smoking gun ... it won't be enough to get a court order," Ms. Daley said, her face burdened with discontent.

"What do you mean? It has to be enough to at least alert the FBI so that they can raid the Central Station," Raydar argued, his voice plastered with frustration.

"Not when it has to go through the state level first and they own the property on which the Central Station stands. If this Inkubus character has our judicial members in his back pocket, not only will they block any attempt by the FBI to issue a search warrant, but they will also unleash a manhunt for Chen. This will put you directly in their crosshairs and me into a body bag, I can guarantee you that," Ms. Daley stressed, her face flushed red.

"You've got to be kidding me," Raydar scoffed, throwing his arms into the air, and turning away in disgust, attempting to control his anger.

"Look, the best I can do is to inform my contact at the FBI of Reem's involvement and provide him a copy of tonight's recording so that he is prepared if in fact they can act in the future. I'm truly sorry, I really am." Frustration was growing in her voice. Then her facial expression shifted, as if a sudden sense of impulsiveness took over her mind, ignoring its status quo. "But ... if you can somehow capture Inkubus and bring him to me alive, then we will have all of the leverage we need to take him straight to the FBI."

Raydar turned back around to face Ms. Daley.

"That suggestion was of course off the record and never came out of my mouth though," she added with a straight face and widened eyes.

"If that's our only option then so be it. I'll see what I can do."

"In the meantime, I will dig up everything I can to try and figure out who Inkubus is and any connections he might have. You have my number so let's keep in close contact and keep each other updated," Ms. Daley said, extending her hand out in front of Raydar.

Raydar did the same, shaking her hand in solidarity.

"Agreed. Let's bring these bastards down," Raydar growled.

Raydar and Ms. Daley parted ways, their mindsets shifted drastically from earlier that night. Though the outcome wasn't as anticipated or hoped, it brought forth a new alliance that could deem itself most critical on the path laid out before Raydar and his team. Just as Siberian Scientist concluded, there was only one undeniable conclusion ... they were going to have to capture Inkubus themselves, no matter the cost.

Chapter 12
The Calm Before the Storm

The two weeks that proceeded Ray and Ms. Daley's meeting were peculiar to say the least, considering the team did not encounter a single soldier of Inkubus's. With the exception of a few domestic disturbances and junkies, the streets had gone radio silent, leaving the team wondering what Inkubus had hidden up that mysterious black sleeve of his. Despite such minimal criminal activity, the team utilized this time to devise a plan to capture Inkubus once and for all. The time had come to storm the demon's lair. It was the only viable option that remained.

The plan was quite simple. Since the team already knew its exact route and timing, the idea was to hijack the DPD armored truck during Reem's weekly inmate transfer to the Central Station, using him as a hostage to give them a free ride directly into the heart of Inkubus's operation. This of course would rely heavily upon the assistance of Ray's internal observation at the precinct as well as Adam's external surveillance to provide precision intel. To further improve that external surveillance ability, Adam had hacked into the DPD's traffic cam system, granting him twenty-four-hour access to several city-wide video feeds. In addition to this, he setup an alert system to notify him of any obscure and abrupt human movements or traffic obstructions that the video feeds witness.

In order to convince Reem to do such an unthinkable act against his master, Siberian Scientist would utilize a handheld laser cutter to create an opening from the truck's cargo pod through to the driver's seat that would be just large enough to insert the barrel of his Kalashnikov and press it into Reem's spine. To ensure such compliance, Siberian Scientist would also mount a tiny camera into the air vent of the truck's dash to observe Reem from a tablet while he and Dreadnight hide in the back. Once inside the Central Station, the goal would be to neutralize any super soldiers present to allow Dreadnight to snag Inkubus while Siberian Scientist rescues Dr. Foster. If successful, they would then utilize the DPD truck as their escape vehicle and return to the Arcane Asylum with their prized prisoner.

Anticipation flowed through the observatory as the team sat at its round table, finishing the final review of their master plan. The moment they had all waited for was just hours away, a notion that ate away at the nerves of each member as they attempted to maintain focus. No further discussions could be had, and all details had already been scrupulously examined to the point of exhaustion. It was time to lay it all on the line and save the city once and for all by bringing down the veil that has darkened its soul ever since the rise of Inkubus.

All that was left was to execute.

Prior to Ray's departure for the precinct, Father Ephrem insisted that the team join hands in prayer. With their arms stretched out across the table, hands adjoined, and heads bowed, Father Ephrem cleared his throat and began his heart felt prayer:

"Dear Lord, our God, and Michael the great, I ask that tonight of all nights you watch over my sons and protect them from the evils they are to face. As they fight an injustice that plagues the souls of many, I ask that you grant them speed, strength, and a steady heart, so that they may defeat all that oppose your holiness. Please, I ask with all my heart and soul that your grace may bless them in the hours to come and that their efforts will not go unnoticed. In your names, I pray ... amen," Father Ephrem proclaimed, lifting his head and exposing his tear bound eyes.

"Amen," the team added in chorus.

The team released their hands from one another, each wearing a solemn expression upon their faces as they arose from their seats. As much as they wanted to block out the lingering pessimism within their wired minds, they knew that there was a chance they might not see one another again, God forbid things happen to go astray. Time and time again, these five heavy hearts proved that family runs much deeper than blood. Family is not determined by birthright or coincidental conception. Family is formed through sheer commitment to the wellbeing of another and an undying will to see such an individual flourish and persevere. Blood does not form such a bond nor dictate such devotion. It is the conscience decisions that we humans make that constitute the principle of family.

Fortunately, Slade's voice broke through that chilling pessimism, bringing the team back to the crucial reality that awaited them.

"Before we part ways, I want to thank you all," Slade said sincerely. "Each one of you decided to sacrifice the life you once led and risk everything on account of the path laid before me. None of you were obligated to make such a significant choice on my behalf, hell most of you didn't even know me. Despite this, you still chose to place the lives of others before that of your own, all in an effort to fight an injustice greater than anything any of us could have imagined. I am proud to call you my family ... I am proud to call you heroes because that is what you all are. With every fiber of my being, I thank you for all that you have done and all that you are about to do." Slade's voice waivered as he finished his speech, fighting to hold back tears of his own.

"Slade, my friend, it should be us thanking you. Your mission has filled a void in each of our lives, voids that had left us lost and confused. It was you who provided us with the path of fulfillment that we had been longing for. You saved each of us from the dread that once consumed our hearts and souls. I know I speak for all four of us when I say we will be forever grateful for the gift you have given us and we will never forget its significance," Nikolai announced candidly.

That statement couldn't have been truer. For Father Ephrem, the mission gave him four sons, sons he never believed he would have had on account of losing his dear Abigail. Slade's brother in blue, Ray, was given the opportunity to clean up the city that had tainted his own family while being gifted the brother he never had. The foreign branch of the family tree, Nikolai, was granted the miraculous news that his best friend was indeed still alive and was provided the chance to seek vengeance against the man who stripped that friend from his life. Last but certainly not least, the brains of the operation, Mr. Adam Keen, was provided a channel to finally be able to put his intelligence and financial resources towards helping mankind in a way he never thought was possible.

It was safe to say that the blessing of the Effigiem Custos was the greatest thing to have ever happened, not only for our heroes, but for the entire city, even though most of its citizens didn't realize it yet.

Overwhelmed by such kind words, Slade was rendered speechless. Words couldn't even describe the pride and joy he felt in that very moment. With a soul filled to the brim with warmth and contentment, Slade looked around with a gracious and humbled smile, a smile that was shared by all.

This only fueled the fire that was already burning bright within him.

"Alright team, tonight is our night, our time. Let's make this happen!" Slade roared, clenching his right fist, and thrusting it out in front of his body.

"Damn right comrade!" Nikolai belted out.

"Let's do this, brothers!" Ray shouted.

The team's jovial and fiery bursts of reassurance echoed throughout the observatory. An ever so fitting scene capturing the city's heroes as they prepared for the battle that could determine the fate of millions of lives.

And so, the team went their separate ways in preparation of the night ahead. Adam immediately went to his monitoring station to prepare the Celestial Shipping truck's GPS route as well as pull up the appropriate traffic cams along said route. Ray suited up and headed to the precinct, hoping the first three hours of his shift would fly by without pause. Their Russian counterpart was just across the observatory from Adam, seated at a tool bench by the east wall, cleaning his guns and sharpening his knife for the upcoming battle. Just as he did every night for the past three weeks, Slade found himself in Father Ephrem's quarters, mentally preparing himself for whatever challenges the night may bring.

"How are you feeling son?" Father Ephrem asked.

"Excited, nervous, and a little scared to be honest," Slade replied as a warm cup of coffee soothed his hands.

"Justifiably so. You have sacrificed so much to get to this very moment, fighting a battle on behalf of those you owe nothing to. Yet here you are, ready to face an evil so great, so horrid, all for humanity's sake," Father Ephrem said, nearly spilling his coffee as his words jolted his body.

"It's a battle I am honored to fight. I can hardly believe that just a few months ago, I would have been spending a night as such contemplating my life over a glass of vodka in a bar of oblivious drunks, and now I have the power to impose justice upon those who feed off the defenseless," Slade replied, his eyes gleaming with pride as the two shared a smile.

"You are forgetting one crucial factor through all of this though son." Father Ephrem raised an eyebrow with implication.

"What's that?" Slade asked curiously.

"You, Slade Allen."

"What do you mean, me?" Slade replied with a look of confusion.

"You must remember the reason you accepted Michael's calling … that which you hold dear to your heart," Father Ephrem said, pointing at the charm hanging from Slade's neck.

Slade lifted his right hand, setting the charm in his palm while looking down at it with hopeful eyes.

"You mustn't forget your own happiness and the dreams that form it. Such dreams are what led you to this very point in time. They are the reason Michael chose you. Without them, all this means nothing. So, when you are out there risking your life yet again, remember that life you told me you hoped for … remember Rachel, and fight for her!"

"I will," Slade said with a grin. "I have been so consumed by the idea of bringing Inkubus down, I almost forgot what led me to this life. It was her ... it was always her." Slade closed his hand, clutching the charm as he pictured Rachel's face.

"Good. Now go out there and make me proud, son."

The two men rose and hugged each other, just as any father and son would in such dire times, both hoping they would be back in that very room for many nights to come.

Chapter 13
Bringing Down the Veil

Only five minutes separated the team from their defining moment. At the precinct, Raydar watched Reem's office door like a hawk, waiting for it to open, an action that would signify it was go time. Just fifty yards away, Dreadnight was perched atop the International Trade Center, his eyes affixed on the precinct's garage door as he awaited Raydar's cue. Six blocks southeast of Dreadnight's location, Siberian Scientist sat idly by in the Celestial Shipping truck at the corner of Sixth and Jefferson, his hand gripped tightly around the steering wheel, ready for action. Back at the observatory, the glow from the monitoring station's vast array of screens lit Mr. Unseen and Father Ephrem's heedful faces as they scanned the area's traffic cams for obstructions.

"Here we go boys! The dog is leaving the pound. I repeat, the dog is leaving the pound," the software's robotic voice announced through the link.

"Get ready guys," Dreadnight said sternly.

After nearly ten painstaking minutes that felt like an eternity, the garage door of the precinct lifted from the cement, breaking the comm link's mind-numbing silence.

"The door is up!" Dreadnight blurted in uncontrollable excitement.

The headlights of the DPD armored truck beamed out into the open as it appeared from behind the rising door. The engine roared as it pulled forward and turned left onto eighth street, the black and blue paint of its reinforced metal panels gleamed as oncoming streetlamps passed by. Just as Dreadnight prepared to take flight, the sound of the observatory's alarm filled the comm link.

"Umm, guys we have a problem," Mr. Unseen announced.

"What? What's wrong?" Dreadnight said with agitation.

"Traffic cam nineteen is showing people flooding out of the Majestic Theater and out into Mack Avenue in utter hysteria. They are screaming that there is a bomb inside," Mr. Unseen said.

What was once a quaint night at the movies was now a real-life terror scene.

Dreadnight's mind raced as he watched the DPD truck pull away, dragging his chance of vengeance along with it.

"Shit! The plan's off," Dreadnight snapped. "I'll be there as soon as possible. Siberian, head over and ensure the civilians clear the area," Dreadnight directed.

"You sure you want to call this off? This could be our one and only shot at ending all of this," Siberian Scientist fretted through his comm, the roar of the Celestial Shipping truck growing with each second.

"If there is but the slightest chance that this bomb threat is real, we have no choice but to act on it," Dreadnight said, bound by his conscience.

"Okay. Then that is what we will do," Siberian Scientist confirmed, entrusting Dreadnight's judgement.

Dreadnight leaped from the north ledge of the ITC and into a sprint toward the opposing end of the rooftop. Full speed ahead, he stepped onto the oncoming cement ledge, using it to catapult himself into the air like a spear. Just as his heavy frame dropped toward the street below, his wings shot out like a parachute and his back arched, causing his body to burst back toward the sky.

"Dreadnight, turn your body northwest forty-five degrees. The Majestic Theater will be about three miles straight ahead," Mr. Unseen said, watching a red dot that was Dreadnight's GPS tracker scale across a map of the city displayed on monitor number three. Quickly, he turned his attention to a second dot, blue in color, indicating Siberian Scientist's location. Utilizing live traffic updates, he plugged the most efficient route into the Celestial Shipping truck's navigation system. "Siberian, follow the route I just transmitted over. It will place you across the street from the theater where most of the civilians are fleeing to," he added with urgency.

"Copy that, on my way." Siberian Scientist released the clutch and slammed the truck's shifter into first gear, throwing him back into his seat as the truck surged forward like a bat out of hell.

Ripping through the air with all his might, the conflicted area was now within Dreadnight's enhanced sight. Zoning his vision in on the street, he saw a flood of people frantically running in a stampede. Pushing and shoving one another, bodies were forced to the pavement to be trampled upon. It was pure narcissistic mass chaos. Suddenly, Dreadnight heard tires squeal in the distance, their rubber screaming with fury.

"Dreadnight, are you seeing what I am seeing?" Mr. Unseen said, his voice growing with anxiousness.

Just as Dreadnight jerked his head toward the abrupt commotion, he saw a black Chevy Impala drift onto Mack Avenue from Cass Avenue just a block east of the theater. Without hesitation, he angled his wings back and straightened his body down toward the civilians, bolting him like an asteroid approaching earth. One hundred yards ... eighty yards … sixty yards, Dreadnight desperately neared. Picking up its own speed, the Impala headed directly toward the fleeing civilians with no intention of slowing. Dreadnight's heart sunk as he saw a family of four with their hands clutched onto one another appear in the car's gleaming headlights. Their young daughter tripped and fell onto the pavement, losing the grasp of her father's hand.

"You guys have to get those people out of there or stop that car somehow!" Mr. Unseen fretted as he and Father Ephrem sat on the edge of their seats watching the horrid scenario unfold.

"What the hell is going on!" Raydar typed anxiously, unable to wrap his head around the situation.

Slamming on the brakes to avoid the hysteria of oncoming traffic, Siberian Scientist slid to a halt a half block south of the theater on the east side of third avenue. Kalashnikov AK74M in hand, he jumped out of the truck in a panic and into an all-out sprint through the oncoming cars and people. Realizing he wouldn't be able to reach the disorderly vehicle now only forty yards away from the people in its path, he jumped on top of a parked SUV on the west side of the street. Lifting his assault rifle up in between his chest and right shoulder, he quickly looked down its notched rear tangent iron sight with extreme focus. His crosshairs were free of innocent bystanders, providing him with a clean shot at the speeding vehicle. Pressing his finger into the trigger, he released a storm of bullets into the side of the Impala, hoping to pop its tires. Holes sporadically coated the car's metal panels as it continued its rampage of dissonance.

POP! Psshhewww!

The rear tire on the driver's side exploded, causing the car to fall onto its rim and toss sparks into the air. The car veered side to side in a sudden loss of traction, but regained stability.

"Dammit!" Siberian Scientist shouted.

With the speeding vehicle now only twenty yards away from flesh and bone, Siberian Scientist lowered his weapon and leaped off the SUV into an all-out sprint toward the seemingly doomed civilians as their inevitable outcome approached.

But hope was not lost.

Out of the darkness and into the light, Dreadnight appeared like an angel from the heavens above. Siberian Scientist, Mr. Unseen, and Father Ephrem, watched as their celestial comrade lifted his wings for a mere split second, hoisting his body upright just before fully retracting them behind his back. At least one hundred feet from impact with nothing left to slow his descent, Dreadnight's monstrous body plunged feet first toward the pavement below.

Only twenty yards from creating human hood ornaments, the gleam of the Impala's headlights engulfed the distraught father as he lunged toward his faltering daughter.

BOOM!

In an earth-shattering blast, Dreadnight's feet crashed into the pavement like an anvil, sending a multitude of cracks in every direction through its foundation. Just a few feet behind him, the frantic civilians braced for sudden impact, their eyes filled with the despair of imminent death. Dreadnight turned toward the speeding Impala. In one swift motion, he released the claws of his feet into the shattered pavement while dropping his body down and straightening his arms out in front of him.

Just as the skin of Dreadnight's palms grazed the paint of the speeding car, he closed his eyes and with the utmost focus he turned his arms to stone. The sounds of screaming civilians and twisting metal filled the airwaves as the car's hood was peeled back like a tin can and its rear end shot up into the air. With his stone hands gripped upon the now mangled front bumper, Dreadnight resisted the force of the car, flexing every muscle in his body as it pushed him backward, causing his claws to screech across the pavement.

"Errraaaggghhh!"

CRASH!

The back end of the Impala smashed back onto the pavement, stopping the vehicle in its tracks and tossing its exposed rim across the street in a rattling skid.

By now both sides of Dreadnight's body were fenced inside of the car's contorted front end as he stood where the engine once sat.

Just inches behind Dreadnight's rippling legs was the brave father, shielding his daughter with closed eyes. Only a few feet away, the rest of their family as well as Siberian Scientist looked upon the sight in utter astonishment.

"Oh my god, he did it! I can't believe he stopped it!" Mr. Unseen gasped.

"Is he okay?" Raydar typed frantically, praying his brother was alive.

"Yes ... he is unharmed ... somehow," Father Ephrem said in disbelief at what he just witnessed.

When Dreadnight opened his eyes and looked up, all he could see was a disoriented man attempting to break free from an inflated airbag and its contents. Dreadnight released his arms from their hardened state, returning them to flesh, then removed his hands from the vehicle's mangled frame. A look of hate consumed his face as he stepped onto what remained of the car's hood. Kneeling in front of the fractured windshield, Dreadnight sent his right fist through the glass and grabbed ahold of the assailant's leather jacket. With one vicious tug, he sent the man headfirst through the windshield, sending shards of glass clanking to the ground as he lifted him high into the air in a standing motion. Looking upon the man's bloodied smug face as he flailed violently to counter, Dreadnight could sense that no humanity remained in the shell before him. He was one of Inkubus's instruments of doom.

This left Dreadnight no choice but to put the rabid animal down right then and there.

Holding the man above him, Dreadnight reached up with his other hand and clutched onto the man's jacket. With an audience of dazed eyes, Dreadnight drove the man's body flat into the car's rooftop, causing it to cave in as if it were a children's toy. The windows of the car exploded from the impact, nullifying the sound of Dreadnight's rage filled grunt.

Coughing up blood, the assailant's head tottered in a futile attempt regain cognizance.

Not on Dreadnight's watch.

With eyes of fury, he drew back his right arm and released the claws of its straightened hand. Like a guillotine, he struck the man's throat, sending his claws through the man's esophagus and jugular, causing blood to spit into the air.

There was no coming back from that.

Pulling his bloodied hand from the fresh corpse, Dreadnight rose and turned around. Stunned and motionless, a crowd of over twenty civilians glared at the beastly creature, acting as if they were in the presence of God himself. Breathing heavily and covered in the blood of the assailant, Dreadnight stepped down from the vehicle's frame and onto the pavement amongst the gawking civilians.

"You saved my daughter's life. You're not a beast, you're a hero!" the distressed father expressed in sheer gratitude, clutching his daughter tightly into his chest.

"Yeah. He saved their lives!" Another voice cried out.

"The media lied!"

"He protected us!"

The crowd voiced their praise for their new-found hero as cell phone cameras flashed one after another as if they were paparazzi. It was safe to say that every man, woman, and child in that crowd now knew that Dreadnight was no threat to this city. In fact, they realized he was their guardian. They just didn't know what he was guarding them from.

"Clear the area ... now!" Dreadnight grunted exhaustedly as he turned and walked toward the Majestic Theater entrance.

"Come on people, move out!" Siberian Scientist shouted as he directed them away from the crash site, his AK74M grazing his side.

With their heads turned back toward their gargoyle savior, the crowd shuffled their way across the street and out of the theater's vicinity, still stricken by the blunt realization seared into their minds.

A grand and glamorous marquee brimmed in multicolored lights above Dreadnight as he entered through the glass doors of the Majestic Theater. "Special Feature: A Warrior's Ascension" was displayed in bold black letters upon the marquee's white porcelain background.

Stepping on popcorn, soft drinks, and fallen crowd control barricades, Dreadnight scanned the barren lobby visually while smelling for any hint of explosive materials. Seconds later, Siberian Scientist walked through the entrance, his gun raised in shooting position.

"The streets are clear of civilians," Siberian Scientist announced.

Before Dreadnight could respond, a sudden burst of loud music filled the room, but the sound wasn't coming from the lobby. Swiveling their heads, they attempted to decipher its origin.

"I think it's coming from the east wing, cover me I'm going in," Dreadnight directed Siberian Scientist who was just steps behind him.

"Be careful it could be a trap," Father Ephrem said as he watched Dreadnight's live feed.

"That's it. I'm coming to back you up," Raydar typed anxiously.

"No, we can't risk your cover being blown. Standby," Dreadnight directed sternly.

A response Raydar was unhappy to hear to say the least, his patience growing increasingly thin as he remained unaware of the full situation.

Lined with three auditoriums on each side, the two cautiously treaded down the dimly lit hallway of the retro theater's east wing as Beethoven's 7th Symphony bombarded their eardrums. In a crouched position, Siberian Scientist swiveled his gun from side to side with each passing auditorium, ready for anything that could pop out. The closer they came to the hall's end, the louder the music became. Only two auditoriums remained, one on each side. Dreadnight stopped, lifting his right hand at Siberian Scientist, signaling him to do the same. Within seconds, Dreadnight motioned his left hand to the left, indicating it was the auditorium in question.

"Siberian, remember those standalone "eyes" I gave you? I think this would be the proper time to use one," Mr. Unseen said into the comm link, referring to five spherical camera units he had given him earlier that night. The very units his "eyes of divinity" assemblies were comprised of.

With the nod of his head, Dreadnight signaled Siberian Scientist that it was a go, then with one large step he backed himself against the wall just right of the closed auditorium double doors. Following suit, Siberian Scientist quickly paced until turning the corner and hugging his back against the entrance's left wall.

A few quiet breaths later, Dreadnight nodded again, ready for his comrade to engage. With steadied hands and the utmost discreteness, Siberian Scientist unlatched a small compartment on his utility belt and lifted out one of the eyes. Smaller than a pea, he held it between the thumb and index finger of his right hand, while reaching with his left hand to grab onto the handle of the door nearest to him. Ever so slowly, Siberian Scientist pulled the door back, using it to conceal himself as it opened. Once opened enough to fit his arm through, he chucked the eye through the slim opening and high into the air of the auditorium, pulling his arm back and closing the door immediately after so.

Hovered in front of the monitoring station, Mr. Unseen and Father Ephrem watched as the glass ball sailed through the air and bounced off one of the seats and onto the floor until coming to a rolling stop. Immediately, Mr. Unseen extended his main monitor to spread its display over all twelve that surrounded he and Father Ephrem, creating a one massive picture. With three clicks of his mouse, he then reversed the eye's playback, reduced its run speed by a factor of ten, and hit the play function. In slow motion, they analyzed the playback, looking for anything out of the ordinary. The dimly lit theater was completely empty, not a soul was present, and nothing seemed out of place.

"It appears to be empty. Proceed with extreme caution," Mr. Unseen said, unsettled by the scenario at hand.

It was obvious to the entire team that Dreadnight was being lured to that specific theater. But why? The bomb had to be a front since Inkubus wanted his adversary alive, not to mention the fact that a bomb may not even kill Dreadnight. It just didn't make sense, any of it.

"I'll head in first and check out the west side of the auditorium. After a ten count, you follow in and cover the east side," Dreadnight directed in a whispered tone. Siberian Scientist agreed with a quick nod, then pulled the left door open for Dreadnight's entrance. With his senses on high alert, Dreadnight entered the auditorium, his eyes shifting in every direction as he slowly crept toward its west side. Just as Mr. Unseen suspected, nothing seemed out of place or unordinary, that is with the exception of the violent piano chords of Beethoven.

Three ... two ... one ... Siberian Scientist marched through the entrance and down the auditorium's east aisle in a crouched position, his trigger finger steadied and ready to fire as the rifle's scout light lit the way. Scanning the seats, walls, and ceiling, they found nothing, absolutely nothing. As they stepped down the aisles, the hair on their necks rose with apprehension, unsure of what they were walking into.

"What the ..." Siberian Scientist shouted frantically pivoting his weapon.

The lights went dark, and the speakers went silent.

"Oh shit!" Mr. Unseen blurted. "Dreadnight what's happening in there?"

His night vision already activated, Dreadnight quickly scanned the area but found nothing irregular.

That was about to change.

Rerrrrr-ing

A panning beam of light projected itself from the rear of the auditorium, illuminating the screen before them, causing the two men to snap their heads forward. Staring them right in the face was a magnified visual of the vile demon himself ... Inkubus, his mask consuming the entire screen.

"Gentlemen, I see you got my calling card," Inkubus's snide voice shot from the speakers, sending a chill down the spine of each team member as its ugliness entered their ears.

"Yeah, and part of it is lying dead with a punctured throat in the middle of a smashed car. Don't worry you will receive your own judgment for this soon enough," Dreadnight snarled at the screen.

"Did the anger come with the claws? Or did someone beat that into you?" Inkubus twisted his head in provocation as his empty eyes stared upon the duo.

Fists clenched and shaking, rage swelled within Dreadnight.

"There is no bomb is there?" Siberian Scientist shouted, his finger grazing the trigger of his gun.

"How'd you guess?" Inkubus said mockingly. "You vigilantes are so predictable. The minute some pathetic little meat suit is in harm's way, you come crashing in guns blazing to save the day. Well tonight at least one of those meat suits is going to die on your watch, and you get the honor of choosing who lives and who dies."

"Enough of these games, how about you face me like a man, coward!" Dreadnight roared.

"Sorry, but I'd much rather watch you squirm. It's truly too much fun!" Inkubus said like the maniac he was. "Let's play, shall we?"

A secondary video feed popped up alongside Inkubus's mask on the left side of the movie screen.

"Here we have exhibit A. Recognize your precious little mole?"

The video feed displayed the disturbing sight of Lainey Ross strung up like a human bullseye to four metal stakes buried into a cement wall, a rag strapped in and around her bloodied mouth. Mounted to an elaborate mechanical fixture just feet away from her, was a loaded shotgun linked to a tensioned cable system. Thrusting her limbs in a desperate struggle to break free from the tightly wound ropes that restrained her, black mascara ran from her weeping eyes and down her flushed face.

"Lainey! What has he done to her?" Raydar feverously punched into the comm software, feeling as if his heart had stopped.

"You see that wire that is caressing that trigger oh so gently? Of course, you do, who am I kidding! Inkubus shook his head like a crazed drug fiend, causing the tentacles of his mask to sway every which way. "Now, you see this red button right here?" Inkubus placed a handheld control unit right into the camera's focus, his index finger aimed at an illuminated red button. "Let's just say there will be a lot of Lainey to go around if my finger gets antsy," Inkubus said animatedly, his hand quivering in embellishment.

"What do you want?" Dreadnight growled, the urge to slit Inkubus's throat swelling within him.

"God you are just so impatient, aren't you?" Inkubus's voice reeked of sarcasm.

A third video feed appeared out the blue and to the right of Inkubus on the movie screen. Gleeful sounds of young children playing and laughing consumed the speakers surrounding Dreadnight and Siberian Scientist as they laid their eyes upon a most disturbing image. An image of six children enjoying one another's company in a hospital playroom, many of them clearly debilitated or cancer stricken. The heart of each team member ached with unbearable affliction as their minds strayed into the darkest pits of despair, all while the six children were unknowingly being watched.

"I said …What do you want?" Dreadnight roared in a furious outburst.

"There you go again with that incessant impatience! Inkubus threw his arms into the air in disappointment. "Trust me you will want all of the time you can get … soon enough. Oh look, a timer!" Inkubus shoved a digital stopwatch in front of the camera's lens, in the middle in big bright numbers was "10:00".

"Guys, what the hell is going on!" Raydar's keys shouted at the team.

"I … I think Inkubus is going to make them choose between Lainey and the children," Mr. Unseen said with hesitation as he looked upon his monitoring station, his jaw nearly on the floor.

"My God …" Father Ephrem gasped just before placing his hand over his mouth.

"I'm guessing you would like to know what the ten minutes is all about, huh? Well, it means that when this stopwatch zeroes out, Lainey's new best friend will say hello and that life sized teddy bear that bald girl is clinging onto … it's going to turn those kids and many others into alphabet soup. Ahahaha!" Inkubus's demented laugh was like nails on a chalkboard to the team's ears as their minds raced uncontrollably and their hearts ached.

"You twisted son of a bitch! Leave them out of this. This is between you and me!" Dreadnight roared, causing the veins of his forehead to bulge.

"It's time for you to decide who lives … and who dies," Inkubus said in a lowered tone. "Who will you choose? Your little undercover birdie or the likes of poor, sick, innocent children," he added mockingly.

The two paneled video feeds flickered into darkness for a split second, until being replaced by the images of two maps, each displaying a bright red indicator.

"Don't think for a second that you and your Russian sidekick can make it to both locations in time. Trust me, only you have the ability to make to one location within the designated time," Inkubus said, his blank obsidian eyes glaring at Dreadnight. "Oh! Speaking of seconds," Inkubus pressed the bright red button on top of the stopwatch, starting its dreaded countdown. "Tick tock … Tick tock." Inkubus said arrogantly, rocking his head side to side, imitating a clock's pendulum.

Without hesitation both Dreadnight and Siberian Scientist turned and bolted toward the auditorium exit, their hearts racing with extreme trepidation.

With lighting speed, Mr. Unseen utilized Dreadnight's eyes of divinity to take snapshots of the two maps and transpose them into his GPS system, calculating all potential routes by car and their respective ETA's. The system's results were like a punch to the gut.

"Guys, location A is the abandoned Chrysler plant off Waterman and Clayton. Location B is the Children's Hospital at Canfield and Sheridan. I'm afraid Inkubus is right, even at a speed of over one hundred miles an hour there is no possible route that can get Siberian to either location within ten minutes by ground," Mr. Unseen said with deep regret.

"That doesn't mean I can't!" Raydar keyed vigorously into the comm system, just before killing his computer's power and jumping out of his chair.

Running as fast as he possibly could, Raydar passed desk after desk as he inserted his comm receiver into his ear and its coinciding microphone to his throat. Co-workers watched in confusion as papers flew off their desks and scattered across the floor from his momentous fly-by toward the precinct's rear exit.

"I got Lainey, you get the bomb Dreadnight," Raydar said, short of air as he slammed through the precinct exit and sprinted down the sidewalk toward the precinct parking lot.

"But you will get exposed. You don't have your mask!" Dreadnight responded concerningly as he and Siberian Scientist raced toward the Majestic Theater's main double doors.

"It's Lainey man, it's Lainey!" Ray said frantically as he hopped into his car and slammed the key into its ignition.

"Okay, let's do this!"

"Raydar, I just uploaded the quickest possible route into your phone's GPS. If you can maintain a speed of at least seventy miles per hour you should get to the Lainey in nine minutes, leaving you one minute to get her the hell out of there," Mr. Unseen said with urgency.

"Copy that. I'll make it ... I have to." Raydar peeled out of his parking space and rammed through the barrier arm of the precinct lot's security gate, shattering it on contact before drifting right onto eighth street.

Immediately upon busting through the Majestic Theater doors, Dreadnight leaped into the air and took flight, heading due east directly toward the children's hospital.

"Siberian, head toward the Chrysler plant and give Raydar some backup, I have a feeling he will need it," Dreadnight said as his wings ripped through the air with might.

"Agreed, Mr. Unseen forward me the coordinates," Siberian Scientist said, sprinting across Mack Ave. in a b-line sprint toward the Celestial Shipping truck.

"Done, the route has been uploaded into your navigation system," Mr. Unseen replied, his hands fast at work as he juggled multiple tasks on a myriad of monitors.

"How much time do we have?" Dreadnight asked, worry eminent in his voice.

"We are at five minutes and twenty seconds boys," Mr. Unseen replied looking upon a large countdown in bright and bold red numbers on his main screen. "I'm pulling up the layouts of both the old Chrysler plant and the children's hospital as we speak to give you both precise locations," he added, flipping from monitor to monitor as Father Ephrem watched Dreadnight and Siberian Scientist's red indicators grow farther and farther away from one another, heading in opposite directions.

Having already hacked into city hall's network, Mr. Unseen sifted through its database in search of building blueprints for both locations. Like a data processing wizard, he located and downloaded the blueprints of both the old Chrysler plant and the children's hospital within sixty seconds. In a flash, the two sets of blueprints popped up onto several of the monitors, the locations split up on the right and left side of the monitoring station. Analyzing the children's hospital prints with diligence, his eyes toggled back and forth in search of its playroom.

"Bingo!"

"Dreadnight, the hospital's playroom is on the third floor, room 302, halfway down the hall on the north side. There is no clean entry point from the outside to that floor and the windows of the patient rooms are too small, you'll have to go through the main entrance," Mr. Unseen said.

"Where do I go from there?" Dreadnight replied.

"Looks like there is a stairwell to the left of the lobby's main desk, take that up to the third floor and take an immediate right. After about thirty feet it will split off to the right, take that right and the playroom will be about one hundred feet down and on the left wall," Mr. Unseen explained.

"Okay got it," Dreadnight said over the rustling wind that deflected off his body.

His foot nearly pressing through the floor and hands choking the steering wheel, Raydar weaved through traffic and blew through red lights, all while avoiding oncoming vehicles and pedestrians in a desperate attempt to make up for lost time.

Come on Ray you can do this! You have to save her ... Raydar thought to himself.

Raydar had never been as determined as he was at that very moment. Nothing was going to take Lainey from him. Even if that meant taking a bullet and sacrificing his own life to ensure her safety.

"Raydar, based upon the images from Inkubus's video, it seems Lainey's located in the plant's old tool room on the ground level at the southwest end. I updated your GPS route to place you right at the most efficient entry point," Mr. Unseen said as he looked upon both the blueprints as well as the latest satellite images of the abandoned plant. "Bust through the second set of windows from the west end, the tool room is directly through the boarded off doorway that will be straight ahead."

"Thanks man!" Raydar blurted as he swerved onto the sidewalk to miss an oncoming car, jerking the wheel back after it passed to get back onto the road to prevent losing speed.

"Three minutes and ten seconds," Mr. Unseen announced anxiously.

Next to Mr. Unseen, Father Ephrem watched the video feeds of both men's eyes of divinity, praying nervously as he clutched onto his red and gold rosary.

"I have the children's hospital in sight," Dreadnight said as he fought through the burning pain emanating through his back and thrashing wings.

Dipping down, he angled back his wings, sending his body bulleting toward the Children's Hospital. Like a meteor hailing from above, the earth's atmosphere morphed around the falling mass leaving condensation trails lingering in the abaft sky. Ripping between the buildings that lined canfield street, Dreadnight quickly approached the hospital's courtyard which led to its main entrance. A few feet before crashing into the courtyard's brick canvas, he opened his wings to their fullest capacity.

WHOOSH!

His body was lifted vertically.

Fwooop!

His wings shot behind his back, ending their resistance and dropping Dreadnight's body as if it were made of lead. Using his descent's ample momentum, his massive feet landed in a running motion onto the brick courtyard, his arms violently ripping through the air. Dreadnight sprinted toward the hospital's main entrance, the thought of innocent children being harmed fueling his tired lungs.

Only twenty yards ahead, he saw a couple with a young child approaching the entrance's automatic sliding doors, an obstacle he didn't have time to maneuver around.

With only seconds to determine a point of entry, it seemed his only option was to create his own. Veering off to the left of the entrance he continued his blitz, now aimed directly at a spanning glass window that bridged the entrance doors to the hospital's brick foundation. Only five yards from the impending impact, Dreadnight leaped forward and turned his left shoulder inward.

SMASH!

The window exploded, sending shards of glass shooting across the hospital's epoxy flooring as Dreadnight's massive body entered its premises. Screams and shrieks of horror filled the air as several visitors and employees panicked from the astonishing sight before them. Disregarding the commotion, he frantically looked for the aforementioned stairwell, still pressing on relentlessly.

"Right there! About twenty feet to your left," Mr. Unseen blurted, watching the eyes of divinity feed.

"I see it," Dreadnight exhaustedly responded. "How much time do I have?"

"Fifty-nine seconds," Mr. Unseen replied with apparent uncertainty in his voice, the countdown staring him in the face.

Leaping onto the stairs, Dreadnight scaled upward and on with powerful strides, avoiding multiple steps at a time as he neared the second level.

"Watch out!" Dreadnight roared, hoping to avoid colliding with those who approached.

Darting out of the beastly gargoyle's way, bodies dove in every direction in unbound fear of his presence. Within seconds, Dreadnight reached the door leading to the third floor, barreling through it like a raging bull and causing it to slam against the wall behind it.

"Fifty seconds, you can do this man!" Mr. Unseen shouted, his head on a constant swivel to monitor both unfolding scenarios at hand.

Blood pumping, lungs contracting, Dreadnight refused to let up as his legs continued to pound against the floor, warning those in his path.

"There! On your right!" Mr. Unseen jolted in his seat.

Dreadnight turned on a dime, knocking two patrons over as he curled into the connecting hallway.

"Coming through! Move out of the way!" Dreadnight's roar echoed throughout the hallway, causing nurses to veer the beds of their patients out of his way and up against each wall.

"Forty seconds ..."

Then Dreadnight saw an overhanging sign on the north wall, with the number 302 engraved in it.

"I see it!" Dreadnight shouted as he stormed toward the room's wooden door.

Slamming down its metal handle, he burst into the room, determined to find that volatile teddy bear. Like a raging fire, chaos spread through the room as the ailing children were filled with terror, screaming and crying incessantly as they scurried away. Ignoring the petrified children, Dreadnight frantically searched for the bear, knocking over legos and crushing toy firetrucks as his eyes jarred side to side and his body twisted in every direction.

Come on, where is it! Panic consumed his body as the seconds ticked away, each feeling like a sword through the chest.

"Twenty-four seconds!" Mr. Unseen nervously blurted as he frantically watched the eyes of divinity feed, searching for the teddy bear himself, sweat dripping from his forehead.

"Behind the wooden chest to your right!" Father Ephrem shouted as he leaped out of his chair, nearly giving himself a heart attack.

Dreadnight turned his head to see a fluffy brown leg peering out from behind a large wooden toy chest that was red in color and plastered with images of clowns. Lunging across the room, he reached down and grabbed the teddy bear's leg. As he lifted his head, his eyes locked with that of a young boy, causing him to freeze up. Shaking in heart wrenching fear, the boy released his grip from the teddy bear and clutched his arms around his caregiver's waist as she hugged the wall, tears flooding from their eyes. An image so unbearable, that no decent man would be able to stomach its haunting.

"Slade get out of there!" Father Ephrem fretted.

Snapping out of his trance, Dreadnight turned and bolted out of the playroom and back out into the hall, the teddy bear swinging back and forth as he gripped it tightly in his right hand.

Only eighteen seconds remained.

"Go left!" Mr. Unseen yelled.

Sliding across the epoxy floor, Dreadnight followed the order as the hospital patrons watched in fear and utter confusion.

"Ten yards ahead turn right!" Mr. Unseen said.

Sixteen ... fifteen.

In two leaping strides, Dreadnight reached the connecting hall, ripping around its corner.

Fourteen ... thirteen ... the suspense continued to mount.

"You got this!" Mr. Unseen's pulse raced as he rose from his chair, bracing himself for what could be his dear friend's final moments.

Amidst the looming inevitability, a glimmer of hope shined through a cascading bay window just ten yards ahead bordering a waiting lounge. Digging deep, Dreadnight pushed his arms back and forth with power as he jetted toward his only escape route.

Ten ... nine

Pushing his left foot into the floor, Dreadnight launched himself into a pencil dive over the lounge furniture and the people inhabiting it.

Smash!

His body blasted through the glass and out into the open air, causing the entire window to shatter into a thousand pieces. Falling at an increasing speed, Dreadnight bulleted straight toward the unforgiving concrete below. Feeding off the thrilling suspense, people flooded out of the hospital and out into the street to witness the superhuman being's feat unfold.

Seven ... six ... timing was running out.

WHOOSH!

Just before painting the street in his own flesh, Dreadnight released his wings, firing him like a cannon up and overtop a neighboring park and to the stars above, producing a wind force so strong it knocked the people below off balance.

"Five seconds! Get rid of that *thing!*" Mr. Unseen screamed.

Dreadnight thrusted his wings like a dragon of myth, climbing the skies with unrelenting might. One hundred feet and climbing, he gritted his teeth as the image of Rachel's face flashed into his mind, the fear of never seeing her again consuming his soul.

Three ... two

"Please God, protect your children!" Father Ephrem cried in a desperate and final prayer.

Dreadnight pulled his right arm back and with every bit of strength that remained in his taxed body, he heaved the plush bear as far into the night as he could.

One ... the adolescent bomb sailed into the foreseeable darkness as Mr. Unseen and Father Ephrem held their breaths with wide eyes.

Just as Dreadnight pushed his wings forward, ending his tear toward the stars, an ear shattering blast saturated the sky, sending an orange inferno slamming into him like a cannon ball as it radiated in every direction.

"Noooo!" Father Ephrem screamed at the top of his lungs.

Smoke and fire consumed the eyes of divinity, cutting off the observatory's visibility and filling Mr. Unseen and Father Ephrem with unimaginable fear.

Fear that would only swell.

Within a second of the explosion, the sound of a shotgun shell clanking onto a concrete floor entered the comm system.

"Raydar!" Mr. Unseen gasped.

~

His tires screaming across the dry pavement, Raydar's car drifted in front of the southwest end of the abandoned Chrysler plant. Slamming the car into park, he scurried out the front seat and dashed toward the graffiti covered building. Four rows of tile glass windows coated the exterior, each set fragmented and tarnished. Launching from an all-out sprint and bracing his arms over his head, Raydar dove through the second set of ground level windows. Tucking his torso in, he rolled across the debris covered floor and popped back onto his feet. Feeding off the momentum, his arms and legs pumped forcefully as he raced toward the boarded off doorway just twenty feet ahead.

"Five seconds!" Mr. Unseen's voice filled his comm receiver.

Turning his right shoulder inward, Raydar leaped into the wooden barrier, splitting the plywood in half and peeling it from the nails from which it was anchored. Crashing onto the floor on his side, he looked up to see the girl he loved strung to a wall only feet away, a fixtured shotgun staring her in the face. Looking over with tearful eyes Lainey screamed helplessly into her gag as she rattled her restraints.

Three …

His hands and feet slipping on the rubble beneath him, Raydar stumbled until regaining traction in a desperate endeavor to reach Lainey.

Two …

Raydar lunged at Lainey.

A red light flashed on the electric transmitter mounted to the right side of the fixture, engaging the pre-tensioned wire that linked it to the gun's trigger.

One … *Click!*

Holding her breath and closing her eyes, Lainey froze, awaiting the cruel welcome of death.

Sliding off balance, Raydar slapped his hands against the wall behind Lainey, halting him directly in front of her. A thunderous crack engulfed the room as the shotgun unleashed a swarm of blood thirsty pellets ripping through the air.

"Aaugh!"

Raydar's body slammed into Lainey's as if he were struck by a speeding locomotive, causing his head to graze alongside hers until smacking violently into the cement wall.

In that very moment it felt as if time was standing still for Lainey Ross as she released an unexpected breath. In disbelief that she was still alive and wasn't feeling excruciating pain, she slowly opened her tightened eyes. But when her eyes finally opened, her heart felt the excruciating pain that she expected her body to feel as she saw Raydar's body pressed up against hers and his head draped against the wall.

In an incessant bout of panic, Lainey screamed Ray's name into her muffling gag, hoping by some miracle of God that he was alive, yet knowing that no one could survive such a lethal impact. Suddenly, she felt a throb where Raydar's neck was pressed against hers.

It can't be ...

"Everything is going to be alright Lainey," Ray coughed in a pained voice, lifting his head.

Blood seeping from a two-inch gash overtop his left brow, he lowered his hands and removed Lainey's gag.

"Ray! How did you … how are you alive?" Lainey stuttered in utter disbelief.

Ray ripped open his police uniform, revealing a bullet proof vest.

"And they say a dog is man's best friend," Ray chuckled with a smirk, as he pulled an army knife from his utility belt.

"How did you know I was here?" She said as Raydar cut through the ropes that bound her.

"I'll explain later, we have to get out of here," Raydar said as he rapidly thrusted his blade back and forth upon the braided nylon.

The final rope was severed, causing Lainey's body to drop freely into Raydar's arms. Before he could even speak, Lainey leaned in and firmly kissed him on the lips, turning a moment that was once consumed by fear and desperation into one enthralled with passion, passion so strong that time itself could not conquer its beauty. It was as if the world had stopped as all of Raydar's pain and anguish melted away in an instant. He had never felt so happy in his life. Everything he had been through, it was all worth it, every second.

But then the world began to turn once more.

Just as their lips peeled away from one another, ending their moment of bliss, Raydar and Lainey heard the sound of cracking glass. When they turned their heads toward Raydar's point of entry, they saw a masked mercenary approaching, his M16 locked and loaded, ready to unleash hell upon them. Glowing faces of joy and love quickly turned to portraits of pure cataclysm. He knew there was no possibility of survival, but Raydar reached for his pistol anyhow. Before his gun left its thermoplastic holster, the ripping scream of bullets and the smell of sulfur consumed the room. Raydar and Lainey closed their eyes and clutched onto each other for one final embrace.

~

Before Mr. Unseen or Father Ephrem could react to the disturbing images they had just witnessed, the Observatory security alarm sounded off, alerting them of a perimeter breach in zone one.

"Shit!" Mr. Unseen shouted, quickly pulling up the security feed for the courtyard facing St. Anne's.

As if the team's current state of affairs wasn't bad enough, what was displayed upon the monitoring station's main screen revealed the cruel intentions of Inkubus's master plan. Eight masked men marched toward the main doors of St. Anne's, in the middle of the rank was Inkubus himself, his mask screaming revenge.

"No No No!" Mr. Unseen shouted, his face dripping with terror. "It was all an elaborate diversion to raid Dreadnight's safe house … they have come for the Effigiem Custos!" He rose and stood, shaking from unbridled nervousness.

Father Ephrem stood in silence in the monitoring station's luminous glow, showing no emotion, his eyes locked open in an austere trance. Mr. Unseen quickly toggled over to Dreadnight and Raydar's video feed.

"Dreadnight, Raydar, Siberian, come in!" Mr. Unseen fretted as panic swallowed him whole.

"I am sorry, my sons, but I fear there is no other option," Father Ephrem said solemnly as his face dropped in sudden sadness.

"What are you talking about?"

"It is not the Effigiem Custos that Inkubus seeks,"

"Of course it is, what else could it be?" Mr. Unseen retorted.

"I love each and every one of you, know that. I am so thankful to have shared in this pivotal mission, it has truly fulfilled my life here on this earth. Take care of one another and never stop fighting," Father Ephrem said with tremendous pride, inducing a gentle smile upon his worn and wearied face.

Father Ephrem removed his ear comm and microphone, setting them atop the monitoring station's lacquered oak desk.

"Wait, what are you doing?" Mr. Unseen said vexedly.

Father Ephrem walked up to Mr. Unseen, stopping beside him. He reached his closed right hand out in front of Mr. Unseen.

"Please give this to Slade. I no longer need it. All of my prayers have already been answered."

Mr. Unseen looked down at Father Ephrem's hand and placed his own underneath, curious to what Father Ephrem was referring to, his mind still racing too uncontrollably to speak. A red and gold rosary was dropped into the palm of Mr. Unseen's hand, its crucifix gleaming of polished silver. Father Ephrem then placed his right hand upon Mr. Unseen's left shoulder, furnishing one final smile. Before Mr. Unseen could render a response or even comprehend the situation at hand, Father Ephrem had already lifted the iron manhole cover leading to the Arcane Asylum.

And just like that, he was gone.

~

THUD!

Human flesh met the cold debris laced concrete. The echoing scream of bullets was quickly replaced by that of two unexpected sighs of relief. Raydar and Lainey opened their hopeless eyes, unsure if they were in heaven or on earth. When they turned their heads, they saw their assailant lying face down in a pool of his own blood.

"Are you alright comrades?"

Standing in the doorway opposite to the now dead mercenary was Siberian Scientist, smoke still curling off his AK74M's chrome lined barrel as he lowered it from its line of destruction. Raydar and Lainey whipped their heads around to see their savior cloaked in his mysterious black and blue mask.

"Am I glad to see you Siberian," Raydar said in immense relief.

Pulling it from the holster on his right hip, Siberian Scientist tossed his Tokarev pistol to Lainey.

"Don't worry, it's Russian, so it's good," he snickered. "We must go now. Let's get to the truck," Siberian Scientist said urgently, signaling them to follow him. "Raydar, provide cover on the back end. Lainey stay neutral until I say otherwise," he added sternly.

Raydar quickly drew his police issued Glock 19, lifting his arms into shooting position in the direction of his point of entry. Using a fresh extended magazine, Siberian Scientist butted the emptied one from the gun's receiver, notching the replacement firmly into position.

Chhk Chhu

Siberian Scientist quickly pulled and released the rifle's operating rod, throwing a bullet in its chamber. Like a Russian Spetsnaz, Siberian steadied his sight and pressed forward like pond water, veering from side to side with extreme rigor as he entered the adjoining room, his side mounted tactical light the only source of visibility. Just as Siberian Scientist stepped across the doorway of the adjoining room, the deafening crack of a double tap shot killed the hush atmosphere, as well as an oncoming mercenary. Raydar's precision shooting created two new orifices in the man's skull, instantly killing him. Before the man's body even hit the floor, a second mercenary appeared out of the shadows to the right of Siberian Scientist, sending the buttstock of his M16 into the side of the vigilante's head.

"Auuggghh!" Siberian Scientist groaned as he stumbled sideways.

Fortunately for him, his mask blunted the striking blow. Beating the merc to the punch, Siberian Scientist stabilized his rifle and buried his finger into its trigger, releasing a blaze of bullets from his hip. Ten bullets ripped into the merc's abdomen, the impact forcing him to stagger backward but not to drop. Assuming his assault had neutralized his enemy, Siberian Scientist relaxed his trigger finger.

Never assume someone is dead.

Seemingly unfazed and undeterred, the merc regained his footing and raised his assault rifle once again to finish his objective. Quick to react, Siberian Scientist lifted his own rifle and aimed its sight directly at the merc's chest. With a lead finger, he choked the trigger a second time, releasing a spray of bullets square into the merc. The merc's arms flailed as he stumbled backward, tripping over rubble and falling to the floor. But Siberian Scientist didn't cease fire, he continued firing in forward motion until the merc's body failed to respond.

P-Taff P-Taff P-Taff

The familiar sound of the Tokarev echoed from three bullets connecting with a third mercenary's right shoulder entering from the building's perimeter to the left of Siberian Scientist. But the wounds would only temporarily neutralize the merc's shooting arm, if only for a mere second. Too quick to think, Siberian Scientist twisted his body toward the merc and unleashed a ten-round lambasting into the masked man's chest. Blood shot into the air from the numerous freshly forged apertures.

That'll finish the job.

"Now we are even my friend," Siberian Scientist said in suggestive appreciation, remaining in his militant stance.

Creeping forward through the hemoglobin painted room, Siberian Scientist neared the building's northwest exit where he initially entered. Following his pace was Lainey, her head on a swivel, trailing approximately five feet behind him while Raydar covered her another five feet rearward.

P-Taff P-Taff

Another headshot served by the hands of Raydar.

"The truck is around the corner against the west wall here. On the count of three, we file out to it," Siberian Scientist announced quietly. "Shoot anything that moves," he added coldly.

Lainey and Raydar nodded in compliance, now only a few steps from Siberian Scientist.

"Three ... two ... one ..."

Siberian Scientist quickly paced in a crouched position through the eroded doorway. As soon as his body met the chilled outside air, bullets zipped by his body as his peripheral vision caught two black masses moving at his two and four o'clock positions, perched up in a brick skywalk connecting the Chrysler plant to the adjacent building. Continuing in a forward motion, Siberian Scientist twisted his upper body forty-five degrees then choked his rifle's trigger.

Five round burst ... twist ... five round burst.

The bodies of the two mercs fell lifelessly out of windowless skywalk, sailing thirty feet through the air until thudding against the concrete. The skull of the initial merc cracked against the concrete while the second merc's legs snapped like twigs after a mid-air flip. A third merc twenty yards northwest of Siberian Scientist met the same fate, thanks to Lainey's rapid firing.

"Cover my right," Siberian Scientist shouted as he redirected his approach westward.

Lainey did just that, rolling eastward as her body met the brisk night air. Raydar continued to cover the interior of the building as he followed suit, exiting its decrepit atmosphere. A rush of 5.56mm bullets bombarded Siberian Scientist's vicinity, slicing through the air and ricocheting off the concrete. Without hesitation, Siberian Scientist dove to his right, rolling on his shoulder into a knelt firing position. Lainey and Raydar simultaneously rolled up against the building brick wall for cover as the stray bullets pierced the concrete, just missing their feet. Standing off to the side of the Celestial Shipping truck's rear hatch was yet another merc, desperate to take down the fleeing vigilantes.

But the merc's tactical skills were no match for Siberian Scientist. Before the merc's line of fire could match up with his positioning, Siberian sent a handful of his own bullets ripping into the man's chest and abdomen, ending his crusade of terror.

"Cover me, I'm going in," Raydar said exhaustedly to Lainey as he slapped in a fresh clip into his gun, immediately cocking it after so. After a powerful exhale, Raydar rolled to his left and around the building's corner edge, his arms horizontal with bent elbows, placing his gun's sight right between his own eyes.

P-Taff P-Taff ... P-Taff P-Taff

Raydar swiveled his arms ninety degrees, sending two double tap shots through the neck and right shoulder of a merc who leaned out to shoot from passenger side of the truck's nose an impressive thirty yards away.

Too slow bitch.

Coughing as he rose, Siberian Scientist felt the sting of two bullets buried into his vest, imitating the impact of two blows to the chest from a sledgehammer. At a nearly identical speed, Siberian Scientist and Raydar paced forward with their heads on a swivel toward their team's truck while Lainey back peddled with haste, ensuring their cover. Keeping his rifle hoisted in shooting position with his shooting arm, Siberian Scientist lifted his left hand and signaled Raydar to flank the passenger side of the truck while he flanked the hatch. Just as Raydar reached the nose of the truck and Siberian Scientist the hatch, a pitch-black Escalade came to a screeching halt in the middle of the street from which Raydar arrived, approximately thirty-five yards south of their location.

Raydar sent a string of rapid-fire shots at the SUV as a myriad of mercs filed out releasing their own storm of bullets at the team.

"Get back, now!" Siberian Scientist screamed, rolling back behind the truck.

Raydar dropped down low and hugged the front of the truck as bullets clanked off the right fender until he reached the passenger side of the cargo pod. Lainey turned and sprinted until pressing her back against the cargo pod.

"Cover your ears," Siberian shouted over the screaming bullets as he reached into his trench coat and walked forward approximately five feet away from the truck itself then faced it.

When he withdrew his hand, it was holding a peculiar device bearing a handle that was capped with a metal canister the size of a beer can.

It just so happened to be an anti-tank stick grenade.

Siberian Scientist pulled its pin then swiftly heaved it overtop the truck and high into the air.

The team waited anxiously with their hands over their ears for the grenade's volatile introduction.

Clink

The grenade bounced off the Escalade's side panel and onto the pavement.

Before a single soul could flinch, a seismic explosion annihilated the swarm of mercs, dismantling each of them into pieces as their now flaming Escalade lifted into the air like a rocket. Raydar and Siberian Scientist quickly rolled around their ends of the truck, their guns aimed and trigger fingers eager to engage. However, when they turned, they witnessed no opposition. Instead, their eyes observed a glowing hunk of metal and plastic crash violently back onto the street amongst a field of human debris. Smoke swallowed the entire sky as the crackling embers seared into nothingness. Lainey joined in on the breathtaking spectacle, her jaw dropping instantly.

"Well, I think that did the trick ... damn!" Raydar said, utterly marveled at the sight.

"Da," Nikolai acknowledged in his native tongue

"Where in the hell did you get a grenade man?" Raydar said half chuckling.

"I have contacts too," Siberian Scientist suavely said, his mask concealing his grin. "We better go before backup arrives."

"Who is this guy?" Lainey said, joking but at the same time not.

"A friend," Raydar replied as he opened the passenger door for Lainey, its reinforced panel laced in pea sized dents.

Siberian Scientist hastily inserted the key to the ignition and turned it over. As soon as the electrical system came to life, a most disturbing cry blared through their comm link.

"Dreadnight, Raydar, Siberian, come in!"

~

The bewildered bystanders of Detroit watched as the mysterious gargoyle appeared out of the atmospheric inferno. People poured out of the children's hospital to witness the phenomena unfold. Nearly one hundred pairs of eyes followed the falling angel as flames streamed off his outstretched wings, the rushing air extinguishing them as his rate of descent surged.

Eyes closed, body at ease, Dreadnight unconsciously sailed through the air, his back heading for the earth below. His body ripped through the branches of a family of trees, splintering them right off their trunks and spitting leaves into the air.

BOOM!

The ground shook as if an earthquake had emerged. The horde of people gasped and braced themselves as the tremor subsided. Looking around at one another, curiosity consumed the hearts of each soul, provoking the crowd to rush toward the crash site. With wings spread wide, Dreadnight's inert body lay in a crater of his own making, implanted in the soil for which he dedicated his life to protecting those who walked upon it.

Within seconds, that very crater was surrounded by the people that once feared him, that once cursed his name. One by one, the hearts of each bystander filled with sadness and regret as they realized the creature before them saved their lives and the lives of many others that night. Ignorance was no longer bliss for the citizens of Detroit ... no, tonight it was a cruel reality.

"He saved the hospital ... the children!" a middle-aged woman cried as her eyes welted.

"It was a bomb. We could all be dead right now!" shouted an elderly man, still shaking profusely from the event.

"What kind of monster would try to kill all those sick children!" a mother abrasively said, her hand clutched onto that of her young daughter's.

"The police were lying to us all along, that ... that creature is a hero!" a teenage boy yelled.

A swarm of gracious and solemn proclamations circulated in the air as humanity's potential beamed through the darkness of the night. However, their savior remained motionless, creating a dreary portrait of uncertainty.

Fifty yards to the east, a returning ambulance came to a screeching halt beside the park on Garner St. The EMT hopped out of the driver's seat, initiating an all-out sprint as soon as his feet hit the concrete. His legs and arms pumping intensely, the man raced toward the scene, completely unaware of what had just taken place or what he was running to.

After weaving through the ever-growing crowd, the EMT's eyes were greeted by the most astonishing sight imaginable, causing them to nearly bulge from their sockets. Ignoring his fears and preconceptions, the EMT quickly dropped to the ground beside Dreadnight's head and reached down to check his pulse.

"You have to help him!"

"He saved our lives ... please."

Pressing firmly into the beast's thick neck, the EMT's heart sunk like an anchor as he felt a rapidly fading heart rate.

"Clear the way. Move move move!" the EMT belted as he popped back onto his feet and rushed through the crowd back to the ambulance.

Within thirty seconds, the sea of spectators parted once more, looking upon one another with uncertainty and heavy hearts.

"Coming through!" the EMT yelled, running full speed with an automated external defibrillator kit (AED), until sliding beside Dreadnight.

Popping its plastic latches, the EMT opened the red and white case. He pressed the device's power button and removed the electrode pads. After removing the first pad's film, exposing its adhesive surface, he firmly placed it diagonally above Dreadnight's right nipple. Tossing the film of the second pad aside, he placed it below the left pec.

Turning his attention back to the device, he waited impatiently for it to analyze the subject's heart rhythm.

"No shock advised, begin CPR," the device announced.

"Bullshit!" the EMT retorted angrily, realizing the device couldn't properly function due to the subject's unique anatomy

Ignoring the device's instruction, he ripped the pads from Dreadnight's chest and swiftly pulled the paddles from the case.

"Screw it!" He manually set the device's voltage to two hundred and fifty joules.

The electric hum of the device commenced a crowd wide silence, charging itself for action.

Gripping their plastics handles, the EMT placed the paddles onto the previously established shock points and pressed down into Dreadnight's chest with all the strength he could muster. The device released its power, but Dreadnight barley flinched.

"Shit!"

The EMT quickly readjusted the device's voltage to four hundred joules, it's max capacity. The crowd gasped as they fretted their hero's demise.

The electric hum of hope filled the air again. *Come on, don't die on me!* the EMT thought to himself just before thrusting the paddles back onto Dreadnight's flesh. As if he had been hit with a bolt of lightning, Dreadnight's back arched profusely, shooting his chest into the air.

No response. The EMT removed the paddles, allowing the device to charge once again.

"You can't leave us after that. You just can't!" the EMT shouted, bracing for the third and final attempt.

~

"Slade! Slade! It's Father Ephrem," a faint voice echoed in Dreadnight's head. "They are going to kill him!"

The paddles sent their electric onslaught through Dreadnight's nervous system, kick starting his heart like a v12 engine.

"Father Ephrem!" Dreadnight gasped as his entire body jolted to life, startling the crowd that encircled him.

The EMT skidded backward, dropping the paddles in fear. Dreadnight sat up and hazily looked around at the awe-struck spectators, until locking eyes with the man who just saved his life.

In fear of Father Ephrem's fate, Dreadnight merely nodded at the EMT as he rose from the ground. Towering over all that neared, he tucked his miraculously unscathed wings behind his back and within the blink of an eye he shot into the air like a rocket and released his wings. The gust of air generated from his take off slammed into the people like a whirlwind, rustling every hair in the vicinity. A sea of hopeful eyes watched as the mysterious creature drifted higher and higher into the dark abyss in pursuit of his next calling, each soul forever thankful for his inconceivable existence.

~

Standing motionless in the marble nave of the cathedral before the alter was Father Ephrem. Any other night he would be kneeling in prayer while in such solitude, but not tonight. No, tonight he was reminiscing. Reminiscing about the night that made his life worth living again, the night the Effigiem Custos summoned the young man who he loved as if he were of his own flesh and blood ... a man named Slade Allen.

Though Father Ephrem knew he may never see his beloved son again, he was not sad, quite the contrary in fact. The past few months had ultimately turned all the pain and anguish he had experienced in his life into nothing more than a speck of dust in the wind, carried away by the enrichment of fulfilling Michael's testament to humanity. A testament bigger than his own life, than his own love.

With the power of a medieval battering ram, two of Inkubus's super soldiers kicked in the cathedral's solid oak doors, busting the iron locks from their reinforced hinges. Father Ephrem didn't even flinch, remaining frozen in thought.

Click Clack ... Click Clack

The oh so familiar sound of Inkubus's lavish dress shoes echoed off the arched vault above.

"And then God said ... any soul who abide not in me shall perish by my breath, forsaken in everlasting fire," Inkubus roared, his arms outstretched with palms facing up and his head tilted back. He then choppily looked all around in an outlandish demonstration of sarcasm. "Yet ... here I am!" He added jovially, lowering his head yet still holding his arms out like a dictator of old.

Father Ephrem turned and faced his aggressors but remained speechless and free of expression. Inkubus walked forward, his eight loyal lackeys close behind him with their assault rifles lowered.

"Really? Nothing to say? No divine warnings or threats?" Inkubus arrogantly questioned as he stood just a few feet away from Father Ephrem, getting no acknowledgement from the aged priest's inscrutable face. "Well, Ephrem ... do you mind if I call you Ephrem? I'm not calling you Father, well cause that's just weird," his sardonic tone counterfeit to his bloodcurdling mask. "You obviously know why I am here, to arrest you for aiding and abetting the worst criminal this city has ever seen ... or so its half-witted citizens believe," he added with laughter.

"From what I have heard, karma is quite the bitch. I think she will have her way with you soon enough," Father Ephrem unexpectedly replied, blank faced and blunt.

"Ha, so he does speak. Boys you know what to do," Inkubus announced, looking back at two of his soldiers.

The two men, their faces concealed by their usual vile masks, skintight and as black as night, approached Father Ephrem. Each pulling a flat paneled magnetometer from their holsters, they collectively scanned Father Ephrem's entire body for any traces of electronic devices.

"He's clean boss," the taller of the two soldiers voiced.

"Of course he is, he's a priest. Time to take this show on the road," Inkubus said, signaling his men to roll out.

The two soldiers gagged Father Ephrem's mouth with a rag and tossed a burlap sack over top his head before tying his hands tightly behind his back with binder twine. Father Ephrem showed no resistance

Click clack … click clack

~

Across the street and behind the Observatory's monitoring station, Mr. Unseen watched with a stomach full of knives as Inkubus's soldiers carried Father Ephrem out of St. Anne's and through its courtyard.

"Mr. Unseen what the hell is going on!" Dreadnight's voice abruptly shot through the comm link.

"Dreadnight, thank God you're alive! Inkubus and his men raided the cathedral and took Father Ephrem," Mr. Unseen frantically replied.

"Why isn't his GPS responding?" Raydar cut in, the sound of his voice providing both Mr. Unseen and Dreadnight a brief breath of relief.

"He removed his ear comm and microphone before he left the observatory for the cathedral," Mr. Unseen said sullenly, dropping his head in regret.

"Wait, why would he do that? He never removes them?" Dreadnight asked sharply, his voice full of skepticism.

The link went silent. Even though Raydar and Siberian Scientist were in the heat of battle, they heard enough of Father Ephrem's speech to know what happened. They along with Mr. Unseen knew that Dreadnight would never accept the decision he took. Then the silence was broken.

"He … he sacrificed himself to protect the Asylum and the Observatory, to protect our mission," Mr. Unseen said despairingly.

"And you let him!" Dreadnight snarled, sending a spine-tingling chill through each of his teammates.

"We need to focus on finding Father Ephrem. Mr. Unseen, check the street cams and keep an eye on the Central Station cams," Siberian Scientist interjected, trying to get his team to refocus. "Dreadnight, double back toward the Central Station. Maybe you can intercept them. Me, Raydar, and Lainey will do the same from our location," he added, his foot pressed firmly into the Celestial Shipping truck's gas pedal.

"You're right. On my way," Dreadnight said coldly, thrusting his wings as forcefully as possible.

"They arrived in three blacked out Ford Explorers and headed north on 18th Street when they left," Mr. Unseen clarified.

Zipping by midtown then the Masonic Temple Theater, Dreadnight's body was like a knife in the wind, tearing through the air with nothing but vengeance on his mind. Though he knew what Inkubus's end game was, he refused to let Father Ephrem sacrifice his life on account on him. Someway, somehow, he was determined to find a way to save Father Ephrem and still protect the city. Even if that meant letting Inkubus capture him in return for Father Ephrem's safety.

Raydar and Lainey braced themselves as Siberian Scientist raced down Michigan Avenue at a speed of over hundred miles per hour. Swerving from lane to lane he headed toward Mexican Town, his eyes toggling between the road and his in-dash monitor. Despite the rampant anxiety and racing hearts, the truck cabin was silent, filled with looming despair that seemed to slowly diminish its oxygen supply.

"Guys, I'm not seeing any sign of Inkubus or his men on any of the streets surrounding the Central Station. Based on my calculations, regardless of their route north they would be there by now. This doesn't add up," Mr. Unseen said, perplexed by the situation as his eyes toggled from screen to screen for the smallest inkling of hope.

Just as Dreadnight's body drifted overtop the junction of M10 and I75, a multitude of beaming lights illuminated the sky just a few blocks east of him near Foxtown. Pushing his wings forward, Dreadnight quickly halted himself vertical. Adrift, he heightened his eyesight and hearing.

"Mr. Unseen, is there anything happening at Comerica Park tonight?" Dreadnight asked, his eyes locked onto the baseball stadium, the source of the lights.

"No. There are never any events scheduled this late there. I double checked online as well," Mr. Unseen replied.

"Check the street cams surrounding the stadium, now!" Dreadnight blurted.

Mr. Unseen quickly pulled up the coinciding video feeds and quickly examined them.

"Son of a bitch. Inkubus and his men are there. They are parked off Brush St.," Mr. Unseen replied, frustrated that he let them slip away.

Dreadnight didn't respond, he remained afloat as his wings steadily maintained his altitude, his mind racing a mile a minute.

"We'll meet you over there Dreadnight. Mr. Unseen, figure out the most concealed point of convergence near the stadium," Raydar strenuously added as he squeezed the truck's grab handle for support while Siberian Scientist swerved onto Vernor Highway, ignoring the on ramp's "do not enter" sign.

"No, you are going to go back to the Observatory to protect it and the Asylum," Dreadnight said adamantly.

"What are you talking about? You are not facing him alone," Raydar retorted, stressed beyond belief.

"Yes ... I am. Inkubus wouldn't think twice before killing any of you. He wants me, and the only way Father Ephrem will walk away from this is if I offer him a trade," Dreadnight said dismally.

"There is no way in hell we are turning our backs on you. Father Ephrem made his decision to protect you and we vowed to do the same," Siberian Scientist proclaimed, his hands choking the steering wheel.

"By the time you get there it will be too late, we both know this. No matter what happens tonight, you need to carry out this mission by any means necessary."

"No, this is bullshit man! This mission means nothing without you. You know he will use that wretched serum on you and use you to rain hell down on this city. What then, huh?" Raydar snapped vehemently.

"Like I said, you will need to carry out the mission by ANY means necessary," Dreadnight stressed, his tone cold and heartless. "I wouldn't be alive today if it weren't for Father Ephrem. There would be no mission if it weren't for him. If there is but a one percent chance that I can save him, I have no choice but to take it," he pressed.

Raydar, Siberian Scientist, and Mr. Unseen were speechless. Each of them knew Dreadnight was dead set on going in alone and that he would follow through, but worse, they knew he was right. Not only would they arrive too late, but they would also be stepping six feet deep into their own graves, ultimately abandoning everything they have worked for. Without warning, Siberian Scientist jerked the wheel to the right, throwing the truck onto Rosa Parks Boulevard heading due south.

At the same moment, Dreadnight dropped his shoulders and angled his wings back, initiating his descent toward Foxtown and Comerica Park.

"We will find a way to get you back. I promise," Raydar said with a heavy heart.

"I know you will, Ray,"

"We all promise, my brother," Siberian Scientist added sternly.

"I'm sorry I let this happen Slade. I'll make this right … somehow," Mr. Unseen said, overwhelmed with regret.

"You have nothing to apologize for my friend, you did the right thing," Dreadnight replied. "You guys take care of one another, and Ray …"

"Yeah buddy," Raydar replied.

"Never let go of Lainey. Hold onto her tightly and cherish every moment you have together," Dreadnight said warmly.

"I will. I promise, brother." Raydar reached over and locked his left hand into that of Lainey's. Looking into her teary eyes, he smiled, embracing that very moment.

"Adam my oldest friend, keep an eye on Rachel for me, will you? Make sure she is safe and if I don't make it out of this alive …" Dreadnight's voice was shaky and unsettled. "Please tell her about me … everything about me." As his body drifted by the pinnacles of nearby skyscrapers, he clutched onto Rachel's charm with his right hand, knowing that if he didn't turn back, he might not ever get the chance to see her beautiful face again.

"You have my word, Slade," Mr. Unseen confirmed, his voice stricken with sadness as he watched his friend's video feed near Inkubus's trap.

As his monstrous ashen figure closed in on the city streets below, the eyes of every soul within a three-block radius shot into the sky as if an alien spacecraft had appeared. Cars slammed on their brakes and into one another as citizens leaped out to view the spectacle. The streets went from a populated frenzy into a gridlock of astonishment. Dreadnight's physical magnitude became increasingly evident as the eyes of the masses followed his graceful descent, sailing past some of the city's most iconic buildings.

Now only ten yards from entering the stadium's outfield, Dreadnight saw a most disturbing sight, Father Ephrem on his knees with a gag in his mouth and his hands in the air. Standing behind him on home plate was Inkubus, his mask as vile and malevolent as ever. A few feet to Inkubus's right was Reem, quivering in fear as he followed his descent.

Just then, a cluster of red laser sights plotted themselves upon Dreadnight's head and chest.

Snipers ...

Dreadnight could hear the heartbeat of each merc yielding a rifle. There had to be at least ten of them based on his calculation, all spread out and hidden in the stadium's vast sections that were conveniently left unlit. Just as his body crossed the stadium's perimeter, still seventy feet in the air, Dreadnight's eyes encountered the beaming flood lights. Unexpectedly, his vision turned into an alabaster blotch of confusion. He closed his eyes and rattled his head as he attempted to maintain his rate of descent, fear swelling exponentially within him. When he opened his eyes, the sea of white turned into a dwindling disarray of spots, allowing his vision to equalize itself with each passing second.

What the hell, Dreadnight thought to himself, as he neared the pitcher's mound.

The heartbeats were no more.

Something's not right.

In ground shaking boom, Dreadnight's feet pounded the sand as his knees bent and the muscles of his legs contracted profusely. Rising from his stoop, he lifted his head, revealing a face so fierce, so vengeful, it could brand the soul of any mortal with everlasting dread. However, as Dreadnight slowly pulled his wings back, he felt a devitalizing weakness spread throughout his body like a cancer, causing his face to loosen for a split second.

"What's wrong beastie? You don't look so well?" Inkubus snidely hissed.

"Well enough to rip your heart from your chest," Dreadnight snarled, his lip curled in fury, exposing his carnivorous teeth.

Within the blink of an eye, the myriad of red laser sights shifted from Dreadnight onto Father Ephrem. Though in a most compromising position, Father Ephrem didn't even flinch. A face vacant of emotion and apprehension remained upon the aged man as if he possessed the grace of an archangel.

"So, this can go either of two ways," Inkubus said, pulling a 9mm pistol from the holster attached to his right hip and aiming it at the back of Father Ephrem's head. "You surrender willingly, and the old man walks away unharmed to wither away like the sands of time. Or you resist and he receives a bullet to the brain. Your choice beastie," Inkubus said, arrogance dripping from every word as he tilted his head and gun from side to side in mockery.

~

The remaining teammates watched in suspense, glued to Dreadnight's eyes of divinity feed displayed in an expanded view upon the monitoring station.

"Raydar and Siberian Scientist, I want you guys to head toward Comerica Park and post up behind the Fox Theater," Mr. Unseen announced. "You guys will need to get Father Ephrem the hell out there if Inkubus lets him walk," he added.

"Agreed," Siberian Scientist replied, immediately grabbing the truck's keys and his AK74M from the Observatory round table.

"I'm going too," Lainey said.

"I rather you stay here and help me with surveillance so that they get back safe," Mr. Unseen retorted, just before nodding at Raydar, modestly revealing his intentions to keep Lainey free from harm's way.

Raydar released a small smile and nodded back, appreciative of the kind gesture.

"He's right, Lainey," Raydar said softly, placing his hand on the sides of her arms before leaning in and kissing Lainey's forehead.

"You better come back to me, Ray," she replied sternly.

"I will, I promise," Raydar replied, pressing his own forehead against hers in a loving gaze. Raydar lowered his arms and walked over to the team's lockers off on the north wall while Siberian Scientist loaded he and Raydar's weapons and replenished the ammo holders of their belts.

Mr. Unseen refocused Lainey's attention back to the monitoring station, explaining how she could assist him.

Moments later … "Let's roll," a deep modulated voice announced, throwing Lainey for a loop and causing her to turn her head in confusion. It was Raydar, suited up in his armored vest and spine-tingling mask.

"Ray?" Lainey softly gasped.

"Yup. That's your man right there," Mr. Unseen replied with a smirk as Siberian Scientist tossed Raydar his utility belt, Glock 19, and an AKS-74U for safe measure.

Seconds later they were gone.

~

"Your heart is still intact, so I believe you have your answer," Dreadnight growled, trying to maintain his composure as his body continued to weaken and his vision blurred.

"You assume I have one, how cute," Inkubus said mockingly as if he were speaking to a child. "I'll tell you what, you let Reem here shackle you up and I'll let you watch your holy friend walk away."

Dreadnight lifted his clenched right hand up to the left side of his throat then straightened his index finger. Before anyone could react, Dreadnight's claw shot from his flesh, grazing across his jugular.

"How about you let him walk now or else I bleed out before your very eyes," Dreadnight snarled, insinuating that he would take his own life. "Just a few pounds of pressure and your precious plan is done for."

"Okay…okay, as you wish." Inkubus raised his opened left hand straight into the air, clenching it closed once fully raised.

Suddenly, all the red laser sights disappeared from Father Ephrem's body. Inkubus lowered his gun and nodded at Reem who stepped up to Father Ephrem and untied his gag before returning back to Inkubus's side like the dog he was.

"Get out of here now! Please. I beg of you!" Father Ephrem cried.

"I'm sorry, but this is my choice to make and mine alone," Dreadnight replied softly, his claw still pressed firmly to his throat.

"Get up old man," Reem blurted.

Father Ephrem hesitantly rose, his saddened eyes pleading with Dreadnight to let him go, to put the city's fate before that of his own.

Heart racing and head throbbing, Dreadnight's finger twitched. It was as if the life was being sucked right out of him, leaving nothing but a mess of flesh and bone.

"Start walking, or die," Reem shouted, causing Dreadnight to growl like a hungry wolf.

With a heavy heart, Father Ephrem lowered his hands and took a step forward, and then another. Dreadnight's clouded eyes were affixed upon his dear friend's grief-stricken face, his soul suffocating from the thought of never seeing him again.

Maybe it was because of his weakened state, or maybe it was nothing more than a miscalculation … but he didn't even hear the shift of the gun amongst the Inkubus's hand nor see the rotation of his shoulder. There was no mistaking the deafening crack of a 9mm bullet erupting from its chamber.

"Noooo!" Dreadnight roared, his face stressed beyond comprehension.

In a knee jerk reaction, Dreadnight fretfully launched forward with every ounce of strength he could muster. As soon as his feet left the ground, he was greeted by over a dozen high caliber tranquilizer bullets, each slicing into Dreadnight's flesh with ease. The effect of their chemical aggression spread rampantly throughout his body, instantaneously nullifying his efforts. Dreadnight's monstrous body sailed sluggishly across the field, arms reaching desperately toward a collapsing Father Ephrem whose eyes were peeled open and glazed in darkness.

In synchrony, the bodies of Dreadnight and Father Ephrem crashed face first onto the grassy field, just a few feet from one another.

"Ephrem …" Dreadnight coughed, his eyes failing as he looked upon Father Ephrem lifeless face.

His right arm still reaching out, Dreadnight fought to remain conscious.

"I'm … sorry … Ephrem…" Dreadnight's eyes shut, sending him into a forceful slumber.

"Lights out beastie." Inkubus lowered his weapon and gazed upon the success of his maniacal endeavor. "Guess you didn't even know your own Achilles heel." He walked up to the beast's inert body and knelt, proceeding to remove Dreadnight's ear comm, mic, and Rachel's necklace.

Within seconds, the DPD armored truck ripped onto the field from a sudden opening in the outfield perimeter wall. Pulling up next to Dreadnight's body, the truck's cargo hatch opened and three masked mercs poured out onto the field, two of which were carrying chains with shackles on their ends. A once pitch-black cargo pod was blasted with a flood of blinding light emanating from four high powered spotlights bolted into each corner of its ceiling. Quickly the two chain yielding mercs slid Dreadnight's wrists into the cold iron of the shackles, clasping them shut immediately.

The third merc pulled a key fab from his pocket and pressed one of its buttons.

A loud clinking noise arose as an electric hoist machine mounted to the front wall of the cargo pod yanked on the very chains linked to Dreadnight's shackles, each chain running through a metal brace fastened to opposing sides of the pod's ceiling. As the chains tightened, Dreadnight's arms were slowly straightened until the pulley system started dragging his body across the grass and eventually up into the cargo pod. Once the machine's function was complete, Dreadnight was hanging mercilessly from his arms, his head drooped, knees barely grazing the floor beneath him.

Inkubus tossed Dreadnight's comm and Rachel's necklace to the ground then lifted the mic up to his own mouth.

"Game over kiddies. You're next!"

~

The hearts of the remaining team members felt as if they had been pierced by an arrow. On the screens before them was Father Ephrem, a hemorrhaging vessel for a beautiful soul set free.

"Fuck!" Siberian Scientist screamed as his fist smashed the in-dash monitor.

The rest of the team remained speechless as their eyes flooded with tears, attempting to grasp the cruel reality at hand.

"Guys, a DPD truck just pulled out of the outfield and onto Adams Ave. heading west," Mr. Unseen said shakily. "Two SUVs are tailing it closely ... another two just pulled out in front from Witherell St."

"We're on it, "Siberian Scientist replied firmly.

Mr. Unseen's eyes shifted to the monitors displaying the Central Station surveillance feeds. His eyes widened and his head shook in frustration.

"Don't follow them, there are ..."

Siberian Scientist bluntly cut Mr. Unseen off, "Are you crazy! We are not abandoning him. I'd rather die than be a coward."

"I have no intention of abandoning him. There are at least thirty of Inkubus's men guarding the grounds of the Central Station. That's where they are heading. Committing suicide does nothing for Dreadnight. We need regroup and figure out how to approach this," Mr. Unseen explained, attempting to calm his teammate.

"He's right man, we gotta be smart here. You know as well as me that an attack fueled solely by emotion is inviting error and misjudgment to the fight," Raydar pleaded.

Siberian Scientist nodded in agreement, too angry to be verbal.

"Wait a few minutes then recover Father Ephrem's body and bring it back to St. Anne's where it belongs," Mr. Unseen said.

So, they did just that. As if the night had not been enough of an emotional rollercoaster thus far, physically seeing the man both Raydar and Siberian Scientist viewed as a father figure lying dead before their very eyes was beyond heart wrenching. With great caution, they wrapped his body in a tarp and laid him in the cargo pod of the truck. As Siberian Scientist latched the pod's hatch and quickly hopped back into the driver seat, Raydar walked toward home plate. Kneeling, Raydar picked up Rachel's necklace from the freshly cut grass.

"You're gonna want this back, buddy."

Chapter 14
The Verge of Total Chaos

As if he had been in a ten-year slumber, Dreadnight's eyes struggled to opened. Eyes that were greeted by yet another onslaught of blinding light. As soon he regained a sliver of consciousness, his arms jerked in distress, causing the chains to which he was shackled to rattle violently. Realizing not only were his arms and legs chained to opposing pillars but also his tail was braced to the epoxied cement floor, Dreadnight released a savage roar.

"Glad you could join us Dreadnight!" Inkubus announced over joyously as he stepped out in front of his feral captive. Hanging from four evenly distributed track fixtures surrounding Dreadnight were eight high intensity spotlights, two on each fixture. Each light was wired to an electric control module headed by Reem on the table hugging the east wall. Inkubus signaled Reem to lower the two spotlights facing Dreadnight, leaving the surrounding six as is.

Slowly, Dreadnight regained his vision, revealing the south end of the Central Station's underground level. Directly in front of him was Inkubus and the industrial cargo door which concealed the secret tunnel leading out to the streets of Detroit. Diagonally off to the right in his peripheral was a cage full of Inkubus's latest test subjects, not including himself of course.

"I'm going to choke you with your own intestines. You hear me? You sick fuck!" Dreadnight shouted ferociously, his eyes as bloodthirsty as ever as the memory of Father Ephrem's death reeled through his mind.

"That's cute, but if you haven't noticed I kind of have you by the balls … or limbs" Inkubus looked downward upon Dreadnight's body realizing he was less human than he thought from the lack there of.

"And yours will be detached from your body when I am done with you."

"I think all of this UV radiation is getting to your head, either that or you're as dumb as you look." Inkubus swiveled his head as he looked upon the array of spotlights.

That's why I felt weak … that's why I couldn't save Father Ephrem, Dreadnight thought to himself, his eyes shifting in contemplation.

"Yes, that's right, I'm not your greatest adversary … no, it's ultraviolet radiation," Inkubus's belted as if he were a Broadway actor.

Dreadnight didn't respond.

"Such a simple yet unorthodox weakness wouldn't you say?" Inkubus tilted his head to the side and stared into Dreadnight's eyes, causing the tentacles of his mask to sway. "But don't worry. Once you have completed my aggressive treatment plan, you will never feel pain again ... or feel anything for that matter."

Dreadnight could feel Inkubus's snide grin through his vile mask, causing his blood to boil.

"No matter what you do ... they will stop you," Dreadnight growled, lifting his head.

Inkubus's maniacal laugh echoed throughout the station, implanting a grin on Reem's smug face.

"Who? The Russian and your two police rats?"

"Yeah, and every other soul on this planet that is good and yearns for justice."

"You just don't get it, do you? See, no soul is all good nor all innocent. Those who embrace the fact are powerful like me, whereas those who attempt to be pure in heart end up being slaves like you and Mr. Foster over there." Inkubus shifted his head to the left of Dreadnight and shrugged his brows.

Dreadnight jerked his body to the left and twisted his head back. Standing beside a gleaming stainless steel laboratory cell was Benjamin Foster, his face weary and unsettled. Dreadnight quickly turned back, acting as if he had never seen the doctor before in his life.

"I'm sure you think I am just another Tyrant, a man with an undying thirst for power ... for control," Inkubus theatrically said, his hands gyrating beside his mask as he paced back and forth just feet away from Dreadnight. "Perception could deem each of those sentiments accurate, however, I am only embracing humanity and its everlasting flaw, otherwise known as free will."

Inkubus stopped in his tracks and lifted his arms high into the air as if he were calling upon God.

"You see, we humans are like maggots, waiting for others to falter, to fail, so that we can feast upon their weakness to satisfy our primal urges. The problem is, for humans there is never enough flesh on the bone, enough blood in the veins. The instant we sink our teeth into another, the hunger becomes insatiable ... unbearable." Inkubus's voice deepened in a belting roar as he clenched his hands out in front of his body, jolting it in the process. "We become inebriated by its taste, its richness," his tone now suave and collected as he paced incessantly once again. "Now there is one glaring difference to recognize here. A maggot eats purely for survival, to carry out the order of nature, whereas humans will keep eating and eating until the bones of their prey are nothing more than dust," Inkubus's hands opened and slowly dispersed away from one another, adding to his dramatic presence. "The kicker … we choose to do this, to live this way. It's our birthright. One that evolution itself could not cleanse from our feeble minds," Inkubus walked up to Dreadnight and grazed the backside of his gloved fingers down the right side of his face. "So, you see, I am no more a monster than you. I am merely making the most out of what life has offered, just as you have."

"I am nothing like you," Dreadnight coughed out, his teeth silently screaming obscenities as his lip curled in fury.

"Ha, not for long," Inkubus scoffed as he pulled his hand back and reinstituted his pace.

"Let me guess … mommy and daddy didn't love you?" Dreadnight sarcastically wheezed with a grin to match, hoping to distract the demon from his objective.

Inkubus stopped his pace mid step and turned away from Dreadnight and rolled his head back in a hanging motion as if a nerve had been struck.

"Not as much as the scabs that cling to this miserable city." Inkubus sneered.

"Just another entitled bitch that never got his fill huh?" A smirk crept upon Dreadnight's face as his head wobbled in a battle for stability.

Zzzt … Zzzt.

Inkubus clenched his gloved fist, causing two metal rods in his sleeve to shift. Like a golden glove boxer, Inkubus twisted around and sent his inhuman might square into Dreadnight's jaw. Blood projected from his mouth as his head whipped across before dropping in gut wrenching agony. The impact was like nothing Dreadnight had ever felt … even in human form. As if he were schizophrenic, Inkubus leaned his head from side to side, cracking his neck until returning to his original demeanor.

"Since your mind will soon be nothing more than my own personal war machine, a carbon copy of my mine if you must, I will tell you a little story," Inkubus poetically said, intertwining his hands out in front of himself as if he were a priest.

"Enlighten me," Dreadnight said before spitting a mouthful of blood containing a tooth onto the checkered floor, hoping that he could develop an escape plan while the maniac rambled.

"Much like myself, my great grandfather was a very powerful man. In fact, he owned and operated this very station, among other less "public" projects of course. His empire ran this city, enslaving the desperate and eliminating anyone who stood in the way of its expansion." Inkubus's voice was stern and dominant, his hands elaborating each syllable. "From heading the city's KKK chapter to organizing the Detroit mafia, his hand was up the backs of every crime organization and gangbanger in the city. If it weren't for the civil rights movement and that God damn twelfth street riot, his empire would have never of been compromised and he wouldn't have been killed by some undercover cop. You know, like your friend Ray Fisher."

Dreadnight's eyes tightened, and his nostrils flared.

"I will surely have some fun once I get my hands on him." Inkubus chuckled like a mad scientist at the thought.

Dreadnight jolted forward in a bout of rage, flexing with whatever strength remained. The chains that bound him rattled violently but their links remained unaltered. Depleted and disheartened, Dreadnight's arms gave way and his body hung in a fragile sway. He knew in that very moment that there was no possible way he was going to physically escape his restraints. Staring at the blood-stained floor, reality crept into Dreadnight's fog ridden mind.

I'm never going to see her again ... she'll never know who I am really am. An unbearable pain crept into his heart. *My family ... I never got to say goodbye.*

Just feet away and rolling a mobile phlebotomy chair to the right of Dreadnight was Dr. Foster. Keeping his external composure yet a bloody mess mentally, Foster frantically contemplated ways to help his one and only hope, the lone soul that could free his family. It was now or never, and he knew he would only have one shot, one that would likely cost him his life.

"I wish I could have met my great grandfather, learned from him, thanked him. But unfortunately, I was raised by his pathetic descendants. His sad excuse of a son, my grandfather, changed our last name and covered up all connections to the original family name. He and my parents squandered the family fortune ... my inheritance, tossing it to the city's less fortunate in some feeble attempt to cleanse their souls of great granddaddy's sins." Inkubus's devious voice intensified. "Unfortunately for them, I found his journals and studied them, embracing every word and vowing to one day resurrect his legacy. So, I cleansed their souls for them ... from this earth."

Dreadnight knew Inkubus was a monster, but to kill your own family in cold blood, that is simply incomprehensible.

"Such a big man, murdering your own family for money," Dreadnight mockingly stated in disgust.

"Oh, I didn't just murder them, I burned them alive."

~

Tension consumed the Observatory as the remaining team members scrambled to develop a plan to break Dreadnight out of the Central Station. The screens in front of them displayed a seemingly impenetrable Central Station perimeter, swarming with masked mercenaries yielding assault rifles. Even if by some miracle of God they were able to reach the interior of the extensive building, there was no way of knowing who or what would greet them.

"I think our only option is to create a diversion to draw out whatever defenses lay behind those walls and to provide Benjamin an opportunity to make a move of his own," Siberian Scientist stated with a discerning look upon his now unmasked face.

"What do you propose?" Raydar replied.

"You've shot a sniper rifle before, right?" Siberian Scientist asked.

"Damn right."

"Well, I say you and I post up on opposing rooftops and just start taking heads off. One way or another it will get Inkubus's attention and will throw a wrench in his plan," Siberian Scientist said sternly with blood hungry eyes.

A smirk crept its way onto Raydar's face, and his eyes tightened. "I like the way you think my Russian brother."

Already a step ahead of his teammates, Mr. Unseen pulled up an aerial map displaying a two-block radius surrounding the Central Station upon the monitoring station. Panning and rotating the imagery he analyzed the entirety of the landscape for concealing vantage points.

"Here and here!" Mr. Unseen blurted as two flashing red dots appeared upon the map, causing both Raydar and Siberian Scientist to snap their heads toward the monitoring station.

"Raydar, I suggest you occupy the rooftop of the old Southwest Detroit Hospital off 20th and Michigan Ave. This spot will allow you to cover the west end of the station." Mr. Unseen did a quick 360 toggle of the building to provide Raydar with a visual of the building's external layout. "Siberian, this abandoned school building off Bagley and Vermont would allow you to cover the east end." The cursor of Mr. Unseen's supercomputer swiftly shifted onto the opposing flashing red dot, maximizing the view of the building.

"Lainey, I want you to drop each of them off at their prescribed locations then park the truck right here." Mr. Unseen placed a flashing blue dot upon a parking lot tucked in between Newark and St. Anne St. which was conveniently surrounded by trees. "Wait there and be ready to move if things go south or either of them need an emergency pickup."

"Got it," Lainey replied, ready for action.

"Alright team, let's load up and ship out!" Siberian Scientist enthusiastically announced just before sliding his mask over his face.

~

Inkubus turned and walked toward his beloved holding cell. Hysteria consumed each of its prisoners as they envisioned ink oozing from the demon's mouth and down onto his thrashing tentacles. Looking away from Inkubus's obsidian eyes, the soon to be super soldiers cowered against the back wall, their faces petrified beyond words. Dreadnight didn't need his celestial perception to know there wasn't a single trace of humanity left in that walking embodiment of ruthlessness, that is if there ever was any to begin with.

If I get my hands on him, I'm going to rip his blackened heart from his chest ... even if it's against Michael's wishes. He must die! Dreadnight thought to himself as he watched Inkubus torture the minds of his victims.

"My children. You are about to witness our greatest achievement," Inkubus raised his open arms as if he were expecting praise. "Not only did David defeat Goliath tonight, he also captured a God among men to create earth's greatest weapon. A weapon that no one shall ever defy. An instrument of total domination!" Inkubus roared like an unrelenting dictator, his hands clenched and jolting out in front of his body. "Oh, I simply cannot wait any longer!" Inkubus turned and walked back toward his prized possession, excitement reeking from his arrogant strut. "Harvey, why don't you shine a little light on our guest, he seems a bit gloomy wouldn't you say?"

Reem readjusted the two forward light fixtures, aiming then directly into Dreadnight's eyes while maximizing the entire light system's power settings. Joy gleamed from Reem's face as Dreadnight groaned in pain and his vision went from blurry to blind.

Bearing down his serrated teeth, Dreadnight grunted as the insufferable sensation of a thousand cuts consumed his body. His sight nothing more than a sea of alabaster emptiness, he closed his eyes and pictured Rachel's beautiful face. It was the only thing preventing him from losing what was left of his obscured mind as it was slowly being melted by the UV radiation. Beneath his withered head, an ever-growing pool of viscous blood crawled along the cement, splintering off into rivers hungering for expansion.

"Doctor, please prepare our patient for stage one."

"Yes sir," Foster replied coldly, proceeding to grab the cold handle of a stainless-steel instrument stand. After pulling the stand approximately fifteen feet, he parked it diagonally to Dreadnight's left side.

"Please be still. We wouldn't want any mishaps, now would we?" Foster said nervously, hinting to Dreadnight that he had a plan as he stepped out in front of him holding onto two wires.

As Foster leaned in with quivering hands, he stuck two wired sensors that were blue and red in color onto the beast's sprawling chest and whispered, "just play along."

Praying that Foster knew what he was doing, Dreadnight did just that to reaffirm Inkubus's belief that he had never met the foreign doctor before.

"Not as still as your body will be once I pull your spine out through your throat, you piece of shit!" Dreadnight growled with exposed blood-stained fangs, causing Foster himself to question the intention of such a terrifying statement.

"See there you go again with the whole ripping the insides out of people's bodies. What is with you?" Inkubus manically yelled, tossing his hands into the air. "Don't make me hook up a few extra lights, tough guy."

Maintaining his nervous demeaner, Dr. Foster adhered four electrodes to Dreadnight's skull, two of which were placed directly on his temples while the other two were placed on the backside of his neck, one on each side of its peak. All the electrodes were connected to multicolored wires which of course ran to the oh so familiar electroconvulsive therapy machine.

Foster stepped back and turned toward the instrument stand, locking his eyes onto his portable EEG machine.

"Brainwave function is stable in a delta state at four hertz," Foster announced.

"Excellent. Reem why don't you come over here and play guard, I don't believe we will need to adjust the lighting system any time soon," Inkubus proclaimed with laughter as he laid back onto the phlebotomy chair locked down just five feet to the right of Dreadnight.

Reem did as he was told, abandoning the control module, and positioning himself to the right of Inkubus's phlebotomy chair. He then removed his 9mm from his holster.

"Ready to administer the pre-op sedative," Foster declared.

"Proceed."

Foster reached over to the instrument stand and grabbed an oversized syringe containing yellow fluid and yielding an eight-inch-long needle. Reem watched Foster like a hawk, assuring he followed procedure. Foster lifted the syringe in the air before applying the slightest pressure to its plunger, causing a small amount of its content to shoot into the air. He flicked the needle twice and lowered the syringe back down.

"Administering the sedative."

Unaware of his surroundings and drained of any strength he once possessed, Dreadnight felt the chilling sting of a needle pierce the skin of his neck, thanks to the potency of the UV rays. Groaning in misery, the seemingly never-ending insertion continued deep into his flesh until he felt a rush of fluid disperse itself into his bloodstream. Before the needle could fully recede from the creature's flesh, Dreadnight fell into an unparalleled slumber.

After setting the empty syringe back onto the stand, Foster grabbed ahold of the second set of electrodes and approached Inkubus. After lifting the small flap on the left side of his master's mask, he adhered the first electrode onto the left temple then reached behind and underneath the mask to adhere the second electrode to the back of Inkubus's neck. Reem stood by with extreme attentiveness, his finger flirting with the trigger of his pistol.

Seconds later, Foster was standing off to the left side of Dreadnight's drooped head with a surgical drill in hand, its bit extensive in length and craving to invade another skull.

"I'll need you to hold the creature's head still," Foster said to Reem.

"Why so that you can drill a hole in my hand on accident?" Reem retorted sharply.

"Do you want him to die? Do you want to be the blunder that foils this bloody plan?"

Reem didn't verbally reply, but his eyes were as murderous as ever as they glared at Foster.

"Do as he says, Harvey. The doctor knows that if he were to try anything funny, I will drop each member of his family from the rooftop of this very building while he watches with eyes wired open right next to their bloody splash point!" Inkubus mockingly emphasized.

Foster gulped down the swelling fear that surged up his throat from the very thought of his family being hurt any worse than they already have been. Meanwhile, Reem inserted his pistol back into his holster and walked up to the right side of the beast's head and firmly gripped one hand underneath its chin and the other on the peak of the back of its skull.

"If you screw with me, I swear I will blow your brains out right here," Reem quietly said to Foster.

Ignoring his arrogant counterpart, Foster carefully positioned the drill against Dreadnight's left temple and took a deep breath. As he slowly exhaled, he steadied his drilling hand while maintaining the other hand's sturdy counterforce against the right side of the skull.

Rizzz

The loud scream of the drill echoed throughout the laboratory as Dr. Foster sent cold metal through the beast's monstrous skull. After what seemed like two exceedingly challenging seconds, the drill finally broke through Dreadnight's unusually thick skin, provoking his tar like blood to slowly seep outward. As the drill bit met fresh bone, the tool's co-axial motor fought to maintain constant torque, deepening the tone of its scream. Once traction was achieved, the steel of the bit slowly disappeared into Dreadnight's skull. By now Foster would be completed with the procedure if dealing with a normal human skull, but that certainly wasn't the case this time. The bit kept going deeper and deeper, still burrowing through bone. The average human skull is only approximately six-point-five millimeters thick, but not Dreadnight's, no, his was at least fifteen millimeters of inhumanly dense bone matter.

Finally, Foster broke through, withdrawing the drill swiftly upon doing so.

"Leave him be now. I can handle it from here," Foster told Reem as the blood coated drill hung from his hand.

Reem immediately let go of Dreadnight's head as if it were diseased, his facial expression clearly displaying his discomfort toward touching the beast. As expected, Reem scurried to Inkubus's side, guarding him like a trustworthy watchdog. Just as Foster set the nearly overheated surgical drill back onto the stand, Reem and Inkubus became suddenly alarmed, their attention fixated on an incoming ear comm transmission.

Apparently, some of their perimeter defenses were being sniped out of action.

Foster made sure to take full advantage of their lapse in concentration.

"Squadron B, hunt them down and bring me their heads!" Inkubus belted through his concealed mic. "The rest of you hold the perimeter. Nothing enters this building, you hear me? Nothing!" Inkubus's back jolted off the phlebotomy chair in a fit of unbridled rage. "Foster, finish this!"

"Yes sir, proceeding with the synapsis serum injections," Foster calmly replied, grabbing a fresh 30cc syringe from the stand and inserting its needle into a vial of the jet-black serum of cerebral suicide. After filling the syringe to its capacity, he returned to Dreadnight and carefully aligned its minuscule needle with the freshly drilled insertion point located on his left temple. Steadying the beast's head with his left hand, Foster gently pushed the needle through the tunnel of bone and released 15cc's of its contents into Dreadnight's frontal lobe.

"Speed it up doctor!" Inkubus growled, his patience rotting away by the second.

Foster withdrew the needle and quickly located the second insertion point located right behind Dreadnight's upper jaw where it met the cheekbone beside his left ear. With a steady hand, he inserted the needle a second time, emptying the syringe into the secondary position.

"Phase one complete, beginning phase two," Dr. Foster voiced as he set the syringe onto the instrument stand.

Dr. Foster reached over to the ECT machine, adjusting its voltage, range, and mode.

"On your mark sir."

"Now dammit!" Inkubus shouted.

Dr. Foster flipped the power switch, but Dreadnight's body remained as still as stone. The same could not be said for Inkubus though.

Foster had reversed the electrical charge!

The phlebotomy chair jarred as Inkubus's body convulsed uncontrollably, his demonic scream striking terror into the heart of his caged victims as three hundred volts of electricity surged through his body.

"No no no!" Reem shouted perilously as he lunged to Inkubus's aid,

The instant Foster's finger abandoned the switch, he darted toward the station's fuse box located on the south wall twenty feet away and to the left of the industrial cargo door.

With the utmost haste Reem ripped the electrodes from Inkubus's skull, fearful of his master's life. Disoriented and hysterical with his eyes rolled back into his head, Inkubus twitched and clenched as he fought to remain conscious.

Only a few feet away, Foster stretched his right arm out to grab the industrial killswitch, his dream of freeing his family within reach.

P-Taff

The ear shattering crack of Reem's 9mm flooded the air.

"Aaaarrgh!" Dr. Foster's sudden scream of pain echoed throughout the cement palace as his body dropped to the floor. Fifteen feet behind him stood Reem, his gun still smoking as its sight marked Foster for a second rendezvous.

A deep-seated groan emerged from Dreadnight as Foster looked back at his assailant, his hand clutching his right shoulder, now gushing blood uncontrollably. The surge of electricity pulled from the power supply and into Inkubus's body dampened the light system's potency just enough to trigger consciousness within Dreadnight. In a groggy stupor Dreadnight rattled his chains as his blurred eyes caught a glimpse of Foster's bloodied state.

"If you fire another bullet, I will strangle you with these very chains!" Dreadnight weakly growled, continuing to fight his restraints, a fight he could not win as the links remained unaltered.

Before Dreadnight could turn to face Reem, the corrupt commissioner shifted his sight and released a flesh mangling round clean through the beast's right forearm from less than eight feet away.

"Aaaarrgh! Errahh!" Dreadnight writhed in unbelievable pain as blood streamed down his arm and onto his upper torso. The trauma instantly revived his cognizance, eliminating any effects that lingered from the sedative.

Foster watched in terror as hope faded before his very eyes.

"Unlike you, we don't need him alive," Reem sneered, aiming his gun back at Foster as his master continued to stabilize himself.

Fighting through the spine shattering agony, Dreadnight continued to drive his body forward in desperation to save the defenseless doctor, causing the flesh of his wrist peel to from the bone. His powerful roar could be felt in the chest of each human that occupied the room.

His mind racing and heart pounding, Foster contemplated betting his life on the trifling possibility of pulling the killswitch before Reem's next bullet stops his heart. As he stared at the barrel of the gun, flashing images of his dear wife and daughter flooded his mind, bringing tears to his wearied eyes.

"For family!" he whispered as he prepared for a most inevitable yet courageous death.

"Oh, how I will enjoy watching you ... awk ... awk!" Suddenly, Reem and the already struggling Inkubus gasped for air, air that was now filled with a warm veil as if the oxygen had been sucked from the room. Reem dropped his gun as his face turned red and purple, causing veins to bulge furiously. Somehow unaffected by the mysterious phenomena, Foster quickly reached upward and pulled the kill switch.

Thwick

The lights were no more. Darkness consumed the room, but only for a brief moment.

In the blink of a blinded eye, a bright white orb of scintillating light appeared before Dreadnight, floating just a few feet away from his face. Weary from exhaustion and immense pain, Dreadnight ended his struggle to break free and glared at the mystical object before him, desperation pouring from his eyes and hate dripping from his bared teeth.

Without warning, the orb bolted into Dreadnight's blood-soaked chest, disappearing from sight. He felt a warm sensation transpire throughout his chest. When he looked down, he saw a glowing aura spreading slowly through the scar tissue that was the brand of the Eiffigiem Custos. As it spanned, Dreadnight felt an overpowering celestial presence course through his entire body. The burns generated from the explosion began to mend and the bullet hole in his arm slowly filled with regenerative tissue as skin expanded over the once mutilated wound.

Still choking strenuously, Reem fell to his knees while his master rolled off the phlebotomy chair and crashed onto the floor just inches away. Both men were just seconds away from total asphyxiation as they scrambled amongst the floor like dogs.

With each passing second, the strength Dreadnight once possessed poured into his veins with unrelenting momentum and each of his senses regained their supernatural capability. He knew exactly what was causing the phenomena, it was Michael's grace that had inhabited his weakened vessel, making it whole again. Dreadnight could feel Michael's mercy and compassion course through every cell in his body.

Foster quickly rose to his feet and stumbled over to Dreadnight, grimacing with every step as he clenched his hand over his bloodied shoulder. Foster stopped and stared in awe at the spectacle before him. A look of calm euphoria had enveloped Dreadnight's face as his brand glowed vivaciously.

PSSSHHEW!

Every particle of light that was being harnessed in Dreadnight's body blasted out into the open like a supernova, blinding all in its path and filling the room with radiance. As quickly as it appeared, the light vanished, returning the station to pure darkness.

HUUAA!

The sound of Reem and Inkubus sucking air into their depleted lungs emerged as they frantically realized they were indeed still among the living, their hands searching for anything to grab onto for balance.

To his disbelief, Foster all of a sudden felt no pain. As his vision went from a sea of white to pitch black, he ran his fingers across his assumingly marred shoulder.

It can't be!

There was no aperture … not even a scratch. The wound had fully healed, and it was as if he had had never been shot!

Aware of Inkubus's consciousness, Dreadnight quickly closed his eyes with immense concentration, activating his night vision. Looking up at the shackle locked around his right wrist, he reached up the chain's links with his fingers, wrapping his hand around its slack.

"Stand back," Dreadnight said to Foster as he wrapped the opposing chain around his left hand. Activating every muscle in his monstrous body, Dreadnight leaned forward and pulled the upper chains with all his might, releasing a thunderous roar that even the likes of Siberian Scientist and Raydar could hear from blocks away. Veins bulging and striations twitching, Dreadnight didn't let up, continuing to drive his momentum forward and down.

A sudden hairline fracture appeared on the right pillar, just under the chain that bound his right arm. In an instant, the chain exploded through the concrete column in a booming crack, sending debris flying as his arm shot forward in freedom.

Startled by the eruption and crashing bits of concrete, Inkubus and Reem dove to the floor, covering their heads in cowardice.

Using his regained mobility, Dreadnight twisted back toward his left side. With one mighty thrust he sent the second arm binding chain slicing through the left pillar and into a crashing slide across the debris laced floor.

A bright light appeared from the direction of his adversaries. Still leaning onto the floor and using his cell phone as a flashlight, Reem beamed it at Dreadnight. Reem's eyes bulged in horror as he witnessed Dreadnight's arms hanging freely and the chains that once bound him draped upon the floor. A powerful rumble emanating from his heavy breath, Dreadnight shot a callous glance at Reem, one that was so fierce it could have stripped the paint from the walls.

In a panicked scramble, Reem redirected his phone to the floor frantically searching for his gun. Dreadnight quickly reached down and snapped the chain from the shackle restraining his left ankle, contorting its connective link as if it were made of plastic. Within seconds, the final chain had been dismantled and Dreadnight had lifted the metal brace bolting his tail to the floor with ease. Gun in hand, Reem helped his master to his feet and aimed his mobile light toward the west wall.

Now free from his restraints, Dreadnight snapped his neck toward Reem and Inkubus, ready to satisfy his thirst for vengeance.

Beginning to run for their pathetic lives, Inkubus tapped his ear comm. "All topside troops to the Central Station now! Slay the Dreadnight, or else you will all … *awk* … *awk*"

Dreadnight whipped the chain clasped to his right arm toward Inkubus, its end coiled around the neck of the demon's mask like a boa constrictor. Naturally Inkubus attempted to break free, clawing and pulling with all his might to loosen its hold, but his nails merely scraped across the chain's rusted surface as his esophagus tightened. Before Dreadnight could yank the chain back, Inkubus engaged his mechanized right arm and grabbed onto chain. Resisting Dreadnight's brute strength, Inkubus dropped his right leg back and pulled the noose with every bit of torque his mechanism could muster. But Dreadnight couldn't be matched as Inkubus's feet slid forward, losing the game of tug of war.

A cascading radiance appeared from the west wall as the sound of elevator doors splitting arose. Standing dead center in the glow was Reem. Turning on a dime and desperate to save his master, Reem lifted his gun, mounting his left hand underneath to aim his phone light. Just as Dreadnight reached forward with his hand and wrapped his fingers around the chain for one for a final bolstering pull, Reem double-tapped his trigger.

"Arrggh!"

The first bullet grazed Dreadnight's chin and crashed into a beaker shelved on the east wall, causing it to explode into a thousand pieces. The second however, sliced through Dreadnight's left cheek and clanked against his gritted teeth. He attempted to fight through the riving pain and pull Inkubus toward him, but the impact of the bullet weakened his efforts just enough loosen the chain and allow Inkubus to squirm free of his hideous mask. The chain crashed to the floor along with the vile mask, causing Dreadnight to stumble backward as blood ran down his face and neck.

Both Reem and Inkubus twisted into a b-line sprint toward the mysterious elevator a mere fifteen feet away. Crouching to regain his footing, Dreadnight launched forward, activating every muscle in his legs as they pounded against the floor with booming force. Only ten feet separating the foes, Reem and the now unmasked Inkubus jumped into the elevator, revealing Inkubus's cue ball of a head. Reem quickly turned and repeatedly slammed the one of the buttons on its switch panel, yet Inkubus continued to face away as the doors began to seal.

Dreadnight leaped toward the elevator door but the light emanating from it vanished right as he landed before it. Without hesitation, Slade slid his claws into the crevice of the elevator door and with all his might tried to pull them apart. Suddenly, a staggering explosion went off, shaking the very foundation of the station. Quickly, he crouched down, bracing himself as he continued to fight the system's interlocks. Seconds later the tremor from the blast ended, leaving the station seemingly undamaged.

"Erraaaahhh!" Dreadnight belted out as he tensed his entire body, the muscles and veins in his arms and shoulders bulging as the two doors inched apart.

CRASH!

The doors shot in opposite directions, slamming violently into the elevators core. Sparks crackled and fell from an overhanging electrical harness as Dreadnight leaned over to look down the elevator shaft to see nothing but debris filling its entirety.

"Of course, it was rigged with explosives!" Dreadnight growled as he gazed at the pile of rocks, gritting his teeth and clenching his fists. "I'll just have to go underground and hunt you!"

His senses on high alert, Dreadnight heard a storm of footsteps heading toward the Central Station from multiple directions.

"Get in the laboratory and lock the door! I'll die before I let them get to you!" Dreadnight hollered across the room as he broke the shackles off his arms and legs.

He needed to protect Dr. Foster first and foremost. It was a promise he would not waiver on.

Foster hesitated as he looked upon his savior with solemn eyes, reluctant to abandoned him as the monsters he helped create marched onward.

"Quickly!"

Foster nodded and sprinted to the laboratory, quickly entering and locking himself inside.

With no time to spare, Dreadnight walked to the center of the room and looked around for a vantage point.

That'll do! He thought to himself as he looked up at the dark abyss that was the ceiling. Leaping up nearly twenty feet off the ground, he grappled his front claws into the ceiling followed by the talons of his wings. Generating strength from his biceps and back, he lifted his body and drove his rear claws into the cement as if they were metal stakes, rendering his body horizontal. Fully secured into position, Dreadnight curled his tail inward, dispersed his wings around his body like a shell, and hardened them into stone, blending him into the darkened ceiling.

Afraid of what was to come, afraid of not being able to protect Dr. Foster, Dreadnight's mind panicked.

Chapter 15
The Stampede

Nestled in a prone position upon the abandoned school's rooftop with his Dragunov sniper rifle nested atop a reinforced tactical bipod, Siberian Scientist had his next victim in his crosshairs. His eye snugged against the adjustable iron sight, he released a steadying exhale as he prepared to unleash an armor piercing incendiary round through the forehead of an oncoming super soldier over two hundred and fifty yards due east. Just as he pressurized the trigger, the super soldier turned on a dime, redirecting his efforts back toward the Central Station.

Maintaining the focus on his target, Siberian Scientist smoothly shifted his aim as the masked man raced full speed back toward his base. Sounding as if the sky had cracked open, the stock of the sniper rifle recoiled violently into his right shoulder. Before the gun could be re-stabilized, the target face planted into the ground as blood shot from the rear of his skull.

"They're heading back to the station in a rush. Something must have happened!" Siberian Scientist urgently said into the comm.

"I'm seeing the same thing. Something has definitely ruffled their feathers other than our bullets," Raydar added quickly.

"The surveillance cameras are showing at least twenty of those mindless bastards heading Dreadnight's way," Mr. Unseen cut in, scrupulously analyzing the four live video feeds covering each angle of the Central Station grounds as each soldier scurried through the trees and across the bordering streets.

"We have to get in there and help him! I'm packing up."

"I second that. Lainey, pick up Siberian then double back for me," Raydar said as he dismantled his rifle.

The sound of the shipping truck's engine turning over filled the comm system.

"Copy that. On my way to you now, Siberian," Lainey confirmed as she sped out onto the street.

~

One after another, Inkubus's super soldiers pooled into the room, each outfitted in their signature mask, tactical gear, and yielding an assault rifle. Foster peered through the looking glass of the laboratory as their shadowy figures passed by, his heart racing and palms sweating. Entering from stairwells in the east and west corridors as well as the cargo door that led out to the railway tunnel, they continued to funnel in. The tactical lights that beamed from each merc's M16 intertwined as they swung their weapons in search of Dreadnight.

As Dreadnight hung cloaked in silence, flashes of light peered through the crease of his wings and the marching footsteps of tens of men echoed throughout the cement dungeon. Unlike previous run-ins with Inkubus's men, this time there wasn't a trace of humanity to be found in the building's vicinity, with the exception of Dr. Foster of course. This absence of humanity meant one thing, and one thing only, that there would no holding back this time … no mercy.

Do not let another innocent life perish at the expense of Inkubus's undertaking! Father Ephrem's death must be avenged! He thought as he prepared to engage his enemies.

Unable to locate him, the mercs moved their attention toward the encased laboratory as a search point, creeping toward its stainless-steel exterior.

Dreadnight closed his eyes, letting go of his fear. *It's now or never*. He withdrew his claws, releasing his anchor from the ceiling. Wings still hardened, eyes still closed, he twisted around as his heavy body plunged like an asteroid directly toward the sea of mercs.

WHOOSH!

Ten feet from impact, Dreadnight released his wings from their hardened state and sent them spanning outward like a bat. The mercs flinched in surprise, unsure of where the sound came from until one of them aimed his gun up and his tactical light revealed a gnarling face of wrath.

"Target located!" The merc shouted as Dreadnight grabbed his shoulders and claws were released deep into his flesh.

Dreadnight turned his wings to stone once again as combustion flashes revealed streaks of bullets flying all around.

Thwack!

Dreadnight's adamantine wings crashed into eight other mercs, leveling them and cracking a few skulls in the process. The merc grappled by his claws crumpled to the ground as blood shot from his freshly pierced flesh. He attempted to kick Dreadnight off him, but his efforts were soon neutralized by a brain rattling headbutt. The surrounding mercs rushed toward the commotion in hope of slaying the beast for their master.

Exhilaration coursing through his veins, Dreadnight pulled his claws from the man's flesh and thawed his wings before swiftly launching through the air straight ahead, barreling through any merc in his way. Bullets followed his path as he latched his claws into an oncoming pillar. Pressing off with his hands and feet, he catapulted himself back into the air toward the laboratory before any of the merc's tactical lights could sight him. As he sailed horizontally across the room, Dreadnight pulled his right arm back and turned his fist into that of stone. Before the targeted merc could aim, Dreadnight shattered his jaw as a slew of teeth shot from his mouth. The shear force spun the merc until his body crashed violently to the floor amongst his lost molars, his face contorted beyond recognition.

    Just as Dreadnight's planted his feet upon the floor, he heard the click of a trigger's ejector six feet to his left. Without thinking, he twisted to his left while whipping his tail around and turning its triangular tip to stone. Before the second bullet left the rifle's chamber, that razor-sharp tip slit the assailant's throat, forcing blood to spray uncontrollably into the air. His finger locked onto the engaged trigger, the merc's arm dropped and flailed as he stumbled back, choking on his own blood. Bullets ricocheted off the epoxied floor, clipping several of the man's teammates until he finally fell to his death.

    A myriad of tactical lights spun in Dreadnight's direction as the tens of mercs attempted to track his movements. Dreadnight dove forward toward the south wall as bullets danced around his feet. Tucking his head and shoulder, he rolled smoothly across the floor and leaped into a low positioned squat. Sensing an incoming blow to his left, Dreadnight pulled his left arm back and thrusted it to that side, delivering an open-handed undercut to the merc's abdomen that sent his claws and fingers deep into the man's innards.

    Hearing rushing footsteps to his right, Dreadnight turned his head to react, but before he could get a visual his jaw was greeted by the composite buttstock of an M16 rifle. The blunt impact barely fazed him, in fact it only fueled his ever-growing rage, causing him to growl and shift his vengeful eyes toward the masked thug. Countering with lighting speed, Dreadnight launched his opposing spike ridden hand into the second merc's mid-section, puncturing several vital organs with ease.

    Before he could remove his entrenched claws, a string of five bullets assaulted Dreadnight's wings. Groaning in pain, he lifted the two impaled mercs and turned to face the gun slinging goon. Using their bodies as meat shields, Dreadnight charged toward his aggressor, releasing a blood curdling scream as bullets penetrated the flesh that separated them and blood projected from their exit wounds. The claws of his feet digging into the epoxy for traction, Dreadnight raced full steam ahead, his arms bulging as they held the two corpses midair. Standing in front of the laboratory door, the merc continue to release hell into the bodies of his allies until they slammed him into the stainless-steel barrier, denting it like a tin can as Dr. Foster jumped back with wide eyes. Face to face as saliva shot from his screaming mouth, Dreadnight lifted the pinnacles of his wings and in a violent downward strike he sent their hooks through the top of the shooter's skull, instantly killing him as his eyes fell into a lifeless haze.

That'll end the mind control!

Thrusting his elbows back and lifting his wings, the bodies of all three masked mercs fell to the floor.

Peering out of the laboratory door looking glass was Dr. Foster. Though his face painted a picture of shock and awe, his heart was overflowing with exhilaration from witnessing the downfall of the rabid weapons his very hands were forced to create.

His face covered in foreign blood, Dreadnight shot a devious grin at Dr. Foster, a grin that perfectly illustrated the fulfillment neutralizing Inkubus's soldiers provided him.

Just as the tactical lights of the remaining mercs located Dreadnight, he launched back into the air toward the north end of the room and again pushed off an oncoming beam with both his hands and feet back toward the center of the room. Mid-air, Dreadnight threw both of his elbows back and straightened his dagger tipped fingers as he barreled toward a trigger happy merc, his night vision outlining the man's vile mask and frame. With insurmountable strength, Dreadnight heaved his arms forward like two harpoons, sending his claws deep into the merc's chest. When the merc's body collided with the concrete floor, it drove the entirety of Dreadnight's fingers deep into the man's body until his claws crashed into the concrete, puncturing his lungs and his heart.

Dead on impact!

Dreadnight leaped onto his feet and pulled his bloodied claws from the fresh corpse. Before he could turn, or even think, he felt the beams of at least twenty tactical lights meet his skin from every direction. With nowhere to run, he had but only one option to avoid the inevitable onslaught of bullets coming his way. As the scent of burning gunpowder and the clanking of over one hundred casings hitting the floor filled the air, Dreadnight swiftly opened his wings and wrapped them around his body. Enduring the sting of at least twenty bullets piercing his flesh, Dreadnight turned his wings to stone, forcing hundreds of bullets to ricochet off his celestial shield.

One after another, every merc's M16 rifle dry fired with an echoing click.

Surrounded by a sea of bullets, Dreadnight remained protected behind his stone shell, awaiting more bullets to follow upon reloading. However, not a single merc reached for a replacement cartridge. Just as he separated his wings to peer out into the open, Dreadnight heard the pull of a grenade pin to the northwest of him.

Shit! Dreadnight thought to himself, unsure if his supernatural state could withstand such a blast. Out of instinct he thawed his wings, leaving his entire body vulnerable.

The unknown merc threw the frag grenade in an underhand toss into the air as it's safety pin fell to the floor. Using his enhanced sense of hearing, he projected the grenade's position as it bounced off the concrete a mere ten feet away. Within a split second, he retracted his wings and spun to his right. Like a wrecking ball, the core of Dreadnight's tail slammed into the grenade, deflecting it into a line drive shot to the merc's gut. Before the merc could react, the grenade released its swarm of shrapnel, tearing his body asunder and dismembering a few of his fellow allies as smoke plagued the room. Bits of flesh and limbs sailed through across the room in every which way while the sound of blood splatting onto the surrounding surfaces filled the air.

The remaining fifteen or so mercs were unfazed, numb to emotion … to fear … to anything other than following their master's all mighty command. Dropping their M16s, they rushed toward Dreadnight with haste.

Dreadnight released a deathly growl, flexing every muscle in his body as his swarming foes collapsed inward with murderous eyes. In one swift motion, he dipped down while curling his wings in front of his body. Just as the mercs stepped within his reach, Dreadnight threw his wings upward and back with the utmost power, slamming them into the five nearest mercs that surrounded and flinging them into the air like ragdolls. A merc to his right threw a line drive punch toward Dreadnight's jaw with his left fist, but the attempt was thwarted by the beast's right hand as it gripped around the merc's right forearm. Maintaining his uncanny grip, Dreadnight tilted to his left and lifted his right knee up into his chest. Like a raging bull, he sent that leg straight into the attacking merc's chest with a side kick, slingshotting him across the room and into a pillar twenty-five feet away. Shards of cement crashed to the floor as the merc's body slid down the now fractured pillar with ribs to match.

Before Dreadnight could reset his stance, a merc from behind sent a five-inch blade deep into the back of his left shoulder while a second merc in front of him sent a haymaker across his jaw. Releasing a pain ridden howl, Dreadnight reeled in pain as he attempted to regain his footing. Before the blade yielding merc could remove his weapon from the beast's flesh, Dreadnight threw his left elbow back, connecting it with the merc's nose. Blood exploded outward as the merc lost his grip upon the blade's handle and stumbled backward. Dreadnight thrusted his head forward, cracking the skull of the merc facing him, causing the man to lose his basic motor skills and tumble to the ground.

Turning around to facing his assailant, Dreadnight lifted his knee then kicked his right leg forward while simultaneously turning his foot to pure stone. Connecting with the merc's midsection, the monstrous kick ripped his body into the north wall, shattering its cement and breaking the man's back.

Sensing a merc charging from behind him, Dreadnight quickly pulled the blade from his own flesh with his right hand as he turned back around and threw his right elbow back before whipping it forward, sending the blade spiraling through the air until it lodged itself into the merc's esophagus. The force of the impact lifted the merc off his feet and in the air until his back crashed onto the floor as he gasped for dear life.

Each using a steel pipe, two mercs struck the backs of both of Dreadnight's knees, causing him to fall onto his right knee as he stabilized himself by driving his right palm into the floor. Continuing to take blows to his wings and back, Dreadnight swiftly turned his wings to stone to curb the impact. Another blade yielding merc lunged forward from Dreadnight's left, striking down at his jugular. Luckily Dreadnight caught the merc in his peripheral vision and threw up his left forearm, blocking the attack. Grunting in sheer rage as he rose, Dreadnight countered with a fierce open-handed uppercut, driving the claws of his right hand up and through the merc's bottom jaw. His claws tucked behind the man's front teeth, Dreadnight released a blood curling growl as he stared into his victim's fading eyes. Jolting his right elbow in a downward motion, his claws slid from the merc's jowls along with a copious amount of blood as the man dropped to the ground.

Even though at least ten of Inkubus's super soldiers had been neutralized, the playing field seemed as ominous as ever as the swarm continued its never-ending assault overtop the dead bodies of their allies.

Twisting to his left, Dreadnight released his wings from their hardened state and swung his left wing back forcefully, knocking the steel pipes from the hands of both mercs. But as he turned to attack them, a third merc ten yards diagonally off to the right pulled a pistol from his utility belt and unleashed a triple tap assault of 9mm bullets into his right shoulder and pectoral muscle. Writhing in pain, his rage was redirected at the shooter. Quickly, Dreadnight gripped onto the nearest of the two pipe-less mercs and with both arms he whipped the man's body through the air and crashing into the shooter, sending both tumbling across the floor.

A leaping merc wrapped his arm around Dreadnight's neck as he forcefully pressed upon the back of the beast in a feeble attempt to choke him out.

Feeble indeed.

Reacting with haste, Dreadnight leaped straight up into the air. His feet at least five feet off the ground, Dreadnight kicked his legs forward while arching his back, rendering his body perpendicular to the floor. In an earth trembling collision, all four hundred pounds of Dreadnight's brick house physique slammed the merc into the concrete floor, shattering his spine with ease.

No chiropractor is going to fix that.

Just as that merc's arms fell from Dreadnight's neck, another was striking downward with a blade, both his hands gripped around its handle for maximum impact. Swiftly, Dreadnight rolled to his left, missing the blade's serrated edge by an inch as it clanked into the shattered concrete. Pushing off the ground, Dreadnight leaped onto his feet. As the blade yielding merc rose to recoup, Dreadnight sent a violent stomp from his left foot directly into the side of the merc's right knee.

Crack!

The masked man's leg buckled, rendering him back to the ground.

Sensing motion to his left, Dreadnight turned to greet another attack, however this time he wasn't fast enough. The cold kiss of a retrieved steel pipe landed across the left side off his face, making contact with the bullet hole in his cheek and cocking his head to the right. Before he could react, the crippled merc in front of him fell forward and drove his blade into Dreadnight's left quadricep. Furthering his agony, the pipe yielding merc swung his weapon back up and across, striking him under the chin.

Disoriented and riddled with pain, Dreadnight stumbled back as another merc lifted a block of rubble and struck him in the back of the head. Falling onto his knees as blood seeped from numerous areas of his body, Dreadnight curled his wings forward and turned them to stone, deflecting any secondary attacks. Fighting to remain conscious, the undying thirst to avenge Father Ephrem's death kept him on the offensive. Again, pulling a blade from his own flesh, Dreadnight returned the favor, sending the blade into its owner's stomach, using his opposing hand to pull the merc forward into the lethal stab.

Stay down!

In one motion, Dreadnight rose and swung back his thawed wings, knocking four barraging mercs back at least ten yards. One after another, punches from every which direction connected with Dreadnight's face and midsection as previously disabled super soldiers re-engaged in battle, ignoring their broken bones and severed limbs.

Unable to see straight as the bloodied fists forced him to stumble backward, Dreadnight blindly lifted his wings, then like two high powered harpoons, struck downward with the hooks upon their pinnacles. Despite feeling an insurmountable rift of pain spreading throughout his body, Dreadnight somehow felt those very hooks grapple into flesh. Instinctively, he lifted the snared prey and threw back his wings. The bodies of two mercs were lifted above Dreadnight's head until he opened the hooks of his wings, flinging the two men through the air and crashing into the various light fixtures nearly twenty yards behind him.

The unbridled mob of fists would not relent however and Dreadnight's patience was all but gone, unlike his burning rage. In a burst of momentum, he grabbed ahold of the nearest merc's skull with both hands, forcing it downward and driving it directly into his right knee. The merc's eye socket shattered like glass but he continued to resist, ignoring all pain as he drove his shoulder into the beast's stomach, attempting to tackle him. His back leg bent as the claws of his foot countered the merc's resistance, Dreadnight sent a five-finger death stab deep into the man's lower back with his right hand, instantly nullifying his efforts.

Returning for more punishment, the merc who sent three 9mm slugs into his torso lurched forward, attempting a pistol whip aimed for Dreadnight's jaw, but he was too quick, too perceptive. Dreadnight swung his left arm in a back-hand assault, sending his claws ripping across the merc's face, tearing his cheek as if he had been mauled by a ferocious bear.

Suddenly, Dreadnight felt cold steel slide into the muscles of his lower back, sending a shocking blitz throughout his entire nervous system and causing him jolt forward, right into an oncoming merc's right hook. The blunt impact twisted Dreadnight around nearly one hundred and eighty degrees as dark blood shot from his mouth and he fell onto his knees. Jutting from his flesh was a two-foot-long rebar, its end jagged from being ripped from one of the pillars Dreadnight had dismantled.

The immense nerve pain emanating from his back kept him conscious as his weakened body fought to stay upright due to the profuse blood loss being sustained. With his vision blurred and continuing to endure a storm of striking blows to every area of his body, he released the most terrifying roar he could muster, causing the ground itself to tremble in fear.

With the last trace of vitality that remained in his veins, Dreadnight reached up and grabbed ahold of the rebar runner's head, placing one hand on the backside of the skull and the other upon the man's jaw.

Snap!

He twisted the man's head, snapping his neck like a twig and cutting the oxygen off to his brain. Releasing his monstrous grip, the merc fell like an anvil to the ground, only to be trampled upon by his comrades who continued their relentless rush to spill the beast's blood.

Hearing the mauled merc lunge forward again, Dreadnight quickly grabbed the very steel pipe that had assaulted his face just moments ago and swung it across like a baseball bat, connecting its alloy with the face of the assailant. The sheer impact twisted the merc's body around. Before the merc could regain his footing, Dreadnight stood while gripping both hands around the opposing ends of the pipe then swiftly lifted the pipe up and in front of the merc's neck which was facing away.

The cold steel of the pipe hugging the merc's esophagus, Dreadnight pressed his right knee into the man's back while simultaneously bending the steel pipe with flexed biceps. Tightly wrapping around the merc's neck as if it were a noose, the pipe crushed his windpipe. Releasing his grip, Dreadnight let the merc fall to his assured suffocation.

Another merc approached from straight ahead. Dreadnight anticipatively lifted his knee and attempted to convert his foot's composition as he drove it into an oncoming merc's chest, however, despite splintering his ribs and sending him soaring across the room, his foot remained flesh and bone. The blood loss was becoming too extensive, not only affecting his ability to fight, but now eradicating his celestial capabilities.

Trying with all his might to endure the spine tapping pain, the disorientation, Dreadnight lifted his right arm, blocking an attack. Quickly he swung his left arm around and drilled his claws into that very attacker's chest, immediately thrusting his arm back.

"Errrraggh!" Dreadnight belted in misery laced rage.

The merc fell to his knees as freshly pumped blood projected from his punctured heart and into the open air.

Spinning, he blocked another pistol-whipping attempt, knocking the gun from the merc's hand before grabbing that very wrist and twisting it back one hundred and eighty degrees, forcing the arm's ulna to tear from its joint and through its skin. Despite the disturbing image, the merc didn't flinch, instead he thrusted his opposing arm forward. Blocked again, Dreadnight countered, grabbing onto the merc's fist mid-air and stopping it dead in its tracks. Holding his ground, Dreadnight released his grip from the fractured arm and like a guillotine, struck the man's neck with a five-claw stab.

Choking on his own breath, the merc collapsed as the beast withdrew his mighty talons.

Just as he heard a merc charging to his right, he was stricken with an unbearable jolt of pain and released an innate howl of agony. An unsuspected merc had struck the semi-embedded rebar with a chunk of concrete debris, driving it entirely through the beast's muscle lining.

Dreadnight fell to his knees with fearful eyes as he realized his strength was no more. Before he could even blink, that very chunk of debris was smashed over his head, shattering on contact. The impact felt as if he has been struck by a wrecking ball, wiping out his night vision and forcing him to collapse onto his hands.

Everything went dark.

Their victory within a striking blow's reach, the eight remaining mercs rushed toward their prey's weakened vessel. Desperate groans of pain bellowed from Dreadnight's core as two kicks to his abdomen knocked him onto his side and a barrage of stomping feet punished his already marred body.

At that very moment, Dreadnight envisioned Rachel's beautiful face as he awaited death's everlasting release ... for the pain and fear to finally cease.

~

"We're coming for you buddy!" Raydar said with fervor, Lainey piloting the Celestial Shipping truck next to him as he and Siberian Scientist buckled their seatbelts.

"Brace for impact!" Siberian Scientist shouted as he clutched onto the grab handle to his right.

The crosshatched road armor mounted to the truck's front end ripped through the industrial cargo door of the Central Station's basement level. The truck rocked violently as it powered over torn sheet steel and metal girders causing the three teammates to tense their bodies and grit their teeth. The beaming headlights immediately revealed the myriad of super soldiers beating their dear friend to a bloody pulp. Lainey slammed on the truck's brakes and threw its shifter into park, stopping it on a dime.

The three heroes leaped from the truck, anxious to save their dear friend. Raydar and Lainey pulled their 9mm's from their holsters and readied their fire.

"Don't shoot!" Siberian Scientist yelled, lifting his hand. "We can't risk hitting him, he has lost too much blood." A fact that was apparent due to the growing reflective pool of obsidian blood underneath Dreadnight's body. He quickly ran over to the east end of the room, scanning the area where the medical instruments and chemicals were located. "I've got an idea!" he shouted as his eyes lined up with a silver cylindrical tank that read "Desflurane Atropine". "Raydar grab that tank and throw it overtop all of them."

Entrusting his comrade, Raydar rushed over to the tank that was no larger than a five-gallon jug, grabbed ahold one of the ringed slits upon its valve guard with both hands, and lifted if from the ground. Meanwhile Siberian Scientist lifted and steadied his AK74M.

Only seconds away from his presumed demise, Dreadnight heard a muffled ringing of undistinguishable noises as the unknown source of light blinded his vision. Barely coherent, he wondered if Michael himself had returned or if Inkubus was back to finish him off himself.

"On my count," Siberian Scientist shouted while nodding at Raydar. "Three ... two." Raydar twisted his body back and to his right. "One ... Now!" Reversing his course with flexed and straightened arms, he hurled the tank around, releasing his grip when it was aligned with the swarm of mercs. The shimmering tank spun sideways as it sailed through the air, unbeknownst to those it approached.

A burst of ear-splitting bullets ripped into the open as Siberian scientist's body rattled from his weapon's recoil. Just as the tank lifted above its targets, the raging bullets penetrated its steel shell. Like a bomb, the tank exploded into a cloud of combusting molecules, leaving behind a thick haze of noxious fumes.

"Quickly cover your mouths!" Siberian shouted as he slowly lowered his rifle, already protected by that of his own mask.

The sound of bodies thudding to the ground arose upon the explosion's echoing remnants as the three heroes stood side by side, watching and waiting with immense anticipation, their weapons drawn and ready to shoot. A growing shadow appeared amongst the haze, filling their hearts with both hope and fear.

Slowly the haze subsided. Standing wearily, covered in a mixture of his blood and that of others, was Dreadnight. With his bloodshot eyes fighting to stay open, Dreadnight began to falter. His teammates holstered their guns and rushed to his side as he dropped onto his knees and fell forward into unconsciousness. Lunging forward, his friends prevented his body from colliding with ground yet again, embracing his monstrous upper body into that of their own.

Instantly they noticed the blood laced rebar sticking out of his back. Without hesitation, Siberian Scientist pressed his hand upon his dear friend's neck. "He's still alive, but his pulse is starting to fade. We have to get him back to my laboratory and get this thing out of him before he bleeds out … or before these monsters wake back up," Siberian Scientist nervously said.

Suddenly, a second source of light appeared off to the right to the team's surprise. Continuing to support Dreadnight's body with his left side, Raydar swiftly drew his 9mm.

"I can take care of him, you just dispose of these abominations," an unsuspected voice announced.

"Benjamin! Is it really you?" Siberian Scientist blurted with wide eyes.

The man stepped out into the open.

"Indeed, my brother," Dr. Foster replied.

"Keep him upright,' Siberian Scientist directed Raydar and Lainey before running over to the laboratory door and hugging his long-lost friend. "Thank God you're alive."

Slapping each other's backs, Siberian Scientist and Dr. Foster brimmed with glee, overjoyed to finally be reunited.

"Let's get Dreadnight into the truck," Siberian Scientist anxiously said as the reality of the situation struck him.

Lainey hurdled over the debris of steel and stone until reaching the Celestial Shipping truck's cargo hatch. Quickly she unlatched it and threw it up into the truck's roof lining. Meanwhile, Siberian Scientist, Raydar, and Dr. Foster hoisted Dreadnight's body off the ground, laying him overtop their backs. Stammering forward, the three men maintained their physical composure, feeling as if they had the weight of the world on their shoulders.

In a way, they did.

With Dreadnight's back claws scraping along the disheveled floor, they reached the rear of the truck.

"Set him on his stomach," Dr. Foster's said. "I'll stay back here with him to keep an eye on his vitals," he added.

Siberian Scientist turned to Raydar and Lainey. "Haul ass back to my lab and help Dr. Foster any way you can, alright?," he said sternly. "I'll stay back and finish what our friend started." Siberian Scientist's icy mask only enhanced his already rigid demeanor.

"How will you get back?" Raydar asked in confusion.

"Call Sandra Daley and tell her to pick me up out front in the circle drive in ten minutes. I think it's time her eyes lay witness to this city's deception."

"Agreed, I'm on it." Raydar turned to head toward the truck's cabin as Siberian Scientist went to depart himself, but Raydar paused and looked back. "Be careful comrade."

"What's the fun in that," Siberian Scientist chuckled with a hidden smile then turned and walked toward the building's electrical kill switch.

Lainey and Raydar hopped into the truck and reversed its course back into the underground tunnel leading to the city streets.

Siberian Scientist flipped the kill switch back into "on" position, filling the room back up with bright UV luminescence. Gazing across the room, he realized the astounding sum of super soldiers that Dreadnight had faced from the bodies scattered all around.

"My God Slade ... how are you still alive," he gasped to himself in utter disbelief. *Time to make sure they stay down!*

Siberian Scientist walked over to the east wall and analyzed the cabinet full of various chemical compounds, both in liquid and gas forms. *Ha, these will work just fine!* he thought to himself as he removed the safety caps from a five-gallon jug of isopropyl alcohol and a coinciding gallon of acetone. He grabbed each container's handle and slowly poured their contents onto the bodies of the neutralized super soldiers. One by one, he connected a highly flammable trail of death amongst the entire army until tossing the empty containers to the wayside. Ending his stroll, he stood behind the glimmering laboratory and faced the super soldiers, ten yards away from a staircase leading to the ground floor.

Though his mask was free of emotion, his heart was full of hate and disgust as Father Ephrem's death reeled in his mind. Pulling a zippo lighter from his utility belt, he flicked his wrist, lifting its cover and sparking its wick.

"This is for you, Father Ephrem," he said somberly before gently tossing the lighter into the air. Landing just a few feet away, the flame splashed into the liquid ignitor, instantaneously spreading its fury rampantly across the bodies. "You'll need to get used to fire where you're going ... demons!"

Siberian Scientist turned and calmly walked up the stairs as the fire engulfed the room, creeping its way toward the east wall and its abundance of chemical compounds. The sound of crackling flames followed him as he reached the main floor and out a door along its east wall. Once outside, he walked over to the very radio tower from which Dreadnight performed surveillance the night the Central Station was revealed as Inkubus's base of operations. After marching a good forty yards he began climbing the crosshatched metal structure.

A series of mass explosions shook the ground at its core, causing his feet to slip from the beam from which they were planted upon. His body swaying midair and crashing against the tower, Siberian Scientist flexed his arms and pulled himself up to regain footing. Behind him as he continued his climb, flames shot through the windows of the stations main floor, blasting glass all around.

A few steps from the top of the tower, Siberian Scientist stopped and removed his right hand from its structure. Maintaining his balance while over forty feet in the air, he reached down and unhooked a reinforced carbon fiber rope from his utility belt. Carefully, he latched one of its ends around the steel beam in front of his waist, then wrapped its other end around his midsection and latched it onto the rope itself, providing him his very own safety harness. Maneuvering his hands onto the bar at his waist, he readjusted his footing and rotated his body one hundred and eighty degrees. Leaning into the rope to eliminate any slack, Siberian Scientist removed his hands from the tower and fell into his makeshift harness, placing him at a forty-five-degree angle aimed at the Central Station grounds.

Amongst the smoke streaming out of one of main floor windows, one of Inkubus's super soldiers who was engulfed in a blistering wildfire appeared. Crashing to the ground, the merc quickly bounced onto his feet and ran toward Siberian Scientist.

Time to have some fun!

Siberian Scientist reached behind his back and lifted his Dragunov sniper rifle overtop his head. Steadying his body with his feet, he pressed the rifle's buttstock up against his right shoulder and lined his right eye up with its adjustable iron sight. Ever so slightly, he followed the merc's movements with the rifle until the man's face was in its crosshairs.

Exhale ... *BOOM!*

Headshot! The bullet split the man's brow, exiting out the back of his skull.

As soon as Siberian Scientist lifted his head to scan the area, a second scorching soldier appeared from a south end window and into an all-out dash toward Mexican Town. Thanks to the Dragunov's gas operated system all he had to do was realign his sights, no need to manually insert a fresh cartridge. With the firm flex of his trigger finger, Siberian

Scientist released another bullet of bereavement through the merc's left shoulder blade and subsequently his blackened heart.

Two of Inkubus's greatest achievements were laid to waste, roasting upon the remains of his kingdom.

Before he could even scan the area once again, Siberian Scientist heard a set of tires scream against the pavement to the north of him. Looking up, he saw a silver sedan parked at the base of the station's circle drive. It was Sandra Daley. She hopped out of the car and waived him down.

That was a bad idea. Siberian Scientist thought to himself as he saw a third inflamed merc, his face nearly melted off, racing toward her with only twenty yards separating them. Twisting his body, he spun the rifle around and quickly nestled his right eye against its sight while closing the other for enhanced clarity. In a bout of panic, Siberian Scientist pivoted the rifle in several directions as he attempted to get the merc in its crosshairs but only saw blades of grass.

Seeing an effervescent glow approaching in her peripheral vision, Ms. Daley's eyes bulged as the searing merc was only ten yards from her vehicle. Flushed in fear she drew her Glock 19 from a concealed holster beneath her suit jacket. Just as she lifted the pistol to eye level, one of Siberian Scientist's deathly bullets ripped bore a hole clean through the man's head from right to left, dropping him before she could release a bullet of her own.

Nighty night scum.

Now that Ms. Daley was aware of the mercs and armed, Siberian Scientist knew that it was time to depart. Lifting the Dragunov overtop his right shoulder he slid the weapon back into its rear mounted sling. Twisting and grabbing onto the carbon fiber rope with one hand, Siberian Scientist stabilized himself so that he could rotate his body around to face the radio tower. After pulling himself forward, he unlatched the rope from his midsection then the tower itself, placing it back around his utility belt.

The double blast of two potent 9mm bullets forced Siberian Scientist to cock his head to the north as he began his descent.

"Oh, thank God!" He sighed in relief as he saw a fourth merc burning face down in the grass nearly thirty yards from Ms. Daley. Hastily, Siberian Scientist continued to climb down, still thirty feet in the air. His ear comm still active, he heard Raydar notify Mr. Unseen to unlock and open the exterior door leading to the observatory, a relieving announcement to say the least.

Relief that would be short lived.

"Behind you!" screamed Ms. Daley, too far away for a clean shot.

Siberian Scientist looked back to see a raging merc rushing toward the tower and emitting a most repulsive scent consisting of burning hair and flesh.

Bring it on.

Refusing to alter his course of action, he continued to step from beam to beam despite the oncoming attack. Now at a height of roughly fifteen feet, Siberian Scientist felt a vibration surge through the metal from which his hands were gripping. He knew it was the relentless merc doing whatever it takes to reach him.

I am going to enjoy this.

Releasing his hands from the structure, Siberian Scientist simultaneously leaped upward and spun his body around one hundred and eighty degrees. In a streamlined free fall, Siberian Scientist's boots slammed into the merc's shoulders, forcing him to lose his grip upon the structure. Driving the burning scum flat into the ground as if he were an anvil, Siberian Scientist landed feet first across the man's chest.

Before the merc could react, Siberian Scientist promptly drew his Tokarev pistol as he rose from bent knees and released a close-range kill shot through the man's eyes.

"Enjoy hell, you bastard," he said as he stepped from the man's now lifeless yet still burning corpse, his hands still gripped tightly around his pistol.

Somehow calm and collected, Siberian Scientist walked toward Ms. Daley and her car, his AK74M and Dragunov Rifle both rattling against his body with each step. Seeing a radiant glow in his peripheral, he swiftly rotated his weapon. After turning a mere ninety degrees, Siberian Scientist immediately double tapped his trigger. That radiant glow was of course another fleeing merc, one that was now bleeding out on the ground from the two bullets lodged in his chest.

Passing the edge of the Central Station, another earth rattling explosion shattered the third story windows, sending glass shards crashing all around Siberian Scientist as flames billowed from their fringe. Ms. Daley watched in wonderment as the raging fire escalated from floor to floor, engulfing the nerve center of her city's crime syndicate. Even though she knew the cause of the fire and the events leading to it went against the laws she pledged to uphold, she couldn't help but smile and feel an overwhelming sense of satisfaction as evil was literally burned to ashes.

Like a meteorite, another merc fell from the fifth floor of the station's north end. Both Siberian Scientist and Ms. Daley twisted and aimed their weapons, ready to unleash hell upon the man. However, to their surprise the fall did the job for them. Though the front of the man's body was embossed into the dirt, his head was twisted around and facing the sky.

With the masked vigilante only a few feet away from her vehicle, Ms. Daley's face wore a look of wide-eyed austerity as she witnessed his exotic and inhuman façade. The wind rustling his long black trench coat and the blue neurons of his mask glistening from the moon's glow, Siberian Scientist looked at her upon stopping.

"Sandra Daley?" Siberian Scientist said politely with a stern nod, before opening the vehicle door and hopping into the passenger seat.

Her face now morphed with perplexity from his nonchalant demeanor, Ms. Daley shook her head, likely refocusing her mind as she got into the car herself.

"And who are you exactly?" Sandra asked bluntly, turning toward the man.

"I'm the ..." he began to say before Sandra abruptly lifted her pistol directly in front of his mask, choking its trigger three times.

Despite his facial concealment, the confounded vigilante turned to his right to witness a new victim of Sandra's Glock 19 lying on the ground in an uncontrollable cremation.

"Damn ... pretty and a markswoman," Siberian Scientist said in admiration.

Ms. Daley lowered her gun and exhaled.

"You were saying?" Sandra hinted, attempting not to blush but failing considerably.

"Yes ... I'm the Siberian Scientist ... and we should probably go," he said suavely.

"Right. Where to?"

"The corner of Woodward and Chicago St. And quick," he replied.

Sandra looked at Siberian Scientist confusedly. *A residential area ... why?* She thought to herself. Nevertheless, she nodded in agreement and shifted the car into gear. Speeding off with a lead foot, the Central Station burning like the Statue of Liberty's torch in the night sky, consuming every inch of her rear-view mirror.

Chapter 16
Never Break a Promise

The metal paneling of the cargo door rattled violently as it flew up into the topside of the Celestial Shipping truck. Facing the truck was the laboratory's examination table, raised to the height of the truck bed with its wheels locked.

"You two, grab his legs," Dr. Foster directed Raydar and Mr. Unseen. "Carefully slide him onto the table in a constant movement. He must not be jarred. We can't risk that rebar shifting into one of his vital organs." Both Raydar and Mr. Unseen gripped their hands around each of Dreadnight's ankles.

"Okay, on my three," Raydar announced, looking at Mr. Unseen. "One ... two ... three." With their feet staggered, the two men cautiously pulled the fallen hero's legs, causing his body to slowly slide from surface to surface until his head was upon the stainless-steel table.

"Right there. That's good," Dr. Foster said, raising his hand in the air. "Let's get him inside."

The three of them wheeled the heavy-duty table through the side entrance of the observatory and into the building with Lainey following closely. As soon as they positioned the table, Dr. Foster immediately wheeled over a mobile vitals cart and hooked its sensors up to Dreadnight's neck and upper chest.

"Shit ... please tell me Nikolai has a handheld magnetic resonance scanner," Dr. Foster fretted aloud, knowing that if he didn't stop the bleeding and fast, Dreadnight would go into cardiac arrest and there would be no bringing him back.

Mr. Unseen ran into the laboratory and scrupulously searched its medical instrument cage. *Bingo!* He located a bright yellow case with a label stating "MRS". He quickly grabbed ahold of its handle and raced out into the Observatory.

"Got it!" Mr. Unseen shouted, hurrying over to hand it to Dr. Foster.

Wasting no time, Dr. Foster opened the case and lifted the device from it. About the size of an ordinary laptop, the MRS consisted of a clear screen mounted to two overmolded synthetic rubber handles, one on each side. Pressing down on a button flushed into the surface of the right-side handle, the screen came to light with encapsulated blue and red LED lights. One could believe they were in the presence of alien technology from its futuristic appearance and capabilities. It was purely astonishing.

Utilizing its touch sensor technology, Dr. Foster hastily pressed the device modules and swiped along the screen, adjusting its settings for the appropriate location of the scan.

"All set. One of you grab it by both ends," Dr. Foster urged, resulting in Lainey stepping forward.

"I got it," she confirmed grabbing ahold of the device.

Dr. Foster then guided her hands to place the device at a precise angle and distance from Dreadnight's wound. "Hold it here and do not move a muscle, his life might just depend on it," Dr. Foster stressed.

"You can trust me, I promise," Lainey said with confidence. Dr. Foster smiled and nodded in gratitude as he pressed one final module on the touchscreen.

The screen transformed into a live musculoskeletal imagery map, detailing all the soft tissue down to its every fiber. Lodged amongst that very tissue was a large cylindrical steel rod, just millimeters away from his liver.

"Holy shit …" Dr. Foster gasped, realizing how close the rebar was from puncturing his liver, an incident that would have killed him within minutes. "Alright, going to have to make sure he stays asleep during this," he added before walking over to the laboratory.

Raydar, Mr. Unseen, and Lainey stood by in utter angst as they gazed upon the MRS, each praying that their teammate would walk away from this. Returning from the laboratory, a syringe in hand, Dr. Foster injected a clear liquid into the neck of Dreadnight.

"That should keep him down for at least another thirty minutes. Time to get this damn thing out of him," Dr. Foster announced. "One of you grab me a bottle of vodka. I'm sure Nikolai keeps plenty around," he added with a grin. "The other, get me a blow torch and the largest metal spoon you can find."

Raydar and Mr. Unseen immediately scattered in search of the requested items. Meanwhile, Dr. Foster walked over to Nikolai's tool and machinery area, grabbing a pair of neoprene wrapped vice grips. Once back to Dreadnight's side, he clamped the vice grips an inch shy of Dreadnight's skin at the base of the exposed rebar. Utilizing the vice grips would provide him improved positioning and leverage in his attempt to pull the object from his friend's flesh. Seconds later, Raydar returned with the requested bottle of vodka, handing it to Dr. Foster.

Dr. Foster poured a generous amount into and around Dreadnight's wound before lifting it and taking a hefty swig of the potent liquor.

"That'll calm these rabid nerves," Dr. Foster said in a sigh of artificial relief.

"Well, don't be greedy," Raydar added, reaching his hand out. Following suit, he too downed a few shots worth of his own.

An out of breath Mr. Unseen returned from Father Ephrem's quarters where the small blow torch was located, presumably to assist in his creation of rosaries.

"Hope this works," Mr. Unseen gasped as he handed the small blow torch and a metal mixer spoon to Dr. Foster.

"We will soon find out my new friends. Let's get this blasted thing out of him," Dr. Foster said with zeal. "Go ahead and get that thing hotter than Hades and have it ready for me," he added, nodding at Mr. Unseen.

"You got it Doc," Mr. Unseen replied, igniting the torch and placing its flame against the mixing spoon.

With an underhand grip, Dr. Foster tightly grasped onto the handles of the vice grips while keeping his eyes locked onto the MRS to ensure the positioning of the rebar avoids any vital organs or major arteries.

Inhale ... exhale ... inhale ...

The sudden sound of gushing flesh arose as the rebar ever so slightly shifted in an upward motion upon the futuristic screen before them. The entire team was holding their breaths on account of the suspense. The further the rebar traveled, the more blood that seeped out. Before that moment, the cruel piece of metal was ironically the only thing preventing Dreadnight from bleeding out.

"Al ... most ... there!" Dr. Foster's arms jerked into the air, along with the jagged metal cylinder coated in Dreadnight's onyx colored blooded.

The instant the metal left his flesh, Dreadnight's heartrate flatlined as blood rushed out of the newly exposed hole, causing the vitals monitor to go into a frenzy.

"Quickly, the spoon!" He shouted, throwing the clamped rebar across the room in disgust then grabbing the now radiantly orange mixing spoon from Mr. Unseen.

"Come on Slade, hang in there!" Raydar blurted, swallowed in fear.

Hastily Dr. Foster pressed the bottom side of the spoon with the utmost pressure he could muster overtop the seeping hole.

"You're not dying on me, not today!" Foster grunted.

The singeing sound of flesh being seared made even the strongest of stomachs in the room queasy as the wound was cauterized before their very eyes.

Dr. Foster lifted the makeshift cauterizer, revealing a raw yet completely sealed area. The blood loss finally ended. He set the spoon down onto the table and snapped his neck to the right to view analyze his vitals. Within seconds the vitals monitor went from a continuous ear-piercing scream to a segmented beep. His heartrate had finally stabilized.

"Phheww, thank god." Dr. Foster sighed as the entire team breathed once again.

~

Rolling to a stop across the street from a two-level Victorian style home surrounded by rustic iron fencing, Sandra shifted her vehicle into park and kept it idling.

"So why here?" she asked curiously.

"You remember the doctor Inkubus kidnapped?" Siberian Scientist asked.

"Yes, of course."

"Well, his family is being held captive in that very house." Siberian pointed in its direction. "I have no idea how many guards are in there if any at all. But, if there indeed is and they are wearing the masks you just saw moments ago, shoot to kill."

Sandra's throat tightened as she attempted to wrap her head around the situation.

"If they are police officers, attempt to neutralize them with non-lethal shots. Above all, we must protect Dr. Foster's wife and daughter and get them the hell out of there," Siberian Scientist said sternly.

Sandra's frantic eyes expressed her apparent jitters as she blankly looked upon the house.

"If you're not up to this, I would understand," Siberian Scientist calmly explained.

"I am. Let's go free them from that sick bastard." Her eyes tightened with ferocity.

"Alright. I promise I'll keep you safe ... plus I owe you one anyhow," he said with a concealed grin, causing a smile to creep upon Sandra's face.

"Mr. Unseen, I need a favor my friend."

"You got it buddy. What's up?" Mr. Unseen replied.

"I need you to hack into the power supply unit that feeds 11887 Chicago St. and shut her down," Siberian Scientist said.

Like a human algorithm, Mr. Unseen typed away, creating his own cyberspace highway on which he severed numerous security fail-safes to allow him to reprogram the system at its very core. Before Mr. Unseen could even provide his own verbal confirmation, the lights went dark before Sandra and Siberian Scientist's eyes.

"Beautiful my friend," Siberian Scientist said.

"I take it the house is no more than an Amish farmhouse now?" Mr. Unseen asked jokingly.

"Yes sir!"

Siberian Scientist nodded to Sandra, signaling that it was time to move in.

"This car isn't a rental, is it?" Siberian Scientist asked, hinting towards a not so obvious notion.

"No. Why do you ... you don't seriously plan on ..." Siberian Scientist cut in before she could even finish her statement,

"Yes ... yes I do."

"You Russians are crazy, aren't you?" Sandra said with a chuckle.

"Well, I guess you will have to get to know me and find out for yourself, huh?"

Grinning from the apparent insinuation, Sandra shifted her vehicle into reverse, backing it onto the sidewalk opposing the house and aiming it directly at the security gate. Shifting its transmission down into neutral, she gripped the steering wheel tightly as she revved the vehicle's engine. Without the slightest warning, she slammed the shifter into drive causing the tires to peel out as the vehicle roared forward like a bat out of hell toward the iron gate.

The front bumper smashed into the gate and its connecting fence lines as Sandra and Siberian braced through the impact, ripping the gates off its hinges, and sending them flying across the yard. Now onto the premises and through the breach, Sandra slammed on the brakes and shoved the vehicle into park.

Both Sandra and Siberian Scientist pushed open their doors and cocked their handguns, both bearing full clips. A police officer rushed out of the front door of the house, his own handgun gripped tightly out in front of him. Before the officer could lock onto a target, Siberian Scientist lifted his tightened arms and released a streamline shot clean through the officer's right shoulder. The officer dropped, releasing his handgun as he gripped onto his freshly formed wound with his opposing hand.

In a prowl like crouch, the new partners quickly paced toward the officer, their heads and guns on a swivel in anticipation of other guards. Stepping up to the officer writhing in pain, Siberian Scientist leaned down and grabbed his abandoned handgun.

"You'll survive," Siberian Scientist said in a deepened tone as he released the gun's clip onto the ground and threw the remaining bullets onto a neighboring yard.

Entering the house, Siberian Scientist motioned Sandra to cover his left as he and his steadied gun probed the oncoming hallway, quickly pivoting to his right to step into the home's living room. With nothing but the moonlight peering through the windows, he checked the room's entirety with his gun on a string. Turning back, he nodded at Sandra to confirm the room was clear. Retracing his steps, Siberian Scientist rerouted himself into the main hallway. With the dining room on the east wall cleared, Sandra followed her partner closely, covering his back side.

After walking approximately eight feet, the hallway ended, veering off to either the left or right of the duo. This time Siberian Scientist motioned Sandra to his right, as he rolled the corner to his left.

Sandra did just that, but no rivals were present. Siberian Scientist pressed forward, walking toward a doorway a few feet away and to the right. Before he could reach it, the outline of a pistol peered out from the darkened entry. Lunging forward, Siberian Scientist removed his left hand from that of his own gun and thrusted it forward. With lighting speed, he wrapped his hand around the barrel of the oncoming shooter's pistol, sliding his thumb through its trigger loop. Before the man could react, Siberian Scientist pulled the gunman toward himself. Alarmed from the unsuspected encounter, the gunman choked his trigger twice, sending two bullets into the corridor wall. Unfazed, Siberian Scientist swiftly lifted and pulled back his right arm before sending its elbow into the bridge of the man's nose twice.

Blood burst into the air as Siberian Scientist stripped the man of his weapon and with a straightened right arm, pointed that of his own at the bleeding bastard's forehead.

Yet another police officer.

"Where are they being held?" Siberian Scientist shouted.

Before the man could muster a response, another gunshot cracked into the air. Jerking his neck toward Sandra, Siberian Scientist witnessed her standing firm with her gun angled upward as a third police officer tumbled down a flight of stairs.

Snapping back to the officer before him, Siberian Scientist's eerie eyed mask instilled a nerve tapping fear throughout the misguided officer, causing him to quiver.

"I ... I don't know man!" the officer stuttered, his hands rattling in the air in submission.

Surely an answer that Siberian Scientist would not accept.

An abrupt ballistic ignition generated a flash of light amongst the darkness. An explosion that was quickly followed by a pain filled squeal.

"Think harder!" Siberian Scientist roared, his gun now aimed back up at the officer's head as the man's left foot bled from the hole inhabiting its topside.

"Okay okay," the officer yelped. "They are in the basement with a member of my squad. Please ... please don't kill me!" he pleaded in desperation.

"Get the hell out of here ... now!" Siberian Scientist snapped, anger dripping from every syllable he spoke.

Not willing to cross the masked vigilante, the officer hopped past him and toward the front door, his hands still shaking in the air as he retreated.

"You too!" Sandra sternly directed the marred officer who was gripping onto his bullet inflicted right arm near the bottom of the stair steps.

The man cowered in fear as he raced toward the home's front door, withstanding a set of broken ribs from the tumble previously taken.

Siberian Scientist and Sandra looked at each other, both feeling a sense of relief yet still spilling over with exhilaration.

"Time to finish this," Siberian Scientist said with fervor. "Follow my lead. I have a feeling this part might get messy," he added.

One after the other, they stepped into the kitchen, its floor newly decorated with blood from the officer's foot. Siberian Scientist prowled toward its south entrance as Sandra back peddled, covering the north entrance. Stepping through the doorway, he swiftly swiveled his gun to his right and to his left.

The hallway was clear.

A few feet to Siberian Scientist's left was the home's backdoor which led to the yard, and straight ahead was a weathered green door. Reaching forward he attempted to quickly turn its etched iron knob, but its lock denied his entry. *That can't be a coincidence*, he thought to himself.

"Stand back," Siberian Scientist announced as he pointed the sight of his gun just above the doorknob. With two squeezes of the trigger, the wood supporting the knob exploded into splinters and the lock securing it became mangled beyond repair. He lifted his knee and kicked the door, causing it to slam open against the wall behind it. Ready to shoot, Siberian Scientist lifted his gun, unbeknownst to what could appear.

No threat was present. However, to no surprise, a staircase leading downward was revealed.

"Mr. Unseen, let there be light again."

Within seconds, the staircase was illuminated. Signaling his partner to press forward, he lifted his right hand and pointed it down the stairs. Cautiously, he treaded from step to step, his gun steadied before him. Maintaining cover, Sandra kept her gun pointed toward the top of the stairs with her right arm as she side stepped downward.

With each step, more of the basement's concrete floor was unveiled, until finally Siberian Scientist's feared premonition came to life.

Amongst an entirely bare room and surrounded by black walls were three individuals. Two of them, a woman and an adolescent girl, were gagged and tied to two chairs that were facing away from one another. The third, a young male police officer standing to the left of them, holding a pistol in each hand, both of which were pressed upon the heads of his prisoners.

The prisoners were none other than Phillipa Foster and her daughter Ava. Their eyes flooded with tears, they screamed into the rags wrapped tightly into their mouths. A sight most disturbing to Siberian Scientist considering they were like a sister and niece to him.

Without a hint of thought, Siberian Scientist placed the officer's face in the sight of his weapon as his feet met the basement floor. Possessing the same innate instincts, Sandra promptly swiveled her gun across, placing the officer in her crosshairs.

"Come any closer and I will shoot them! I will!" the officer stressed in a frantic shout. His guns scraped along the skin of Dr. Foster's wife and child's scalp as they wept and shivered.

Both Siberian Scientist and Sandra froze like ice.

"Is that why you became a police officer? To kill an innocent mother and child?" Siberian Scientist said harshly, hoping to awaken whatever fragments that remained of the officer's conscious.

"What are you talking about? They are family members of an international terrorist," the officer argued, his face tightened in contempt.

"And who told you that? Commissioner Reem?" Sandra said sharply, cutting in. A question to which the officer didn't answer with words but instead by the abrupt shift of his eyes. "You know who I am right? she asked bluntly.

"Should I?" the frantic officer answered.

"She's the city's district attorney, and soon she will be your only hope of staying out of a federal penitentiary." Unexpectedly, Siberian Scientist lowered his weapon and stepped forward.

"I told you not to come any closer man! Don't press me!" the officer stressed, tears emerging in his own eyes.

"Do you have a wife or child of your own?" Siberian Scientist asked empathetically, causing the already rattled officer to remove the gun pointed at little Ava are redirect it toward Siberian Scientist.

"Stop! I won't tell you again man!" the officer shouted, his gun tremoring within his palm, answering the masked vigilante's question without knowing it.

Siberian Scientist paused, then tossed his own gun aside, sending it clanking off the concrete floor. "If you take the life of another tonight, I can promise that you will never see them again," Siberian Scientist said earnestly, now unarmed with a 9mm pointed directly at his face.

The officer's throat tightened as he continued the ruthless battle between his mind and conscious.

"But if you set your guns down, you get to walk away. You get to go home to them, to hold them, to never let go of them." The officer lifted the gun pointed at the masked vigilante, pulling it back and pressing its hammer against the top of his own head, now looking at bare floor in tormenting contemplation. His other gun still pressed against Dr. Foster's dear wife.

"It's your choice."

Losing the battle to his conscious, the officer lowered both guns to his side and opened both of his hands in surrender, causing his guns to crash to the ground. Turning his head, the officer stared blankly at Siberian Scientist's emotionless mask, unsure of what would happen next.

"A man is only as good as his word. Get out of here and stay the hell away from the precinct," Siberian Scientist said sternly.

The officer nervously nodded and stepped toward the mysterious vigilante and the district attorney, her gun still steadily aimed at his forehead. Too ashamed to make eye contact, the officer bowed his head as he walked in between them. Once past them, he raced up the steps and out of the house as if he were being chased.

The second the officer left the room, Siberian Scientist rushed over to little Ava while Sandra tended to Phillipa. Kneeling, Siberian Scientist pulled a switchblade from his utility belt and quickly detached the gag from her mouth, setting loose her screams of utter distress.

"It's okay it's okay," Siberian Scientist said gently in a valiant attempt to calm the young girl that didn't quite catch. Unexpectedly, Siberian Scientist ripped the mask from off his face, revealing his identity. "See it's me ... uncle Nik!" he said joyously with a smile, an action which wiped the fear from Ava's once fretful face.

"Uncle Nik!" Ava shouted gleefully with eyes lit up like a Christmas tree.

"Nikolai is that really you?" Phillipa asked in ecstatic curiosity, attempting to whip her head around to see him.

Overpowered by curiosity herself, Sandra ceased cutting one of the ropes to witness the reveal. Looking up, she saw Siberian Scientist's kind face glaring up at the once helpless child. Catching her glance, Siberian Scientist's eyes shifted over, connecting with hers, forcing an adoring smile to emerge upon his face. A smile that would be met by a blushful grin of which Sandra attempted to suppress as she quickly redirected her attention back to the rope that bound Phillipa.

"Yes, it's me, Phillipa. How about we get you two out of here," he responded, easing the mother and daughter's anxiety.

Within a matter of seconds, the two-year imprisonment of the Foster family came to an end as Phillipa and Ava stood from their once restrained state. Overwhelmed with joy, little Ava wrapped her arms around Siberian Scientist's waist as Phillipa rushed over to embrace both her daughter and dear friend.

"I missed you guys so much," Siberian Scientist's eyes began shedding tears of joy as a sense of relief overwhelmed his heart.

"Where is Benjamin? Please tell me he is all right?" Phillipa asked as her mind processed the new reality at hand.

"Yes. We will take you to him now." A response that brought life back into the woman's soul, a soul that had been desolate for far too long. "It's over. You are all safe and I promise I will never let anything happen to you again," he added with zeal.

Just feet away, Sandra marveled at the heartwarming reunion. One not of blood, but of pure love for one another. Such a spectacle only reaffirmed the verifiable truth that it is not shared genes nor hereditary traits that define the conception of family. No, it is an incalculable equation consisting of undying loyalty and boundless commitment. An equation that simply cannot be denied and is forged from the pureness of humanity.

Chapter 17
Seeing is Believing

Exiting Father Ephrem's quarters, Nikolai felt the unforgiving sting of reality as he realized it would soon be uninhabited, no longer graced by his dear friend's presence. Noticing Nikolai's sudden display of sadness, Sandra wondered how he could feel anything other than joy after such a tremendous rescue. Disheartened and curious, she placed her hand upon his shoulder.

"What's wrong?" Sandra said softly.

Nikolai paused and his mouth trembled as he attempted verbalize his troubling thoughts.

"The priest who lived in that very room was like a father to me ... to all of us ... and he was taken from us tonight by Inkubus!" Nikolai's eyes though swelling with tears, shifted to that of pure hate by the thought of that vile demon.

"Oh God, I am so sorry Nikolai!" Stepping out in front of him, Sandra wrapped her arms around his neck, overpowered by a desire to console him.

Though surprised, Nikolai dropped his head into her shoulder, closing his eyes as her warmth eased his plagued mind. For a brief moment, all the anger, the heartache, vanquished from their kindred souls. Right there in that musty stone sheathed hallway, fate had twisted in more ways than one.

Pulling back, Nikolai placed his hands upon Sandra's shoulders and looked into her hazel eyes while tightening that of his own.

"He took your father from you ... and now ours," Nikolai said in a tempered tone. "It ends tonight. All of it!"

"For our families," Sandra said in reverence with an austere expression upon her face.

"And for this city," Nikolai added sternly. "I think it's time you see what we do here."

Continuing past Slade's quarters and the storm cellar door, Nikolai and Sandra entered the murky underground passageway.

"Where does this lead to?" Sandra curiously asked.

"You will soon see. But first you must put these on," Nikolai said, handing Sandra his voice modulator and a black ski mask.

Puzzled, Sandra laughed at the seemingly ridiculous gesture.

"You're kidding, right? Why would I need these?" Sandra replied light heartedly, hoping Nikolai was being sarcastic.

"You need to conceal your identity for this next part," Nikolai said with a grin.

"Oh God, you are serious." Sandra grabbed the pea size voice modulator and stuck it underneath her jaw near her vocal cords then slid the ski mask overtop her head.

"I look ridiculous, don't I?" Sandra's now modulated voice asked.

"I don't think you could, even if you tried," Nikolai said with a smirk, causing Sandra to smile.

Pulling a skeleton key from the inside of his trench coat, Nikolai unlocked the door then pulled his mask over his face. The screeching of the metal hinges echoed throughout the passageway as light began to peer into its vastness. An eruption of roaring voices and unrest slammed into Siberian Scientist and Sandra as they stepped through the doorway. A visual of rows of screaming inmates caged in narrow cells sent Sandra's mind spiraling.

How is this possible? How could two men do all of this? Sandra thought, feeling as if she were living out a movie scene.

"Welcome to the Arcane Asylum, home of the city's finest citizens!" Siberian Scientist said animatedly, lifting his arms.

"So, this explains the sudden surge in missing person reports," Sandra said, the disbelief of the situation apparent in her voice. "Wait ... I recognize a lot of these guys," she added as they walked past the first two rows of the cells.

"You should. Many of them have been in and out prison, slipping through the cracks of this city's justice system while backed by the likes of Commissioner Reem and Inkubus," he said in disgust.

"Whoa, what's with the gash down each of their faces, are you torturing them?" Sandra said apprehensively.

"No, it is merely a permanent reminder of who brought them down and why they should never repeat their offenses ever again."

Though impressed with the results of Raydar and Siberian Scientist, Sandra couldn't help but feel disturbed by the conditions of the asylum and the physical harm inflicted upon its prisoners. Such tactics went against everything she swore to defend, hell, the basis of her whole career.

"You know this is wrong, don't you?" Sandra asked earnestly.

Siberian Scientist stopped mid step and turned to look at Sandra. "Is it though? You see, here there is no getting out on account of good behavior, there are no bribes, and money is of no influence. There is only justice," he said with pride.

"And what about a fair trial?" Sandra's skepticism grew the more Siberian Scientist elaborated.

"Their actions were the fair trial, and our eyes the jury."

"Maybe that's how you handle things in Russia, but that's not how our system works," Sandra said sternly, cradling the letter of the law.

"So, the same system that got justice for your father's murder? Or my dear friend lying dead, wrapped in a tarp upstairs? The system that allows a rapist to roam the streets again because he underwent some therapy and behaved in a cozy prison?" Siberian Scientist countered with passion.

Sandra didn't respond … she couldn't. Deep down she knew he was right, otherwise she wouldn't feel as if her relentless efforts to save this city from those who corrupt it have fell upon deaf ears and blind eyes. She wondered if any of it truly made a difference, surely no more than was made tonight from freeing the Foster family.

"We don't want to be the law. We only want to correct its mistakes," Siberian Scientist said.

"I believe you," Sandra replied with a slight smile.

"Come, this is only the tip of the iceberg."

Chapter 18
Beginning and Ending

The screeching noise of the Arcane Asylum's iron manhole sent an elating chill up Dr. Foster's spine. After years of torment, of feeling hell's scorching flames incinerate his soul, liberation was finally upon him. This was the moment, the ray of angelic light that kept him from embracing death's releasing touch. This was the beginning of a new life.

Surfacing from the tunnel was Nikolai, unmasked and unscathed.

"Is it true? Are they really here?" Dr. Foster exclaimed joyously.

"Yes, my brother. They are resting in Father Ephrem's quarters," Nikolai said with a brimming smile as he helped Sandra up from the tunnel's notches. "Let me take you to them."

Shifting her gaze from Nikolai's inviting eyes, her own bulged as if they had seen a ghost, rendering her body frozen in time.

"This one's all yours Raydar," Nikolai chuckled, before he and Dr. Foster stepped down into the manhole to be reunited with their family.

"Is that ... oh my ..." Sandra gasped, the monstrous gargoyle known as Dreadnight a mere ten feet away, face down on an examination table.

"Yes, it's him," Ray cut in, unmasking himself in the process.

"Is he alive?" Sandra asked.

"Very much so," Ray replied with a grin.

"How in the world did you capture that ... that beast?" Sandra's face still ridden in disbelief from the creature's presence as she spoke.

"Capture?" Ray chuckled. "That beast is the heart and soul of this operation," Ray said with pride. "He's the reason we are all here, the reason Dr. Foster and his family are finally free," he added with fervor.

Sandra's face quickly turned from a portrait of disbelief to one of confusion.

"Wait ... what are you talking about," Sandra questioned Ray's statement.

So distracted by the site and story of Dreadnight, Sandra never realized what was right in front of her eyes.

"Hold that thought ... I recognize you. Aren't you a cop?" Sandra asked, perplexed by the ongoing revelations taking place. "And so are you?" she added, noticing Lainey.

"We're the good kind," Ray replied with a smirk.

"It all makes sense now. How you were able to be one step ahead of your prisoners ... how each of them got their mark," Sandra said as she gawked at Dreadnight's claws.

"Trust me, it took a lot more than my badge and his ferocity to bring all of those scumbags down," Raydar said, motioning his hand toward the monitoring station. "I would like you to meet Adam Keen, AKA Mr. Unseen. I have a feeling what he is about to show you will clear things up a bit for you."

Adam stood from his captain's chair approximately ten feet to the left of Sandra then walked over to greet her.

"Nice to finally meet you ma'am," Adam said, reaching out to shake her hand. "Come, let me show you the nerve center of our operation," he added directing her toward the array of monitors, her eyes still glued upon Dreadnight's beastly presence.

Stepping in front of the monitoring station, Sandra's eyes widened yet again in awe at the spectacle before her. From live street cams to private storefront surveillance feeds, Adam had eyes all over the city, eyes that revealed the team's technological capabilities. A few clicks of his computer mouse later, Adam merged four of the monitors into one grand display at the center of the arrangement.

"This is where it all began ... this is why we fight," Ray said, pointing to the display, now demonstrating an electronic depiction of Slade's "Wall of Injustice".

Sandra analyzed the elaborate web of facts and figures, following each of its intertwining strands of collusion. For a moment, the room was silent as Sandra soaked up every little detail laid out before her.

Moments later that silence broke.

"So, this whole time the beast this city has been demonizing ... was the one saving it all along," Sandra said, ashamed by her former judgement of the hero. "But why?" she added, now pondering how someone could risk their life on such a grand scale on behalf of others.

Ray wasn't shy in his response.

Starting with the night of May 23rd, he explained in great detail the origin story of Dreadnight, otherwise known as Slade Allen. From the near fatal encounter with Adam Knight to saving the children's hospital from total devastation, the near thirty-minute awe-inspiring story of a seemingly ordinary man turned celestial vigilante rendered Sandra dazed in a jaw dropping stupor. She felt as if she were living out a dream of biblical proportions. Stomaching the remorse of past convictions, a tear fell from Sandra's eyes as she realized the magnitude of Dreadnight's sacrifice for a city filled with so many underserving souls.

"As you can see, if it weren't for Dreadnight's incorruptible fortitude, Inkubus would have bled this city dry and turned its bones to dust, only to continue his infection upon the rest of this country," Ray said passionately.

Looking back upon the unconscious creature, his back laced in half dried blood, Sandra was now overwhelmed with concern for the hero before her. She couldn't believe that she once feared Dreadnight, yet at that very moment she couldn't wait to express her gratitude to him.

"So, what happened to him? Is he going to be alright?" Sandra asked.

"He was captured by Inkubus just hours ago," Ray said somberly.

"Oh my god!" Sandra gasped.

"But thanks to Dr. Foster's bravery, Inkubus was unable to inflict any of the synapsis serum's evil upon him," Nikolai added unexpectedly, rising from the Asylum manhole, Dr. Foster right behind him.

"I however could not stop the onslaught of super soldiers that beat him to a bloody pulp, sticking him with a damned steel rod," Dr. Foster said angrily. "By some miracle of god, that angelic brute fought them off by the masses before my very eyes," he added, his heart filling with astonishment as his mind relived the event. Astonishment that was shared by the likes of every soul in the room as the team attempted to imagine what Dreadnight endured. "Thank God you three showed up when you did, otherwise he would have surely perished before my eyes," Dr. Foster said with a smile directed toward Nikolai, Ray, and Lainey.

"By the way, how did you know that tank of whatever that was would neutralize Inkubus's super soldiers?" Ray asked Nikolai curiously.

"I didn't," Nikolai said bluntly, triggering Ray and Lainey to chuckle in amazement. "I knew that desflurane atropine was a powerful anesthetic compound in relation to an average human being, but I had no idea if it would have any effect upon someone who was fully converted by the effects of the synapsis serum," he added, still shocked by the results of his impulse action.

"That's the ironic bit," Dr. Foster chimed in. "As smart and calculated as Inkubus is, he never once thought that the very compound that grants him cerebral incursion could be the very thing to paralyze his prized soldiers."

"Oh, the irony!" Nikolai laughed as the remainder of the team stood by and attempted to decipher the scientific banter taking place.

"Then that chemical is all that we need to take down those monsters?" Sandra asked in misguided innocence.

"If only it were that simple," Nikolai responded. "Take Dante Jones for instance," he added, pointing back at the digitized "Wall of Injustice".

"You actually brought down Dante Jones?" Sandra said in amazement, as she analyzed the information blocks and pathways dedicated to him.

"Indeed," Ray replied.

"I have been trying for years to bring that bastard down, only to be blocked by the city's chief judge," Sandra said in frustration.

"No surprise there. Judge Compton is as crooked as they come. You should see the police reports that he blatantly ignores or alters," Lainey chimed in.

"You see that red X in the corner of that block there?" Ray said, pointing at the showdown between Dreadnight and Jones.

"Yeah," Sandra replied with intrigue.

"That indicates he was one of Inkubus's super soldiers," Ray stated.

"In other words, he had to be put down," Nikolai added coldly.

"Had to be?" Sandra asked in disgusted skepticism.

"In fact, yes." Dr. Foster spoke up. "If a subject's brainwave pulsations reach a constant level of at least eighty plus pulses per second, they are at a point of no return. Over time, the subject will be rendered into a catatonic state while the pericytes in their brain rot into nothingness, eventually leading to a complete loss of cerebral blood flow," Dr. Foster elaborated as Sandra, Lainey, Raydar, and Mr. Unseen stood by in utter amazement at his genius. "In other words, they are greeted by an inevitable death."

Sandra was speechless, as if the information previously revealed wasn't enough to wrap her head around, this was surely one for the books. But then again, she did have to kill two of Inkubus's soldiers less than an hour ago, a fact that surely put things into perspective.

"So, there's no cure?" Sandra asked.

"Not for those whose brainwaves have exceeded the rate of eighty pulses per second," Dr. Foster stated solemnly.

"But … for all others there will be," Nikolai countered to Dr. Foster and Sandra's surprise.

"Are you saying you have formulated a cure ... but how?" Dr. Foster said in excited disbelief.

"Yes. But in order to complete the vaccine, I need stem cells belonging to none other than Inkubus himself," Nikolai replied.

"Well, what are we waiting for, let's go take them," a deep and unexpected voice declared.

Taken by surprise, the team turned to an awakened Dreadnight lifting himself up off the table in a groan of pain.

"Man is it good to see you upright again," Ray said in relief as the team gathered around their wounded friend.

Standing with his hand clutching his lower back, Dreadnight grunted in anger as he looked to his right and saw the tarp covering Father Ephrem's body.

"He burned his family alive." Dreadnight growled in disgust.

"Who?" Nikolai asked, his face bewildered by the statement.

"Inkubus. He was just a kid," Dreadnight began to elaborate. "That's how he inherited his wealth ... his influence, and he doesn't even feel the slightest bit of remorse," he added, still shaken by the matter.

The team was speechless, just when they thought their perception of humanity couldn't get more dismal, a story as such arose from the depths of this hellish earth. Unexpectedly, Adam turned away from the group and rushed back over to monitoring station.

"Adam, what is it?" Nikolai asked in confusion.

"This is what we have been waiting for!" Adam said in excitement as he furiously typed away.

"What is?" Raydar replied.

"We finally know something about Inkubus! Something that we can use!" Adam explained.

"My God! You're right," Dreadnight said, his head still buzzing from the sedative.

"I'm running a search module in the public records database as well as the precinct's core server for all deaths resulting from a fire. Once that is complete, we can narrow the results to any involving children that survived," Adam detailed while putting his computer expertise on display, a spectacle that drew the entire team back to the monitoring station.

As Sandra watched the computer algorithm sift through thousands of records, the wheels in her own mind began spinning. Something about that story was familiar, but she couldn't quite pinpoint it. With the room's atmosphere filled with anticipation, the search had finally completed, leaving a list of a few hundred names upon the main monitor. Modifying the existing algorithm, Adam integrated a keyword function to identify cases involving a child. Initiating the search once again, the information upon the screen shifted as words were whipped to and from the screen in a storm of data transference.

Ping!

Silence consumed the observatory. It was finally time. Time to find out if that one fragment of that vile monster's past could unmask him once and for all.

Narrowed down to a mere thirty names, every set of eyes in the room scrupulously analyzed each name before them. However, not one name seemed to strike a chord with any of the team members. That is until Sandra's eyes made it toward the bottom of the list.

"Oh my God!" Sandra gasped, breaking the mind-numbing silence.

Flooded with curiosity, the team twisted their heads in her direction.

"It was right in front of me the entire time," Sandra said with astonishment.

"What was? What is it?" Several of the team members blurted, the room now filled to the brim with anticipation.

"Wayne and Linda Potts," Sandra said, her words still dripping with shock as she blankly stared at the monitoring station.

The minds of the team reeled a million miles an hour as they attempted discern the significance of those names. Like a flash of lighting, the mystery that was Inkubus's identity was no more.

"Norman Potts ... AKA the Mayor of Detroit!" Dreadnight growled.

It all made sense, almost too much sense. The influence, the funds, the boundless connections ... the answer they were looking for was so obvious yet so intangibly obscure that the team never considered it.

"Son of a bitch ..." Ray uttered as he rehashed the numerous encounters he had with Mayor Potts over the course of the past few years, a feeling and mental state that Lainey shared as well.

Turning to his technology as he always did, Adam pulled up a full screen image of Mayor Norman Potts for all to see. The man's cue ball head and maniacal grin were unparalleled yet incredibly fitting for that of a criminal mastermind.

"That story sounded familiar, but I couldn't quite put my finger on it, that is until I saw that last name," Sandra began to explain. "I now remember Potts' inaugural speech where he spoke of the "tragic" loss of his parents to an arson attack and how it molded him into a man that would dedicate his life to making this city safe and prosperous," she added sneeringly.

"And as always, I'm guessing the people just ate that line of bullshit up and followed him blindly into hell. Just like most of this world has with its egotistical leaders," Nikolai said, shaking his head in disgust.

"Yes. Except this tyrant can no longer hide behind his fortress of lies and deceit. This tyrant will face a most certain doom, one that will be less than forgiving," Dreadnight snarled. "It's time we go hunting, boys!" he roared with blood thirsty eyes, bolstering a storm of exuberant support as Nikolai, Ray, and Adam jolted with pumped fists and turbulent cheers.

Keeping her composure, despite her own restlessness to bring Inkubus to justice, Sandra contemplated where they would even start.

"I don't mean to rain on your parade, but do we even have any idea where Inkubus might be?" Sandra asked, interrupting their surge of motivation.

"Well, I know he went underground and I'm assuming that is where he plans to stay," Dreadnight said.

"Like literally underground?" Sandra further asked.

"Yes, he took an elevator down at least fifty feet before he triggered a failsafe that filled the elevator shaft with rubble," Dreadnight clarified with a most serious expression upon his face.

"Hmm, well that takes the sewer system and any type of maintenance tunnel out of the equation," Ray added, pondering where that elevator could have led to.

Instantly turning to his computer, Adam pulled up the Central Station blueprints as well as the latest land survey for the surrounding areas. No dice. Neither route provided any suitable options or pathways.

"Wait, isn't a large portion of this city sitting on a massive salt mine?" Lainey asked with a crunched face of reverie.

The eyes of every team member grew upon the riveting question.

"Holy shit! You're right …" Ray shouted excitedly. "There are miles and miles of tunnels that run underneath the entire city," he added.

Before Ray even finished his statement, Adam had already pulled up an article discussing the sale of the Detroit Salt Company, scrupulously reading through its text.

"It says here that the Detroit Public Works Department purchased the land back in 2013," Adam announced.

"In other words, the city government. Which we now know is under the full control of Inkubus," Sandra added with a scornful tone.

"So, the question becomes, how do we get access to one of these tunnels?" Dreadnight pondered aloud, triggering Adam to check public records for any blueprints or land surveys relating to the Detroit Salt Company or any salt mining operations in general.

"Looks like any record relating to the layout of those mines has been wiped. No surprise there," Adam said sarcastically. "The main points of entry would most likely reside in River Rouge where the mines were started. I'm certain all other entry points are well hidden or securely closed off," he added.

"Knowing Inkubus, those main entry points are either heavily guarded or rigged to explode," Nikolai said.

"Agreed, we need to find another way down there. One he wouldn't suspect us to find," Dreadnight said, his pain still apparent in his words.

Stumped by the current predicament, the team racked their brains for any rational solution that could grant them access to the tunnel system. However, nothing was coming to mind, even for the heroes that were native to Detroit.

"It's a damn shame your city never built a subway system like me and Nikolai have back home. Could easily be used to smuggle drugs and such to an obscure location like a salt mine," Dr. Foster proclaimed with a hint of sarcasm.

"Yeah, if only it were that simple," Ray added.

"Actually, it might just be that simple," Lainey said unexpectedly, deep in thought as she stared at the floor.

The team turned their heads toward Lainey, thrown off by her statement.

"Wait, what do you mean," Ray interjected, beating the rest of the team to the obvious punch.

"Detroit did start a subway project back in the 1920's, even dug out a few of the initial tunnels. However, the mayor nixed the project from rumored pressure placed upon him by the owner of the Central Station," Lainey explained.

"Inkubus's great grandfather," Dreadnight said, causing the team to look at him with curious faces. "He revealed to me that his great grandfather once ran the Central Station, along with the rest of this city for that matter," he added.

"Well, that explains a lot," Sandra said. "Any idea where these subway tunnels were?"

"One of them yes. Over on Zug Island, where Detroit Steel Corporation used to be located. The main function of the subway was going to be to shuttle workers to and from the steel mill, salt mines, and the Ford plant," Lainey explained.

"Well, aren't you just a fountain of knowledge," Dr. Foster exclaimed, impressed by her historical know how, a feeling shared by all in the room.

"Both my father and grandfather worked at that steel mill for decades and they always had a story to tell regarding its history," Lainey said, smiling from the memories of her family.

"Ha, what do you know, the Detroit Steel Corporation and all of its land was sold to the Detroit Public Works Department for agricultural research," Adam said with a chuckle filled with irony.

"What are we waiting for? Let's get over to Zug Island and hunt us a demon!" Dreadnight roared, energizing all but one team member.

"You really should wait until that wound has had more time to heal. Not to mention there is no possible way you could hunt Inkubus down and be back before sunrise," Dr. Foster said in genuine concern for Dreadnight's wellbeing.

"I have waited long enough. All that matters is that we capture him. If I don't make it back and my future is that of stone, then so be it," Dreadnight proclaimed with pride.

"But the wound …" Dr. Foster began to say.

"I have survived worse. Not to mention it's already starting to feel better," Dreadnight explained, more than intriguing Dr. Foster who just pulled a steel rebar from his flesh moments ago.

Regardless of Dreadnight's confidence, Dr. Foster walked over to him and peeled back the dressing he had adhered over top the sealed wound to prevent infection.

"What in the bloody hell!?" Dr. Foster shouted, his eyes as wide as the ocean.

"What's wrong?" Dreadnight asked sharply, overwhelmed with a sudden surge of fear.

"That's the crazy thing, nothing is wrong. The wound has already scarred over … but how?" Dr. Foster said in awe, awe that spread across the faces of the rest of the team, even Dreadnight himself.

"Whatever Michael's essence did to me must have amped up my healing ability," Dreadnight said.

"Yeah, you ain't kidding bud." Ray laughed.

"See, I told you, I'm good to go." Dreadnight smirked. "Raydar and Siberian Scientist, it's time we end this once and for all. Let's load up the truck with all the fire power we got and ship out."

"I'm coming too!" Sandra blurted sternly.

"No. I can't risk you dying. You are the only one who can bring the law down upon Inkubus and his organization," Dreadnight said. "Dr. Foster before you say anything, because I know you were going to, please stay here alongside Lainey and help Adam. You have already risked your life enough on account of our mission. It's time you and your family remain safe and hidden," he added earnestly.

Though it was a statement that neither Sandra nor Dr. Foster liked to hear, they both knew he was right. It had finally come to the point where they both needed to think ahead to the future instead of solely focusing on the present while throwing caution to the wind.

Already rummaging through their weapons closet, Ray and Nikolai grabbed an assortment of weapons, ranging from their handguns to knives and even grenades. As Ray wrapped his utility belt around his waist, he felt an unexpected hand upon his shoulder. When he turned, he was greeted by the gentle face of Lainey, her eyes glossed over.

"What's wrong Lainey?" Ray said softly as her hand grazed down his shoulder until grasping onto that of his own.

"Nothing … I just … I can't believe that we finally have the chance to be together and you have to run off risking your life for this city," Lainey replied with sadness.

"As long as you are in this city, I will never stop protecting it," Ray said with a smile of confidence, forcing a smile upon the young woman's face.

"You better come back to me Ray Fisher. I can't imagine ever being without the one I love. Not now, not ever," she said before wrapping her arms around Ray and hugging him.

As Ray embraced that very moment in her arms, his heart fluttered in bliss as his mind realized the implication that the girl of his dreams just made.

"Did you just say what I think you just said?" Ray replied innocently as they stared into one another's eyes.

"Yes, and you better not forget it when you're out there bringing that monster down," Lainey replied sternly with a grin.

"I love you too Lainey, always have," Ray said softly, holding back tears of joy as he leaned in to kiss her.

Back at the monitoring station, Dreadnight exchanged hugs with Dr. Foster and Adam, hoping he would soon see them again. Turning to his right, he grinned as he made eye contact with a seemingly contemplative Sandra Daley.

"Thank you for showing up tonight Ms. Daley. I hope this means you will be joining our little team going forward," Dreadnight said.

"I am the one that should be thanking you. If it weren't for you, this city would have never had the chance to fight back and all the sacrifices my family has made to bring justice upon Inkubus's organization would have been for nothing," Sandra said earnestly.

"Well don't thank me quite yet. And can I consider that a yes pertaining to becoming a team member?" Dreadnight said with a chuckle.

"Of course ... friend." Sandra reached out and shook Dreadnight's monstrous hand, a hand that was over twice the size of hers. Both Dreadnight and Sandra knew that this newfound friendship would be of great importance in the future to come as if they were destined to join forces all along.

With the truck now packed with enough fire power to wipe out a small country, the now seven-member team said their hopefully temporary farewells as they prepared to split off once again. The atmosphere of the observatory was that of angst and anticipation. Tears were plenty, yet so were hearts full of hope and love. The upcoming hours would not only determine the future of these seven significant beings, but that of the entire city and quite possibly the world if Inkubus were to continue his reign of terror upon the minds of the shameless. That is, considering there was a future to be had.

As the hopeful souls released one another from warm hugs and sturdy handshakes, a boisterous alarm coming from the monitoring station seized the entire team's attention.

"You guys better get moving. Time is of the essence ... now more than ever," Adam stated aloud.

The alarm was no mystery, it was their warning that there were only three hours till sunrise, a most likely timeframe until Dreadnight was as much flesh and bone as the Effigiem Custos itself.

Roaring from its ignition, the Celestial Shipping truck's engine was preparing for its journey to Zug Island as the Observatory's industrial door slid upward. Like a spark in the wind, both the Celestial Shipping truck and Dreadnight vanished from the Observatory, slipping back out into the cruel world they knew all too well.

~

Speeding down the tattered Detroit highway, Raydar clutched the steering wheel as he and Siberian Scientist sat in anticipative silence, each of their minds dreaming of what could be. For Raydar, a life with Lainey free of restriction yet full of unbridled potential. One where their roots become one and he starts the family he had always yearned for.

For Siberian Scientist, life as it once was where Dr. Foster's family regains everything they had lost and he can personally ensure it stays that way. A life where he lets his guard down and opens his heart to another once again … maybe even to Sandra. Baffled by a mere two hours of interaction, Siberian Scientist could not help but be enamored by Sandra. Not by the likes of her beauty alone, but also by her fortitude and moral ambitions. For a man with such strong and immovable ideals, this was surely a rare yet comforting occurrence.

Meanwhile, flying over one hundred feet above, Dreadnight's mind was in a trance of its own. Though riddled with flashes of a reality without Father Ephrem, he couldn't help but think of Rachel, of the day where he finally sees her face again … a day where he gets to tell her who he really is.

Could that day be just around the corner?

Though all three men wore tough exteriors and held vigilant aspirations, not one of them could imagine a life without love. A coincidence that begs the question, is there a purpose to life without love? Apparently not for these three heroes.

"Alright guys. You are going to want to turn left onto Springwell Court and drive until you approach the only standing bridge on the left," Mr. Unseen said over the comm link as he monitored the GPS.

"Copy that Unseen," Raydar acknowledged.

"Looks like there are some wooden barricades along with some water barrels blocking the pavement halfway down the bridge. You think that truck can handle a little front-end adversity?" Mr. Unseen said with a hint of sarcasm.

"Oh, don't worry, my baby's got this!" Raydar said with a chuckle, tossing a grin upon Siberian Scientist once sullen face.

Raydar turned the truck onto Springwell Court, he and Siberian Scientist's adrenaline levels spiking as they prepared for some fun. Bending the curve that followed along the Detroit River, they passed numerous abandoned factories and patches of dead grass. Just another reminder of the city's current state, as if they needed more.

Now in the final quarter mile stretch of road, Raydar increased the pressure upon the gas pedal, steadily pushing the truck's speedometer meter further to the right. With the bridge and the road's end approaching quickly, Raydar veered the truck toward the right shoulder of the lane.

"Here we go!" Raydar shouted until finally whipping the steering wheel back sharply to the left, turning the truck at the fastest speed possible onto the entrance of the bridge without tipping it, inciting he and Siberian Scientist to yell excitedly.

Their bodies rattled back and forth until the truck stabilized into a straight assault toward the oncoming roadblock. Raydar slammed the gas pedal, throwing both he and Siberian Scientist back against their seats.

Thirty feet … twenty feet … ten feet.

Raydar and Siberian Scientist braced for impact, their jaws clenched, and muscles tightened.

Like a missile, the reinforced front end of the truck shattered the wooden barricades into splinters as water shot into the air. Barely losing momentum, the truck ripped across the bridge's midway point, its frame and passengers remaining unscathed.

"Hell yeah! That's what I'm talking about!" Raydar shouted, flooded with adrenaline.

"Wooooh!" Siberian Scientist yelled, enjoying every second of the impact.

Sharing their excitement, Mr. Unseen nearly jumped from his chair and Dr. Foster pumped his fist into the air as they watched the event from Dreadnight's "Eyes of Divinity".

"Ha yes!" Mr. Unseen blurted. "Now, once you have crossed the bridge, the tunnel will be one hundred and ten yards ahead and on your right. Based on the latest satellite images, it is covertly sealed by presumably a lift gate of some sort. It may take some force to open it from the outside," Mr. Unseen explained, analyzing the imagery.

"No worries, I'm feeling extra strong tonight," Dreadnight chuckled as he began his descent toward level ground.

As the truck came to a halt before the specified location, Dreadnight's enormous and sprawling wingspan consumed the moon's presence, its glow adorning his outline as he drifted toward his teammates. Landing in a steady trot, Dreadnight threw his wings behind his back, folding and relaxing them.

"What should we do now?" Dreadnight asked Mr. Unseen through the comm link.

"Based on my calculations, if you take ten steps to your right you should be literally standing on top of whatever is concealing the entrance," Mr. Unseen replied.

Dreadnight stepped to his right, counting each step as he went.

Three ... two ... one, he counted in his head, before kneeling onto the ground.

"What are you thinking?" Siberian Scientist asked Dreadnight, curious to what he was doing.

"I'm thinking it's time I see what underneath here," Dreadnight responded, leaving the team perplexed as to how he planned to do so.

Before any of them could ask, Dreadnight's right elbow shot into the air and within an instant his fist surged down, slicing through the earth as if it were nothing.

Thud!

Dreadnight's fist slammed into a solid structure, his forearm now halfway into the dirt.

"Bloody hell!" Dr. Foster gasped, unknowing of the extent of Dreadnight's abilities.

"Found it." Dreadnight grunted, the rest of the team still awe-struck what he just did.

"Uh ... yeah you did." Raydar chuckled with wide eyes.

Keeping his arm down into the ground, Dreadnight pulled his arm toward Raydar and Siberian Scientist while dragging his claws along the seemingly steel structure, in hope of finding its edge. He stepped sideways as his arm tore through the grass and dirt for several feet, that is until his claws finally felt the softness of the earth again. Turning his body around so that he was facing the structure's edge, Dreadnight lifted his left arm and swiftly thrust that fist down into the ground to match the other. The jaws of his team members remained on the floor as they continued to be blown away by his strength.

Twisting his hands around, Dreadnight wrapped his palms around the lip of the steel then squatted down and lifted his chest. It was apparent to all exactly what he was about to do, despite how impossible it seemed.

With a deafening and stomach-churning grunt, Dreadnight jolted his body upward, causing every muscle and vein in his body to bulge as he fought the structure's resistance. His legs shaking, he pulled with all his might, only intensifying his strain filled grunt as the ground beneath him slowly peeled apart like sod. As this phenomenon occurred, the ratcheting sound of a linked pulley system arose.

"Oh my God! It's working, he's really doing it!" Mr. Unseen shouted.

Rushing to help their brother, Raydar and Siberian Scientist ran to Dreadnight's side, both grabbing onto the structure's edge, mustering whatever strength they could as they pulled. Within seconds the now exposed liftgate was angled above Dreadnight's waist and rising at an increasing rate. The screams of the three men filled the comm link as the team members back at the observatory watched with diminished breaths.

The liftgate now level with his chest, Dreadnight flipped the positioning of his hands around, pronating them. With the strength of twenty men, he heaved the liftgate above his head with such force that it shot from his hands, rocketing upward until its chain crashed against the peak of the system's vertical track, locking into place.

With exhales of relief and exhaustion, Dreadnight, Raydar, and Siberian Scientist were standing before a paved ramp leading down into a seemingly endless black hole. One large enough to drive a semi-truck through. Angled above was the lift gate, nearly twenty feet long, ten feet wide, and composed entirely of concrete lined with reinforced steel beams.

"Well, I guess we now know where all of Inkubus's contraband has been hidden this entire time," Siberian Scientist said sarcastically.

"Yeeeahhh. Who knows what we are going to see down there," Raydar added.

"Let's find out boys," Dreadnight grumbled as he firmly closed his eyes, activating his night vision.

With eyes full of ambition, Ray and Siberian Scientist nodded in agreement before turning and heading back to the Celestial Shipping truck. Just shy of reaching the driver side door, Raydar stopped and pulled a small object from his utility belt before turning back around and taking a few steps toward Dreadnight.

"Slade," Raydar announced as Dreadnight stared down the tunnel.

"Yeah brother?"

Raydar tossed the object into the air toward him.

"I have a feeling you will want that for this next part," Raydar said with a smirk.

Looking down at his hand, Dreadnight's face loosened, and his heart skipped a beat as he felt a surge of tranquility flow through his body from the sight of Rachel's charm.

"You know me too well man. Thank you," Dreadnight graciously replied as he clasped the charm around his neck. "Now I'm ready," he added with a smirk.

Seconds later, the truck's headlights cascaded light upon their beastly ally as he walked toward them, creating a chilling silhouette that only Dreadnight's form could conceive.

WHOOSH!

In a nimble yet mighty leap, Dreadnight sailed overtop the truck's cabin.

THUMP!

His monstrous feet landed atop the cargo pod. Both Raydar and Siberian Scientist smiled as the truck's engine turned over.

Rolling forward, the truck approached the breach in the ground. Turning to the right, the squad was now aligned with the entrance. Crossing the breakpoint from dirt to concrete, Dreadnight dropped into a plank atop the cargo pod, the skin of his wings just grazing the cold steel of the liftgate. Sloping downward upon the ramp, a concrete corridor running at least fifty yards long before leveling off was revealed. Presumably, this must have been intended to be the escalator ramp to the railway.

His hearing on high alert as he hugged the cargo pod, Dreadnight heard voices arise amongst the echoing roar of the truck's engine.

"Sir, there has been a breach on Zug Island and a vehicle is approaching!" shouted an unseen merc.

Dreadnight honed in on the voice, blocking out all other sounds. Within a second's time he faintly heard an explicit response.

"I don't care what you have to do! Blow it to fucking hell!" screamed a raging Inkubus through a comm link.

"Yes sir!" the merc obediently replied, showing no fear in his voice.

Before Dreadnight could even notify his team, he heard the racking of four semi-automatic rifles.

"Alright boys. It appears we have four mercs with semi-autos at the bottom of the ramp and there isn't an ounce of humanity left in them," Dreadnight said into the comm with joyous anticipation apparent in his tone. "Time to spill some blood!" he added, the truck now a mere five yards from exiting the corridor.

"I'll take the two on the right, Raydar you level the two on the left," Dreadnight directed.

"My pleasure, brother!" Raydar acknowledged eagerly as he slammed his foot down onto the truck's accelerator causing the engine to roar.

The front end of the truck violently scraped against the connecting concrete, sending sparks flying and rendering the vehicle parallel as the team was greeted by four tactical lights and a slew of bullets. Bullets which ricocheted off the armored exterior in a clanking fury. Thirty yards ahead and standing on opposing sides of the subway platform, the truck's headlights revealed four mercs, beside them a rail trench lined with spikes. Cloaked in darkness and ready to pounce, Dreadnight pushed his body up into a crouched position, calculating the right moment when to strike.

Just as Raydar aggressively whipped the vehicle to the left, Dreadnight leaped to the right with claws thirsting for flesh, his targets fifteen yards ahead and standing only five feet apart. Like a scene from a horror film, Dreadnight's gnarling teeth and vengeful eyes were a split-second sneak peek of their doomed fate amongst the muzzle flash of their rifles. Before they two men could take another breath, they each felt the choking grip of a monstrous hand around their throats as they were lifted off the ground into a blind flight of ambivalence. Sailing downward into the ten-foot-deep trench, Dreadnight's grip did not falter. That is until the bodies of the two mercs were impaled by a multitude of rail spikes, each driving through the entirety of their flesh, forcing blood to spit from the newly formed orifices as well as their mouths.

Using his arms as stabilizers, he landed on his feet in a prowling stance overtop the withering degenerates.

"You can take this train straight to hell!" Dreadnight growled as he released his grip upon their now collapsed throats.

THUD!

The grill of the truck pulverized one of the two remaining mercs, killing him on contact before his skull was cracked open like a walnut by its oversized wheels.

Raydar swung the driver side door free, reinforcing it with his arm as it slammed into the second merc, sending him rolling off the platform's edge and down into the rail trench, just missing its spikes. The rubber of the truck's tires screamed as Raydar slammed upon its brakes, bringing it to a screeching halt. His AK74M already gripped firmly in his right hand, Raydar leaped out of the vehicle and swiftly located the fallen merc with his tactical light.

Before the merc could aim his rifle, he was greeted by the piercing sting of four lethal bullets to the chest. Standing at the platform's edge was Raydar, his mask's fierce gaze striking down upon the merc. But that triumphant moment was short lived as a string of foreign bullets clanked against that very door, forcing Raydar to dive behind it for cover.

Following his protective instincts, Siberian Scientist whipped open his door, slid down behind it, curled his assault rifle around its edge, and released heavy cover fire to thwart the assault upon his comrade.

Alarmed by the unsuspected gunfire, Dreadnight leaped into the air, landing square in the middle of the subway platform, sending cracks through the cement surrounding his inhuman feet.

Quickly realizing the beast's presence, two tactical lights at least thirty yards ahead on opposing sides shifted onto Dreadnight's darkened skin. Naturally, Dreadnight flung his wings open like a mythical dragon, before wrapping them out in front of his body and turning them to stone. Walking forward without a sliver of fear, an onslaught of bullets clanged off Dreadnight's stone shields as if he were leading an army into hellfire. However, that walk quickly increased in gait, and within a few strides, a full out sprint. Using his enhanced hearing ability, he gauged his enemies' proximity, as they continued to wastefully empty their clips.

Twenty yards ... ten yards... *WHOOSH!*

Dreadnight's wings were transformed back into flesh as he thrusted them back with all his might. In a flash, the bodies of the two mercs sailed across the rail trenches, slamming into opposing walls like pinballs and leaving human shaped craters behind as they crashed to the ground. Knowing that the impact alone wasn't enough to kill the merc, Dreadnight leaped back down into the right-side trench, landing just steps away from the now disoriented man who was attempting to stand.

But Dreadnight's left hand gripped the hair upon the man's head before he had a chance to lift his rifle. Leaning down, the very beast the merc vouched to kill drew its right arm back then jolted it forward like a trident, sending five claws straight into the soulless man's heart. A heart, that was nothing more than an automated machine fueled by deceit.

Both rolling around the truck doors, Raydar and Siberian Scientist focused their tactical lights on the left side trench.

"Got em" Raydar blurted as the merc's military jacket popped up in his lighted sight.

Tracking side by side, Raydar and Siberian Scientist relentlessly tapped their AK74m triggers, unleashing strings of hell upon the now lone merc, quickly knocking him back down onto the ground in a bloody backpedal.

"Clear," Raydar loudly said, realizing their targets had been eliminated.

Back at the observatory, Mr. Unseen, Dr. Foster, Lainey, and Sandra watched the projected live feed with heart racing angst, each wishing they could be there to fight alongside their teammates. Witnessing Dreadnight's ferocity for the first time, Sandra was so enthralled by his inhuman abilities that one could have sworn her eyes didn't blink once throughout the entire subway slaughter. She could now fully grasp the fact she was truly in the presence of a celestial being. A being unlike anything that had ever graced God's green earth.

Three hundred yards and twelve slain mercs later, the Celestial shipping truck came to a rolling stop before what seemed to be a large dimly lit industrial elevator shaft planted dead center in the platform. On both sides of the platform, the trenches came to an abrupt halt, where two rigid walls of dirt and rock presided, ending the abandoned subway's path. Raydar and Siberian Scientist hopped out of the truck and walked up beside their leader, standing just before the elevator's mesh gate.

"Well I guess this is it, huh? Our chariot into the demon's lair," Siberian Scientist said half-jokingly.

But no one laughed. The three heroes just stood in silence, each knowing that their defining moment was upon them. A silence that was soon interrupted.

"Guys, if you descend any further, the link between your comms and the observatory network will be severed. In other words, you'll be on your own," Mr. Unseen said solemnly.

The stomach of every team member churned as the severity of the moment sank in.

"Understood, until next time my friends," Dreadnight said softly.

"Godspeed brothers," Mr. Unseen responded, his face stricken cold as he realized those could very well be the last words he every says to them.

The last sounds the observatory heard were the screech of a metal gate sliding open and the ratchet of a chain link. Then, like the snap of a finger, everything went silent and their visual flatlined into darkness.

Standing in a ten-foot by ten-foot cage of steel, the bodies of the three heroes were motionless yet their hearts we nearly beating out of their chests as they slowly became surrounded by the earth's mantle. The ride down into the unknown seemed endless as they travelled hundreds of feet toward the earth's core. Looking upward, the men watched as the faint light emanating from the subway tunnel faded into a mere speckle, a faint reminder of the world they could be leaving.

The subtle sound of an exhale or the rattle of ammunition was to be expected during such an austere moment as they stood shoulder to shoulder awaiting certain danger, but not the sound that popped up out of nowhere. The eyebrows of both Dreadnight and Siberian Scientist peaked as they turned their heads. Playing it cool with a smirk was Raydar, humming a peculiar tune.

"Really man?" Dreadnight chuckled.

"What? It just didn't feel right without the elevator music," Raydar said sarcastically, about to burst out laughing.

"I'm over here getting ready to light some bitches up and you go and do that?" Siberian Scientist said, trying as hard as he could to keep his voice from wavering.

The team lost it. Such a statement being delivered with a thick Russian accent set off a chain reaction of laughter that had them reeling. As amusing as the scene was, nothing compared to the sight of a monstrous gargoyle leaning back as it laughed its ass off.

"Oh, you funny Russian bastard, you!" Raydar howled, slapping his hand on Siberian Scientist's shoulder, who was now in tears from Dreadnight's uncharacteristic reaction. No one would have guessed that a day filled with tragedy and pain would lead to such a heartwarming moment of brotherhood.

Unfortunately, that moment was short lived as they felt a gravitational shift from the platform abruptly decreasing its rate of descent. The laughter ceased and Dreadnight focused his hearing. Raydar and Siberian Scientist gripped onto their rifles, anticipating warfare.

"Just heard the racking of at least fifteen rifles. They know we are coming," Dreadnight said sternly, his face back to its resting rageful state everyone was so accustomed to.

Light began to peer into the cage from a sudden opening at their feet like an eclipse, dropping their hearts into their stomachs.

"Get behind me now!" Dreadnight shouted as he turned to face the rear of the cage.

WHOOSH!

Dreadnight's wings consumed the cage as they separated his teammates from the ever-growing light that encroached upon them. Raydar and Siberian Scientist heard a crackling noise transpire, then right before their very eyes they witnessed the flesh of Dreadnight's wings harden into stone in a breathtaking display of celestial glory.

Before the gate had even unlatched, a storm of bullets bombarded the cage and all that surrounded it, relentlessly clanking off the steel mesh and Dreadnight's stone wings.

"This shit is getting real old!" Dreadnight growled in annoyance, looking at both Raydar and Siberian Scientist who were nervously hunched underneath his wings.

The gate automatically slid into the side wall, leaving nothing between the opponents. The storm didn't relent as the mercs continued to empty their mags into Dreadnight's impenetrable appendages, continuing to deflect their wrath.

One after another, the mercs ran out of ammo, only to change their mags while the others continued their assault, leaving Dreadnight no window of opportunity to counter-react.

"They probably have endless ammo … down here," Dreadnight groaned as a bullet snuck in between the crack of his wings, sticking the back of his left leg. "Grrrr! How do you guys propose we proceed? We need to act fast before they realize they need to move onto bigger weapons," he added sharply, growing more impatient by the bullet.

"Umm … shit!" Siberian Scientist ducked nervously as a ricocheting bullet sliced into the wall just above him, spitting dirt onto his mask. "I have had enough of this! Can you do a one eighty and walk out of this box of bullets without taking any damage?" he added with a tongue of rage.

"I think so. What did you have in mind?" Dreadnight replied with unbelievable calmness as he continued to be a not so human shield.

"Using your back as cover while you walk forward, me and Raydar can slowly inch around your wings, taking mercs out one by one as they enter our crosshairs."

"I'm down. I just want to get the hell out of here!" Raydar added pressingly, yet somehow exhibiting a hint of wit despite the circumstances.

"I like it! Let's do this!" Dreadnight snarled with widened eyes.

In one swift yet sleek motion, Dreadnight rolled his body into his left wing of stone while relieving the other and folding it behind him like an accordion. Continuing to rotate while shielded by his left wing, Dreadnight unfurled his thawed wing, striking it forward like a sword now that his teammates were tucked safely behind his back. The not-so-subtle crackling noise returned as that wing was returned to stone once again. Dreadnight was now facing the clan of masked mercs, his hardened wings curled out in front of him.

Bullets continued to ricochet off in every direction as Dreadnight blindly stepped forward in a slow but steady pace, his enhanced hearing his only guide.

Before Dreadnight could even take a second step, both Raydar and Siberian Scientist had peaked around the curvature of Dreadnight's wings, their AK74m rifles pressed into their shoulders as their trigger fingers trembled with anticipation. As if it were perfectly choreographed, two strings of encapsulated lead were shot from behind Dreadnight's wings, both connecting with the most outward located merc on both sides of the mine shaft.

Chest shots! The two mercs crashed to the ground as their blood shot into the air.

Two down!

Raydar and Siberian Scientist simultaneously inched further around Dreadnight's wings while swiveling their rifles. Releasing another three bullets each, the duo dropped another pair of mercs with lethal shots to the neck and head. With each step Dreadnight took, mercs continued to fall to their demise by the hands of Raydar and Siberian Scientist as they curled around the entirety of their comrade's wings.

The salt mine was the stage as the echoes of rifle blasts and dying breaths created chords of justice for a symphony of perpetual carnage.

WHOOSH!

Dreadnight's wings returned to flesh and were folded behind his back as the gunfire ceased. The three heroes stood side by side as they gazed at the bloodied field of bodies just feet away, each feeling great pride in the score they settled.

"Yeah, good plan indeed!" Dreadnight said with a chuckle, compelling his teammates to nod their heads in silent agreeance. "Let's press on," he added, reverting to his usual sternness.

With claws drawn and rifles steadied, the team walked deeper into the alabaster cavern, guided by the occasional industrial light and Dreadnight's inhuman senses. Beneath their feet were large tire tracks, presumably from cargo trucks transporting drugs and weaponry. Approaching side tunnels, Raydar and Siberian Scientist paced to their respective walls, hugging their backs against them as they neared the intersection of the tunnels. Despite not hearing any nearby mercs, Dreadnight decided to use himself as bait to draw out any potential threats in order to keep his teammates free of danger. As soon as his monstrous feet crossed into the intersection, Siberian Scientist signaled Raydar to advance. Like trained spetsnaz, they rolled around the corner and rapidly swiveled their rifles, using their tactical lights to check the area.

"Clear!" "Clear!" Both Raydar and Siberian Scientist announced.

Clear of mercs that is ...

Stacked three tiers high were a myriad of wooden crates, unmarked and untarnished. *Let's see what we have here,* Raydar thought as he walked up to the nearest crate that was at waist height. Flipping his gun around, he pulled it back then thrusted its buttstock into the side of the crate. The gun's high strength plastic splintered the wood and what seemed to be a plastic liner. Before he withdrew the gun, a stream of white powder poured out of the crate and onto the tunnel floor.

"Seems like we found some of their cocaine stash," Raydar said. "Sandra's gonna love this shit!" he added with laughter.

"Take some photos for proof. But do it quickly, we gotta keep moving," Dreadnight said as he kept an eye and ear out for potential threats.

After Raydar snapped a few photos with his phone, the team pressed on, checking four other adjacent tunnels, all riddled with various illicit substances ranging from opioids to crystal meth. It was a drug den like no other known to man, one that could soon be exposed and eliminated once and for all.

Near the end of the tunnel, there appeared to be a second elevator shaft placed in its center. However, the team soon realized that the cable system had been cut, rendering it inoperable.

"Wow, he must be really losing his touch if he thinks a little drop is going to stop me." Dreadnight chuckled.

"He's not able to rig these shafts to blow like the one in the Central Station. He would risk compromising the structural integrity of this entire mine, and all that lies above it for that matter," Siberian Scientist added.

"Did you say a little drop? That's gotta be over one hundred feet, at least!" Raydar said as he pointed his rifle's tactical light down into the seemingly endless shaft, baffled by Dreadnight's casual demeanor. "How do you propose we get down there?" he added with a touch of skepticism.

"By jumping, of course," Dreadnight said with a face of austerity, that was until a smirk appeared upon it.

It was a good thing Raydar was wearing his mask, otherwise his comrades would have seen a face as pale as a ghost. A ghost that looked as if it were going to vomit.

"Uhh ... what!?" Raydar replied shakily, triggering Siberian Scientist to chuckle as he knew full well what Dreadnight had in mind.

"Friends, tonight you get to take a ride on the Dreadnight express! The destination ... revenge!" Dreadnight theatrically said.

"Ahahaha!" Raydar's fear turned into side splitting laughter. Laughter was soon shared by Siberian Scientist and even Dreadnight himself.

"Yeah haha. I know ... as soon as I heard it out loud, I realized how bad it sounded." Dreadnight chuckled, shaking his head in embarrassment.

"All aboard!" Siberian Scientist bellowed, imitating a conductor, adding insult to injury.

"You asshat." Dreadnight chuckled.

Yet again, the team shared unexpected laughter just moments before facing the unknown.

Remembering that time was of the essence, the team grounded themselves as they prepared to take a leap of faith. Dreadnight unfurled his wings, slanting them in an upward angle before kneeling onto the tunnel floor, just inches from the sizable pit before him. He directed both Raydar and Siberian Scientist to wrap their hands around the claw hooks upon the pinnacles of his wings and to leverage themselves by placing their feet upon the main sections. They did just that, rendering both suspended from Dreadnight's wings as if he were a mountain and they were rock climbers.

"Here goes nothing!" Dreadnight said in a winded exhale filled with anticipation.

Dreadnight's feet left the ground as he leaped forward. Before his body crossed the barrier of darkness, he curled the ends of his wings inward to ensure clearance from the shaft's sidewalls. Gravity's initial pull dropped the trio like an anvil as they disappeared from sight. Freefalling, Dreadnight's wings fought the pressing air, acting like parachutes and abating the descent. He firmly closed his eyes, activating his night vision as he bowed his head down, revealing the elevator cage approximately fifty feet away.

"Shit shit shit!" Raydar shouted blindly, awaiting the inevitable impact.

"Wooh! Hell yeah!" a fearless Siberian Scientist hollered, adrenaline coursing through his body.

Like a bat in the night, Dreadnight sailed through the air, until ...
BOOM!

Dreadnight's monstrous feet landed atop the elevator cage floor, leaving his imprints upon its alloy. Crouched with knees bent, dust consumed the air as Dreadnight stabilized his body and his teammates held on for dear life, their bodies tensed beyond belief. Beaming through the veil of dust were small rays of light that grew with each waking moment.

Just as Dreadnight peeled his nictitating membranes back behind his eyes, the landscape before him was revealed. But this time, instead of fifteen semi-automatic outfitted mercs, there was one lone wolf standing approximately twenty-five yards from the elevator ... a rocket launcher pressed into his shoulder no less.

"Behind me now!" Dreadnight roared at the exact moment the rocket propelled projectile peered from the merc's weapon.

Within a millisecond's time, Dreadnight's flesh turned to stone as the missile exploded into his midsection, creating a blazing cloud of fury that poured along his wingspan and against the surrounding walls, just missing Raydar and Siberian Scientist as they cowered behind his back. The shell of mangled steel that remained clanked against the cage floor as smoke replaced the dissipating flames that wrapped around the now stone figure. His eyes still in their humanoid state, Dreadnight realized he and his comrades were clear of danger, triggering him to return to his natural state.

As the smoke cleared, the once confident merc saw the outline of a beastly figure, a figure that was on the move. Reaching down, the merc scrambled for a second rocket as Dreadnight's feet stomped into the ground, picking up speed as he raged toward the merc. Just as the merc completed loading the launcher and looked up to aim, Dreadnight's gnarling teeth were within arm's reach. Like a creature of habit, the merc pulled the trigger in a knee jerk reaction. However, Dreadnight's counter was far too quick. Covering the end of the rocket launcher's barrel was the freakishly large hand of Dreadnight, solidified and bolstered by a matching locked right arm.

"Blast off!" Dreadnight snarled as he stared into the merc's eyes.

A burst of exhaust flames shot from the rear of the launch tube as the rocket was propelled forward. In a flash of uncontainable combustion, the rocket launcher peeled apart as a cloud of destruction filled the air. Standing unfazed and unscathed was Dreadnight, drenched in blood with smoke culminating around him. Relaxing his arm, the stone disappeared as he lowered it back down to his side.

THUD!

A sound of unknown origin arose as the smoke cleared. Dreadnight soon realized it was the bottom half of the merc's body hitting the floor. The missing half was scattered amongst the tunnel, fragmented beyond any recognizable form.

Already alongside their teammate, Raydar and Siberian Scientist stood with their jaws to the floor from the inconceivable sight.

"Holy sh …"

"Shh! Quiet," Dreadnight blurted. Stuck in trance, his head was tilted and eyes fixated upon the floor. "I hear at least ten additional mercs about one hundred fifty yards ahead and to the left. It seems they are planning a poor attempt at an ambush." Dreadnight snickered.

"How should we approach this one?" Siberian Scientist added as the team looked around curiously, each trying to devise a strategy.

"I have an idea, but I am not sure if you're going to like it," Dreadnight said while looking over at a rustic mining cart fifteen yards ahead to their right.

"What is it this time …?" Raydar sarcastically replied.

"I launch you guys down the tracks in that mining cart. When you cross the path of the storage tunnel they are hiding in, they will become distracted and will begin firing. Meanwhile, I will swoop right into them and begin disabling them. Once their attention is on me, you two can rise up and start knocking the mercs down with bullets.

"In other words, we're bait?" An uneasy Raydar said.

"Yes, but bait that will be concealed behind bulletproof steel."

"Good point. Alright, I'm down," Ray replied.

The team walked up to the mining cart and quickly checked its structural integrity. It seemed sufficient to carry out Dreadnight's diversion. Raydar and Siberian Scientist hopped into the cart and situated their rifles, ensuring they were properly loaded and positioned for sudden engagement. All three men looked at each other and confirmed their readiness. It was time.

With a head full of steam and a heart full of rage, Dreadnight took off in an all-out sprint, his right hand gripped onto the rear of the cart as it coasted out in front of him. Picking up speed with each giant stride, the wheels of the cart spun so fast they appeared to have changed direction. In a matter of seconds, Dreadnight had already covered thirty yards of ground and had reached his maximum speed by foot. Drawing back his right arm while maintaining speed, Dreadnight's muscles flexed as his body twisted. With all his might, Dreadnight drove his arm forward and released his grip upon the cart, sending it rocketing forward as the sound of screeching iron filled the airwaves. Maintaining his speed, Dreadnight dove into the air like a spear, releasing his wings before thrashing them with might which sent him soaring ahead.

Only twenty yards separating the heroes, their vessels cruised toward the impending battle with nothing but darkness leading the way.

Sixty yards ... forty yards ...

With distance unknown to Raydar and Siberian Scientist, they tensely tucked their heads beneath the cart's iron rim, that is until they heard a slew of bullets clank off the side of the cart, the sound violently assaulting their ear drums which were just inches away from the points of impact. Attempting to maintain his composure while remaining low, Siberian Scientist reached forward and pulled the cart's brake lever, releasing an iron-to-iron scream.

WHOOSH!

Siberian Scientist and Raydar felt a gust of air rush over them despite the descent of the cart's speed.

His body flush with the crystalline ceiling above, Dreadnight turned his wings to stone then dipped his shoulders down, targeting the trigger happy mercs. In a two second blitz, Dreadnight's wings pummeled several mercs as his claw-stricken feet impaled a random merc's chest that was now being used as a landing pad. Reverting his wings back to flesh, Dreadnight twisted to his left as his night vision caught a glimpse of a recovering merc lifting his assault rifle.

SNAP!

Dreadnight reached forward, gripping his hands upon the man's head and jerking them in opposing directions, snapping his neck and instantly killing him. Before the man's body reached the floor, a second merc ten feet straight ahead had already steadied his rifle. Just as he squeezed its trigger, Dreadnight grabbed the nearest merc to his right, pulling him out in front of his beastly body. The first few bullets sliced into Dreadnight's flesh, however the remaining ten or so found a home in his fellow merc's back causing his body to rattle with each impact. Lifting his knee, Dreadnight kicked his right foot forward as he released his hands from his human shield sending the merc slamming into the gunman and the tunnel wall behind them.

Two mounted lights appeared from his left followed by strings of bullets, neutralizing the mercs to the rear of him. Pushing the corpse of his collaborator that he just struck down, the merc facing Dreadnight rose for more abuse. Before the merc could stand straight, Dreadnight stepped forward, lifted his wings, and struck the hooks upon those wings down into the mercs shoulders. Within the blink of an eye, he flipped his wings backward and released his hooks from the man's flesh, sending him crashing into the wall to his rear. The instant the merc's body touched the ground, it was met by a finishing jackhammer stab to the chest from Dreadnight's now stone tipped tail.

Swiveling their weapons, Siberian Scientist and Raydar scanned the tunnel for any surviving mercs, but instead laid witness to Dreadnight delivering the finishing blows to that of two failing mercs desperately attempting to recover their footing. As soon as their feet touched the ground from leaping from the iron cart, the two teammates were greeted by their beastly leader, now covered in a fresh layer of blood from his enemies that only accentuated the dried remnants of his previous victims.

"Enough of these games. It's time we take the head off this snake." Dreadnight growled, his brow stern and his breath heavy.

Another seemingly endless void separated the three heroes from what they hoped to be the final stage of this elaborate game of hide and seek. Leaning his head overtop the sabotaged elevator, Dreadnight closed his eyes and focused his hearing. At first, he heard nothing, not even the rattle of an ammunition cannister. Could Inkubus have fled the mines already?

Combatting a surge of anxiety, Dreadnight took a deep breath then slowly released it, clearing his mind. As subtle as a single raindrop upon a blade of grass, the silence was broken, even if only for a split second. One of Inkubus's soldiers made a fatal error, but it wasn't just any soldier. The sound was that of a shaking set of handcuffs, meaning that the soldier was none other than Commissioner Harvey Reem himself.

"Oh, the sweet irony." Dreadnight chuckled.

"What? What is it?" Raydar asked.

"Inkubus is down there. I heard Reem's handcuffs, which means Inkubus is right by his side."

All three men smiled as they realized they were minutes away from the final faceoff. Or so they hoped.

"If the fiasco at the Central Station taught us anything, it's that Inkubus always has an escape plan. We can't allow him to slither away again. we need to scour this level before we make a move and find out whatever means he plans to use when we neutralize his army for the last time," Dreadnight said with power and fortitude.

"Agreed. Raydar and I will check the east wing out while you comb over this area with your night vision," Siberian Scientist said.

"Copy that," Dreadnight confirmed.

Siberian Scientist and Raydar headed toward the east tunnel that forked off from the main tunnel that they had just sped down. Raising their rifles upon reaching the fork, they trekked forward in a swiveled crouch with their tactical lights leading the way in case they ran into any surprise guests.

Simultaneously checking each white walled section of the level, the team searched for any clue of an escape elevator, but Siberian Scientist found something much more interesting. As he turned yet another corner into another cavern, he located four wooden crates stacked in two rows of two.

"Raydar, I think I found something. Go grab Dreadnight," he shouted to Raydar who was checking the opposing wall. Lowering his rifle, Siberian Scientist approached the crates, all seemingly unmarked and standing approximately seven feet high. Twisting his gun while pulling his arms back, he struck the side of one of the top crates with its buttstock. The AK burst through the crate's wall, splintering it with ease. Repeating the motion twice more, Siberian Scientist created a football size hole, revealing an extensive amount of packaging foam. Reaching through, he hastily pulled the foam from the crate until his hand felt something cold that resembled metal.

"What did you find?" Dreadnight asked, just as his comrade pulled a steel canister from the crate.

"I think I found us some new toys," he said with a smile as he turned and revealed a can of tear gas.

Dreadnight lifted the crate off the others and set it down on the ground before them.

"Umm that's not the only thing you found," Raydar said with eyes as wide as the pacific as he stared upon the empty space that Dreadnight had just created.

When Siberian Scientist and Dreadnight turned, they were greeted by the visual of the corner to what seemed to be an old wooden door.

Dreadnight removed each of the three remaining crates from the face of the door before cautiously turning its aged iron handle. Just as he expected, a prime yet poorly hidden escape path was revealed. Encased in century old wood planks was a three-foot-wide staircase also consisting of the same material, a visual that only Dreadnight could depict thanks to a complete lack of lighting within.

"What is it?" Siberian Scientist excitedly asked, brimming with anticipation.

"It's exactly what we were looking for my friends."

"You already have some wise ass plan, don't you?" Raydar said sarcastically.

The smirk upon Dreadnight's face was an obvious answer in itself.

"You won't mind if I borrow your AK for a little while, will you?" Dreadnight asked Siberian Scientist, adding a wink to that smirk, causing he and Raydar's brows to rise.

His plan was to utilize Inkubus's own supply of tear gas to disorient the mob of mercs awaiting his arrival then to mow them down with Siberian Scientist's AK, ultimately leaving Inkubus and Reem no other option but to retreat via the wooden stairwell where Siberian Scientist and Raydar would be patiently waiting for him. Though edging brilliance, the plan was another that not only impressed his teammates but also deeply concerned them, knowing that Dreadnight would be placing himself right in the line of fire and God knows what else. However, they knew to follow their fearless leader and to trust his celestial instincts as that very leadership and those instincts were exactly what got the team to this point, hell they were what gave them their lives back in the first place.

Walking in synchrony back toward the presumably final sabotaged elevator shaft, a crate of tear gas in Dreadnight's arms, the heroes were primed and ready to go.

"You ready for this man?" Raydar said as the three heroes stared down into the pit of darkness, each holding two cannisters of tear gas in their hands and out in front of them.

"It's go time." Dreadnight growled. Curling the tops of his wings overtop his shoulders, Dreadnight inserted the hooked claw from each wing through the loophole of each cannister's pin.

Schlick

Dreadnight lifted his hooks, removing both pins before releasing his grip from the cannisters. Raydar and Siberian Scientist followed suit, removing the pins from their cannisters and sending them free falling into darkness.

"Go get em, brother," Siberian Scientist said as he tossed his AK74M to Dreadnight.

As soon as the AK was in his hands, Dreadnight stepped from the pit's edge, sending his body slicing through the air like a knife, straight and streamlined. Just as Raydar and Siberian Scientist heard the cannister's begin to hiss, spraying their toxicity into the air, Dreadnight was gone, consumed by the darkness.

With his night vision capabilities in full effect, Dreadnight tracked the six cannisters as he neared their fumes. Before he knew it, he felt the sting of the initial residue from the release of his cannisters, signaling him to release his wings.

FWOOP!

Dreadnight forcefully drove his wings downward, pushing the oncoming smokescreen away from his body and into a funnel against the salt lined walls. Repeating the motion in a steady yet timed fashion, he continued to thrust his wings and reduce his rate of descent, ensuring his position above the tornado of poison he created. Solid ground only one hundred and fifty feet away, Dreadnight gripped his hands into shooting position on the AK, preparing for a shootout.

One hundred feet ... fifty feet ...

BOOM!

All remnants of the tear gas blasted from the pit along with a storm of dust as the earth shook violently.

The ground beneath him a map of detritus crawling in every direction, Dreadnight's legs flexed as he straightened his stance and lifted his firearm into shooting position. His eyes shifted ahead to the unknown cavern.

The echoing boom from the impact was quickly replaced with that of chaotic discord.

~

Inkubus and Reem stood idle as twenty super soldiers stood before them, covering every inch of the fifty by fifty-foot cavern they inhabited while staying as silent as a mouse.

Clink ... clink ... clink ... clink clink clink

Six metal cannisters bounced off the ground in the elevator pit Inkubus and his men were facing. The soldiers were of course unfazed, fearlessly holding their positions. The same however could not said for Inkubus and Reem who dove back toward the west wall, expecting grenade blasts. Face down with their bodies tensed, both Inkubus and Reem peeked out from under their arms, no explosion nor even gas to be seen, just their array of soldiers standing attune.

"What the ..." Reem began to say.

BOOM!

That voice was replaced by that of a guttural scream as tear gas appeared like a sandstorm, swallowing the entirety of the cave.

"Awk awk ... shit ... it's tear gas!" Reem choked, crashing back down to the ground and attempting to cover his mouth with his uniform.

His mask protecting him from the airborne onslaught, Inkubus quickly rose to his feet but before he could utter any command, the boom of a triple tiered chamber release arose.

SPLAT

Inkubus jerked his head back and frantically swept his hand over top his mask, feeling as if something had struck him, but quickly realizing it was only the blood of a super soldier just feet in front of him as its body collapsed to the ground, blood pouring from its cranium.

"Fire! Kill that son of a bitch!" Inkubus roared in a fit of rage.

Coughing incessantly with their vision on the fritz, the super soldiers guarding Inkubus blindly fired erratically, without the ability to aim or even hold their position. The synapsis serum may be able to numb one's mind to pain and fear, but it can't change how one's organs function or respond to chemical stimuli. The cavern became a fuming cesspool of bullet casings and muzzle flash.

~

His finger nearly snapping the trigger in half, Dreadnight choked his rifle, teeter tottering its sight from one super soldier to another as their twitching bodies shot blindly throughout the cave. Groaning as three stray bullets became plugged into the flesh of his chest and abdomen, the words of the late Father Ephrem reverberated in his mind, *Be aware of each and every one of your gifts. Use them and they will guide you to glory.*

Clink clink clink

Bullets ricocheted off the now stone wing shielding the left half of Dreadnight's body. Releasing another triple tap assault, Dreadnight dropped another pair of super soldiers to his right from a fatal head and chest shot while the third bullet unfortunately only struck another soldier's leg. Swiveling to his left, Dreadnight swapped wing positions, releasing the left from stone and dropping it while raising the other and turning it to stone.

Triple tap … swivel … triple tap … swivel

Dreadnight repeatedly swapped the wing shielding him, deflecting a slew of bullets from the spastic soldiers that were coughing their lungs out while neutralizing them one by one in a scene that would forever be known as the salt mine slaughter.

Cowering behind the nearest meat shield still standing, Inkubus watched as his army of twenty strong became that of a debilitated half dozen and his right-hand man choked away on the ground.

"You don't really think this is over, do you?" Inkubus arrogantly bellowed for which no response was given. "I am always a step ahead of you. Always! Soon your head will hang from my wall you mutant bastard!"

Dreadnight's only response was that bullets and bloodshed, continuing his strafe, wings transforming into shields one after the another amidst the constant muzzle flash.

Inkubus's overreaching confidence came to an abrupt halt as his meat shield's legs buckled from blood loss and the count of six super soldiers was chopped down to a mere three. Quick to react, Inkubus wrapped his arms underneath that of the collapsing soldier's, holding him up while backpedaling to the rear wall of the cave. Reem watched in utter confusion and crawled in a panic behind his leader.

"Aaargh!" Inkubus groaned, taking a bullet to the front of his left shoulder just as the final living super soldier collapsed to the ground, leaving only a dispersing cloud of tear gas and Reem's spastic body between the foes. "Until next time," Inkubus insolently said, releasing his grasp upon the now human corpse filled with bullet holes.

As soon as his left wing dropped, Dreadnight turned to follow Inkubus's voice, but instead only saw a large wooden door coming to a slamming close. Just inches away from the door was Reem, his arm outstretched in desperation and his face displaying the trauma that could only be the result of pure betrayal. Pushing the toxic gas away from himself, Dreadnight pushed his wings forward while stepping over the myriad of deceased super soldiers spread amongst the cave floor on route to Reem.

Dreadnight stood over the trembling commissioner who was unable to stand or even scream from the gas' noxious effects.

"Seems like your commission is over little man." Dreadnight snidely growled before thrusting the buttstock of his rifle square into Reem's forehead, sending his head bouncing off the floor and into an unconscious stupor.

~

The sound of rushing footsteps along with the coinciding creek of aged wood was suddenly an earshot away as both Raydar and Siberian Scientist stood side by side along the pitch-black stairwell, their pistols in shooting position. The stomachs of both men twisted and turned as they awaited the arrival of the team's nemesis ... or at least they hoped. The footsteps became louder and louder, causing the grips upon their pistols to tighten in anticipation.

"Three ... two ... one!" Siberian Scientist whispered.

A storm of blinding light beam from underneath the barrels of their pistols as the two teammates clicked on their HD tactical lights. Lights that revealed the masked tyrant himself. Quick to react, Inkubus reached for his pistol but just as his hand pulled it from its holster, he was greeted by the numbing sting of three tranq darts, two to the chest and one to the arm.

"Gotcha bitch!" shouted Raydar, adrenaline running rampantly throughout his body.

Fighting the toxins now coursing through his bloodstream, Inkubus continued to sluggishly lift his gun, but his legs buckled. Losing all neurological control to his limbs, the pistol slid from Inkubus's paralyzed fingers, crashing to the ground seconds before his face shared the same fate.

Raydar and Siberian Scientist steadily paced forward, their guns still pointed at Inkubus who was groaning in a failed attempt to speak. Stopping and standing overtop their prey, the teammates smiled at the victorious sight before them.

P-Taff

"Stay down ... bitch," Siberian Scientist playfully mocked his comrade after sending a fourth and final tranq dart into Inkubus's back.

~

The time was 5:15 a.m., the smell of coffee and vodka loomed as Mr. Unseen, Lainey, Dr. Foster, and Sandra Daley remained alert yet attempted to suppress their utter anxiety while sitting around the Observatory round table. There had been no trace of their teammates nor any of Inkubus's men since their trek down into the depths of the salt mines. Such a moment was where Father Ephrem's presence was surely missed. When uncertainty is but a plague upon the hearts of many and doubt is cast into the souls those hearts inhabit, that is when faith shields us from the darkness and guides us towards the light.

"Mr. Unseen come in," an abrupt yet scrambled voice shot from the observatory speakers, filling the hearts of its inhabiting team members with exhilaration.

"Oh my God! Raydar, is that you?" Mr. Unseen shouted, bolting up from his seat.

"Get our VIP cell ready cause we have bagged us a demon my friends!" Raydar excitedly announced as he and Siberian Scientist dragged Inkubus and Reem toward the Celestial Shipping truck after appearing from the initial elevator shaft.

The Observatory erupted in pure elation as joyous cheer and congratulative hugs consumed the room and those within.

"Wait! Where is Dreadnight? Is he okay? The sun is going to rise in less than fifteen minutes!" Mr. Unseen blurted in a sudden spur of panic, bringing the team's celebration to a halt.

"Yes. He is already rushing out of here to try and make it back to the cathedral before it's too late," Raydar confirmed.

"Oh, thank God!" Mr. Unseen sighed in relief as the Observatory reverted to its joyous state.

~

The dawn of a new day was upon the city of Detroit as the horizon cracked at its seam, swallowing the darkness before it. Dreadnight's eyes swelled in fear as he glided toward St. Anne's Cathedral, it's steeples within sight. Daylight was once again the essence of his greatest dream as well as his grimmest nightmare.

A mere one hundred yards from the place he called home, Dreadnight felt a spine numbing tingle emanate from within. The ritual had indeed begun! Angling his body down while pushing his wings with every ounce of strength that remained in his body, he speared toward the rooftop that changed his life forever. Like a wave upon an ocean shore, light cascaded over his body. At that very moment his feet felt a sudden heaviness, looking back he witnessed stone consuming his very flesh. When he lifted his eyes, he saw Mr. Unseen, Lainey, Dr. Foster, and Sandra Daley rushing onto the rooftop, anxious for his arrival.

The sensation now spreading up his legs and a distance of twenty-five yards remaining, Dreadnight pulled his left arm in and clasped Rachel's charm with his hand knowing full well what was going to happen next.

"Come on Slade! You can make it!" Mr. Unseen shouted as he watched his dear friend bulleting straight toward the Effigiem Custos.

Just as the stone reached his wings, Dreadnight tucked his head into his right arm. The rooftop ledge exploded as his body ripped through its brick and mortar before violently skidding across the floor and crashing against the statue which gave birth to his form.

By the time Mr. Unseen and the others had sifted through the dust and debris to reach Dreadnight's side, the ritual had already ceased, leaving but a celestial statue bearing eyes full of fear, its hand wrapped around a glimmering necklace. Not a soul upon that rooftop felt certain that their dear friend had made it back in time, filling their veins with the most haunting sense of angst imaginable. Every second felt like a minute as they prayed for Slade's return, unable to envision a world without him.

Chapter 19
Facts of Existence

"Rachel!" shouted the unexpected voice of Slade as his upper body shot up off the phlebotomy chair in the observatory, wires running from his chest and his hand still clutched onto Rachel's charm.

"Slade! Oh, thank God!" Ray shouted as he and the other five sleep deprived team members leaped from their round table seats, rushing over to their teammate's side.

Covered in sweat and shaking profusely, Slade's head and eyes toggled every which way, seemingly unaware of where he was or why.

"Relax relax, it's okay Slade. You are back in the Observatory," Dr. Foster exclaimed, placing his hands upon Slade's shoulders, attempting to calm him as he witnessed a spike in his heartrate from a rush of cortisol into his bloodstream.

"Shit man, I thought I was goner. I don't even remember making it to the rooftop!" Slade exhaustedly said, shaking his head in relief.

"Man, you didn't just make to the rooftop, you straight up crashed through it," Ray said with a laugh for which was shared by the entire team, releasing their tension as they relived the astounding moment in their mind.

Sitting there surrounded by those who had risked their lives for him, their gazing faces full of love and support, it finally hit Slade … it was all over. They had finally ended Inkubus's reign of terror, completing their mission. Slade's breath vanished and tears flooded his eyes as he sat there speechless, his heart overwhelmed with unbound relief and pride. It was all worth it, every sacrifice, every ounce of blood … redemption was finally upon him.

"We did it guys. We actually did it."

A rush of emotions overcame each soul as a feeling of pure solace washed over the Observatory, a new reality hitting them like a tidal wave. There wasn't a dry eye in sight as Slade stood up from the phlebotomy chair, ripping the sensors from his chest before embracing his dear friend Ray.

"It's over man, it's finally over," Ray said in a relieving sniffle.

A sentimental display as such was shared amongst each and every team member as they basked in the glory of victory.

A victory that of course came with a price …

Just as Nikolai pulled a bottle of vodka from his locker, proposing a celebratory shot, Slade shot a glance past the round table, redirecting his attention toward his Russian friend. But as his eyes shifted, they locked onto to a most sobering sight. Slade's face dropped, rendering him mute and statuesque.

"Adam, grab the … Slade?" Nikolai quickly noticed Slade's sudden dilapidated state.

"Is he in there?" Slade coldly asked, causing the entire team to shift their attention toward Slade's point of contention, a point that just so happened to be a rustic wooden coffin.

That dilapidated state was now promptly shared by all.

"Yes, my friend. We thought he would want a proper burial and decided to make the appropriate preparations. I hope you don't mind," Nikolai gently explained.

At first Slade remained silent, just nodding his head as if he were deep in thought. However, that silence was short lived. "You're right. Thank you, brother. I know exactly how and where we should honor him." A small smile crept upon his face he envisioned a most fitting ceremony. "You guys have some energy left to do a little project with me?"

~

Raindrops poured upon the wooden surface of the coffin, each sounding as if a drum had been struck in honor of the late Father Ephrem. Slade, Ray, Nikolai, and Adam stepped outside of the Observatory and into the downpour, each donning a black suit with a white dress shirt and black tie. The rain pelting their unmasked faces, the team clutched onto the steel rails of the sarcophagus, sorrow dripping from their skin as they curled around the building toward the cathedral, toward … his home.

It was the first time in what felt like years that Slade had stepped foot out into the open air in his natural form. He surely never imagined the day he had been dreaming of would end up being the very day he buried the man that was like a father to him. The sun's presence was but a mystery that day as clouds tainted not only the sky, but the hearts of those enduring a day of darkness.

Soaked with the chill of reality, the team carefully stepped through the cathedral's cellar doors and down into its basement. Each member's eyes shifted in the direction of Father Ephrem's office, tightening each of their bleeding hearts. Twisting to their left upon leaving the final step, the team headed down the tunnel toward the Arcane Asylum entrance. With each step, both Slade and Ray were reminded of the monumental day their paths collided and became one, a day that was solidified by Father Ephrem and his unwavering kindness.

Paused half the distance from Inkubus's place of imprisonment, the team stood underneath a string of four small spotlights, all shining upon a freshly burrowed aperture in the stone encrusted north wall. Rotating, Slade and Ray aligned the rails of the coffin with a pair of polished steel tracks bolted into the base of the tomb. With cautious ease, the four men slid the coffin forward, stopping before the second half of its wooden surface could become enveloped in darkness. Stepping back, the four friends stood side by side in silence as water dripped like blood from their somber faces. The subtle creaking of aged oak ended that silence as Father Ephrem's newly embalmed body was revealed, initiated by that of Slade's reaching arm.

That sight, the living nightmare coming to fruition, inherently choked the breath right from Slade as his mind relived the very moment Father Ephrem's soul left the body lying before him. A body at peace with a face that somehow seemed to be wearing a smile of relief. It took every ounce of strength within Slade to not simply march over to Inkubus's cell and beat him to no end for the gut-wrenching pain he was feeling at that very moment. However, Father Ephrem's voice of reason was always guiding Slade away from such temptation, from the evil within.

Not a dry eye could be found in that damp tunnel of dirt and rock as the team hung their heads in remembrance. Sliding his hand into the front right pocket of his suit coat, Slade pulled Father Ephrem's favorite rosary from within, wrapping it around his right palm as its cross dangled freely. Seeing such a symbolic keepsake of his dear friend calmed his anger, changing the tides of his emotions.

"Just months ago, I was trapped in an endless war between my heart and my mind. A war that neither wanted to survive … a war that I was about to end once and for all," Slade began to say in reverie, his head bowed as he stared upon the golden rosary. "A prisoner of my own memories and of my own shortcomings, I felt alone, I felt powerless."

Slade lifted his head and looked at his team.

"Yet here I am … surrounded by the best of friends … by my brothers, and my past no longer dictates my present. This and everything we have accomplished is a direct result of Father Ephrem's intuition and his incorruptible conscience. Men like him are the only reason this world hasn't turned to cinder despite its endless greed and insatiable thirst for pleasure. He is the reason I will never stop fighting for those who feel just as I did, for those who deserve the world as it is intended to be," Slade powerfully said, his eyes tightened.

"I know I speak for the rest of the team when I say ... neither will we brother," Raydar added with confidence, causing both Adam and Nikolai to nod accordingly.

"He's right, my friend. And even though we have exorcised the demon from this city, the mission is not over as there are others like him still plaguing this world. We must find those who share our convictions, the few who are willing to place the greater good above that of their own ... the Father Ephrems of the world.

Such words of kinship placed a smile upon Slade's weary face as he looked back down upon the rosary, memories of their pre-transformation discussions fresh in his mind. Reaching into one of inner pockets of his coat, he removed the beloved picture of Father Ephrem and his late fiancée Abigail. Stepping forward, Slade gently placed both the picture and the rosary into the breast pocket of Father Ephrem's clerical jacket, located fittingly above his heart.

"God I'm going to miss him ..." Slade said somberly, tears streaming down his face.

"You know what, my friend?" Nikolai placed his hand upon Slade's left shoulder. "Father Ephrem wouldn't want us to be sad. He would want us to celebrate his life, to celebrate saving the city he vowed to serve and protect," he added before taking a few steps forward and to the left of the burial site. Reaching down, he lifted a small wooden box from the dirt floor and turned to face his team. "He would want us to propose a toast!" Nikolai grinned as he opened the boxed, revealing a familiar bottle of vodka and four coinciding shot glasses.

Such a sentiment could not be renounced as each man in that dreary tunnel knew that is exactly what Father Ephrem would suggest during a time of affliction. Nikolai proceeded to hand each of them a glass then filled them all to the brim with their drink of tradition.

"I think you should do the honor, my friend," Nikolai kindly said with a wink.

Slade dried his eyes and took a deep breath as he shifted his eyes away from Father Ephrem and toward the team.

"I propose a toast. To a man that dedicated his life to improve that of others. A man that not only saved my life but also gave it purpose. He enriched the soul of every person in this room effortlessly and with charisma that only an angel could possess. His deeds, his teachings, will live on through us as we continue to fight those who tarnish this earth."

Slade lifted his glass into the air. "To Father Ephrem, a saint among men. May he rest in peace, basking in the glory of heaven alongside Michael the great."

"To Father Ephrem!" Ray, Nikolai, and Adam chanted in synchrony, lifting their glasses, and clanking them against one another before shooting back the vodka's bite.

Chapter 20
The Bitch that is Karma

It was sufficient to say that single bottle of vodka was only the beginning of the memorial drinks that day. For the next three hours, the original four plus Dr. Foster and Lainey sat in the cathedral kitchen and drank to the memory of the hero whose name was Ephrem. Shot after shot, the team reminisced over the joyous times shared and the sage wisdom inherited thanks to that very hero. A priest that not only spoke the word of God, but also followed in the footsteps of the most powerful angel that ever was and ever will be. Despite the inebriated hiatus, the mission remained and the moment our dear doctors had been waiting for was on the horizon.

The time had just passed 6:00 p.m., meaning only six hours remained until the long-awaited final step of the team's mission would be initiated ... using the synapsis serum on the very man who resurrected its vileness, along with extracting some of his stem cells. Both Dr. Foster and Nikolai headed to the lab in preparation for the big experiment, hopeful and drunkenly giddy. Upon entering the lab, the two men arranged all the necessary instruments, machines, and chemicals around the phlebotomy chairs in anticipation for the cerebral incursion procedure. Once everything was in its proper place, the doctors moved onto the second phase of preparation, the script.

Since the doctors couldn't simply convince Inkubus that he couldn't lie, due to the factors surrounding Dreadnight as well as Dr. Mueller's journal, they would need to carefully manipulate the man's mind to compel him to admit to his crimes while remitting certain knowledge regarding his enemies and his method of recruitment. For the next three hours they did just that, writing out the exact verbiage to use along with the potential mind blocks Nikolai should expect while treading through Inkubus's subconscious. Ultimately, they wanted this treatment to be a one and done, consisting of the optimal combination of serum dosage and time under incursion to prevent any potential delays.

Like clockwork, once the time struck 11:00 p.m., the entire team, now including Dr. Foster and Sandra Daley, compiled in the cathedral kitchen for supper, carrying on the tradition brought forth by Father Ephrem. Ray and Lainey harmoniously cooked a delicious yet odd mixture of pizza, burgers, and pancakes, a collection of the team's favorite foods. Of course, no meal at St. Anne's cathedral would be complete without copious amount of coffee, especially considering the long night ahead for our team of heroes. For nearly fifty minutes the team discussed not only the detailed plan for the night ahead, but as well as the coinciding contingency plans in case certain aspects didn't go as hoped. The sight of the seven-member team huddled in preparation was one that would surely make Father Ephrem weep from the heavens above. The sight was perfection on earth.

Just minutes prior to midnight, the entire team headed up the spiraling staircase to the cathedral rooftop where they stood before the Effigiem Custos, awaiting Slade's transformation, an experience that would be a first for both Sandra and Dr. Foster. Slade stepped forward in front of the statue, facing his teammates without a trace of fear in his blood as he stood proud and astute.

"Everyone knows what they are to do tonight, right?" Slade said attentively, evoking a collective yes from the remaining six teammates before him. "Tonight we drive the final spike through the heart of Inkubus's empire. Tonight ... we fulfill Father Ephrem's commitment to this city and to all of humanity. This and everything we do going forward is for him as he is the reason we are all here together tonight."

Just as the final syllable exited Slade's mouth, the sky became consumed by swirling gray clouds and the air became cold and dense ... it was time.

In less than a minute's time, Slade had become Dreadnight, his vast wings and godlike frame as profound as ever. Despite Sandra and Dr. Foster's previous encounters, the transformation left them astounded, yet made them fully aware of the supernatural essence tied to the Effigiem Custos and Dreadnight.

"Let's do this!" Dreadnight growled, his fists clenched, and eyes tightened.

~

The ratcheting scream of chain links bounced off the Asylum walls as its cargo door peeled from the cement floor, crawling into the ceiling above. It seemed as if only darkness lied beyond the steel passageway as the Asylum's prisoners watched in anticipation, that is until the glow of two alabaster eyes pierced the blackness of the night. Stepping into the light, Dreadnight approached the one and only cell sheathed in metal shutters which both Raydar and Siberian Scientist stood attentively by. Immediately upon his entering, the cargo door sealed itself back upon the Asylum floor.

Standing before that very cell, Dreadnight grinned at his teammates as he relished the moment at hand.

"Mr. Unseen, how about we let some light into cell number eight?" Dreadnight said through him comm.

"My pleasure," Mr. Unseen replied as he typed the appropriate passcode into his security system.

Within seconds, the metal shutters folded upward, revealing an unmasked Inkubus. No longer yielding his prized mechanical sleeve apparatus, he sat leaning forward with his hands intertwined underneath his chin. Emotionless and still, the man didn't bat an eye as his three adversaries stood before him.

"Welcome to the Arcane Asylum Inkubus ... or should I call you Norman?" Dreadnight snidely said with a grin, triggering no response from the ordinarily vocal foe. "Mr. Unseen, open her up," he added.

The cell door's electric latch shot across causing a metal-on-metal crash that echoed throughout the room. Dreadnight slid his fingers in between the bars of the door then flung it across its tracks as if it were weightless before stepping through the doorway and into the cell. Towering over his nemesis, Dreadnight glared upon the human responsible for his dear friend's death.

"I think you know what happens next." Dreadnight snarled, still unable to trigger a response from Inkubus. "You are truly a coward, aren't you? Without your mask to hide behind, your fabricated strength, your serum to compel others to worship you." Dreadnight paused then tossed an old newspaper article onto the floor in front of Inkubus. On the front page of that very article was a picture of Inkubus's parents from the story of their mysterious death by fire.

"You have become what you have always feared ... a failure!" Dreadnight hissed.

"Eeerrraagghhh!" Inkubus screamed in a sudden bout of rage as he bolted from his bed toward Dreadnight. But just as he stood, his neck was greeted by that of Dreadnight's gargantuan hand, lifting him from the ground and thrusting back against the cell bars behind him.

Holding Inkubus midair, Dreadnight wrapped the edges of his fingers around the cell bars behind his foe's neck, rendering the man defenseless, grunting in raged filled desperation.

"You're nothing but a weak and pathetic little man, just like your great grandfather!" Dreadnight roared, his teeth screaming at the flailing and powerless Inkubus.

"Finish this, you pussy! Come on! Kill me!" Inkubus belted, his face red and bulging with hatred.

"Ohhh no, that would be too easy … you are about to experience a taste of your own medicine!" Dreadnight grinned with widened eyes, enjoying every second of retribution at hand.

"Fuck you!" Inkubus screamed like an unhinged psychopath before a syringe was plunged deep into the flesh of his back by none other than Siberian Scientist, instantly knocking him unconscious from sedation.

"And to you … bitch," Dreadnight chuckled as he released his grip, allowing Inkubus's numbed body to crash onto the cell bed.

Within moments, Inkubus's body was strung mid-air as it was pulleyed up into the Observatory, all of his loyal subjects watching in disarray as they realized his true identity and his ultimate demise. In the Observatory, Nikolai was already seated in the appropriate phlebotomy chair with the necessary electrodes and sensors attached as Dr. Foster pulled Inkubus from the Asylum manhole. Seconds later, Dreadnight and Raydar joined the party and Inkubus was situated opposite of Siberian Scientist, strapped in next to a rolling table holding, an ECT machine, a surgical drill, and of course a fresh dose of the synapsis serum.

"Let the fun begin," Dr. Foster said with a grin, followed by the sudden scream of the surgical drill.

For the next ten minutes, the team thoroughly enjoyed the sights and sounds of Inkubus's skull being probed by cold steel and that of the violent convulsions brought forth by the ECT machine's electric assault. Such an occasion however felt short lived, considering the months of pain and suffering caused by the now powerless man, but it was finally time for karma to unleash its wrath upon Inkubus's mind.

"Are you ready my friend?" Dr. Foster asked Siberian Scientist.

"Ready as I'll ever be," Siberian Scientist replied calmly despite the anticipation reeling through his body.

"You know what to do. Now let's get our revenge mate," Dr. Foster said firmly.

"Go get em' brother," Dreadnight added with a smirk.

Siberian Scientist nodded, matching that very smirk before Dr. Foster placed the once mysterious spray nozzle into his mouth and released its potency, instantly sending him into a subconscious journey that would change history forever. For the next twenty mind numbing minutes, Dreadnight, Raydar, and Dr. Foster waited with frayed nerves as their dear friend's mind travelled into the vile core of their enemy.

~

For Siberian Scientist, those twenty minutes felt like two hours. Travelling down the blackened hallway of Inkubus's mind in search of its epicenter, he witnessed the man's most twisted and sadistic memories. Memories that would haunt Siberian Scientist for days if not weeks to come. Unlike the minds of Inkubus's subjects, his memories were not locked away or suppressed. No, they were waiting to be shared, doused in pride like that of a true Satanist. Memories filled with abuse, murder, rape, and even pedophilia. The evil within knew no bounds. Despite this mental house of horrors, Siberian Scientist remained focused as he walked past each door until he was greeted by one of bright red color, wet with what appeared to be blood.

Pulling down upon the steel handle, Siberian Scientist opened the door, revealing a most startling sight. A gust of flames shot through the doorway causing him to leap backward in fear, covering his face for protection. Crouched a few feet back, the flames still burning vigorously in the doorway, he lowered his arm and looked upon his body in disarray. He could have sworn he had been engulfed by the fire. However, he felt no pain and his clothes were untarnished.

Stepping toward the entrance, he witnessed the fire burning precisely in the room before him without seeping into the doorway, as if it was a controlled burn of sorts. Standing mere inches away, a theory popped into his head. Reaching forward ever so slowly, he sent his right hand across the chasm and directly into the fiery abyss.

Siberian Scientist's once wincing face eased, morphing into a smile as he reached his arm further, twisting and turning it. He felt absolutely nothing. Proving his theory correct, that this was nothing more than an illusion. Siberian Scientist then stepped across the chasm and into the faux inferno. Looking around, he realized that there was much more to the room than fire. It was a vivid portrayal of the interior of a Victorian style home, its contents turning to embers as smoke culminated upward.

This realization was only the beginning, however. As soon as he focused his eyes on the middle of this portrayal, he locked onto the sight of Inkubus, bare faced yet dressed in his traditional attire. He was standing upon a chair engrossed in flames, a noose wrapped snuggly around his neck with its rope anchored into the darkness above.

Inkubus immediately heard Siberian Scientist's footsteps forcing him to hinge his neck toward him.

"Who's there?" Inkubus fretfully shouted. "Please help me!" he pleaded as he awaited a face to peel away from the darkness.

Now only ten feet from Inkubus, a sudden burst of flames shot upward in a ring around the man as Nikolai stepped through and out in front. But it was not Siberian Scientist that Inkubus saw. No, he instead saw a flawless depiction of his dear great grandfather, bearing a top hat, a tailored black suit, and a face bearing a thick gray mustache with a cigar hanging from its disdainful mouth.

Inkubus's face changed its tune into that of shock and awe.

"Great grandfather ... is that really you?" Inkubus cried as if he were a child again.

What the hell ... he thinks I'm his great grandfather. Siberian Scientist thought to himself as he paused in front of his enemy. Then it clicked, he knew exactly where they where and why Inkubus was seeing what he was seeing. They were reliving the night young Inkubus killed his parents, and he was envisioning his great grandfather because his greatest fear was that he would never live up to the man's accomplishments ... that he would become a failure.

The serum was doing exactly what it was intended to do. All Siberian Scientist had to do was play the part and seize the moment. Luckily, he knew enough about Inkubus's great grandfather to harness the serum's potential.

"Yes, son. It is I."

"Please help me down!" Inkubus pleaded, expecting sympathy as he watched his great grandfather remove the cigar from his mouth and light it with the flames beneath his feet.

"Help you? You mean like you helped them?" Siberian Scientist said, acting perplexed.

Siberian Scientist snapped his fingers.

Suddenly, two bodies fell from above, each landing with a thud beside Siberian Scientist and into a flesh-eating blaze. Gut wrenching screams consumed the air as the pair flailed desperately.

"Why son? Why?" the body to the right of Siberian Scientist cried.

"We gave you life, and you killed us!" the body to the left of Siberian Scientist screamed.

It was indeed Inkubus's late parents burning to death playing out before his very eyes, their flesh peeling as it was singed from their bones, their bloodied arms reaching toward their son. The sight contorted Inkubus's face in dread and confusion. He attempted to wiggle free from the noose, but frantically stopped when the burning chair beneath began to tip and its flames burned his bare feet.

"Why the fuck am I here?" Inkubus screamed, the pain of his flesh burning convincing him that the situation was indeed real.

The serum was now in full effect.

"You are here because you have failed, my son. You are here to be judged," Siberian Scientist coldly replied.

For the next fifteen minutes, which felt like an eternity to Inkubus, Siberian Scientist dismantled the demon's psyche, destroying him with his own weapon. Still mirroring the image of Inkubus's late great grandfather, Siberian Scientist convinced his fragile mind that Dreadnight was a mere illusion, a false enemy created out of his fear that God himself would come after him for the killing of his parents. An enemy spawned from coming face to face with the Effigiem Custos upon the cathedral rooftop during the funeral of his parents.

The manipulation didn't stop there. Further utilizing Inkubus's immense guilt from not living up to his great grandfather's testament, Siberian Scientist convinced him that the serum itself never existed. Instead, it was merely an elaborate accomplishment that his melted mind had conjured, one that provided false supremacy from coercing others to follow him. This revelation created a reality within Inkubus's mind that aligned with the truth at hand, that he was nothing more than a thug that relied on fear and money to obtain power ... that he was insane, constantly living out dreams within his own tormented mind.

~

Siberian Scientist's jolted forward off the phlebotomy chair, short of breath and tremoring.

"Holy shit that felt real!" he blurted out as his head jerked toward his teammates.

"Well, in many ways it was, my friend," Dr. Foster replied with a smirk.

Siberian Scientist collected his breath and centered himself, removing the sensors from his body.

"Was that enough time?" Dr. Foster asked.

"Yeah, I think so."

"So ... how did it go?" Dreadnight asked with great anticipation.

"I think it's safe to say that he's our little bitch now." Siberian Scientist chuckled, providing relief to the team while lighting up their faces. "He's been convinced that he is incapable of lying and that any knowledge of Dreadnight, our team, and our operation was merely an elaborate dream created to feed his ego," he explained smiling.

"Hell yeah, brother!" Dreadnight roared, drowning out the sounds of the surrounding cheers.

"As far as the man once known as Inkubus is concerned, an unknown group of vigilantes were the only thing that stood in his way, continually blocking his attempts to overtake the city," Siberian Scientist added.

The team rejoiced as Siberian Scientist hopped from the chair, overcome with both joy and comfort as they inched closer and closer to getting justice for Father Ephrem's death, from getting redemption for the city. However, the night was far from being over and despite the momentous accomplishment just achieved, there was much work to be done.

Refocusing, Dr. Foster adjusted Inkubus's phlebotomy chair upright while Siberian Scientist attached a portable medical stand out in front of Inkubus's chest. Mounted to that very medical stand was a new toy that Dr. Foster and Nikolai were extremely excited to use. That toy was a TMS machine, also known as a Transcranial Magnetic Stimulator. And what was the function of this nightmarish machine one might ask? Simply put, to aid in the extraction of stem cells ... the missing ingredient to Siberian Scientist's cure!

Dr. Foster proceeded to place the chin of the still unconscious Inkubus atop the TMS machine's rubber placement pads and adjusted the machine's positioning frame to align its secondary placement pads with his subject's forehead. The TMS machine's power unit, much like that of the ECT machine, was on a separate roller table just feet away.

"Would you do the honor, Lainey?" Dr. Foster asked, holding the handheld Magnetic Resonance Scanner (MRS) out in front of his body. Lainey of course nodded in agreement, then Dr. Foster guided her hands and the scanner into the appropriate position.

RIZZZZZZZ!

The familiar scream of the surgical drill filled the laboratory as Dr. Foster held it into the air, a smirk engrained upon his face as his moment of long-awaited redemption neared.

"Time to continue karma's bidding," Dr. Foster said as he placed the camera guided drill bit just behind the tip of Inkubus's right ear.

The team members stood by intently watching.

Reviving the scream of the drill, Dr. Foster pressed into its trigger, ripping a .25mm hole through the skin and making contact with Inkubus's skull. Toggling his eyes back and forth, Dr. Foster observed both the MRS and the monitor displaying the guidance camera as he steadily sent the drill bit through bone matter until reaching the desired crevice within the flesh of the brain, provoking him to quickly withdraw the drill. Next, he placed the drill back onto the roller table and grabbed a small syringe yielding a lengthy needle matching the diameter of the newly placed hole. Closely monitoring the MRS, he inserted the needle, cautiously gliding it until the tip of the needle was one and a half inches deep.

Dr. Foster paused, causing the team members to cease breathing, each filled with anticipation. With a quick plunge of his thumb, Dr. Foster injected magnetic nanoparticles into the subventricular stem cell zone in the lateral wall of the right ventricle located in the forebrain, targeting neural stem cells. He withdrew and discarded the needle then removed the handheld magnetic coil unit from the TMS machine, placing it above Inkubus's forebrain at the precise location of the injection. After signaling Lainey to power down the MRS, he adjusted the TMS machine's settings on its touch screen monitor.

"Go get em," Dr. Foster said before pressing the machine's start function.

For the next three minutes, the TMS machine provided a constant and targeted electric current that aided the magnetic nanoparticles in pursuing and latching onto Inkubus's neural stem cells. After which, Dr. Foster removed the now adjoined material through the means of a magnetic syringe. Anxious as ever, Dr. Foster swiftly injected the adjoined material into a sterile petri dish. Last but not least, Dr. Foster injected Neuropeptide Y to the cell material to stimulate cell proliferation … in other words, duplication.

The core of the stem cell project was complete. All that remained was to allow the newly mixed material to incubate for six hours before removing the nanoparticles through the process of magnetic agitation, leaving nothing but untainted stem cells.

Much was to be done during these six hours however …

First and foremost, Siberian Scientist and Dr. Foster spent two hours performing synapsis serum treatments upon both Reem and Chen, ensuring their minds were in line with that of their newly reborn master. Within a matter of just a few hours, the team had subconsciously subdued three men who they fought for months to capture. It was hard to believe that these kings of crime were now nothing more than ants beneath their boots. All that remained was one final task, a ruse if you must, one the team would surely savor and never forget.

~

Handcuffed vertically from the ceiling of the Celestial Shipping cargo pod were the likes of Chen, Reem, and of course Inkubus. Heavily sedated, their heads hung, and their bodies swayed from side to side as the Celestial Shipping truck cruised down Corsa Street on route to the infamous Crimson Rapture. Gliding through the fog of the night was Dreadnight, monitoring from on high as Mr. Unseen viewed the live stream of the eyes of divinity.

"How's it looking, boss?" Raydar asked as he and Siberian Scientist neared the alleyway at Ninth and Corsa Street.

"As clear as can be," Dreadnight responded as his head continued to swivel. "Haven't seen a single cop or anything. Seems like Inkubus's loyal followers have hid like rats."

"Yeah, no surprise there. The remaining police force won't be taking any action without orders from Reem the dictator." Raydar scoffed. "Alright, we're here. It's go time boys!" he added excitedly.

"Get those masks on guys. I'm sure there will be some cameras near the entrance," Mr. Unseen said throughout the comm system.

"Doing it now brother," Siberian Scientist confirmed as he and Raydar followed Mr. Unseen's suggestion, however the masks they slipped over their faces were not of their own, instead they were bearing the vile black guise of Inkubus's followers.

Raydar and Siberian Scientist turned and looked at one another as the truck creeped down the alleyway.

"I'm not going to lie my friend, that mask makes me wants to punch you in the face," Siberian Scientist said before breaking out in laughter.

"I know the feeling." Raydar chuckled.

Siberian Scientist brought the truck to a cautious halt in front of the Crimson Rapture's once secret door, leaving the engine running as they placed their handguns in their holsters.

"Time to set the stage," Raydar announced to the team as he and Siberian Scientist opened their doors and stepped out onto the blacktop.

The cargo pod door slid upward and out of sight, revealing the team's prized prisoners, all incoherent as the chains of their handcuffs rattled like loose change. Raydar and Siberian Scientist unlocked the restraints and proceeded to set the three prisoners carefully onto the floor of the pod. Raydar stepped out of the truck bed and dragged a now re-masked Inkubus out of the pod until lifting him and placing his arm around his own shoulder, propping him upward. Siberian Scientist followed the same procedure but instead with Reem's body.

"We are going in. Keep an eye on the truck," Raydar directed to Mr. Unseen as well as Dreadnight who was circling above.

The duo approached the door with their "guests". Siberian Scientist reached out and knocked upon the rusted red door. Seconds later, a small slit opened at eye level in the door.

"The password?" a mysterious voice asked from behind the aperture, triggering Raydar and Siberian Scientist to look at one another, hesitant about what to do next. Luckily Raydar was quick witted.

"Our boss needs no password," Raydar's muffled voice sternly replied as he leaned Inkubus's body toward the door slit.

No response was provided, instead the door was opened, revealing the lavish interior of the elite whore house as well as the brick house of a security guard that now towered over them.

"What happened to them?" the guard asked in a deep voice full of skepticism.

"Seems like the boss and the commish had a bit too much sauce, you know," Raydar suavely replied, an answer that didn't seem to mitigate the man's doubts.

"It's the commish's birthday. We figured we would give them something nice you wake up to, you know?" Siberian Scientist replied, doing his best to imitate an American accent, an attempt that nearly made Raydar break out in laughter.

"Well, then you brought them to the right place," the guard chuckled, easing the minds of the minds of Raydar and Siberian Scientist as well as the remainder of the team listening through the comm system.

"You got a VIP room free for them?" Raydar asked.

"For them, of course. Straight back past the bar and behind those curtains," the guard answered as he turned and pointed toward the northeast end of the first floor.

"Thanks bro," Raydar casually replied.

Literally carrying on, Raydar and Siberian Scientist continued to prop up Inkubus and Reem as they walked through the lavish interior of the Crimson Rapture. Neither of them could believe their eyes as they gazed upon the egregious paintings and chandeliers that hung throughout while oversexed skanks sent seductive gestures in their direction. Before they knew it, they were behind the sleek red curtain and in the VIP room, the very room where Inkubus had mangled Antonio's hand.

"How we looking, boys?" Raydar asked Mr. Unseen and Dreadnight.

"You're good, but you only got five minutes before we start cutting this close," Mr. Unseen said.

"Things are clear from up here," Dreadnight confirmed.

"Ditto. We are finishing up know," Raydar replied as he and Siberian Scientist set both Inkubus and Reem upon an Italian leather couch in the middle of the gaudy room.

Exiting the room, Siberian Scientist walked up to a pair of the same skanks that were eyeing them, pulled out one thousand dollars, and told the women to undress Inkubus and Reem a bit in preparation to surprise them when they awake. Before they departed with the money toward the room however, he explicitly directed them not to remove Inkubus's mask otherwise there would be severe repercussions, a sentiment they clearly understood.

With their primary objective complete, Raydar and Siberian Scientist casually walked out of the crimson rapture but weren't quite ready to flee the scene. They headed to the back of the truck once again where Chen remained asleep upon the cargo bed floor.

"I'll let you do the honors my friend," Siberian Scientist told Raydar with his accent back to its natural state.

"Gladly!" Raydar said joyously before pulling Chen's body from the cargo pod and tossing it like a ragdoll onto the ground in front of the Crimson Rapture's door.

"He will be quite the welcoming mat for them huh?" Siberian Scientist chuckled.

"Da," Ray answered in the same demeanor, adding to his teammate's laughter.

With only a minute to spare, the duo hopped into the Celestial Shipping truck and drove off, heading back to the team's headquarters as Dreadnight scoured above.

Within thirty minutes following Raydar and Siberian Scientist's departure, two blacked out armored trucks arrived outside of the Crimson Rapture, trucks that belonged to the FBI. This and all that followed was thanks to an anonymous tip made by none other than Mr. Unseen. At roughly 4:00 a.m., ten FBI operatives raided the once classified whore house where they discovered much more than the illegal solicitation of sex and drugs. To their surprise, they found not only an unconscious and half naked commissioner wearing a prostitute for a coat, but also the praised mayor of Detroit in the same preposterous state bearing a villainous mask.

This monumental uncovering compelled the Federal Government to invoke the Michigan Attorney General's executive responsibility over Detroit's city law enforcement, in other words Ms. Sandra Daley was now calling the shots at the DPD. Immediately upon the order, Ms. Daley not only placed Reem and Inkubus behind bars without a chance at bail, but she also placed the entire DPD staff under federal investigation. That is with the exception of Ray Fisher and Lainey Ross of course, stating that both had been assisting her with her own investigation into the Mayor and the DPD.

The veil of the DPD had finally been lifted and Ms. Daley was dead set on turning the police force into a symbol of hope and integrity. A symbol that the citizens of the city deserved.

Chapter 21
The Light of Day

The next morning when Slade awoke, he sat up in bed feeling lighter than normal, as if the weight of the world had been lifted from his shoulders. In a way, such a sentiment was true now that the quest that had once consumed every fiber of his being had finally been conquered. A quest that had put both Inkubus and Commissioner Reem behind lock and key, freeing the city from the corruption that had plagued it for over five years. Exhaling as his eyes toggled his basement quarters, Slade couldn't conceive the sheer gravity of reality.

His heart thumping and his mind overwhelmed, Slade stood and got dressed before heading to the kitchen to begin his daily routine. Halfway up the stairs, he stopped suddenly as a rush of excitement flooded his mind and body. It was in that very moment that he realized he was free. He no longer needed to hide in his dungeon of solitude and was finally able to live a life as a human again, a concept that still seemed too unbelievable to grasp. He dashed up the stairs and to the large oak doors of the church's entrance. With a burst of might he pushed through the doors with both arms, slinging them open as he stepped out onto the sun-bathed courtyard.

Slade's feet froze as he leaned back and soaked in the heat from the sun. The glow of the light reflected off his cheeks as they slowly flushed a tint of red. This was the first time since the day of the stabbing that he had seen the light of day.

Now it's over, now I'm awake, Slade thought to himself as he closed his eyes.

Slade had never appreciated the sun as much as he did in that very moment. Its brimming radiance was the essence of beauty, through and true. Happiness coursed through his veins as he was reborn amidst the world he had longed to rejoin. That happiness came to a quick halt when it dawned upon him that Father Ephrem would have loved that very moment, and that he should have been right there by his side. He dearly missed that old man, and he would be forever influenced by his teachings and wisdom. But he knew Father Ephrem was up above looking down at him, sharing this very moment with him in spirit.

Now seeing the world with new eyes, Slade walked the cathedral grounds, observing his home from the outside for the first time all while attempting to figure out what to do with this newly found freedom. Stopping and staring upon the face of the cathedral, Slade placed his hand upon his chest, feeling the risen embodiment of his brand and Rachel's charm which grazed above.

"Today is the day I see Rachel. No more waiting, no more fear. It is time I return what is hers," Slade said in a burst of courage.

This was the day he had longed for … the day he dreamt about constantly … the day that kept him pressing forward.

He pulled his phone from his pocket and rapidly tapped its screen. Lifting it to his ear, Slade paced as he bit his fingernails in anxiousness.

"Good morning man," Slade cheerfully said, continuing to pace.

"It sure is Slade. How are you my man?" Ray replied.

"The best I have been in a long while. Look Ray, I was wondering if you could do a big favor for me," Slade replied with a nervous shake in his voice.

"Do you even need to ask? Name it, and consider it done!"

"Well … I want to go see Rachel and would like you to take me to her. I really didn't want to journey it alone," Slade shyly said.

"Good for you man! I was hoping this day would come. I'll be right over. Give me twenty minutes," Ray proudly replied, the sound of Lainey giggling in the background becoming obvious, bringing a smile to Slade's face.

"Thanks Ray. I don't know what I would do without you brother!"

"Oh, you would still be a creepy ass gargoyle saving the city's skin at night and all … you just wouldn't have as much fun doing it without my badass presence," Ray replied, chuckling through every word.

The call ended in obvious laughter, leaving Slade filled with excitement for what was to come. One of the many things Slade could always count on Ray for was a good laugh. It was one of the few aspects of his day that had kept his spirit up throughout the team's trials and tribulations.

Realizing the big moment was within an hour's time, he headed back into the church to clean himself up, meaning he would be shaving for the first time in weeks. Knowing that he must make a worthy second impression with Rachel, Slade pulled out the nicest outfit from his limited closest which ironically happened to be a red and black flannel shirt, blue jeans, and an old pair of converse shoes. An outfit he could thank a donation from Ray for.

It'll have to do. Slade chuckled to himself, knowing he didn't have time to spare. He had to see Rachel right away.

Shortly thereafter, Ray pulled up to the courtyard. Slade hopped into his car and the two men joyfully nodded at each other before driving off. He handed Ray the directions to Rachel's home, directions that Slade had held onto dearly for months. Not much was said during the course of the ride. Ray knew Slade had a lot running through his mind, and Slade merely appreciated Ray's presence as it provided him with a much-needed sense of calm as he ran potential scenarios though his mind.

Approximately thirty minutes had passed when the car stopped in front of the quaint house Slade recognized oh so well. Its exterior consisted of multi-toned brown brick and sharp triangular peaks which hovered over its doorway and main sections. Slade's heart pounded as reality sunk into his twisted stomach. Ray reached over and placed his hand on Slade's shoulder.

"You ready man? Ray said.

"As ready as I'll ever be I guess," Slade nervously replied.

"Just relax. You got nothing to worry about. She is going to be really happy to see you, trust me. Now go get her!"

Slade energetically nodded, took a deep breath, and reached behind his neck to unlatch Rachel's necklace.

"Here goes nothing ... or everything," Slade said with a slight chuckle as he exited the car.

Ray just smiled as Slade headed up a few steps and onto Rachel's front porch, the necklace hanging from his right hand. Slade raised his other hand to knock on the door but paused, holding it stagnant in the air.

"Come on man, you got this!" Ray said aloud as he watched attentively.

Slade forced his hand forward, knocking three times against the thick oak door. Impatiently waiting, Slade heard footsteps approaching from inside the house, causing his heart to immediately sink like a ship's anchor into his stomach. As the door slowly opened, he saw Rachel's raven hair appear, followed by her flawless pale skin. Her eyes peered out beside the door.

"How can I ..." Rachel said before pausing wide eyed and stunned.

She covered her mouth with her hands as her eyes swelled.

"I believe I have something of yours," Slade said softly as he reached forward, showcasing Rachel's silver necklace as it hung from his hand.

"Oh my god. I thought you were dead!" Rachel muttered with tears flowing from her eyes and cascading down her cheekbones.

She lunged forward, wrapping her arms around Slade and embracing him.

"I thought I would never see you again!" she said with a shaky voice.

Surprised by her reaction, Slade was speechless as he froze in place. He loosened his body allowing his arms to drop around her back and his head to rest against hers. He was overtaken by a sense of relief and safety. As they embraced each other, tears of joy flooded Slade's shoulder.

"I had to make sure you were okay. I'm sorry I didn't come sooner, but you have to trust me when I say I couldn't have".

They released their arms from each other and naturally held each other's hands. She took the necklace from his hand, opened it, and placed it around his neck, latching its clasp.

"I want you to keep this close to you. Somehow, I feel as if it guided you back to me and for that I am forever grateful," she said with a growing smile.

"Thank you, Rachel. You should know this necklace and the thought of you is what kept me going these past few months. It is what kept me alive."

"I should be the one thanking you. You saved my life, and I don't even know your name!" Rachel said with a hint of uneasy laughter. "I owe my life to you. I can only imagine what could have happened if you wouldn't have showed up that night." Rachel paused, choked up from the memory. "There hasn't been a day that has passed that I didn't think of you or picture your face. I have had so many sleepless nights fearing that you didn't survive and that I would never see you again," Rachel cried, her voice becoming overpowered by her uneven breaths.

"I'm here now, Rachel, and I don't intend on ever leaving you again!" Slade responded staring intently into her piercing brown eyes.

Their eyes locked, Rachel lifted her body ever so slightly and leaned in, pressing her lips into Slade's. As they stood there, eyes closed, lips locked ever so firmly, euphoria washed over Slade's body. He had felt a sense of love before, but nothing like this. He would have gladly relived all the trials and tribulations thus far to hold on to this feeling. It was perfection. Many seconds later, the two untwined, keeping their foreheads pressed against one another.

"My name is Slade, Slade Allen," he said softly.

"Slade huh ... well would you like to come inside for some coffee, Mr. Allen?" she replied with a beaming smile from ear to ear.

"I would love to, Ms. Winston," he joyfully replied with the same exuberant smile on his face.

"That's my boy, hell yeah Slade!" Ray cheerfully shouted as the two proceeded inside the house.

Ray then drove off, knowing Slade wouldn't be leaving anytime soon.

Entering her house, Rachel insisted that Slade make himself at home directing him to the living area off to the left as she headed to the kitchen directly ahead. As she prepared the coffee maker, Slade sat on the nearby couch and studied the room around him. Rachel's place was very clean and immensely organized. The walls were covered in antique windowpanes which incased images of what seemed to be her family and others with a cat that faintly resembled a bobcat. Unexpectedly, he felt something land onto his lap. He looked down to see that very cat from the pictures. He enjoyably petted him.

"I see you've met Ollie. I hope you don't mind cats."

"No, I actually love cats. I hope to have one myself soon."

"That's great! Then my Ollie could have a play date." Rachel giggled.

"Sounds like a plan to me," Slade replied with a brimming smile.

"Would you like cream and sugar in your coffee?

"Just cream please. Thank you."

She walked over, handed him his cup of coffee, and sat next to him. Before he even could start to sip on his coffee, he felt compelled to ask her something.

"If you don't mind me asking, how did you end up in that alley that night? I'm sorry if I'm overstepping my bounds. You don't have to answer if it is too uncomfortable," Slade asked shyly.

"Oh, it is quite alright. I guess it started like any other weekend night with my friends, if you could call them that. Per the usual, they wanted to go out for a night on the town, essentially to get hammered and meet random guys as I sit by contemplative and uncomfortable."

Sounds familiar, Slade thought to himself.

"As the night progressed, I became more and more agitated until right before midnight when I convinced my friend Cassandra, who had drove with me, to leave. I didn't want to walk back to my car alone, not in that city at least. We were almost half our way back to where we had parked when Cassandra received a call from one of her other girlfriends pleading her to come meet at a nearby bar. In a slur of acceptance, she agreed, telling me I would be fine and that she was sorry as she scurried away barely able to keep her footing. Let's just say I never spoke to that skeeze again."

Though Slade's face appeared calm and collective, his insides were stewing in a pool of anger. *How could that girl be so careless and stupid? She almost got Rachel killed.* He thought to himself. Fighting his anger, he continued to intently listen, giving her his undivided attention.

"At that moment I panicked. I knew where I had to go but never felt safe in that godforsaken city. I walked along, but moments later an arm burst from the shadows and pulled me into that very alley you had found me. I tried with all my might to resist, but the man was beyond strong. And his eyes ... his eyes were pitch black. It was like nothing I had ever seen before. Before I knew it, he had forced me up against a wall and began choking the life out of me ... that is until you appeared."

She paused, briefly looking down into her coffee.

"I'm so sorry you had to go through that. Nobody deserves to endure such an event. I'm just glad I was led to you that night," Slade replied.

"What do you mean led to me?" she asked with an intrigued look.

"Well, it's hard to explain but ... my night started almost identically to yours. Another wasted night entertaining the ideas of some so-called friends while contemplating my life ... my purpose. For some reason, I was overcome with an impelling urge to leave that night. Usually I would stick it out, but not that night. It was as if I was being drawn away from the bar and guided to that alley. Thank God I was though, regardless of whatever force was pulling me to you that night!" Slade explained.

At that moment Rachel was rendered speechless as the two looked at each other in awe. A peculiar sparkle filled each other's eyes. Rachel set her coffee down onto the table and reached over to grab onto Slade's unoccupied hand.

"I just can't believe you are here, that you survived. I watched you get stabbed and bleed out for over fifteen minutes. The blood was everywhere ... it just doesn't seem possible," Rachel said, her voice beginning to crack from sadness. "What happened after the priest and I took you to that rooftop?" she added, showing apparent concern in her voice.

"Well, that night is still a bit hazy, but the first thing I remembered was waking up in pain as my body convulsed."

Rachel's eyes widened and her brow lifted.

"Father Ephrem was pressing his hand against my forehand while chanting something into the sky. Before I knew it, a bolt of lightning struck my chest, knocking me unconscious again. Moments later, I hazily saw Father Ephrem's figure crouched beside me talking about how I must prove myself worthy to my maker and of a chance to be redeemed."

At this point Rachel's eyes were about to pop out of her head as her mouth hung in awe.

"I woke up the following morning next to a gargoyle statue, unscathed with merely a charred shirt. It was as if my skin had never been pierced. Sounds crazy, huh?"

"But ... how? What saved you?" Rachel urgently asked.

"Beside the fact that you sought help and carried me to safety ... I swear I am not lying but ... Father Ephrem performed an ancient ritual from a grimoire which healed me, ultimately sparing my life."

Clearly flabbergasted, Rachel's jaw seemed to be clamped down whilst her eyes remained glued open as Slade anxiously feared expected skepticism.

"You know, nothing is beyond believable at this point. The mere fact that you are sitting here with me is a miracle in itself. Everything else is dust in the wind to me," she said softly before wrapping her arms around his shoulders, embracing him once again.

For the next six hours the two rekindled souls opened the floodgates of their hearts, narrating the books that were their pasts and inevitably dousing the fire that was their future with fuel. Memories poured into the air like the coffee filling their cups as their words danced with laughter and even cried from the sorrow caused by the pain their scars once concealed. It was as if a lifetime had come and gone as the two became one, bound by everlasting passion and virtue, gilded in Michael's grace.

Exhausted from the emotional outpour, the two fell asleep, with Rachel snuggled underneath Slade's arm and Ollie the cat stretched across both of their laps.

Several hours later, Slade awoke, feeling as if he had been pulled from a most amazing dream until looking down and realizing the dream was in fact the reality of one becoming true. He felt the smoothness of her skin as his fingers slowly grazed her arm, causing a tingling sensation to surge through his body. Even though the moment was real, Slade was beside himself. It was hard to believe that after everything he had been through, he finally felt content in life. Sitting there with the most beautiful girl he had ever laid eyes on, a girl he thought he might never see again, was simply euphoric bliss.

That bliss however came to a screeching halt when he realized it was completely dark on the other side of the living room windows. In a panic, Slade reached into his pocket with the hand that was free and jimmied out his phone. Shaking, he frantically pressed the power button on his phone, fretful of what its clock might read. Feeling the sudden commotion, Rachel hazily awoke.

"Is everything alright?" Rachel sleepily asked, just as the screen of Slade's phone lit up reading a time of 11:20 p.m.

Slade exhaled, causing the pins and needles within his mind to fall.

"Sorry. Just a false alarm," Slade responded, despite the time becoming alarmingly tight for his return to the cathedral and the fact that he wouldn't have time for Ray to retrieve him.

"Oh, good," Rachel said, smiling as she nestled her head back into Slade's shoulder.

This of course placed Slade upon quite an impasse as he had to choose between coming clean about his alter ego or lying to the woman he loved more than anything. Despite the potential ramifications, Slade had his answer before even finishing the thought.

"Rachel?" he asked softly, his voice donning a faint nervousness.

"Yeah, Slade?"

"Would you mind coming to the St. Anne's cathedral with me? I have something important I need to show you," Slade asked as innocently as he could.

"Of course I will. I would love to," she kindly responded.

"Great. We just have to make it there by midnight, okay?"

"No problem, we will leave now."

The two quickly arose, put on their shoes, and headed to Rachel's car, easing Slade's anxious mind. After a twenty-five-minute drive filled with nothing but matching smiles and clutched hands, Slade and Rachel arrived out front of St. Anne's cathedral. The time had just crossed 11:50 p.m., leaving Slade less than ten minutes to get to the rooftop without consequence. As Rachel exited the car, her eyes met the face of the cathedral, instantly filling her mind with memories she had spent months suppressing.

"You ready?" Slade softly stated as he stood in front of the car with his handoutreached toward her.

She merely responded by nodding with an innocent smile, unable to speak from the rush of emotions surging through her body as she reached out and grabbed onto Slade's hand. The two crossed the courtyard and entered through the etched oak doors that were all too familiar before beginning their journey up the spiral staircase. Looking down, Rachel faced a most disturbing image, a faint yet visceral blood-stained reminder that trailed up each and every step. Rachel paused, her eyes frozen as her heart sunk to the depths of her body.

"You okay, hun?" Slade asked gently, placing his hand on her back. He followed her gaze realizing what triggered her respite.

"I … I just can't imagine how you survived … this," she replied, her eyes tearing up as she stared upon what was once fresh blood.

"Come. I will show you," Slade said softly, lightly tugging her arm, breaking her trance and resuming their pace upward.

Slade opened the rooftop door, revealing the Effigiem Custos to Rachel. Its soul jarring scowl sent her mind twisting and turning through a cognitive black hole filled with memories and speculations.

The creature from the news … the shadowy figure I thought I had seen near the water tower … this statue, Rachel's mind reeled as it attempted to distinguish fact from what could only be perceived as fiction, however her heart felt as if they could be one in the same.

Could he be …

"Do you trust me, Rachel?" Slade asked, his face tightened with worry as he turned and faced her, placing the statue directly behind him. The question pulled Rachel from her altered state.

"Of course, Slade, with my life," she replied with a kind smile, looking up to see not only Slade's face, but that of the statue's in the background. The striking resemblance was undeniably breathtaking, rendering her stunned.

Feeling the hair on the back of his neck rise from the suddenly chilled air, Slade looked to sky to see gray clouds beginning to swirl. Releasing his hand from Rachel's, he stepped back placing himself beside the Effigiem Custos, knowing the time was near. The wind began to pick up, tousling her hair and giving her the chills.

Staring into one another's eyes, Slade's right arm suddenly snapped like a twig, sounding as if the sky itself had cracked open. Just as Rachel began to scream, his shoulder followed suit, popping from it socket. The transformation was indeed underway.

"Please … erragh! Don't be afraid!" Slade groaned, his voice nearly unrecognizable to Rachel.

With tear bound eyes, Rachel clasped her hands over her mouth as she watched Slade's body contort in unimaginable torment with screams to match.

"Slade!" Rachel screamed before lunging forward.

"No! You must stay back!" Slade coughed out, thrusting his mutated arm out to stop her while stricken to his knees with his opposing arm driven into the concrete floor. Fighting her maternal instincts, she did just that, stepping back toward the rooftop ledge as his face morphed and his teeth turned into daggers. The buttons of Slade's shirt trickled onto the cement as his shirt split at its seams from the exponential expansion of his once humanoid frame. Adding to the horror of his screams, the newly formed claws upon his feet scraped violently along the rooftop floor as he fought to maintain his balance despite the unnerving agony. Seconds later, bones popped through the raw grayed flesh of his back as his wings mapped themselves across the rooftop like that of a dark angel.

Despite the horrific event taking place, Rachel wasn't afraid for her own sake but instead for that of his. Watching his body continuously mangle then repair itself sent her on an emotional roller coaster ride of worry and unstable relief. Shaking as tears poured down her face, she covered her mouth, continuing to hold back her urge to scream. It felt like the longest sixty seconds of her life, a mere minute that felt like an eternity.

Unanticipatedly, Slade's head dropped and the clouds above dispersed. With wings now fully formed, Slade retracted them while rescinding the daggers that were his claws from the concrete beneath him.

"Oh my god, Slade?" Rachel gasped as he slowly lifted himself from the floor, triggering her to rush to his side. Sliding her arm under that of his and the other around his back she attempted to assist him as he continued to rise. "Are you okay?" she asked.

"Don't worry, I'm better than okay," he responded with a grin, now standing tall and looking down at Rachel.

"It was you all along. This whole time you were saving this city and protecting us all," she said empathetically, lifting her arm and placing her hand upon Dreadnight's cheek.

"I'm sorry I didn't come to you sooner … that I didn't tell you," Dreadnight began to say with sadness apparent in his voice. "I just couldn't bear the thought of my enemies knowing that we were connected. I couldn't risk them discovering what is was that brought us together," he added with regret.

"It's alright Slade, I understand. You were only protecting me, like you always have," Rachel said smiling.

"I'm gonna lift you up now," Dreadnight said cheerfully, lifting her off the floor as he clutched onto her sides. Rachel giggled as her eyes neared that of his, exhilaration seeping from her gleeful face. "Wrap your arms around my neck, okay," Dreadnight added, his beastly smile still growing.

"Okay," she said innocently as she did just that.

"Don't worry, you're safe with me. I got you."

Rachel simply nodded as they glared into one another's eyes. Dreadnight wrapped his arms around her waist and slowly bent his knees, dipping them ever so slightly. Within a split second, Dreadnight had launched himself and Rachel twenty feet into the night sky, however for Rachel it felt as if time had stood still, making their surroundings inconsequential. That however quickly changed the moment Dreadnight unfurled his wings, revealing their angelic vastness before thrusting them to and fro.

As the powerful gusts of circulated air blew past her skin, she swiveled her head, immediately bringing her to the realization that they were indeed flying.

"Oh my god, I can't believe this is real!" Rachel gasped in astonishment.

"Me either Rachel … me either," he replied, sharing her astonishment.

They gazed upon the city lights as the earth itself became smaller and smaller, knowing that the future was theirs, theirs alone … and nobody would take that away from them. Slade vowed to ensure that.

Floating over one hundred feet above the cathedral rooftop, Dreadnight and Rachel's eyes met once again as they leaned in and engaged in a kiss for the ages. As their bodies hung seemingly motionless, they were illuminated by the moon's glow and for the first time the minds of both Slade and Dreadnight were finally at ease.

Chapter 22
The End of an Era

  The six months that followed laid the foundation for which the city of Detroit would be rebuilt. Despite past stints in the limelight of the national media, the city found itself yet again in the eye of the storm, tainted by the word "scandal". Contending this storm of assumptions and conspiracies was Sandra Daley. The once seemingly unknown district attorney became the prosecuting lawyer in the nation's biggest court case. While Nikolai and Dr. Foster administered their newly synthesized cure to each and every one of the Arcane Asylum's inmates, only to then covertly "release" them into the DPD's custody, Ms. Daley was engaged in over two hundred hours of court proceedings to expose Inkubus's once powerful empire.

  Meanwhile, Slade and the team continued their siege against the remnants of Inkubus's following. It was business as usual, researching, hunting, imprisoning, then repeat. However, the days were far from usual for Slade given the fact that he spent the better half of each day's light making up for lost time with his love, Rachel. For months Slade had slowly forgotten how beautiful life could truly be, how becoming one with another could awaken a once withered soul. Within a matter of days, Rachel had decided to move herself and Ollie into the cathedral with Slade, unwilling to spend but a single night or morning without him, even if that meant merely hearing him through the comm system during a night's hunt. The two were undeniably inseparable, a sheer reflection of true love's portrait.

  "The People vs Norman Potts" was one hell of a trial to say the least. It showcased a level of corruption and collusion that the city and country had never before laid witness to. Over one hundred hours of testimonies and deliberation consumed television news broadcasts and those whose eyes and ears followed. But unlike before, these followers now filtered everything that was presented with a healthy level of skepticism resulting from years of misleading and even outright fabricated information spewed by its presenters. Rightfully so, this monumental trial legitimized that very skepticism.

  Using the vast flow of intel provided by Mr. Unseen, Ms. Daley went on the offensive, launching a prosecutive onslaught for all to see. Shaky and uncertain, Norman Potts could not evade his adversary's crosshairs … not this time. Bound by his own weapon, the synapsis serum had created a mental prison within, preventing lies from escaping and leaving only truth to be told. Unable to bite his tongue, Norman Potts spewed his secrets as if he had suddenly been stricken with turrets syndrome, increasingly hating himself as his case crumbled away. The criminal kingpin once known as Inkubus had finally become his own worst enemy, and it was a beautiful sight indeed.

On March 3rd, 2016, Norman Potts pled guilty to twelve counts of first-degree murder, twenty counts of racketeering, seventy-six counts of bribery, fifteen counts of drug trafficking, and of course arson, his original sin. These and other charges resulted in the federal judge sentencing Potts to two hundred years in a maximum-security prison, in other words a life sentence. The unprecedented judgement sent shockwaves throughout the country as a once untouchable elite was actually brought to justice, unable to manipulate those around him or the system itself.

With the case closed and all connections to Inkubus within the city of Detroit severed, Dr. Foster and Nikolai utilized the synapsis serum on one another to purge each other of the knowledge behind Dr. Mueller's vile treatment, only leaving details of the cure to remain. Upon completion, the team gathered to witness the insidious journal of Dr. Mueller be set ablaze, ending its control over humanity once and for all.

Just two weeks following the verdict, Ms. Daley was appointed interim Mayor due to the vast lines of corruption that were uncovered in the local government. She was to hold the office until mid-year when the official local elections were to take place, an election she was determined to win. A position as such would ensure Dreadnight and his teammates' ability to keep the streets of Detroit clean all while establishing a police force free of corruption and chaos.

Despite the fact that the enemy had been defeated, there would always be more evil peering out of the darkness just ahead. It was the end of an era, but the beginning of this team's destiny.

Chapter 23
A Bid Farewell

Three weeks had passed since the trial of the decade had concluded, leaving the city of Detroit in astonishment yet hopeful for a better tomorrow. Meanwhile, their former mayor was behind lock and key at the Michigan State Penitentiary. Unmasked and powerless, he was no longer able to slither his tentacles around the necks of others. Though locked in solitary confinement to avoid collaboration with his former lackeys, Potts was far from alone, spending every waking moment with the karma he had averted for decades.

On March 22nd, interim Mayor Sandra Daley approved and signed for the official transfer of Norman Potts to a federal maximum-security prison as recommended by the FBI.

This transfer, however, was unsuccessful …

The DPD armored truck transporting Potts went missing during the operation, assumingly hijacked while its escort cruisers were intercepted and diverted from their mission.

An event that went exactly how Dreadnight's team had hoped. An event that the federal government so conveniently covered up, keeping the media, local government, and of course the public in utter darkness.

It just so happened that Mayor Daley's uncle was a "retired" Marine Corps General. A man who had been exposed to the intricacies of US government operations … a man who laid witness to more corruption and lies than his stomach could take. The death of his half-brother and the cover up that followed certainly topped that very list. Enlightened by such troubling knowledge, he vowed to use his connections and influence to clean up the mistakes of the nation and cleanse himself of past sins.

His name, General Clark Dukat. When Potts' trial had commenced, General Dukat contacted his niece to warn her of the risks of allowing such a high-profile criminal to remain tied to the US justice system, insisting that one day he would again roam the streets untethered if matters weren't taken into their own hands. His recommendation was to "transfer" Potts to his very own secret facility that resided underneath an old nuclear missile silo in the mountains of Montana, or as far as the US Government was concerned, his retirement ranch out in the middle of nowhere.

Sharing such legitimate skepticism, the team was certainly concerned that Potts would fall through the cracks of the justice system, allowing financial or political pressure to one day release the demon from his cage. It was a risk they were not willing to take. After a few days of deliberation, the team accepted General Dukat's proposal, with one condition however, that Slade visit the facility upon Potts' imprisonment.

~

Footsteps echoed throughout the dimly lit cement dungeon as Slade exited an industrial elevator shaft, forcing a myriad of prisoners to turn their heads in fear. Walking down a designated aisle, Slade remained indifferent, ignoring the plight of the inmates as they pleaded for forgiveness on route to a secluded cell at the structure's end. Sitting in that very cell and clad in orange was Norman Potts, arms leaning upon his thighs with folded hands as he stared at the floor beneath him. Expecting the warden, the man we know as General Dukat, Potts lifted his head with eyes full of arrogance.

Those eyes quickly changed their disposition.

A flood of confusion and curiosity struck Potts as he analyzed the approaching man, the feeling of odd familiarity growing with each of the man's steps. He could have sworn he had seen this man somewhere. His face seemed to be seared into his memory, but he simply could not link its origin. Knowing he was the man's point of interest, Potts rose from his bed, suppressing his emotions to the best of his ability.

Bearing a sneering grin, Slade stopped before the cell bars. Though silent, his face fully expressed the joy of seeing his arch nemesis right where he belonged.

"Who the hell are you?" Potts said with apparent anger as his confusion continued to swell.

Slade simply chuckled, soaking up the glory of his victory as he witnessed karma eat away at its prey.

Potts approached Slade, clutching onto the bars that separated them as his face boiled over with rage.

"Answer me!" Potts shouted, unaware that he was only inches away from the man responsible for his incarceration.

"Don't worry, you will have plenty of time to think about it," Slade replied, verbally backhanding Potts, before turning and walking away.

"Come back here!" Potts screamed, his face pressed against the iron bars.

Slade stopped and turned around.

"Tick ... tock ... tick ... tock," Slade mockingly said, rocking his head side to side, before turning back and walking out sight.

With a mind on spin cycle and unable to conjure words, the vile monster once known as Inkubus glared in disarray as the lights above flickered into darkness.

More justice to be served in
"Kleenup Krew: Vigilantes' Creed: Book Three"